WHAT'S A KING TO A GOD

TEENAGE MAFIA

PART ONE

HENRY F. TYLER III

outskirtspress
DENVER, COLORADO

Teenage Mafia Part One
What's a King to a God

Outskirts Press, Inc.
http://www.outskirtspress.com

ISBN: 978-1-4787-2940-2

PRINTED IN THE UNITED STATES OF AMERICA

Chapter 1

It all started with two friends named Steven Ward and Lewis Jackson. Growing up, you could not find one without the other. They both lived in the grand city of Los Angeles, California. Steven, a young black teen, did not know his real parents. He was adopted by a white couple, Barbara and Tim Ward, when he was only an infant. Barbara and Tim did not have much, but they gave Steven what they could afford. They lived in a very old, small, and tattered gray-colored house. It only had two bedrooms, one small kitchen, one small bathroom and a small living room. In rainy weather, rain would drip from the ceiling. The house didn't have any insulation, so when it became cold their house would almost feel like being outside. Barbara and Tim owned a beat-up black 79' Chevrolet Caprice with the paint peeling off. You could hear the car squeaking every time it got on the road.

Lewis and his parents were a little different from Steven's family. Lewis's family was doing great things with their lives. His mother, Jessica Jackson, was a high school teacher who taught English III. His father, Sam Jackson, was a well-known doctor in the community. They all resided in a two-story reddish brick house with four cars parked in the garage. Sam was the owner of two cars, a black 2009 Mercedes Benz CL500 and a gray 2009 Cadillac CTS-V. Jessica also had two cars, a red 2010 Infiniti M and a white 2010 GT BMW F07. The home was filled with extravagant material and highly expensive paintings that any celebrity would envy. It also had four bedrooms with one master bedroom. Lewis and his parent's home were sitting on two acres of land. Sam was also the landlord for three other homes which his father left to him in a will.

Although Lewis and his family were filthy rich and everything seemed wonderful on the outside, the family contained a dark secret. Lewis was continuously being sexually abused by his father. Sam would fondle Lewis between his legs and then force Lewis to rub his penis. The sexual abuse went on for more than six years. It started when Lewis was six years old and it still continued to happen on a regular basis. Jessica knew about the molestation, but sadly she never did anything to stop it.

Steven and Lewis were now eighteen years old. Steven's height was 5'11. The color of his skin complexion was Honey Brown and the color of his eyes was Coffee Brown. Steven also kept his hair cut in a bald fade.

Lewis height was 5'10. His eyes were light gray. Lewis had short black hair. His arms were muscular, his chest was big, and was blessed with a natural six-pack. Lewis was so handsome that he could be mistaken as Brad Pitt.

On a beautiful sunny day, Lewis walked over Steven's house to sit down and chat with him like they normally did. He went into Steven's bedroom and took a seat by him on the bed. Lewis started off by saying "I'm tired of my parents controlling my life. Everyone thinks I'm rich. It's too bad that they don't see the pain I go through at home almost every day. Both of my parents treat me like shit." Steven responded, "Well, at least you're not living under the poverty line. You know how ashamed I am about my house. My parents are up in age and they don't think I need name brand clothes. Can you even tell me that you know what it feels like to have nothing? I'm not ugly and still no girl in school wants to talk to me." Lewis responded, "Your parents love you and my parents treats me like I am not their real son. My dad is a drunk. He beats on my mom. Then she would turn around and take her frustration out on me. My parents tell me I will never accomplish anything because my grades are low. I guess I won't be going to college." Lewis wanted to cry and his eyes became watery. Steven was shocked to hear how cruel Lewis was being treated. Lewis wanted to tell Steven about the times his dad would molest him, but he didn't feel comfortable talking about that subject. Steven said, "How can we fix our problems?"

Lewis stated angrily, "We should take whatever we want by any means necessary as Malcolm X said. We both need some money to put ourselves in a better position. My parents couldn't put me down anymore if I became successful. Why become a King, when you can become a God?"

Steven told him, "We have to put our minds together. I bet something great will come up."

Lewis said, "Well, I'm getting ready to go home. We'll sleep on it." After conversing some more with his best friend, Lewis left to go home.

Two days later, Lewis came up with a plan that would change their lives forever. Walking home after leaving Rosa Parks High School, Lewis told Steven about forming a six-man crew. He was going to select two guys and he wanted Steven to pick two guys. The crew's mission was to get money any way they could. Steven and Lewis's choices for their gang had to be trustworthy and loyal. Once Lewis finished telling Steven about his ideas, they split ways.

Steven really liked what Lewis came up with and he instantly thought about two fellows that he would like to join the gang. Eric was the smartest guy in their school and James barely went to class. Steven would find a way to meet up with them. Eric would be the easiest to find because he came to school every day. Steven usually saw James in the restroom because that's where he went to skip class.

On the other hand, Lewis had Willie and Johnny Moffett in mind. Both of them played on the school's football team on defense. They randomly bullied other students by taking their money and forcing them to give them their homework. Willie would turn in another student's homework and pretend as if it was his. Lewis loved their size because he figured they could knock-out fully grown men. He knew the best time to catch them was before or after football practice. The hard part was going to be convincing them to join the crew.

The next day at school, Steven was inside of his first period Science class. He was wondering if James Nelson could be in the restroom skipping class. He asked the teacher for permission to use the restroom. Ms. Taylor told him he could go to the restroom. Steven walked out the class, down the hall, and into the restroom. He didn't see James. He decided to use the urinal, anyway. Steven washed his hands, then he walked towards the door. Out of nowhere, a tall guy with braided corn rolls, caramel brown skin, sandy brown colored eyes, and sagging pants walked into the restroom. It was James. Today he wore a purple and yellow Kobe Bryant Los Angeles Lakers jersey with a white t-shirt underneath it, blue pants, and a pair of purple and yellow Nike Zoom Kobe V shoes.

Steven said, "Some things never change. I haven't seen you in a minute. We go back like M.C. Hammer with those baggy shining pants. You are "real" and that's what I like about you the most. I got this new idea to stack some "paper". You wanna be a part of it?

James replied, "Since there is money involved, you can count me in."

Steven stated, "I must warn you that this is some gangsta' shit. We are not going to different houses selling lemonade or Boy Scout cookies."

James burst into laughter. "You can count me in. Just don't try to play me out of my money. If it's really some gangsta' shit, I already know what's gonna to happen. The whole school knows my reputation. As long as you keep it real, we can definitely do some business together." They shook hands and separated. The handshake sealed the deal.

Steven had to find a way to get in touch with Eric. He thought Eric would be able to give him whatever he needed for the crew. Eric had some connections. Steven had known Eric and James since junior high school, but he never knew them on a personal level. Steven decided he would look for Eric after school. Eric was highly intelligent. His name stayed on the honor roll list every six weeks in school. He was also a senior in high school.

After school, Steven waited on the roadside in front of the school. He was beginning to get frustrated because there were so many students coming out together. Finally, Steven spotted Eric walking out. His height was 5'10 and he was very skinny. He was wearing a pair of Harry Potter shaped eyeglasses. His hair was blonde and he had blue eyes. Eric wore casual clothes every day. His attire would consist of polo shirts, long-sleeved button up shirts, dress pants, Eastland boots, and he kept his shirt tucked in his pants.

Steven walked up to Eric and asked him, "Do you still have the hook-up?"

Eric answered," Of course I still have it. There must be a party going on and you need some booze?"

Steven told him, "No."

Then Eric asked," Are you trying to get high?"

Steven told him, "No".

Then Eric asked Steven, "How many females do you want?"

Steven told him, "No! What about the guns you once told me about? The women do sound good, though."

Eric responded, "Damn! You are trying to "smoke" some-one. I know a guy who would give me a couple of "heaters". He keeps a gun on him like it's helping him to breathe. I'll talk to him and see what I can come up with. If you plan on shooting the school up, let me know something in advance."

Steven told Eric, "I don't want to "light" this place up. Besides, there are a lot of girls here that should be having my baby."

Eric stated, "I like a man with a good sense of humor." They shook hands and split ways. Eric was a nerd who was desperate to change his wimpy image. He wanted to become a tough guy so bad. Eric's only connection was his cousin Redd. Redd would supply him with anything he wanted. Eric was also addicted to sex. He would spend his last dollar on a piece of ass. He had so many prostitutes' phone numbers that you would think he was a pimp. No one else knew about his addiction.

Friday evening, Lewis was thinking about the two guys that could possibly join the crew. He didn't know much about his choices. He only knew that they were 12th grade bullies and were football stars. He didn't have any history with them. Willie and Johnny were very intimidating figures at school; both guys were black. Johnny was bigger than his cousin Willie; his height was 6'4. He was a 250-pound monster and some people would instantly think of the comic book character, Hulk, when he walked by. Johnny was in very good shape. He could easily bench press 400 pounds. He played the Defensive End position. His hair was always cut in a two-inch Mohawk with the rest of it faded. His skin color was dark brown. He was always wearing a t-shirt with a pair of pants and a pair of white Chuck Taylor's Converse shoes. Johnny's jersey number was 56.

Willie, on the other hand, played the Linebacker position. His height was 6'2 and he weighed 210 pounds. He might be blacker than Wesley Snipes. His haircut was always designed with stars all over his head. His jersey number was 51. He was always wearing t-shirts and pants with a pair of black Chuck Taylor's Converse shoes. He was also very muscular and strong. The only reason why Willie and Johnny didn't get expelled was because the school was depending on them to help win a state championship in football. Johnny was more feared than Willie. He didn't give a damn about anybody, but himself.

At least Willie cared about his teammates. Willie really

didn't like bullying other students and he only did it because Johnny wanted him to. Johnny never lost a fight at school. Everybody thought he was a young Mike Tyson.

Lewis already knew recruiting the two cousins was going to be a challenge. He decided to stay close by the school after it closed, so he could go by the football stadium when practice was over. He didn't have a clue what he was going to say to them. Lewis knew there was a possibility that things could backfire on him. They could try to fight him. Willie and Johnny would be tired, so he could run away if he had to.

When practice ended, Lewis saw them leaving the football stadium. He was nervous; the butterflies were in his stomach. He built up enough courage to approach them. Lewis walked up in front of them while they were tired and sweaty said, "What up guys? I know y'all don't recognize me. My name is Lewis. I got something you two may be interested in."

Willie gave Lewis a mean look and replied, "Man, do I even know you?"

Lewis said, "No. But if you join my team, you won't regret it."

Johnny stepped into the conversation. "Your team?! Man, you must be gay! I don't swing that way, so back the hell off!"

Lewis answered, "No, man I'm not gay either; I just thought ya'll may be interested in making thousands and thousands of dollars. We will split everything, right down the middle."

Willie became curious. "First of all, what kind of team you're talking about? We don't play basketball."

Lewis stated, "This is not a basketball team or any other kind of sports team. Y'all supposed to be bad, so show me what ya'll got. Taking money from students is giving you little petty cash. Get with me and I will make both of you ballers."

Johnny realized what he wanted them to get involved in. "You want us to help you break the law. I don't want to be locked up in jail."

Lewis told them, "Yes. We will be breaking the law. The money will be coming in, so fast; you wouldn't know what to do with all of it. We can get together and discuss this some more."

Willie asked, "Why us? You don't even know us. How do we know you can be trusted? Lewis, you are a complete stranger. Trust doesn't come over night, man. It has to be earned."

Lewis said, "You are right about that. But the chances of anybody double-crossing y'all are slim to none. No one in their right mind would do it. I'm not insane."

Johnny agreed. "You do have a point. Nobody wants to fuck with us. Give us a few days to think about it. Willie and I will discuss this first. You can find us right here after or before practice."

Lewis told them, "Alright, I will be looking forward to doing business with y'all." Willie and Johnny walked away. Lewis felt that his chances were good to make them a part of the crew.

While walking home Willie and Johnny spoke about the offer. Willie said to Johnny, "We can use the money. My mom and dad don't give me shit. They are for themselves."

Johnny said, "This is serious business. Breaking the rules at school and breaking the law is two different situations. I don't want to kill anybody. I must admit this Lewis guy seems to be very confident. I want to hear his plans. Personally, I'm down with whatever. His ideas must be legit for us to get involved. Going to jail or prison isn't a joke. There are men in jail bigger and stronger than us. I don't want to fight anybody who could beat me."

Saturday afternoon, Lewis went over Steven's house to go over their recruits. When Lewis told Steven that Willie and Johnny could join their crew, Steven disliked the idea. He asked, "Why would you ask them to be a part of our group? You have never socialized with them dudes before. The deal was to find two people we can trust and not two people who would whip our ass and take the cash from us."

Lewis said, "I knew you would feel that way. Like it or not, we need their help. We don't really have the size. They must earn our trust and we must earn theirs too. Once the money starts to roll in, everyone will be happy. So who did you decided to bring along for the ride?"

Steven answered, "Eric Hall and James Nelson are my picks."

Lewis said, "That James Nelson is a bad boy. He is a perfect choice. James doesn't mind getting his hands dirty. James and I had some conversations in the past. He could become a true soldier and he doesn't take any shit from anyone but why would you put my life in the hands of a fragile nerd like Eric? He needs to just stay in a classroom where it's safe."

Steven told him why. "Eric could give us whatever we need. He is not physical, but he is the key to our operation. He will give me some guns."

Lewis said, "Wow, the nerd must be living a double life. I

never would've guessed he could get his hands on a gun. It's always the quiet ones."

Steven said, "I can't wait to get everybody together, so we can kick this thing off. We have to be clever. Any mistake can cause our demise or some serious prison time. I don't want to be anybody's bitch. Can you feel where I'm coming from?"

"I can definitely feel where you coming from. Willie and Johnny will be the muscles of the crew. Once they agree, we can't be stopped. The minute those two giants tell me something I will let you know. My stomach is running on E; I'm ready to go home and eat. Take it easy, Steven," Lewis said. He walked out of Steven's room and went home.

Barbara came into Steven's bedroom. She told him, "You and Lewis have been hanging out a lot lately. He is a great kid."

Steven answered, "He is a good friend. Lewis is like the brother I wish I had."

Barbara said, "Let's eat dinner. Tim is already at the kitchen table waiting on us. We are having chicken, rice, biscuits, and sweet potatoes."

Steven responded, "That sounds good." Steven, Barbara, and Tim ate dinner together.

Lewis arrived home with his mind on finding something to eat. He unlocked the front door with his key and then he walked into the living room. Lewis wasn't surprised when he saw his dad on top of his mom. Sam was trying to choke her, squeezing both hands around her neck. Lewis wrapped both of his arms around Sam's waist from behind him. Lewis used all his strength to lift Sam up and slammed him on his face and stomach. Sam lay there motionless. Lewis turned around to check on his mom. She bashed his head with a wooden vase. Lewis fell down on his back, holding his head. Jessica dropped the vase and started kicking him in the stomach. She screamed, "He is still your dad, you bastard! Don't put your hands on him, again!"

Sam got off the floor and stood up. Then he yelled at Lewis, "You must want to die! I will kill you, faggot!" Sam and Jessica went to their room.

Lewis slowly got up. He thought, *What the hell just happened?* He rubbed his head, noticing there was a knot on the top. Lewis was livid. He wondered, *How could my mom do this to me? I was just trying to help her. That fool must have the magic stick between his legs. Why else would she come to his rescue the way she did?* Lewis got a small towel out of the bathroom and some ice out of the kitchen's refrigerator. He wrapped the towel around the ice, then placed it on his head.

Lewis began contemplating something that never crossed his mind before -- making his Mom and Dad disappear. He lay in the bed thinking about what had happened, until he fell asleep.

Chapter 2

On Monday morning, Willie and Johnny stopped Lewis by the cafeteria. Willie said, "We have been doing some thinking. We decided to accept your offer."

Lewis told him, "I know where an abandoned building is at with a good location. There's one behind Bozeman Store. We can discuss our business there. Bozeman's Store has been out of service for a long time. It would block the hide out from traffic. Bozeman's store had a lot of good snacks before it close down. I haven't told y'all this, but the crew will have six members. Once I get all the kinks ironed out, we all will work as one. I think we need to have a meeting tonight at the abandoned building."

Johnny said, "It's all about the money. Willie and I have hopes and dreams like everybody else. Cash makes the world go round. Everything has to go down right to dodge jail time. We all must know our roles."

Lewis told them, "I'll get things ready for tonight. How does 8:30 sound?"

Johnny answered, "It is okay with me." Then Willie said the same thing. The conversation was finished when Lewis told them he would catch them tonight. Then they went to their first period classes.

When Lewis saw Steven on the first break, he couldn't wait to give him the good news. Lewis said, "Willie and Johnny agreed to join us. We will have a meeting tonight at

8:30, to get this thing "popped off". There is an abandoned building behind Bozeman's Store; it will become our hide out. You need to bring your guys and I'm going to bring my guys."

Steven said, "A meeting tonight would be good. Before school is out, I will get in touch with James and Eric." The bell rang for their next class and they had to separate.

Steven was in his history class, sitting down. He asked the teacher if he could use the restroom and she said 'yes'. Steven was hoping to find James in there once again. James was inside the restroom looking at a few porn magazines.

Steven asked, "What are you doing studying in the restroom?"

James replied, "I'm not studying. I'm checking these hoes out in these Playboy magazines."

Steven said, "Let me get a look at them. Those bitches are Michael Jackson bad."

James said to Steven, "Damn man, you are foaming out the mouth like you have never seen a piece of ass before."

Steven was still a virgin. He lied, "I done had plenty before, homie. On a different subject, we are having a meeting tonight behind Bozeman's Store. It will be held at 8:30."

James told Steven, "I know where that place is at. I was wondering when you would holler at me again. A thought ran through my mind like you didn't want to do anything."

Steven said, "I had to get some other things straight, first. The crew will have six members including you. I'm sorry for not telling you at the beginning."

James stated, "I trust you and that won't make a difference with me. Plus, the more people we have the more we could do. Hopefully, they are serious about getting this "cheddar" just like us. At 8:30, I will be there. I'm skipping class right now and I'm trying to enjoy my magazines." That was a hint that James wanted to be left alone, so he could finish looking over his Playboy magazines.

Steven said, "See you tonight, James." Then Steven went back to his history class.

After school, Steven quickly spotted Eric in the parking lot. Then he caught up with him. "What are you doing tonight? We are having a meeting at 8:30. Can you show up?"

Eric said, "Well, I don't have anything scheduled for tonight. I have a big test coming up. I'll squeeze some time in to be there. Where's the meeting?"

Steven replied, "The building behind Bozeman's Store."

Eric said, "I don't know where that place is at."

Steven said, "Give me your phone number on a piece of paper." Eric took out a single sheet of paper and a pen. Then he wrote his cell phone number down on the paper. "I'm putting together a six-man crew. Do you want to be down with us? Don't be scared. You'll have an easy job. Eric, your hands will never get dirty. Your job title will be the "connection man". Bring us what we need."

Eric was stunned that Steven would even offer a deal like that. Even the thought of being a criminal scared him. At the same time, it was an opportunity to show he was not a wimp. Eric stated, "I'm a nerd and you are trying to turn me into the next Makaveli the Don. If my hands stay clean we got a deal."

Steven replied, "I can respect that." After they finished talking, Eric got into the green 2010 Chevy Malibu LS with his mom.

While Steven walked home, many thoughts crossed his

mind. *Will I go to jail? Is this going to work? What am I going to do with my part of the money? Are Willie and Johnny going to kick everybody's ass and take our money? What kind of car I want to drive? How can I help my parents out by making life easier for them? What name brand clothes will I buy?* Steven felt that a lot of money was the answer to his problems.

As he got closer to his house, he could see red and blue lights. Steven started running. He ran past the police officers and then he saw Tim, the only father figure he ever had, dead on their front lawn. Steven dropped to his knees; he was devastated. Tim was laid out with his eyes and mouth open. The police officers were trying to calm Barbara down because she was screaming and crying, "They killed him! They killed him!" Steven closed Tim's eyes and mouth with his right hand. Steven got off the ground and went to Barbara. Then he asked Barbara, "What happened to Dad?!"

After she finally calmed down, she replied, "The police officers surrounded him with guns. He grabbed his chest and fell to the ground. I saw the pain in Tim's face before he died. They tried to bring him back with CPR. He was dead before the ambulance showed up. They had mistaken him as someone else. We were outside together at first. I went inside the house. Then I heard yelling outside and the police sirens. I went back outside as quickly as I could. Then I watched him fall. Tim was a good man. He never did anything to nobody."

Steven wanted to seriously hurt an officer. He knew he would have to become the man of the house. An officer came up to them and said, "We are really sorry. Tim really looked like the guy we were looking for."

Then one of the paramedics told Barbara after taking her blood pressure, "Your blood pressure is too high. We have to take you in for further examination."The paramedics took her to the hospital.Tim left the yard in a body bag inside of a black hearse. Steven went inside the house.

Steven was thinking about vengeance and getting it any way possible. He wanted to start a war against the police officers but he knew he had to slow his roll. A war against the boys in blue would be suicidal. So it would definitely be a bad idea. He still wanted them to pay for what happened to his dad, because sorry would not bring Tim back.

Tim was a retired housekeeper at Motel 6. His retirement money was the only reason their bills were getting paid. Tim worked there for 25 years. Steven needed some great ideas as soon as possible to keep the utilities on at home. He wished tonight's meeting would shine some light on how he was going to get the bills paid.

Steven found himself looking at some of Tim's pictures hanging up on the wall and on the living room's table. All those old memories came back like when he was 7 years old; his dad taught him how to ride his first bike. Every Christmas, Tim would make a lot of sacrifices ahead of time to give Steven a gift. Sadness overwhelmed him. It was just too hard for him to take, his dad never coming back. The way his dad died was unbelievable to him. He looked at the clock on the wall – it was 8:23pm. He called Eric and gave him the directions to the hide out. Then Steven walked out of his house, on his way to the hideout.

Everybody was there waiting on him. Johnny snatched both nailed boards off the door before they got in. After a 20-minute walk, Lewis met him at the door. Lewis asked, "Why did you take so long to get here? I was hoping you didn't get cold feet."

Steven replied, "It's a long story. I'll tell you once the meeting is over."

Lewis said, "Alright. I brought some candles, so we won't be in the dark." The one-story abandoned building was once a welfare office. It was a brick building with all the windows boarded up. There were three small offices and one large office. The large office had a large table, a dirty mirror with an egg shape, purple cotton made chair with wooden legs, the brown wallpaper was coming off the walls, a blue and red ceiling lamp was hanging over the table, and the floor was black. The other offices were empty. The entire building was dusty and spider webs were everywhere. Old newspapers were scattered all across the floor.

Everyone gathered inside the large office and then Lewis stood on top of the table. He lit the ceiling lamp with a few candles with a cigarette lighter. Lewis got off the table. He started the meeting by saying, "I'm glad everybody came out. We are all here for the same reason. That reason is to get this cash and live large. We could have everything we ever dream of."

Steven told them, "Lewis and I are the head of this operation. Putting this crew together is our idea. We must work hard as a team. The key is not getting caught. We have to be smart to pull this shit off. Everyone must be on the same page. If we are not on the same page, a lot of us will be in jail becoming somebody's girly man." Everyone began laughing. Then Steven continued to speak, "I was thinking we should start small and then we should go on to bigger and better things." L

Lewis asked, "How small are you talking about?"

Steven responded, "Robbing people at some ATM machines, we could break in houses whether people are there or not, and we could jump out of a car and start beating some folks heads in and take their money." Everybody realized that Steven had a criminal mind.

Lewis thought, *He didn't go over none that stuff with me. I want to know how big he's thinking.* So he asked him, "How big are you talking about?"

Steven answered, "Hitting a few corner stores and a bank. The bank would be the hardest but most rewarding." Lewis liked all Steven's ideas, but he disliked the fact that Steven didn't discuss anything with him as planned. Lewis did not let his true feeling known. Steven said proudly, "Hey, I almost forgot to introduce y'all to the man who will be the main factor in our future success -- Eric Hall. Eric has been so quiet that I almost forgot he was here."

Johnny looked at Steven and thought, *Man, have you lost your mind?*

Eric looked around at everybody and then he said, "I'm the connection man. Our guns should be coming in very soon. Whatever we need, I will try to get it for us. It's going to take a while before y'all take me seriously. That is no surprise to me, at all. I have to handle my business first and then everybody will feel differently."

Willie said, "Johnny and I will be the strength that this crew needs. Have anybody here other than us heard of lifting weights before? I'm just kidding, folks. We are going to get this bread and live comfortable. The pigs are the only people in our way."

Johnny responded, "If the pigs get in our way, we have to

turn them into bacon. We really don't want to take anybody's life. If my life is in jeopardy, you can bet your bottom dollar that I will bomb first. Before we get started on any mission, a plan has to be laid down to perfection. There is no room for errors. The money will be split equally because that's the correct way to do things. We have enough people here to get a lot accomplished." James didn't say anything; he just wanted to listen to everybody. Steven said, "All of us will meet here tomorrow night. Our first mission will be to catch someone at an ATM machine. Eric is the only person who doesn't have to get his hands dirty. We would be wasting our time if nobody shows up at the bank we choose to watch. Tomorrow night will be our debut, so let's make it happen, guys."

Everybody shook hands and left, but Lewis and Steven stayed to chat. Lewis asked Steven, "So what happened that made you late for the meeting, tonight?"

Steven replied," My dad died today. I came home from school; the police officers were in my yard. They were looking at him on the ground, dead. My mom told me the officers were yelling at him with their guns out. They scared him into a heart attack. He was mistaken for the wrong person."

Lewis told him, "That's fucked up. Your dad was like a father figure to me. I want to get some kind of payback on them. We can't let that shit slide, Steven."

Steven responded, "What can we do? They are police officers and we are just high school students. The pigs gave an apology. That apology doesn't mean shit to me." Lewis became anxious to do something about Tim's death.

Lewis told Steven, "Bro, I'm your right hand man. I promise that they will not get away with it. In the future,

I'm going to need a big favor from you. We have to help each other out. Tim always treated me well; he should've been my real dad. He was a great and down to earth man. Tim had a lot of love for me. They got me hot about this situation and I really want to do some damage. If you come up with a plan before I do, just let me know. I'm down with it already."

Steven said, "We have to focus on getting this money first and then we will deal with them bastards. My dad was bringing home most of our income. I have to bring the bread home, now. He died before I could help him and mom financially."

Lewis said sadly, "It will be hard on Barbara and you for a while. Steven, please stay strong for her. Keep your head up because things will eventually get better."

Steven thought about his mom and got worried. He said, "I have to go and check up on my mom. Her blood pressure went up. We will hook up here, tomorrow night." Then both of them left the hide out.

When Steven went home, Barbara was already there. She was sitting on the living room couch. Steven walked up to Barbara and gave her a hug. He said to her, "Everything will be all right. You look exhausted; getting some rest may not be such a bad idea."

Barbara agreed, "I can use some rest, son. Today has been a very long day. The good Lord will help us through our time of sorrow. I'll see you first thing in the morning." She went to bed extremely depressed.

Steven also went to bed, but not to sleep, he wanted to think. He was feeling so stressed out; he caught a headache. After one hour and a half of tossing and turning, he finally fell asleep.

Chapter 3

The next day at school, Eric approached Lewis during lunchtime under the gym's bleachers. "Look inside my book bag, Lewis." Lewis took the gray book bag from Eric and then he looked inside of it. He saw a silver 9mm Beretta IPX45 Storm double with a black polymer grip. Before that moment, Lewis had never seen or touched a gun before. Eric asked, "Are you going to take the gun or do you want me to hold on to it?"

Lewis replied, "I will take the heater." As Lewis held the gun, he began to feel very powerful. He aimed the 9mm at the wall trying to get a good feel of it. "Damn, this gun feels good. It looks brand new. What kind of gun is it?"

Eric replied, "It's a 9mm that has 17 rounds. Be careful now, this baby is loaded. I already had this one. I'm still going to get some more."

Lewis placed the gun into his pocket. "Thanks for getting me connected, Mr. Connection Man. It's cool; this gun will do for right now. Don't tell Steven about this gun; I want to surprise him with it." Lewis felt very excited to have a gun in his possession.

After school, Lewis went over Steven's house. He knocked on the door twice. Then Barbara came to the door and let him in. Lewis gave her a hug and said, "I feel sorry for your loss. If there is anything I can do for you, just let me know."

Barbara responded, "I'm doing fine and you don't have

to worry about me. Everything is in God's hands. My faith in God is very strong, Lewis. Steven is in his bedroom."

Lewis said to Barbara, "It's been a pleasure to speak with you." He gave her another hug and then he went to Steven's room.

The bedroom door was already open, so Lewis walked on in. Lewis greeted him, "What's up, dog?"

Steven said, "I'm kind of scared because we have never done anything like this before. What if we get caught? I haven't come up with a plan for tonight yet. Sitting around crying over my dad all day is not helping."

Lewis suggested, "Don't fall apart now. Tonight will be the beginning of the end of our problems. Get yourself together, man, because we need you to be a leader. We are the master minds that will lead this crew into doing big things."

Steven agreed, "I guess you're right, Lewis. It wouldn't look good at all for me to change my mind. I'm one of the main reasons the crew is pumped up. What time did we plan the meeting, tonight?"

Lewis answered, "At 8:45, hopefully it's an excellent time. Do you remember all those times me and my family went on trips to Colorado to go skiing?"

Steven replied, "I remember that because my parents would never let me go. They thought it was too dangerous for me. Damn, my parents were too old-fashioned. I probably would've had the time of my life."

Lewis said, "Yeah, you would've had fun. Well, I got four white ski masks that we used on those trips. We can use the ski masks to protect our identities."

Steven said, "I'm supposed to be smart and I never

thought of that. It's a good thing I'm sharing this leadership with you."

Lewis thought about telling Steven about the gun Eric gave him. He decided not to say anything about it, yet. Lewis told him, "I hope tonight goes smooth."

Then Steven asked," What if we have to kill someone? Taking another person's life just isn't right. We will conduct a lot of beat downs, but killing is something I hope I would never have to do."

Lewis responded, "Killing would be going over the edge, though. Johnny said it best; if your life is in danger, you have to bomb first. It could be the only way to survive. The odds of us killing someone are very high. The more people we rob, the more likely it will happen. We have to go all out for our lives to reach new heights. Stop thinking about others and worry about your mom. We are the common people worst nightmare, gangsters. Get use to it; we are "Gs", that is how we are going to roll."

Steven asked, "How are you staying so calm and relaxed about everything? It seems like you are very brave or very crazy."

Lewis replied, "I'm a little of both. We need to go outside before I really go crazy. It's a pleasant day."

Steven and Lewis went outside to catch some fresh air. Barbara watched them outside through the window. She had a strange feeling something was going on. They were usually laughing and talking loud, but now they whispered, while talking in private. Plus, Lewis had never come over that often before. She could only wonder what they were talking about.

Willie was at his ranch home, thinking about his million

dollar dreams of playing football for the NFL. He picked up his cell phone to call his cousin, Johnny. Johnny's kid sister, Toya, answered the house phone. Then she yelled for Johnny to come and get the phone.

"Hey Johnny, this is Willie. I'm just checking up on you. Tell me, what you really think about all the stuff we are getting into?"

Johnny replied, "I really think we have a shot to get the job done. The only problem I have is splitting the dough six different ways. Eric is not getting his hands dirty. He doesn't deserve a dime. While we are getting down, Eric is not breaking a sweat. I should slap those glasses off of his face because that is some bullshit."

Willie said, "Johnny, you're never lying. Why are Steven and Lewis calling all the shots? They must think we are jocks with no brains."

Johnny said, "Let's sit back and do it their way. We have to find out how smart these guys really are. Once we start doing big things, then we will put our two cents in, Willie."

Willie said, "Yes, we can fight, but both of us are capable of doing much more. I had a feeling we would be on the same page. Even though we don't fully trust them, we have to focus on making this shit work. I want to get rich or close to being rich."

Johnny said, "I want the same thing. I'll get back with you because it's my turn to wash the dishes." Both of them hung the phone up.

Eric was at home, receiving oral sex from a prostitute. He met her twice a week most of the time. His dad moved away when he was three years old. Eric's mom worked the night shift as a nurse; her only off days were Tuesdays and Wednesdays.

Eric's sex addiction led him into calling prostitutes. He couldn't have them over while his mom was still at home. All the prostitutes he fooled around with already knew to call him when his mom left the house. The prostitute he had over his house called herself, Honey. She was a 24-year-old white girl with a banging body. Honey had light gray eyes with blonde hair. Her measurements were 35D-25-35. Honey was so fine; she would make a preacher want to lose his religion. After she was finished pleasuring him on his bed, she lay down. Eric wanted to cuddle with her. He held her from behind. Honey said to Eric, "I'm sorry, but this is a business. Call me when you get some more money, baby." She went into her black purse and took some red lipstick out and a small mirror. She watched herself put the lipstick on. She climbed out of his bed and grabbed her fifty-dollar bill from the top of Eric's dresser. She gave him a kiss on his forehead and then she told Eric, "Bye." Honey walked out of his room and left Eric's house.

Eric thought, *Wow! She really showed me a good time. I need to hurry up and get some more money.*

James was at home, angry. He had a serious gambling problem. James was over a friend's house and lost $80 playing pool. He didn't know why he loved gambling so much. James had lost more than he had won in the past. He had lost money on professional basketball, football, and baseball games. He normally played air hockey, pool, and bowling very well. It seemed like when money was on the line, he found a way to choke.

It was getting close to 8:45, so everyone was heading to

the hideout. Lewis and Steven were the first ones to make it there. They also discussed the plan while walking to the hideout. The rest of them made it there almost at the same time. Once everybody walked into the main office, the meeting started. Lewis made it his job to light the ceiling lamp candles before every meeting. Lewis told them, "It's show time, folks. The Treasure Bank isn't that far from here. The first person that we see use the ATM machine, I want Willie and Johnny to force them to cough up $400. Four hundred dollars is the maximum they would be able to get out at one time. This is what I like to call just practice. That kind of cash isn't much. We are trying to get warm up, right now. I have four ski masks to keep our faces covered. The bank should be surrounded by cameras. The store across the street called "Kasey's" doesn't have any at all. We are going to hide behind Kasey's. When we see someone trying to use the ATM, bomb rush them. Try not to say too much because we don't want anybody to catch our voice. Put enough pain on them, so the person won't get up while we are getting away."

Steven asked, "Does anyone have a question?" No one said anything. Then Steven said, "Let's go out here and make it happen. This is easy, like getting Jennifer Lopez to marry you. If you got butterflies, fuck it because I have them too. So let's get on down there and make things happen."

They took twelve minutes walking to Kasey's. Eric was very nervous; he had sweat dripping from his face. Every time they saw a car driven by the bank, their hearts started to beat faster. James was getting frustrated. "We have been out here for a little over an hour and a half. No one has stopped there, yet."

Willie told them, "It looks like a car is getting ready to stop." The car was a red Dodge with a 28-year-old white male behind the wheel. The guy parked his car and headed to the ATM machine. Everybody got real quiet, so they wouldn't be heard. Johnny and Willie put on the ski masks and ran towards the guy with almost no sound at all. The man never saw or heard them coming. Johnny placed his large arms around the guy's neck. The man was afraid and he pissed on himself. Willie told him, "Give us $400 or you will not see tomorrow." He made the money come out as fast as he could, four- hundred dollar bills. Willie took the money out of the machine and then he punched the guy in the stomach. Johnny let him go and he dropped to the ground. Johnny kicked him in the head like he was kicking a field goal. The powerful blow knocked the man out. Both of them ran back behind Kasey's. Willie and Johnny took the masks off. Then everybody left together, heading back to the hideout.

While walking back to the hideout, Lewis spotted another person at a bus stop. He said to the crew, "We are not done, yet." The man they were looking at was fifty years old. Lewis and James placed ski masks on their faces. Willie, Johnny, Eric, and Steven watched them from behind. Lewis and James were looking around to make sure no one was coming. They slowly crept up behind him. James hit him with a solid punch to the jaw; a tooth flew out of his mouth. Then he fell to the ground hard on his back. Lewis turned him around and placed his knees on the back of the guy's neck. The guy's face was touching the ground. Lewis yelled, "Move and I will kill you! Granddaddy, please don't try anything stupid." Lewis had the .9mm handgun in his pocket. He wanted to use it on him, but decided not to. James checked the man's entire pocket and found a brown wallet. The guy was still dazed; he didn't know what was going on. Lewis and James walked back to the rest of them and they went to the hideout. Everybody was happy -- they got away with everything.

The crew was in a bragging mood. Johnny told them, "Did y'all see when I kicked the shit out of that dude. I don't think Randy Orton could've footed someone that hard. His head almost came off. He even pissed on himself; he should've been wearing a diaper."

James added, "That wasn't nothing compared to the sucker punch I gave Pops in the jaw. The worst hits are the ones you don't see coming. The old denture-wearing bastard didn't see it coming. As y'all saw, I'm more of a finesse puncher. It's a work of art the way I knock people out. I almost forgot; let's see what is inside of this wallet." They saw a driver license, a golfing membership card, and a debit card. Then James pulled the zipper back. They took the money out and counted $353. They were surprised that there was that much cash inside the wallet. In all, it was a $753 night.

Steven was glad but not satisfied. He let it be known, "Don't forget, this is only the beginning. There are many others who will soon feel our hunger for money. Guys, this is the beginning of a dynasty. We won't stop until everybody is straight for life."

Lewis split the cash as even as possible. Then he put the ski masks on top of the purple chair. Lewis said to them, "When we walk home, please walk calmly. Looking suspicious is the last thing we should do. We need a car because it's not good to be walking around with the police officers everywhere."

Steven said, "I think I have a good idea for the next time. Eric, add a car on to the list with the guns. Hook it up, Mr. Connection Man. For right now, let's get the hell out of here."

Eric wondered, **Where in the hell he thinks I can get a car from? I don't even own a car. Shit!**

Lewis's parents were at home thinking about him. Sam told Jessica, "Look at the time; Lewis is not home yet. I hope he don't believe we are stupid. It's going on 11:30 and he is probably getting into a lot of trouble. Our son is almost retarded and could become a major problem. We have given him the world and look how he repays us. He's going to try to make staying out late a habit, watch'em."

Jessica said, "He could have a good explanation for being out too late. Lewis has never been the type to get in trouble."

Then Lewis walked through the front door. He was not expecting them to still be awake. Jessica said with concern, "Where have you been? We were very worried about your safety. I thought about calling the police to look for you."

Lewis was still upset about his head getting smashed with the wooden vase. He kept on walking without giving her a response. Lewis's silent treatment made his dad angry. He yelled "Answer her right now, you piece of shit!"

Lewis walked up the stairs like no one was speaking to him. He lay down in his bed wishing they would leave him alone. Sam wasn't ready to leave him alone. He ran up the stairs and into Lewis's bedroom. He said angrily, "Boy, you must have lost your muthafuckin mind! I'm waiting for your sweet ass to try me again. The last time, I had my back turn. Now try that bullshit face to face, Bitch!"

Lewis finally spoke, "First of all, I'm far from being a

bitch. I was just hanging out with some friends of mine. I don't make the honor roll, but I am smart enough to know when someone is just bullshitting. Some people call it blowing hot air for nothing. Don't even act like you care about me. Your true colors have been showing for years, abusive blue and child molesting red."

Sam became hotter than a coffee pot on the stove, "We really don't give a fuck about you. Lewis, you are a disgrace to our family. Your dumb ass barely can read. I actually paid a couple teachers to pass you. Being illiterate has been your weakness since birth. I have friends who are lawyers, doctors, and police officers. When we hook up, they tell me about their children doing well. I have to make up lies about you. You don't deserve to live here. Only smart people should be living in luxury."

Sam's words cut through Lewis like a knife. Lewis's feelings were crushed and Sam had won the verbal battle. He put his head down in shame. Lewis's right hand was around the handle of the .9mm handgun that was in his pocket. He wanted to put a few holes in his dad. Jessica came into his room and she didn't make things any better, "Lewis! Never stay out that late again! You're not grown, so as long as you are under our roof, respect the rules. A person with some kind of sense would've called home. This better be the first and last time a stunt like that gets pulled. Do you hear me? I said do you hear me!"

Lewis answered, "Yes, I heard you loud and clear."

Jessica replied, "Straighten your act up or I will straighten it up for you." Then Sam and Jessica walked out of Lewis's bedroom.

Lewis went from lying down to sitting straight up. Lewis felt they rob him of the little pride that he had left. If looks could kill, he would be a serial killer right now. He did some pondering. *The only thing my parents seem to be good at is bringing me down. I'm their only child and they have never showed me any love or compassion. My child molesting, drunk, and abusive dad wants to talk about me like he is perfect. He doesn't mean shit to me. As far as I am concerned; I am father-less. My mom is foolish for worshipping the ground he walks on. He uses her as a punching bag. The next time they get into a scuffle with each other, let the best asshole win. I won't break shit up. I hate both of their guts more than ever. God should've given me Steven's parents. Being poor is better than going through this shit almost every day.*

When Steven arrived home, Barbara was already asleep. He went into her room and gave her a kiss on the forehead. Steven really believed that he and Lewis had put together a criminal dream team. The crew had a combination of strength in numbers, brains, and muscles. The only thing Steven had to do was keep coming up with good ideas. He could get his mom into a better house and car in no time. After a shower, he went to bed.

When Eric made it home, his mom was already at work, as usual. He pulled out his cell phone and called Honey. She really did not want to answer her phone, but she did anyway.

"This is Eric; I wanted to know would you come over here tonight. I have some more money and my dick is hard," Eric said.

"I am tired, Eric. Call me back tomorrow night," Honey said.

"Alright, I'll get back with you," Eric said. Then he called a prostitute named Strawberry, on her cell phone. Her measurements were 32D-24-35. Strawberry was 22 years old and her height was 5'5. She was a very gorgeous brunette with light blue eyes. The only time Eric gave her a call was when Honey was not available. Strawberry said, "Boy, I haven't heard from you in a minute. Where have you been, lately?"

Eric replied, "All of this homework is catching up with me. I'm a senior who is trying to graduate number one in my class."

Strawberry said, "That's sounds very understandable. Your brain is like a computer chip; you can remember everything the teacher says."

Eric said, "I know it is pretty late, but can you come over to my crib. I have a big surprise for you. We need to rekindle our flame tonight."

Strawberry responded, "It's never too late for some good backbreaking sex. I'm on my way to your house, Eric. You better keep a hard on for a long time, too. I don't want to come over there in the middle of the night for some few minutes shit. Give me your all or don't call me at all."

Eric said, "My front door will be open for you."

Strawberry took sixteen minutes to arrive over Eric's house. Eric was already naked under his covers. She came into his bedroom with a red silk robe on. When she saw Eric under the covers, she took the robe off. Strawberry was wearing some Victoria's Secrets lingerie, a purple see through bra and panties. Her body was flawless and sexy. Strawberry placed her hand behind her back and then her bra fell to the floor. She climbed in bed with him and got under the covers. Then she got on top of him and they began French kissing. Out of nowhere, she started crying. She lay down beside him.

Eric had a very disappointed expression on his face. Eric felt super horny and his plans of getting some was looking very dim at the moment. "What's wrong with you?" Eric asked.

"My real name is Rebecca Smith. Every since I was thirteen years old, I've been selling my body. My mother was a prostitute, as well. Both of us were having sex for money to supply her drug habit. She lied like the drugs were saving her life. It is the reason she's no longer with us today. I been doing this for so long; it's the only way I know to survive. I'm very sorry, Eric. You were expecting a great time and I let you down," Rebecca said.

Rebecca's story had made Eric feel sorry for her. He put his arms around her from the back. "Everything is going to be alright. I will take good care of you. You will never have to sell your body to anybody else again," he said.

Rebecca wiped the tears from her face with her hands. "Come on, Eric. You're not just saying that to get some?" she asked.

"No. I will prove it to you. My mom will arrive a little after 7:00 in the morning. Please stay as long as you want before she gets here. We don't have to have sex. You and I could just cuddle the night away, baby." Eric said. Eric feelings for her went from lust to love. He thought they were close because she opened up about her story. Eric and Rebecca cuddled all night long.

When James went home that night, he started looking at all the L.A. Lakers and Chicago Bulls upcoming schedules on the Internet, using his laptop. James was hoping he could bet on their biggest games. Once James got off the computer, he called a few buddies to play pool for $20 a game with him. James had lost $80 today already. For some reason, he thought he could bounce back and start winning. He was the biggest loser in his friend's circle. If someone was having a bad gambling day, they could almost depend on getting some of their money back by playing him. James even fell asleep, thinking about new ways to gamble.

Johnny and Willie were so tired. All of the running and walking caught up with them. They went straight to bed as soon as they made it home. Johnny was kind of surprised. He didn't know robbing was going to be easy. He thought every robbery was like playing on a slot machine that you could not lose on. Johnny began thinking about making it a career. He thought a 9 to 5 job was nothing compared to fast money. Then he didn't know shit in school, Willie was there giving him answers. *College was a dumb move, if you can't do high school work,* Johnny thought.

Chapter 4

In the morning, Steven woke up to the pleasant smell of breakfast. Steven went into the kitchen and he saw pancakes with syrup, scramble eggs, and sausages served on two plates. Two cups of orange juice were next to the plates, on the table. Barbara said, "Good morning, Son. Steven, I was wishing you would not let this delicious food get cold or go to waste. You must have made it home late last night. I don't remember seeing you at all. Lewis is starting to come around a lot. I don't have a problem with that at all."

Steven told her, "Lewis and I are getting closer. We were hanging out talking about dad, school, and the future. By the way, when is Dad's funeral?"

Barbara replied, "I have to get everything together. Which church to use? What time will it start? Which cemetery will we use?" Lewis took a seat and started eating his food.

Eric woke up and Rebecca was gone. She had left a letter on his dresser which read: "I can't wait to spend some more time with you. I want a chance to know you better. I didn't want to wake you up and say goodbye because you was sleeping too good. P.S. You better be a man of your words."

Eric imagined her how she looked last night with her bra and panties on -- she could have been a model for Victoria's Secret. All the other times he fooled around with her, the light was off or dim. He finally saw her amazing body with the light bulb shining bright. He couldn't wait to stand next to her again.

Unlike Steven, Lewis woke up to find his breakfast cold. Sam and Jessica didn't wake him up to eat. Jessica made scrambled eggs, grits, bacon, and toast, but they didn't leave one slice behind. They did not care whether he ate or not. Lewis had to fix his own food and put it in the microwave. When his food got hot enough, he ate it at the kitchen table. Before he got up from the table, he saw a $100 bill under his shoe. He looked around before he picked it up. He knew it belonged to Sam, but Lewis was going to keep it anyway.

Sam came into the kitchen with an open bottle of Crown Royal. He was drunk and staggering with every step he took. He told Lewis, "I ate the rest of the toast. Learn to get your ass up in the morning. Please try not to be an idiot all your life. Jessica and I will not be around all your life. Learn to make better small decision. Sooner or later, you will be making big decision like me. Clean these dishes too; your mother is tired of cleaning up after you!"

Jessica heard Sam rubbing it in about the toast. She didn't say anything. He told Jessica when she came into the kitchen, "Move out my way, bitch, you are the one who gave birth to this retarded boy!"

Jessica looked at Steven and told him, "Damn, you just find ways to get under his skin." She rolled her eyes at Lewis like he was the person who gave Sam the bottle. Then she walked away with disgust written on her face. Lewis shook his head. Sam and Jessica did not know they were pouring fuel to his fire. Lewis wanted to go over Steven's house to find some peace.

Lewis washed all the dishes, then went over to Steven's house. Steven was already outside. The first thing Lewis asked Steven, "Are you my brother?"

Steven answered, "You are my brother forever. The clouds are turning gray; I really don't want it to rain. So what's on your mind? You haven't come over my house this early in a long time."

Lewis replied, "My house looks like heaven, but hell is going on inside. I need to free myself from both of my parents. What's our next mission going to be? My money has to be saved because those assholes are pissing me off."

Steven stated, "You never had money problems before. At school, it wasn't a day that went by with you not having plenty of snack money."

Lewis replied, "My wino dad could lose an arm while he's drinking and wouldn't notice it was gone. When he's drunk, he could lose anything. Fortunately for me, my dad loses cash all the time. He can't remember what he did with that $50 bill. Basically, I steal from him."

Steven told him, "It sounds strange; they won't give you any money and they have so much."

Lewis told Steven how the stealing begun, "One day, when I was about eleven years old. My dad dropped four $1 bills. He placed his hand inside of his pocket and then the money fell out once he took his hand out of the pocket. I was timid about taking it. He would've tried to kill me if he knew I stole from him. As the days went by, he never asked about those dollars. I've been finding cash on the floor and under the couch pillows. Man, I have found hundreds of dollars over the years."

Steven thought the story was funny and he said, "Wow! That is a serious and hilarious story. I would find pennies, nickels, and dimes around my house. There was this one time when I found a $10 dollar bill. The money was given back to my dad; who lost it. Let's get back to business, man. We might do the same thing again. Practice makes perfect and we are not professional criminals, yet. Eric probably can't get us a car; it was a big favor to ask him for. If he get lucky enough to find us one, it would be great. Damn great. I know with your slice of the pie you're going to move out. If Dad was still alive I would move in with you. We would have ourselves a bachelor pad. Women would come in through the front and back door. Our home would become another version of the Playboy Mansion. Welcome to Freak City, USA."

Lewis said, "We were supposed to talk about a plan. Your mind is in the gutter, Steven. Let's speak about getting paid again. Don't lose me again with your freaky desires. What if I borrowed one of my parent's cars and used it for the crew?"

Steven kept on joking, "We could turn your dad's Mercedes Benz to a hotel on wheels. My honey and I would take the back seat while you and your chicken head get busy in the front seat."

Lewis stated, "Boy, something is wrong with you. Maybe, your ass has been in the sun too long; it's starting to fry your brain. The story would've gone like this; you would've been kicked out the car while, me and those ladies would've had a three some. We would let you masturbate and watch us through the windows."

Steven gave Lewis a hug and said, "Show me what you're working with, big boy."

Lewis said, "Get your gay and sensitive ass off me, dude. I'm going to tell the guys to call you, Steffi. Real talk, this joking around, made me feel much better. You haven't told me anything about Tim's funeral. I want to be there to support you and Barbara."

Steven responded, "The funeral is going to take place Friday or Saturday. My mom will let me know something when she gets everything together."

Steven and Lewis went inside the house and took a seat on one of the living room sofas. Steven picked up the remote and turn on the TV. A male news reporter named Jessie Ross was talking about a robbery that took place at a bus stop on Davis Street. He said, "A fifty-year-old man named Joe Ronald was assaulted and robbed. Joe couldn't identify any of his attackers and if anybody saw or knew anything contact the police. Joe did acknowledge that it was more than one person. Doctors are expecting him to make a full recovery. Who would do such a terrible crime?" Then the weather lady began to speak.

Steven and Lewis looked at each other, at the time same time, but they had different thoughts. Steven hoped the police officers wouldn't find out about it but Lewis was happy to see the robbery make the news. It gave him a thrill to become an outlaw. Lewis told Steven, "Our group needs a name. We would really give these people something to talk about."

Steven didn't want the crew to have a name because they wouldn't be together for a long time. He didn't see a reason to have one. Steven told him, "Longevity in this game will get you killed or jailed. This is real life and not something you saw on TV; your life doesn't have a sequel. Once you are dead, there is no coming back. Once these pigs have you sur-rounded, it's the end. The fast money sometimes comes with a big price. If we get a chance to hit a bank, I will leave this shit along. We could have enough cash to chill forever. A bank would be like our super bowl; it's all or nothing. The crew would have so much dough, we could swim in it."

Lewis said, "I can definitely see myself driving a Range Rover or a Jaguar. Living in a mansion with a few stories is good enough for a person like me. I'm used to living in luxury and I can't have it any other way. I would buy everything from expensive clothes to the latest video games. The one thing I always wanted was to become more successful than my punk ass dad. My granddad left my dad some land when he died; my dad was smart enough to get a few houses build on them. Sam is the worst dad ever in history, but he's a good doctor. A certified doctor has to be pretty smart."

Steven told him, "You want a lot of extravagance things; have you been taking notes from Jay-Z? Well, getting to his status is almost impossible; he made it that way."

Lewis told him with a serious face, "Why can't I become the next Jay-Z or anybody else who is balling out of control? Everyone should want to live their lives to the fullest."

Barbara came into the living room and then Steven and Lewis quit talking. Barbara said, "I'm on my way to the store. If a guy calls by the name of Fredrick Lee, tell him to leave a message. He will give me the information I need for Tim's funeral. Please don't forget it, Steven. I'll see y'all later."

Barbara left the house and drove away in her car. She was thinking about Steven and Lewis. *They were talking non-stop, but I couldn't hear them. I should've had my hearing aid in. They became quiet once I step into the room. They could be out there looking for trouble.* Then she started to feel like the worrying was for nothing. Barbara spotted a Wal-Mart and then she drove over there to get some things.

When Barbara left the house, Steven told Lewis, "Man, that was a close call; she came out of nowhere. We didn't hear any footsteps."

Lewis replied, "We should not talk about our business where she could possibly hear again. Tomorrow, we have to let the crew know, Friday or Saturday our next meeting will take place. Don't forget about the big favor I will need from you."

Steven was curious. "What kind of favor will you need?"

Lewis answered," It's a secret for right now. I'll tell you when the time is right." Lewis shook Steven's hand before he went back home.

Steven wondered, *The secret is something huge because Lewis is always up front about whatever he wants.*

Chapter 5

James was over his friend Alex's house, playing pool in his game room. The other two guys who were supposed to come didn't show up. All the pool games that were played between James and Alex went by fast. James played pool on this day like the Black Widow. James beat Alex three straight times, very dominantly. Normally, James would lose every game and every dime he had. But today, Alex gave James $60 because they played $20 per game. Alex was a sore loser; he couldn't believe James beat him convincingly and he didn't want to pay.

Alex started hating. "The next time you won't have luck on your side. I still have more wins over you than you have over me. Use the $60 to get you some better clothes. You look like you robbed a homeless person on the streets."

James became tired of him running his mouth, "Look here, Alex, you will swallow your teeth fucking around with me. When you were winning, everything was cool. Now that you have lost, you're acting like a bitch. Just step your game up next time, so you won't have to hate on me. I'll give you a chance to win your cash back. After you get smashed by me again, the respect has to get handed over. Hater, let's play bowling for $20 per game."

Alex confidently answered, "You must smoke crack, James. I'm the best at bowling and you are the worse at it. Let's make the deal sweeter; we could play for $30 per game."

You won't win one game against me. We could use the mall's bowling alley. In the great words of Ric Flare, 'to be the man, you have to beat the man'. Your chances of beating me in bowling are very slim."

James said, "On Saturday we will settle this shit. You better eat your Wheaties, homie. For now, I'm going home to enjoy my $60. Tell them other guys their ass whipping is coming too." James left Alex's house and went home.

Alex could not wait to bowl against James; he felt there was no way he could lose. Alex said to himself, *Today was a fluke; I want to see how he does at the bowling alley this Saturday.*

Willie and Johnny were doing well on the football field; a lot of scouts would talk to their coaches after the games. Willie had his mind on going to college. Johnny was losing his love for football; he believed no one cared about him unless he was on the football field. Scouts were also coming to their practices, as well. Willie had dreams of playing for UCLA and then play for an NFL team, San Francisco 49ers or Oakland Raiders.

After practice, Willie and Johnny were asked to take a picture for the newspapers by a journalist. Willie was on the right, Johnny was on the left and Coach Thomas was between them. The journalist told them, "The picture will make the front page of the newspaper. The title at the top will read in bold letters, 'State championship, here we come!'" Johnny was leading the state in sacks and force fumbles, twenty-four sacks and fourteen force fumbles. Willie was considered the second best defensive player on the team, behind Johnny. Most of their classes were put together by Principal Washington.

Willie's grade point average was a 3.2 in school and Johnny's averaged 2.9 before he stopped studying in the tenth grade. If a player could not average 2.0, they wouldn't be eligible to play on the team. Willie was giving Johnny answers on all the major testes. Rosa Park High School was very big on football since they get close to the big game every year. Without Johnny, the defense would not hold up. No defense, no state championship everybody thought. Even the teachers wanted them to win; they would let Johnny cheat off of Willie's paper to keep Johnny's grades up.

After practice, Willie and Johnny were walking home. Willie thought about Johnny's performance at practice. He asked, "What's wrong with you? Any other time scouts on come out, you would play like its NFL auditioning day."

Johnny replied, "It wouldn't make a difference whether I make it to college or not. I'm not smart enough to do college work. A matter of fact, without you I would stay behind in my work in most of my classes. Principal Washington set up our classes, so you could help me. In college, Willie, you will not be there to give me answers. College is for smart people like you. Yes, my playing skills on the field can get me a scholarship, but without book smarts, it is a waste of time. I wish all the scouts would watch Willie Moffett and not Johnny Moffett. This might sound crazy, but the street life is giving me hope. I could rob my way to the top."

Willie told him, "You should want more than a street thug lifestyle. We decided ahead of time that this thug shit wouldn't last forever, only until we have made us enough money to get a head start in life. The thug life is not a profession. Personally, I think you could make it in college. When I started helping you, studying was no longer an option in your mind. Maybe, there is a way to put you on the same level as a normal senior."

In Johnny's heart, he was no longer an athlete. Johnny still wanted to stay thugged out for a while. "How is anybody going to learn 10th, 11th, and 12th work in a few months? It's too late for me to hear all that school talk. My life could go in a different direction than yours. I can make it without going to college. Handle your business and I will handle mines." Willie and Johnny split ways. Willie was unsuccessful in making Johnny believe in going to college.

Eric was at home watching porn movies. In his closet, there were twenty-six porn movies and over one hundred porn magazines. Eric kept the volume low while his mom was at home. When Eric was at home chilling in his room, he was always masturbating and fantasizing about having sex with the finest girls in school. While he was masturbating, Honey gave him a call. "I'm sorry; I missed you last night. Maybe, tonight we could make up for lost time."

Eric was horny from watching all those flicks. "Come on over, baby. We can definitely get down and dirty." Honey didn't care about Eric too much -- she just liked him. Honey called him with dollars signs in her eyes. Last night Honey told Eric she was tired and it was a lie. Honey was in bed with another guy. Eric contacted her when she was finished with him. The other guy was one of her highest paying customers. "When your mom leaves, I'll come over there to fuck your brains out. Leave the door unlocked, please. There isn't anyone who could freak you like me" Honey said.

"Hurry up and get your freaky ass down here. Don't let me and my dick down; both of us are depending on you. I can't wait until my rocket explores your universe," Eric said.

"I'm on my way to see you, Eric or should I call you Mandingo. Stop jerking off and save some energy for me. Give me a few minutes, I'll be there," Honey said. Eric and Honey hung their cell phones up.

Eric was blinded by her good looks and charming ways. He just realized he'd made a big mistake. He was thinking with his head between his legs and not the one on his shoulders. He was supposed to keep it real with Rebecca, since his feelings had grown for her. When he thought about Rebecca, he didn't want to fool around with Honey. He didn't want to mess things up between him and Rebecca.

Later on when Eric's mom went to work, Honey came over. Eric and Honey were lying down on Eric's bed. Eric was trying his best to avoid any sexual contact with her. Honey was wondering why Eric was not all over her like he normally would be. Honey was tired of talking and she wanted to get paid. She started running her right hand through his hair. Eric told her, "The weather was kind of warm today. I hate warm and hot weather. If it was my decision, late October weather would stay all year around. Did you see the new Snoop Dogg video? He should be the greatest rapper of all time. S-N-double-O-P. doesn't forget about the L.B.C." Honey used her right hand to rub his chest. Eric kept trying to change the mood, "No one seems to understand Snoop's struggle. He was a member of a Crip gang in Long Beach. His song called 'Drop it, like it's hot' is inspirational to me." Then her right hand went from his chest to between his legs. She gave him a kiss on the lips. Eric was caught in the moment and gave her a kiss back. Eric could no longer fight the temptation; he began taking her clothes off. Then he "beat it out the frame". Honey was screaming so loud she could've wakened the dead. For two hours, they did every position twice.

When the freaking was over, Honey wanted to cuddle with him. Eric had really done a good job this time; she'd had six orgasms. She placed her arms around Eric from the back. He thought about Rebecca and he climbed out of the bed. Eric told her, "It is time for you to leave because my mom is coming home early to night. I'm sorry I forgot to tell you."

Honey became confused. "She hasn't come home early before."

Eric said, "Well, she is coming home tonight. There's nothing I can do about it. Here is your money and let me walk you to the living room door, goodbye." Both of them put their clothes on and walked towards the living room door. Honey had a hurt expression on her face. She couldn't believe Eric would make up a lie just to get her to leave. The most shocking part of all, he said the word goodbye. Goodbye to Honey meant he didn't want to see her anymore. Eric had never shown any kind of backbone before. He always acted like he was deep in love with her. On the way out, she started counting her money. By the time Honey made it out the door, she noticed Eric shortchanged her. She said to him, "Wait a minute, Eric. This is not all the money you were supposed to give me. I have $80 and you know I charge $120 for this kind of occasion."

Eric just wanted her to leave because he felt that he was not honest with Rebecca. He still wanted to become the man that he thought she needed. Eric told her, "Take it or leave it." Then he slammed the door in her face.

Honey became furious. She was thinking about killing Eric. She took her .22 handgun out of her purse. The gun was for her protection against any customers who wanted to force themselves on her and for customers who refused to pay. She decided not do anything to him for right now. She placed her gun back into her purse and then she went to her car and drove away. In a weird way, she liked the fact that Eric pushed her away. Eric proved he wasn't weak minded. No guy had ever treated her like she wasn't anything before because she was so beautiful; it kind of turned her on. Eric earned some respect from her and it made her want him even more. She still wished he'd given her the $40 that he owed.

Eric ran back upstairs to call Rebecca on his cell phone. Rebecca answered her phone by saying, "I haven't heard from you any today. Did you read my letter?"

Eric replied, "Yes, I've read the same letter four times. You have been on my mind all day. Do you need anything from me because I'm here for you?"

Rebecca said, "Maybe last night I was too emotional. I want you to shower me with love and not to take care of me. It's a good thing you was willing to take care of me, though."

Eric was excited just to hear her voice and he wanted to hang out with her again. "Last night seems like a long time ago. When can we meet again, Rebecca?"

Rebecca was a smooth con artist; she could make anything believable. She told him, "Right now, I'm cleaning my home and I have other things to straighten out. I will explain it to you later. Don't worry; no one else will taste my strawberries, but you. We will get together before you know it. Holler at me later on, baby."

Eric said, "All right." They got off the phone with each other.

Rebecca knew she had Eric right where she wanted him. Eric was such a good guy; she didn't know whether to be real with him or just use him for his money. Last night, everything she told him about her mom was true, but her crying was acting. Once she hung up her phone tonight after talking to Eric, she climbed into bed with three guys. Just like an Aladdin bitch, she granted any wish they wanted. On the other hand, Eric believed Rebecca was the one for him. He didn't have a clue that she was not sure about him.

The next day at school, Steven saw James at the water fountain before class started. Students were still going to breakfast. Steven approached him and said, "What's up?"

James jokingly responded, "The sky is what's up. I'm kidding. Do you have anything new to tell me? Your boy is ready to get back into the ring."

Steven responded, "Either Friday or Saturday night, it will go down again. We might do the same thing, but our location got to be different. Lewis and I had a long talk; we hope Saturday night could be the night for us. We have to keep y'all informed about what's going on."

James told him, "I'm ready to put in work on any given day. I'm also ready to eat breakfast on any given day; let's go into the cafeteria.

The cafeteria workers were serving pancakes, scrambled eggs, and bacon. Willie and Johnny came into the cafeteria behind them. The ladies made sure all the football players got extra food on their plate. Steven, James, Willie, and Johnny were all at the same table eating. James realized Willie and

Johnny had more food than the rest of them, "Damn, they gave y'all enough food to feed a giant. Maybe, I should've played football."

Willie responded, "Our bench stays cold a lot; we need someone to keep it warm."

James replied,"That is very funny. You better slow down before you eat a part of the spoon. Fuck CPR, I'm going to let you choke on it and die."

Johnny thought he was the "roasting" king, "Let me get in this. Let me get in this, please. I'm not going to let you handle Willie. James, you are so ugly that you would give Freddy Cougar nightmares and bad daydreams."

James told Willie and James, "Y'all look sweeter than Prince and Little Richard put together."

Steven didn't know how to "roast" so he just laughed at their jokes. He said, "Friday or Saturday, I'm having a party. Y'all guys are welcome to show up." Everybody automatically knew what Steven was talking about. Then the bell rang and everybody went to class.

Lewis stayed at home; his parents were at it again. Jessica called in sick from work because she wanted to confront Sam. Jessica suspected Sam was cheating on her. They were standing face to face. Jessica asked, "Who are these different women calling the house for you? They won't leave their names or messages. You must think I got a peanut for a brain?"

Sam responded, "You are a college graduate and a high school teacher; you are far from being dumb. I know you're very bright." Then Jessica slapped him so hard that the people in Sacramento could've heard it. Jessica should've been bright enough to know better that a man sees a slap as being very disrespectful.

Lewis was watching the whole thing, thinking, **This bitch is crazy; she probably should've punched him, instead. Can she smell the alcohol all over him? He's probably drunk.** The right side of Sam's face had a red handprint. Sam retaliated with a vicious back handed slap which sent her sliding across the kitchen table and then hitting the floor. He got on top of Jessica and started slapping her, over and over again. Lewis was getting ready to grab Sam from behind, but he stopped himself from helping her. He went to the refrigerator and got some popcorn with a glass of grape soda. He took a seat on one of the kitchen's chairs. Lewis pretended like he was at a championship boxing fight. Lewis chose to do nothing because Jessica hit him with a wooden vase across the head the last time he tried to help her. Plus, she told him to never put his hands on Sam again. After about two minutes of slapping Jessica down, Sam became tired and stopped. He looked up and saw Lewis enjoying their fight. Sam wanted to put everything on Lewis and he did. Sam asked Lewis, "How could you sit there and watch this happen? Dummy, you could have broken up the fight before it got out of hand." Jessica was laying there with both hands over her face, crying. Sam kissed her on the lips and apologized, "Baby, I'm very sorry about what I just did. It will never happen again because I love you with all my heart. When I'm drunk, the real Sam isn't there. Our son doesn't love us; he watched the whole thing eating popcorn." Then he helped her off the floor. Sam continued to make Lewis a part of their problems, "Lewis must have found us hurting each other very entertaining."

Jessica tried to attack Lewis, but Sam held her from behind. Jessica was irate because Lewis didn't break the fight up. She screamed repeatedly, "So you think this shit is funny?! So you think this shit is funny?!"

Lewis was sitting down with a big kool-aid smile on his face. He replied, "Check this out, my dad is the one who whipped your ass. Now you are mad at me like I'm the one who pimp slapped your face off. Do you remember the last incident? You told me to never put my hands on him again. My dad is full of surprises. He is a drunken child molester, an abuser, and a cheater. I swear I thought he couldn't get any worst. I'll never get between y'all again."

Jessica started yelling, "Please, let me go! Let me wipe the smile off his face!"

Sam held her even tighter, "Don't worry, baby; he will get what is coming to him. He's not worth it, just cool down."

Lewis left them in the kitchen and went to his bedroom. He began thinking about how they took their frustration out on him. *When everything goes wrong, they love to point the bullshit in my direction. I should have gone to school. My parents are very pissed off at me. The way dad was talking, he may have something up his sleeves. I don't have a clue what it is. As long as I'm staying under their roof; it will always be them against me.*

Eric came across Steven while they were changing classes. Steven told him, "Saturday or Friday, I'm throwing a party and you are invited. I'll get with cha after school." Then they went on to their next class. Eric remembered he had not spoken with his cousin, Redd, about the guns. He had been too busy talking and fooling around with prostitutes. Sex had been his main priority. Eric had never told anybody about his cousin, Redd, who was affiliated with a Piru Blood gang. Redd's real name was Shannon Wilson. Eric and Redd were real close at school. Redd was always two grades ahead of him. He helped Redd to graduate from high school and Redd introduced him to some prostitutes. He hadn't heard from Redd in five months.

Eric's mom Molly had warned him about hanging with Redd. She said in her own words, 'Redd is a ruthless killer and being with him is dangerous; a bullet doesn't have a name on it'. Eric didn't want to get close to him again. He had to communicate with Redd, so he could get the guns from him. The .9mm handgun he gave Lewis came from Redd. Eric decided to call Redd once he made it home.

After school, Steven caught up with Eric at the front of the school. He asked Eric, "Do you have the guns yet? I'm not trying to rush you, but we will need them soon."

Eric confidently responded, "I've been working on it. We will have three or four of them by Wednesday of next week. Don't worry about nothing, consider it done."

Steven asked him, "Have you seen Lewis today? I looked for him and I didn't find him. Maybe I'll give his house a visit."

Eric said, "I can use my mom's 2007 Toyota Land Cruiser. It has enough room to fit all us inside. My mom will be at work."

Steven told him, "Thank you, Eric. Giving us a car to handle our business is a big favor. Nothing will happen to your mom's car; that is my word. Just let me know, when you get those guns." Eric and Steven went their separate ways.

Steven decided to go over Lewis's house to check up on

him. He knew about Lewis's dysfunctional family. As he got closer and closer to Lewis's house, he saw someone standing in the yard. Steven realized he was looking at Lewis. Steven finally made it to Lewis and he asked, "Why didn't you make it to school today? I was looking for you all day long."

Lewis answered, "My mom and dad were arguing this morning while I was getting ready for school. My mom accused him of cheating. She was questioning him about the different women calling the house. The women who were calling the house would never leave their names or messages, which raised her suspicion. My dad was drunk -- his eyes were red and the alcohol smell on him was very strong. She was stupid enough to slap him in the face. Then he slap her back; she must of flew crossed the kitchen table. He got on top of her and slapped her senseless."

Steven asked him, "Did you help her out?"

Lewis replied," She hit me with a wooden vase the last time I help her ass out. The bitch even kicked me when I was down. She told me the last time to never put my hands on my dad again. I slammed his punk ass face first to the floor, the last time. Both of them were mad at me because I let them fight without doing anything. I ate popcorn while watching the fight."

Steven's eyebrows rose. He was shocked because Lewis did something like that while a serious matter was going on. "You actually watched while eating popcorn. I could only imagine how disappointed they are in you. Lewis, you may have to hire a bodyguard for protection to live at home. Your parents will not let that shit slide. Basically, you poured fuel to an already blazing fire."

Lewis felt cocky, "I also had some grape soda to go with the popcorn. He has been beating her ass for years. I'm not scared of them. They are the ones who will need a bodyguard to walk around the house if they keep on fucking with me. Sam is the problem in our house."

Steven was worried about what could happen at Lewis's house. He had a bad feeling someone would get hurt or killed. He told Lewis, "Try to avoid contact with them until things cool down."

Lewis responded, "That seems like the smart thing do. It's impossible; we live together."

Steven gave him some good news. "Eric and I had a little talk after school. He will let us use his mom's car, so we won't have to walk. Eric also said we will have the "heaters" on or before Wednesday. Everything is going in our way. Somehow you have to stay focus; we need you at your best."

Lewis said, "I'll be o.k. My family has been jacked up for years; it will not change in a few days. In my house, being insane is being normal."

Steven told Lewis, "Be careful, man. Your life is like a real soap opera, full of drama. Call me if things get out of hand, Lewis."

He told Steven, "I can take care of myself. You don't have to worry about me. Homie, I have everything under control. Nothing will happen to me unless I let it happen. There is not a chance in hell I would let something happen to me. You are trying to show me some sympathy and it is for the weak. Steven, you should know that I'm strong. It is an insult for you to console me like I'm a bitch. For some strange reason, you don't think I'm man enough to take care of myself. I'm Ford stuff, man."

Steven felt like his advice had backfired on him. He was trying to help Lewis through his problems at home. Lewis was hard-headed and he hated for anybody to tell him how he could handle his business and he didn't even care if it was good advice. Steven realized he was stubborn. Steven pretended to agree with him, "Lewis, you are right. Everything is under your control. It was crazy for me to doubt you."

Lewis was kind of upset, but now he started to calm down. Lewis stated, "Eric is coming through for us in a big way. You were correct when you said Eric is the key to the operation. We couldn't do much without him supplying us with everything. We have a car now so let's try to avoid a high speed chase with the police officers."

Willie and Johnny were at football practice. Johnny was back to his beastly ways, again. No one on the offensive line could stop him from hitting the quarterback. Coach Thomas decided to do something he never did before. Without telling Johnny, he made Willie a part of the offensive line to protect the quarterback. The quarterback hiked the ball and Johnny moved one player on the defensive line out of his way. The quarterback was in his sight and Johnny ran full speed toward him. He thought he was getting ready to make a sack and then Willie came out of nowhere and put Johnny on his back with a shoulder to chest hit. Everyone on the team was shocked to see Johnny on his back for the first time in practice. Johnny didn't know who or what hit him. While Johnny was lying on the ground he saw a hand reaching out to him. Johnny held on to the hand with both of his hands. Willie was helping him get up off the ground. Johnny asked, "What happened to me?" Willie had a huge smile on his face. He was trying his best not to laugh at Johnny. Johnny said, "Willie, it was you who ran me over."

Finally, Willie couldn't hold back his laughter. He snickered in Johnny's face. Willie told him, "It was Coach Thomas's idea to place me on offense." Everybody on the team started clapping their hands because they thought Willie did the impossible. The whole team surrounded him like he was a hero. Johnny became jealous because the team never showed him any love. Johnny hadn't realized Willie and the rest of his teammates had already established a good relationship. Johnny was the only black sheep on the team. The team knew Johnny only cared about his stats and getting his face in the newspapers, so all eyes could be on him.

Johnny felt like fighting everybody on the field, including the coaches. He went into the locker room to take a shower. He waited until after practice to let Willie know what was on his mind. Willie and Johnny were walking home and Johnny said, "You stabbed me in the back today. How could you let Coach Thomas turn you against me? Willie, you could've given me a warning."

Willie relied, "Coach Thomas is the head coach; we have to do whatever he says. Johnny, you are a special player. He had to do something different against you. Every practice you put somebody on their ass and you was fine with it. Now your back has met the ground and you want to act foolish. I've been put on my ass plenty of times; you don't see me complaining."

Johnny and Willie got face to face and Johnny warned him, "Don't let this football shit get to your head." Willie walked past him and Johnny held his arm and he said, "I'm not finished talking to you, yet. My own cousin took a cheap shot at me during practice. You would sell your soul for a scholarship to UCLA. Don't get mad at me because you don't want to "box" at all. Put your set up, Willie!" Willie put his guards up and then Johnny put his guards up too. Johnny was trying to see if Willie feared him. Willie showed him he was ready to rumble.

Johnny didn't want to battle and he began singing another tone, "Willie, you was right. I overreacted about everything. I'm very sorry, man. We are cousins and it wouldn't make sense for us to fight." Willie and Johnny shook hands and both of them went home.

James was at home watching Sports Center on ESPN. He wanted to know what teams were good and what teams were lame. James kept a small black notebook. He would write down all the teams he thought were good. He would also keep up with their scoring averages. Teams who had great defenses, he would write down their opponent's averages against them. He knew about a sports bar called "Touchdown". All he had to do was come up with five teams, but they would have to make the point spread in order for him to win some money. Fifty dollars is the maximum anybody could gamble with there. With a $50 bet, he could win $600. James was only seventeen; not old enough to gamble. A guy named Frank would always take up his bets. Frank was a 55-year-old black male who worked at the bar. James and Frank were cool with each other.

James was getting ready to call Frank, but Alex called him before he could dial Frank's cell phone number. Alex had revenge on his mind because James had manhandled him in pool the last time they met.

Alex arrogantly told James, "I hope you been practicing because there will be no excuses for getting embarrassed by me."

James responded, "No one needs to practice bowling to get a win over you. You couldn't beat me if I was blindfolded with one hand tied behind my back."

Alex replied, "Everyone gets lucky once in a while. Come on now, James, do you really think your chances of beating me are great? Man, you are far from being crazy because my trophies and plaques say a lot about my bowling skills. I'm a bowling legend."

James said, "All those trophies and plaques are great to have, but you won them with a team. Individually, you can't cut the mustard. Those awards don't mean anything to me. When Saturday comes, my skills will do the talking for me. The word lucky won't come out your mouth anymore."

Alex knew now that he couldn't get under James's skin. He told James, "Bring your A- game. It still won't be enough for you to win."

James responded, "I'll holler at you later. All the hating is making sick." Then Alex hung the phone up in James's face.

James thought, *Alex has changed since he lost to me in pool. The white boy is a very sore loser. I never saw him acting like this before. He was always winning and that is how he hid his real characteristics. It could become a bad idea to keep in touch with him if I win Saturday.*

James called Frank's cell phone number. "This is James and I was wondering would you put in my bet for me?"

Frank replied, "All the cash you lost last year, I'm surprised you're back for more."

James begged, "Please give me an opportunity to win my cash back from last year."

Frank told him, "You are a great kid. Having a gambling problem could cost you a lot one day. I'll work with you."

James was happy to hear him say that. He asked Frank, "How will you work with me?"

Frank answered, "If you start losing too much money, I will pull the plug on your operation. Good luck, James."

"Thank you for giving me another chance. I really appreciate your help. Have a nice day." James was thrilled to receive another crack at gambling there again. He had to get smarter with his picks this time around.

Eric made it home; he just came back from the store with a few snacks in his hands. He had Rebecca on his mind. Molly told him, "Keep up the good work, Son. Your cleaning skills are almost better than mines. Well, I'm in a hurry. Make sure the house stays looking good."

Eric said, "Alright, Mom." Molly went to work at the hospital where she nursed; she was running a little late. Eric called Rebecca on his cell phone and she didn't answer her phone. He dialed Redd's phone number and Redd answered his phone by saying, "All C's down, blood. What's up, kinfolk? I haven't heard from you in a minute."

Eric replied, "I can tell from the sound of your voice you're doing well. I'm getting ready to finish school soon. It seems like yesterday when we were kicking it around the school campus."

Redd told him, "It has been a long time; those days feel like two decades ago. How is your momma doing? Is she still tripping over me gangbanging?"

Eric answered, "Well, Mom is doing fine. She will never get over the fact that you are taking a part in gang related activities. Personally, I don't care. Handle your business and don't let your business handle you. I need a favor from you. Is there any way you can give me three or four guns?"

Redd responded, "Three or four is a lot of heat. Is someone after you? Tell me; I'll "get after" them fools."

Eric told him, "I just want to feel protected. Plus, I'm a gun fanatic."

Redd said, "I can bring the guns over your house tomorrow; when your mom leaves."

Eric said, "That sounds good to me. I'll hook up with you tomorrow." Eric knew Redd would agree to give him the guns. Redd touched so many guns that you would think he was a part of the USA Army. Eric had a lot of love for Redd, but he could never be close to him again. Redd would not let the red bandana go. Eric really didn't know what he was getting himself into dealing with Redd. Even though Redd was nice to him; he was still a cold blooded killer.

Eric focused his attention back on Rebecca. He tried to call her again and she didn't answer her phone. Eric was wondering why she wouldn't answer her phone. He was losing his mind thinking about her. Then it seemed like a light bulb came on over his head. He thought, **Rebecca could still be prostituting. It's the only reason I can come up with for her not to answer my calls.** Eric's cell phone started to ring and he looked at his phone and saw Rebecca's name and phone number. He was angry, but he wanted to keep his cool.

Eric answered his phone. "What have you been doing? I

called you twice and you didn't answer your phone. The other night you were supposed to be busy."

Rebecca wanted to earn his trust back. "I was taking a shower. You know I want to smell good tonight. All that cleaning made me tired the other night. We will hang out tonight, I promise."

After she told him they would be together tonight, Eric forgot he was mad at her. He said, "I'm sorry for overreacting. You're the only one I'm thinking of. Just the thought of losing you drives me crazy."

Rebecca knew she had his heart back in her possession. She stated, "Tonight, all those silly thoughts in your head will get put to rest. I'm going to show you better than I can tell you." She sounded very convincing to Eric. Then she told him, "Let me dry off and I will see you later."

Eric said, "Okay, Rebecca." Eric thought everything was back to normal. The real reason she didn't answer her phone was because she just didn't want to talk with him. Eric wanted to ask her was she still prostituting, but he did not. He wanted to get laid tonight and a question like that would probably kill her freaky mood.

Steven was at home sitting down with Barbara. Barbara told him, "Fredrick Lee called me today with the information we need about Tim's funeral. He said it would be cheaper if we use his funeral home, The Fredrick Lee's Funeral Home. He has the cheapest deal going. The autopsy took too long; they wanted to make sure it was a heart attack that killed Tim. The heart attack did kill him. The funeral will take place Friday at Fredrick Lee's Funeral Home to save money. Some of his former co-workers may show up."

Steven's mood went from happy to sad. "We have every-thing ready for him. He will live on through us now, Mom. You and I are going to miss him a lot. We will mourn him until we join him. In the meantime, we are going to be alright. I will make sure of it." Barbara didn't have a clue about what Steven meant when he said he was going to make sure they were going to be alright. Barbara went to her room.

Steven wasn't going to let anybody stop him from pro-viding for his mom. He still wanted a piece of the police offi-cers. He couldn't let what happen to Tim slide. **He did some thinking.** *What if I shoot up a few police stations? It's a perfect idea; I just want to piss them off. I don't even want inside the station. Without them there, I would avoid a shoot out with the police. Some kind of way, I will cause a diversion. The police station will get left unattended, hopefully. The shooting must be done very fast. The pigs wouldn't know who did it. They would probably think the shooters could come back for more. Just like they terror-ized my dad, I'm going to terrorize them.*

Later on that night, Eric waited for Rebecca to call. She never called or came over his house. Eric had his hopes high about her coming over to chill with him that night. He called her over and over again, but he did not get an answer. He fell asleep waiting on her. Once again, Rebecca was out getting her freak on. Eric was the last thing on her mind while she was bending over getting pounded by another customer.

The next day, Molly left home on her way to work. Redd came over to Eric's house driving a black '64 Chevy Impala with the convertible roof and hydraulics. Redd was mixed with black and white. He had tattoos on both of his arms, three tattoo tears under his left eye and a tattoo of the Lord's Prayer on his chest. He kept his head cut bald and his eyes were dark gray. Today he was wearing a tank top, a pair of khaki pants, and a custom made LA Dodgers cap (all white with a red LA sign), and a pair of all red Converse Chuck Taylor shoes. Eric opened the door and let Redd walk in. Redd begin looking around the living room. He was noticing all the changes that had been made. Redd said, "There used to be a picture of me and you on top of the TV. What happened to the picture, anyway?"

Eric replied, "My mom must of taken it down; she is really angry with you. Mom probably hates your guts now, Redd."

Redd responded, "I hate her fine ass too with that big booty. She was a secret crush of mines. Every time she walked her hips would swing from side to side. I remember when I walk in on her taking a hot shower. I would have traded my dope money to become those drops of water hitting her soft and beautiful breast."

Eric said, "That's my mom you're talking about. She is also your aunt; dude, that's nasty to see her in a sexual way."

Redd told him, "Molly is my aunt by marriage. If Molly was willing to give me a piece, I'll give you a little sister or brother."

Eric was uncomfortable with Redd speaking about his mom sexually. He changed the subject. "So what's in the bag?"

Redd answered, "Eric, you already knew what's inside of this garbage bag." Redd took the guns out the bag one by one. He brought two .45 Caliber Semi Automatics, also known as a Ruger and two 380 Caliber Semi Automatics. Redd told him, "Don't shoot your eyes out kid. I hope you can handle these toys. The .45 handgun is very power; hit the weight room before you squeeze the trigger. All these guns are fully loaded with the serial numbers scratched off. Plus, there's even more bullets inside the bag; most of them are still in the original boxes."

Eric stated, "I really appreciated you for given me some guns."

Redd said, "If you ever get ready to kill someone let me know. We are all soldiers in God's eyes. I wouldn't let anybody tell me different. This is the life for me, fucking hoes, drinking Colts 45s, and hitting switches in my Chevy Impala. If you think about becoming a real G, let me know. I'll holler at cha later, kinfolk. The suburban life could fuck up my street credibility. I like to wake up and go outside to smell the sweet fragrance of gun powder."

Eric replied, "Redd, you must have all the juice. You will get a call from me soon." After Eric and Redd dapped up each other, Redd opened the door and exited the house

Once Redd left, Eric started picking up the guns and looking at them. He began thinking, *Are these guns on safety? Redd has a lot of juice; the only thing I need is a couple of sips. I will become thugged out, soon. Everybody in the crew is "sleeping" on me, but I'm going to wake them up.* Eric put all the guns back into the bag. He carried it to his bedroom and then he hid it inside the closet. Eric took his cell phone out of his pocket and then he called Steven.

Steven answered the phone," Easy money, what's good?"

Eric responded, "I have the heat like it's the winter time."

Steven told him, "You're dependable. Don't tell me about what kind of guns you have; I like surprises. We have to get in touch with everybody and let them know what's going on. I will call a meeting tonight to go over our weekend plans. You are going to be our driver, Eric, AKA Jeff Gordon."

Eric was proud of himself because he delivered on his word. He cheerfully said, "Well, I am the Connection Man; it's my job to bring us whatever we need. Let me know when you need something else, homie."

Steven laughed and replied, "You need to put those Snoop Dogg CDs away. Just act like yourself and everything will be okay. I wish I had your smarts. You've been making good grades forever; that's how you become cool for real. Almost everybody in our class voted for you, the most likely to succeed."

Steven was truthful with Eric, but he didn't want to hear it. Eric had been a smart nerd most of his life. Being fascinated with science and chemistry was starting to get boring to Eric. He was tired of his soft image. Eric told him, "My accomplishments in school were great. I'm on another mission now."

Steven said, "Don't let your new mission take you away from the books. Knowledge is power, Eric. You have the power to become someone great."

Eric stated, "Alright Pastor Steven, I received your message my brother. I'm still going to college. It is time for me to try different things because my life isn't too fun. Enough about me, let's get back to the mission at hand. We should be getting in touch with the crew right now."

Steven told Eric," Okay. I get the hint for me to get off your back. At 8:45 tonight is a great time for our meeting. I'll holler at you there, Eric."

Eric responded, "Take it easy, man."

Steven replied, "The next time we meet bring the thug manual with you. Rule 48 states, a nerd can't become a thug. I'm just fucking with you; I had to sneak that joke in."

Later on, Steven spoke with Lewis and they went to the hideout together, on foot. Steven and Lewis were joking around on their way to the hideout. They walked through an alley between two brick buildings. The alley was a short cut to the hideout. A middle aged black man came out from behind a large trash can and scared both of them when he popped up out of nowhere. He was shaking and scratching himself. The guy was 6'2 with gray and black hair on his head and beard. His clothes were dirty with a lot of holes in it. Steven and Lewis stared at the guy and he stared back at them. The man spoke, "Do anyone of you have some crack? Y'all look like two drug dealers to me."

Steven replied, "We don't sell any drugs."

The man wasn't ready to believe them. "We can do this the easy way or the hard way. Make a wise decision, if you know what's good for you."

Lewis told him, "We don't have any drugs. Go find someone who does sale drugs, man. My partner and I are not looking for any trouble. Let us bounce from around here."

The man was getting frustrated because he was craving crack. They could see the anger in his face. Then he said, "If I don't get what I want, the only thing that will bounce is y'all heads." He walked in front of Lewis and then he punched him in his face. Lewis fell down on the ground. Steven hit the crack head behind the head. The guy turned around and swung at Steven. Steven duck down and gave the guy a football tackle. Steven was on top him, but the man was too strong. He overpowered Steven; the man rolled over and got on top of Steven. The guy was trying to choke the life out of Steven. Lewis got up off the ground. He delivered some solid blows to the crack head behind his head and on his back. The man still had Steven on the ground choking him. Lewis just realized he had a .9mm handgun in his pocket. He took the gun out and then he aimed at the crack head from behind. Lewis thought he could shoot Steven if he was not careful shooting. Lewis walked in front of them to prevent shooting Steven. Lewis started shooting the crack head; he shot him three times in the chest. The guy fell backwards off of Steven. Steven was trying hard to catch his breath and he slowly got back on his feet. He saw Lewis standing over the man with a gun in his hand. Lewis put his hands on the man chest and he didn't hear a beat. Then Lewis put his ear by the man's mouth; he couldn't feel or hear him breathing. The man was dead.

Once Steven caught his breath, he asked Lewis, "Where did you get the gun from?"

Lewis answered, "Eric gave me this gun; I told him not to tell anyone. The gun was supposed to become a surprise. Well, are you surprised, Steven?"

Steven was still stunned about what had happened. He said, "I thought the crack head was going to kill me. You saved my life, Lewis."

Lewis said, "You are my brother; I can't let some crazy muthafucka hurt you." Lewis began searching the man's pockets. He checked all of his pockets until he found some money. Lewis said, "Let's get out of here. We will count the money later, after the meeting tonight." On the way to the hideout, Steven and Lewis tried to straighten up their appearance. They didn't want anyone to know what had happened.

As they walked in Lewis told them, "We are here, guys." Steven came in behind Lewis. He was feeling kind of sad because he saw a man get killed tonight.

Before Steven and Lewis made it there, everybody was wondering what was taking them so long. Steven said, "I'm sorry we took too long; we weren't paying attention to the time."

James said, "It's almost 9:15pm; y'all conversation must have been real good."

Steven told him, "Lewis and I were talking about some of the best looking girls in our school. I don't know about y'all, but Lewis and I want to fuck every dime piece there."

Willie said to Steven, "You are sweating a river, dude."

Lewis stated to Willie, "I thought it was kind of warm in here. Let's talk about what we are here for."

Steven asked Eric, "Would you show everybody the heaters?" Eric pulled all the guns out the bag and laid them on the table. Steven became "crunk". "Now, that is what the fuck I'm talking about! I made Eric a part of this crew! Saturday night, we will get it on. Eric has supplied us with guns and a "ride" to handle our business with. The M.V.P. of this crew is E.R.I.C. We have all the tools we need to work with." Everybody took turns holding the guns. Steven kept on talking. "Lewis is the only one of y'all that knows about my dad's death."

Johnny said, "I'm sorry to hear the bad news. What happened to him, anyway?"

Steven responded, "The pigs yelled at him and they pulled their guns out on him too. All of that bullshit caused him to have a heart attack. They came after the wrong muthafuckin man. We need to shoot up a police station."

Everyone became quiet very quickly. Willie was worried, "Steven, you must have lost your damn mind. We are trying to stay away from the police as far as we can. Your dad's death was very tragic. You would put every one of us in jeopardy. We won't have a chance in a shoot out with the police officers. Most of them are trained to become straight shooters. They also out number us by thousands. Steven, think it over."

Lewis told them, "I'm ready to stand by Steven no matter what. I'm down with "lighting" their station up. Steven, count me in."

Eric saw an opportunity to put his wimpy image in the trash. Eric walked up to Steven and told him, "I got your back and I will not hesitate to shoot, fuck them bitches." Eric took everybody by surprise. He stepped up to the plate before James, Willie, and Johnny.

James was curious about Steven's plans and he didn't want to look scared. He told Steven, "If you come up with a good plan, count me in too? We shouldn't develop into dumb criminals."

Johnny wanted to show his toughness too. He always wanted to do something crazy like that, "Hell yea, I hate the pigs anyway. They are always harassing young black men. Come on Willie, stop acting like a coward."

Willie looked at Johnny and told him, "You are calling me a coward and I'm no coward. This is a real dangerous move Steven is suggesting that we should make."

Steven said to Willie, "I'm not forcing you at all. If you won't take a part in this, it's fine with me. There's no pressure on you, so make your own decision."

Johnny jumped into the conversation again, "Stop being too soft, Willie. You are acting like a little punk."

Willie asked Johnny, "What is your problem?"

Johnny stated, "Willie, you are the problem. We should boot you out of this crew. Grow some nuts and step your gangster up."

Everybody was wondering why Johnny was coming at his cousin Willie. Willie couldn't take any more of Johnny's trash talk. "Since I am a coward; we can go at it right now. I bet I will beat the shit out of you. They are going to see who the real punk is."

Steven stepped between them as the peace maker. He told Willie and Johnny, "We can't let y'all fight. Everybody hear would love to see who would win, though. Our crew has to grow into a brotherhood. Everyone here has to watch the other person's back, at all times. Y'all need to put all of that energy into Saturday night. Eric, since you want to become "bout-it". You will be Lewis's right hand man this time around. Willie, you will stay in the car behind the wheel, but normally Eric will do the driving. James and Johnny will team up together. The backup man is my position, just in case something goes wrong."

James said playfully, "Steven is our Phil Jackson. He's coaching us on how to become the best criminals. Lewis is our Kobe Bryant. Johnny is our Paul Gasol and I would become our 6th man, Lamar Odom. Hell, Willie and Eric would not come off the bench."

Everybody started laughing, but Eric didn't think it was funny. He took the joke as if James was telling him he wasn't tough enough to roll with them. Eric wanted to bust James in his mouth. James didn't know he gave Eric more motivation. Saturday night, Eric would try to prove he wasn't weak.

Steven ended the meeting by saying, "This meeting is over with; everybody knows their roles."

Johnny gave Willie an apology and he accepted it. They left the building together. Eric left with a smile on his face but he was pissed off inside. James exited the building laughing. Lewis and Steven were the only ones who stayed after the meeting.

Lewis pulled the money out of his pocket and then he noticed three $20 sacks of crack. The sacks looked like very small Ziploc bags. The money was wrapped around the cocaine. Lewis hurried up and placed the cocaine back into his pocket. Steven was watching everybody leave. Lewis called Steven and he came to see what Lewis wanted. Lewis told Steven, "Here's the money." They counted $79 in all, two twenty dollar bills, two ten dollar bills, and nineteen one dollar bills. Lewis took $40 and Steven kept $39.

Steven said," I can't believe we killed someone tonight. I hope we didn't leave any evidence behind. That crack head was begging for trouble. I was feeling sorry for him, but fuck him; he was trying to kill me."

Lewis didn't give a damn. "I killed someone trying to defend myself. I'm happy to get a murder under my belt. We might see a lot of dead muthafuckas soon."

Steven said, "You're actually happy to kill someone. We didn't get in this to kill, only to stack paper."

Lewis responded, "Man, you need to wake the hell up! We are gangsters, thugs, and criminals or whatever society wants to call us. Killing is a part of this job. Have you ever heard of a mailman who didn't deliver mail? What about a policeman who won't make an arrest? What about a gangster that never put in work on the streets? The answer to all the questions is no. You may not be cut out for this shit. It is not too late for you to quit. I would take over as the sole leader of the crew."

Steven responded, "I'm not going anywhere. Have you been carrying that gun around almost every day since you hid it from me?"

Lewis answered, "No, I've been carrying it around every day. You should stay a true leader or move your save-the-world ass out of my way. Stop being a nice guy; it's time to get rough and raw. Choose one, saint or sinner. I'll pick sinning because it just feels better."

Lewis left the hideout without saying bye to Steven. Steven said to himself, *There's no reaching him now. Someone should've told him gangsters don't live too long.* Steven realized he had to keep his eyes open for Lewis and Johnny. Both of them were snapping on their crew members. Steven looked at his shirt; he saw a few drops of blood on it. Steven came to the hideout with Lewis and now he was leaving by himself.

When Lewis arrived home, his parents were gone. He went to get a plate from the kitchen. He brought the plate to his bedroom. Lewis put the plate on his bed. He took all the cocaine out of the sacks by pouring them out on the plate. He lay down in the bed with the plate of cocaine in front of him. He used his pinky finger to move the coke; he made a small line. Lewis took a $20 bill out of his pocket and rolled it. Lewis started wondering how he saw it done on TV. He always wanted to know what it felt like. Lewis held down one of his nostrils and placed the rolled up $20 in his other nostril. Lewis started to inhale the coke. His first hit was very long. He was amazed because he didn't know it felt so good. Lewis said to himself, *This is some good shit. I should've been tried some coke a long time ago. I want this feeling over and over again.* He went ahead and finished the rest of the cocaine. He went back into the kitchen to wash and dry the plate. Lewis put the empty sacks in his pocket. He was going to throw them away, while walking to school. Before tonight, Lewis had never done any drugs in his life. Now he was willing to experiment with coke and other drugs, trying to reach an ultimate high. Lewis heard his parents' car outside and then he ran up the stairs. He went into his room and lay down under his bed covers. Lewis pretended to be asleep to avoid Sam and Jessica.

About seven minutes later, he heard his bedroom door open and close. Sam was trying to see whether Lewis was in his room or not. Sam went in the kitchen and told Jessica, "Lewis is in bedroom sleeping. He doesn't have a clue what we have in store for him. We are going to pretend everything is fine, for now. I'm going to strip him of something that no real man would want it to be taken."

Jessica added, "When it goes down; I'm going to watch the whole thing. After this, he will never play around with us again. We have done our best to raise him; sometimes your best isn't good enough."

Sam said, "Enough about him, our dinner at IHOPS was good. When I saw the IHOPS commercial on TV, I just knew it would taste great."

Jessica responded, "Sam, you were always good at picking the right dining places."

Sam held Jessica's right hand and told her, "I think we should go in our bedroom and make love."

Chapter 6

When Friday came, Barbara and Steven knew it was going to be an emotional day. The Funeral took place at 12:00pm. Barbara and Steven were sitting down side by side at the funeral home. Tim's casket was three and a half feet in front of them. Fredrick Lee was also the preacher. All of their neighbors showed up to the funeral. Tim's casket was brown with gold handles. Tim had on a white three piece suit with a black tie. Barbara thought the white suit made him look heavenly. Barbara was wearing a black dress with a black pair of high heels shoes. Steven was wearing a black three piece suit. He had on a gray long sleeve button up shirt under his jacket. He also wore a pair of black dress shoes and a black tie.

The funeral lasted two hours. At the end of the funeral, Fredrick opened the casket for everybody to see Tim for the last time. Everyone who attended the funeral walked up to the front to see Tim. Barbara and Steven were the last people to get up to see Tim. Barbara gave him a kiss on the cheek and she said, "Goodbye." Steven told him, "I will love and miss you forever." Fredrick closed the casket and told the pallbearers to get ready to carry the casket. Six of Fredrick's hand-picked pallbearers picked up the casket and took it to the black hearse. Barbara told Fredrick, "My son and I had enough for one day. We don't want to watch the burial." Steven did not cry at the funeral because he wanted to stay strong for his mom. Barbara's tears were running down from her face non-stop; the only man she ever loved was getting put to rest. Barbara and Steven went home in her car.

Once they made it home, Barbara and Steven looked through a few photo albums to relive some memories. They went from page to page while sitting on one of the living room couches. Barbara told him, "Thank you for being so strong for me today. I guess one of us had to be."

Steven responded," Dad would've wanted me to stay strong."

Barbara told him, "I'm so tired right now. Maybe I can get a good nap in; lying down is relaxing."

Steven said, "You should go and get some rest. I'll just stay here and finish looking through the photo albums." Barbara gave Steven a hug and she went to her bedroom to take a nap.

Steven started crying like a newborn baby. He wanted to cry during the funeral. Now that he was by himself, Steven didn't have a reason to hold his tears in. He turned on the TV in the living room. He had the remote in his hand, flipping the channels. As he was flipping the channels, Steven stopped when he heard Jessie Ross the reporter say, "Jack 'The Rat' Harold body was found with multiple gun shots wounds to the chest in an alley. He was assaulted. There were some bruises on his back and the back of his head. Jack had a high level of cocaine in his system. The bullets that killed him came from a .9mm handgun; the autopsy was done and it revealed that. The Police say most likely, he was killed trying to attack someone. He has been on the run for three years. There's a lot of controversy about his escape from prison. Some people expected an inside job. He was wanted in California and Nevada for the murders of seven people. The police officers are ready to speak with any witness or someone who knows something about what happened to him."

Steven pondered, *A killer was murdered, damn. If Lewis hears about this making the news, he will get ready to pop a cap in somebody else. It will also feed his want to be hard ego.*

James decided to skip class, again. He was inside the arcade section of the mall. He was playing four of his buddies in Street fighters, Pac Man, and NBA live. He wanted Alex to come there, but he was a no show. Every game was worth $10 and $20 a piece. James was unstoppable in all the games. He was wining game after game. He was taking all of his friend's money. James couldn't lose a game even if he tried to. The guys who came to the arcade were playing against each other too. Every time one of them would play against James, he would add a loss to their records. James won $320 and he wanted more. His buddies were astonished because James had never had a winning streak before. Everybody was ready to leave and James gave them a message, "Go and tell Alex I'm ready for our bowling match up Saturday. Stop bragging about his little trophies and let his skill speak for him."

One of the guys said, "I will give him the message, James. The next time you won't be so fortunate. You were Michael Jordan today, but soon you'll go back to being Sam Bowie." James didn't know how he became so good at everything. He planned on keeping the winning streak going for as long as possible. When he started walking home, James decided to call Frank.

Frank answered the phone, "Hey, how is it going?"

James replied, "Everything is going well for me. I wanted to make a $50 bet on the football games this Sunday."

Frank responded, "Just have your list of teams and your money ready before Sunday. Alright dude, good luck and I will see you later."

James had been studying all the NFL teams. He felt like his picks were guaranteed to win and make the point spread. His $50 bet would win him $600; it would become the most money he ever won gambling on the point spread. James's cockiness was building up his ego like he couldn't lose.

Willie and Johnny were on the school bus going off to play in a playoff game. Everybody was excited about their chances of winning. Johnny was quiet and Willie was more vocal. Willie felt like a general leading his troops to battle. Willie became the team's real captain. Willie and the rest of the team were repeating "We can't be stopped! We can't be stopped!"

Johnny thought, *Willie needs to close his mouth. He is trying too hard to gain everyone's respect. All of this screaming is irritating.* If their team won tonight, they would play in the championship game.

Coach Thomas noticed a change in Johnny behavior. It seemed like he just didn't care anymore. Everybody on the bus were laughing and joking around. Johnny had a straight face, not showing any happy emotions. Coach Thomas wanted to speak with him. He decided he would have a chat with him after the game. He knew it would take a team effort to win. They could lose if Johnny played like he didn't care. The team had a lot of seniors on it; they would be mostly 10th graders next year. Coach Thomas had to strike while the iron was hot. Who knew when they would have another opportunity to win a championship again? Coach Thomas was sitting by a window on the front of the bus. He had an assistant coach sitting by him; they were going over different plays for tonight.

Eric arrived home from school. Molly was looking everywhere, trying to find her work shoes and a pair of earrings. She cooked fish and French fries so Eric wouldn't have to cook. Molly went to work three hours early because she wanted some overtime money. Her normal work schedule was 7pm to 7am. She gave Eric a hug and said, "I love you." Eric went into the kitchen while Molly exited the house. He went inside the refrigerator to get some ketchup. Eric poured some ketchup on his food. The door bell rang and he said to himself, *Maybe Mom left something behind. She was in a rush when she stepped out of the door.*

When Eric opened the front door his eyes became wide open and his bottom lip even dropped. He was stunned to see Honey. He wasn't expecting to see her again. She walked inside without being invited by him. Honey had never come over his house without telling him she was on her way. Eric and Honey stared at each other for a few seconds. Honey told him, "Don't treat me badly again. Now give me my $40."

Eric went into his bedroom and took $40 dollars of his money from under his mattress. He came back down stairs and gave Honey the money, two $20 dollar bills. Honey wasn't finished talking to Eric, "You better treat me with some respect for now on. I thought we were better than that. Maybe you fell on your head or something. For some crazy reason, you pretended to not care about me. We made passionate love that night. You acted like a real jerk after it was over."

Eric had to think hard about what he was going to say,

"Did we make love? I thought we were just fucking. Girl, you are talking like we had a relationship. It was business and you know it. We had our fun, but it's over with."

Honey wasn't going down without a fight. She gave him a hug and looked into his eyes. She said, "Ever since we stopped talking I've been stressed out. We need to let the past go and look toward the future." Eric noticed when Honey placed her arms around him she was very soft and smelled good. Eric looked in her eyes and then all those feelings came back. Eric held her with both of his hands on her waist. She even hugged him tighter. Honey had fallen in love with Eric. Honey held Eric's right hand and walked him into his bedroom. Eric didn't give a rat's ass about Rebecca at this moment. Honey and Eric made love in his bed. After they were finished making love, Honey cuddled with him. Eric held her like she was his wife. It was no longer about the cash with her anymore.

While Eric was lying down, he realized that he had a new problem. Honey or Rebecca, which one he loved the most. He had fallen in love with two prostitutes. Eric was far from a player, but it was just the way things were going for him. Honey and Rebecca were very attractive women. Eric thought, *One day I will have to decide which girl I want. For right now, I want to have fun with both of them.*

Lewis was in his bedroom thinking about getting high. He knew one person who sold drugs. Three $20 sacks of crack (soft) was what he wanted. He also wanted to take over the crew. Steven just wasn't gangster enough to him to stay a leader. He wondered could he come up with better ideas than Steven. Lewis's cell phone began ringing, Steven was calling him. Lewis really didn't want to answer his phone, but he answered it anyway.

Steven asked, "Did you watch the news today?"

Lewis replied, "No, I have not watched the news." Steven said, "Well, the guy who attacked us was wanted by the police. He probably killed seven people."

Lewis stated, "He received a dose of his own medicine. The bastard tried to put us on his list as numbers eight and nine. Tomorrow night will work in our favor; I can feel it. How do you come up with all those "tight" ideas? I've known you forever; you never showed any signs of being a clever criminal."

Steven replied, "It comes to my mind easily. A lot of shit crosses my mind, both good and bad ideas. Shooting up a police station is a bad idea. We won't get paid for doing it. Making Eric a part of the crew is a good investment. I was smart enough to see that he could become a big factor in our operation."

Lewis thought Steven was bragging on his accomplishment. Lewis stated, "What wasn't an idea of yours? You act like all the good ideas came out of your mouth. Don't forget, it was me who recruited two of the toughest guys from our school to join the crew. It was me who convinced you we could do this. Putting this shit together came from me. I'm my own leader."

Steven thought, **Here we go again**. He told Lewis, "Look man, making Willie and Johnny a part of the crew was a genius move. I'll give you a round of applause for that move. We are both leaders, not just me. Everybody is an important piece."

Lewis was still jealous because Steven was better than him when it came down to coming up with a plan. He had been envious for years over the fact that Steven's parents loved him so much and his parents loved him less. Lewis said, "The next time, explain yourself better, so we won't have another misunderstanding."

Steven wanted to keep himself calm. "I can feel where you're coming from. It is a good thing to have someone like you to help me out with everything. We have a dream team on our hands. We will get things "popping", Saturday."

Lewis told Steven, "Everything is going to be alright. Keep in mind; you are not the sole leader. I'm not trying to stop you from coming up with ideas. I respect what you have done. Tomorrow night, Johnny and I will take the lead in assaults. I'm more trigger happier than a crooked cop in the ghetto. The rest of you will follow our lead. If another clown approaches us, we will turn him into ashes. I'm going to use my "tools" to take them apart. The guy we fought in the alley gave us a good fight; we gave him a chance to beat our asses. We will deliver the haymakers for now on."

Steven told him, "If things get out hand, I want to kick some ass too. The crack head in the alley tried to choke me out. To say he was a bomb on the streets, he was mighty strong. Watch over Eric for me; we can't afford for him to get hurt. Everything would go down the drain if someone breaks him in two."

"I'll keep the nerd safe. He seems ready for war; I hope he's not "stunting". If he leaves me behind, it would be the last mistake he will ever make. Hopefully, he won't coward out at the wrong time. No one said anything, but who believes someone that skinny is capable of handling his business on the streets. He will have to show me a killer instinct. I'm not talking about the video game call Killer Instinct, either," said Lewis.

"Don't worry about Eric. Believe it or not, he wants this almost as bad as you do. I had a talk with him; he could be over anxious to fight this war with us. In our last meeting, he was second behind you to support me in shooting up a police station. In my opinion, Eric is going to surprise a lot of y'all," Steven said to Lewis.

You are the one who placed him into this battle. If something happens to him, his blood will dry on your hands," Lewis said.

"I knew it was a risk to bring Eric into this. At first his hands wasn't supposed to get dirty. It was him who decided his hands should not stay clean," Steven added.

Lewis asked, "How was Tim's funeral?"

Steven answered, "It was like all the other funerals. Seeing my dad in a casket was difficult for me. Mom and I have to move on with our lives."

Lewis suggested, "Seeing my dad in a casket would be easy for me. That faggot deserves to die."

Steven said, "Wow, you're on some Eminem type shit. I know you don't really hate Sam. If something bad would happen to him, I bet you would lose your mind. Parents are supposed to get on their children's nerves. It is the unwritten law, Lewis."

Lewis said, "I would lose some stress. My pockets would look pregnant. I would never have to look for a job. Living like a Don, I can get used to that lifestyle. Can you picture me rolling in my 500 Benz?" Steven didn't know what he just sparked up. Lewis already had his thoughts of getting his parents out of the way. He made Lewis visualize what life would be like without them. He thought his life would get ten times better. Lewis told Steven, "I'm still going to need a big favor."

Steven didn't give the big favor a lot of thought. Steven knew about Lewis's problems at home, but he didn't know how dreadful it really was there. Steven said, "I'll get back with you tomorrow, it has been a long day." They both hung their phones up.

Later on that night, Willie and the rest of the team were celebrating their 30-14 victory on the football field. Coach Thomas walked up to Johnny and whispered, "I have to speak with you. When we get back on the bus, take the seat next to me; so we can talk." Johnny wasn't aware of what he wanted. Once everybody was on the bus, Coach Thomas and Johnny began talking. Coach Thomas said, "I've been watching you for a while. It seems to me your passion for football is vanishing. All of us were joyful about this game because we knew how close it is to the championship game. What happened to you, Johnny? Boy, you were the face of the team. I thought you were showing tough love, but the team doesn't even cross your mind. Look at the guy sitting behind us in the third row, next to the window."

Johnny turned around and said, "Oh that is John."

Coach Thomas said, "Yes, that is John sitting right there. The kid looks up to you. He is a really big fan of yours. He knows all your stats starting from the freshmen year to now. John wants to play football as well as you do."

Johnny was amazed because he didn't think anybody

cared about him on the team other than Willie. Johnny would not talk to his teammates outside of football. Johnny responded, "I was wondering why in practice or working out in the gym, John would watch my every step. Let me be honest with you; my love for football is dying. Different colleges want me to play for them. My grades would stay low and my college days will become short. Willie will not be there to help me out in class and my grades will descend. Why should I keep on playing football; it won't help me none?"

Coach Thomas replied, "You are supposed to play football because you love it. I thought about you going to college. College would get hard on you without a lot help. There are tutors on every college campus. If college doesn't work out for you, I would give you a job as an assistant coach under me."

Johnny asked, "Coach, you would do that for me?"

Coach replied, "Of course, the rest of the staff and I don't look at y'all as just business. It's a lot of love and caring that goes with this job."

Johnny began to wonder again about which lifestyle would suit better for him. *An honest living has no risk with a normal lifestyle. The thug life has a lot of risk and if things work out, I would start "balling out of control". No one should really gamble with their lives.*

Johnny had to make a big decision. Coach Thomas's little chat with Johnny did him some good. It motivated him to start treating his teammates the right way. Johnny was happy to play football again. He wanted to place the championship trophy in Coach Thomas's hand. Willie was sitting on the fourth row on the left. He saw Johnny and Coach Thomas sitting side by side. Players don't sit next to coaches. Willie thought Johnny was in some kind of trouble. Their trip took thirty five minutes long, coming and going. The bus driver took all the players home and the coaches were taken to the parking lot outside of the school.

Chapter 7

In the morning, Steven woke up with butterflies in his stomach. He knew what was on his agenda for tonight. Steven didn't want to hurt anybody, but it came with the job. His mother had to get taken care of and the bills had to get paid. His back was against the wall and he was depending on the robbery money to get it off the wall. Steven wanted out of the robbery business, but he had to stack his dollars first.

Lewis was thinking about the same thing. He was a little tense, but he would never tell anybody. All the violence and media coverage gave him excitement. Lewis had his mind on his money and his money on his mind. He wanted enough money to last forever. As long as he could become more successful than Sam, he was cool with that. With a lot of money, he would have an unlimited amount of drugs, some nice cars and a large house. He wanted to get high as a falcon. Once Lewis had his mind set on doing something, he would not stop until his goal was reached. Lewis knew he couldn't continue to commit crimes forever. But he couldn't wait to cause some havoc tonight. Lewis felt like he was put on this earth to rob people -- no one could tell him anything different.

James was thinking about closing Alex's mouth, while he was taking a shower. James and Alex agreed on playing bowling for $30 per game. James was feeling mighty good because he was on a long winning streak that he believed couldn't get broken. James would move on up like the Jeffersons if his football teams made the points spread and take all of Alex's money but only if everything worked out tonight. Every dollar he got his hands on, he planned on gambling with it so the money could multiply into even more dollars. James realized Alex and him picked a day, but not a time of the day. When he stepped out of the shower, he dried off and called Alex to set a time.

Alex answered his cell phone. "I thought you were going to get out of our deal. I'm a professional bowler and you are an amateur bowler. It's not too late for you to throw in the towel."

James relied, "Throw in the towel; you are talking crazy. I'm calling to set a time for our bowling games today. We never agreed on what time we were going to meet up at the mall. Trust me; I'll never back down from you. Even when I was losing, I would keep on playing until I was broke. I'll love the feeling of taking all your money and laughing in your face. Let's set this time, so the best bowler could win today."

Alex responded, "Just because you beat me in a few games of pool, it doesn't mean you has an edge over me in bowling. I received the message you sent me through a friend of mines. Why are you begging me to embarrass you? I'll give you a little credit; the winning streak of yours is impressive. They say all good things must come to an end. Your streak will be broken like an axes going through a board. On my life, you will get your ass kicked today in bowling. How does 11:30 sound to you, James?"

James replied, "It sounds good to me." Alex loved to gamble as much as James did. James would take his loss like a man but Alex hated losing; he always wanted to fight for his money back.

James and Alex met at The Sunshine Mall's bowling alley around 11:30am. They played nine games, which all came down to the wire. Alex kept his word, he broke James's winning streak. James had won seven games and Alex had won two games. James was the better man today. His winning total was $150. Alex was extremely angry. He thought about taking his money back with force. Alex knew he couldn't win a fight against James. Then he started to feel real stupid, watching James put the cash into his pockets.

James started bragging, "Who is the bowling champion now? Boy, you are the bowling chump. You talked more shit than Muhammad Ali. Two games isn't shit to me. Thanks for the bread, homie. I saw a fresh pair of Air Jordan shoes that would look "clean" on my feet. The next time you think about beating me, you better think twice, loser. If I was you, I would throw those bowling trophies into the trash can."

Alex just stared at James with a smirk on his face. The smirk hid his real mood. Alex pretended like losing wasn't a big deal to him. Alex said, "Congratulations, you deserved to win. Nobody has beaten me like that be for in bowling. There's probably a four leafed clover in your pocket. I guess I'll show good sportsmanship this time." Alex reached out his hand to James.

James shook his hand and told him, "I'll give you a chance to win your money back. This time, my selection is air hockey. Take it or just leave it, man. I swear you are making my pockets fat." James laughed in Alex's face. Alex took the laugh as disrespect. Without giving Alex a chance to think about the offer, he walked out of the mall.

James had his list with five teams written down in his

pocket; he thought they were going to win and make the point spread. He was walking towards "Touchdown" to give Frank the list. After about fourteen minutes of walking, he made it there. He used his cell phone to call Frank.

Frank playfully said, "I wasn't expecting to see you today. Give me a few minutes; I'll come out there shortly." Frank already knew he was outside. After five minutes, Frank went outside to meet James. James gave Frank the list and he looked at it. Frank told him, "You have a good chance to win. Hopefully, the Dallas Cowboys don't screw everything up for you. Jerry Jones might have to fire Tony Romo." James gave Frank $50. Frank said, "Wow! You are betting that kind of money. Whatever happened to $20 and $10? James is trying to have all the money. With $50 on the line, you must be one hundred percent sure about your picks. You are going for the big pay day of $600. Why did you decide to bet, so much money? In the past, you would've never put $50 on the line. Maybe you feel even luckier this time around."

James said, "I know everything about football. It's not that I feel lucky; I just know who's going to win. Tony Romo always plays his best games against the Philadelphia Eagles. It took me two months to save this up and it could take one day for me to lose it." Frank said, "I wish you good luck, Lewis. Dallas is a shaky team. We'll see what happens Sunday." After he was finished talking to Frank, James went home.

Eric was on the phone talking to Honey. "I will never disrespect you again. What was I thinking about? You have always meant the world to me, baby. The way we made love the other night, it felt like we were already married. It was the true meaning of heaven on earth."

Honey responded, "I care about you more now than ever. I have fallen deep in love with you. It is not about the money anymore, Eric. We need to stay together forever. I wasted a lot of time fooling around with those other guys. You are my true love, I'm sorry I didn't know it at first. Give me a chance to leave prostitution. You got me and I am what you need."

Eric told her, "I believe you would leave prostitution for me. When are you coming back over to my crib? We have to make a sequel in my bedroom. Let's make it better than part one, if that's possible."

Honey laughed and said, "Why do you say some of the craziest things? Some of that stuff probably came off the internet. I like the fact you are always trying to make me laugh."

Eric stated, "I don't steal nothing, my lines come from me. You can say my jokes are original. I'm wishing we could hang out soon. I will give you a call tomorrow, baby." Honey told him, "Okay Eric, take it easy. I love you."

Once they got off the phone, Rebecca gave him a call. Eric didn't want to speak with her because he knew she was full of lies, but he still wanted to have sex with her, "Girl, I haven't heard from you in a few days. The last time we had a talk, I thought you was coming over my house. I waited all night for you and I didn't get a call or nothing."

Rebecca replied, "On that day, it was my mother's birthday. It was too emotional for me. I cried all night long. I'm surprised you even answered your phone. I'm very sorry for standing you up. Will you ever forgive me?"

Eric didn't believe anything she said. He thought she had more excuses than George Bush Jr. but he was dying to see Rebecca drop her panties. Eric told her, "I forgive you. No one is perfect. Most of the time, you are cleaning when I call you. I am very messy person. My clothes are all over the place when my mom is not around. They say opposites attract like magnets. So when can we connect? You could pick me up and we would go out to eat."

Rebecca liked the idea of going out to eat, but too many guys were paying her top dollar. Rebecca liked Eric, but she loved money. Rebecca was making almost $2,000 per week. She was making more money than she ever made in the past. Rebecca didn't want to miss out on any money. Rebecca responded, "Going out sounds good, but we can set up things for another day. I don't know which day. You don't want to have sex with me tonight."

Eric asked, "Why would I turn it down tonight?"

Rebecca lied, "I'm on my period. Some guys wouldn't mind running a couple red lights. You are not nasty like them. When I do give you a piece, trust me; it's worth the wait."

Eric told her, "Damn, I have to beat my meat tonight. When you come off your period give me a call. I haven't even seen you in a while. The last time we were together, I thought we had something very special. I care about you a lot. All of this time apart, can break us apart. Our future is in your hands. Please, make the right decision. Get back with me sometime soon."

Rebecca said, "Don't worry about nothing. My pussy is always good; you would be glad to wait for it. You'll get a call from me soon, baby. Bye."

Eric was getting tired of all her excuses. He wanted to give her a little more time because he still had some feelings for her. Eric heard his mother say, "I'm going to work, so keep my house clean. Don't forget to pull the trash out on the side of the road. Take your time and wash the dishes. Those dishes are having more grease on it than Popeye's chicken." Eric heard the door slam; his mom walked out the house. Then Eric heard her crank up the car.

Eric went into the kitchen to get a head start on washing the dishes. Eric knew he wouldn't feel like washing them after he came home tonight. He was washing the dishes at a fast pace. Within fifteen minutes of cleaning the dishes, he heard the door bell ringing. He went to answer the door. He opened the door and he saw his troublesome cousin Redd standing outside of the door. Redd said, "What up, blood? Why are you looking, so surprised to see me? I came to check on you, kinfolk. Are you going to let me in or not? Don't let your momma's bad judgment get between us."

Eric didn't want Redd back over his house anymore, but he had to pretend like he did want him over. Eric put a smile on his face and he told Redd, "Come on in, man. My neighbors would have a stroke just by looking at you."

Redd walked into Eric's house. Redd told him, "I miss the old days; we used to kick it like brothers. You were doing our homework and I supplied the women and beer. We were tag teaming like Scott Hall and Kevin Nash, The Outsiders. It's our time to relive some of those memories. Do you have some of those prostitutes' contacts in your phone? Call two of them over here, so we could smash those hoes. You are probably falling in love with them. I should've trained you not to show them any feelings; it's pimpin' or die trying. All of those freaks want some money, that's it. They would feed you a lot of bullshit to make you think differently. I left the keys to the game in your sensitive hands."

Eric said, "I'm not falling in love with any of them. A matter of fact, I have not heard from none of them in five months. Falling in love with a hoe is crazy. You are supposed to have more faith in me than that."

Redd asked, "What are you doing tonight? We could bring some women over here while your momma is gone to work." There was no way Eric was going to let Redd bring some women over his house right now. He had big plans for tonight, already. Eric pulled one of Rebecca's numbers by coming up with an excuse, "I'm real busy tonight; my mom told me to get this place clean while she is at work. I was washing dishes before you came over here. My house is very dirty. There's a good chance I'll be tired when I finish cleaning the house. Give me a call before you come over, next time."

Redd looked around the living room and everything looked clean to him. He figured the rest of the house must be dirty. He told Eric, "Go ahead and do your thing around here. One day, we are going to hook up. We are family. We have to stay in touch with each other. My clique can use another member. Let me stop sugar coating this shit. Do you want to get gang affiliated with the Piru Bloods like me?"

Eric said, "I would have to pass on that offer right now. My mom would kill me before the Crips will. Being paranoid every day is not the life for me. The fear of getting murdered doesn't have much of an effect on you. I am scared to gang bang."

Redd thought Eric sounded weak. "You need to stop acting scared. My "road dogs" will have your back. We are a small army. If your mind changes, the offer is still on the table. I'll holler at you later." Redd walked out the door and went to his 64' Chevy Impala; then he drove off. Eric had to hurry up and get back to cleaning the kitchen. He would have been done with everything if Redd haven't come over. When Eric became finished with the kitchen, he pulled the trash can on the roadside, so the garbage men could pick it up in the morning. He went back into the house.

Steven gave him a call. "Eric, we are going to meet at the hideout, around 8:30 tonight. Maybe you are getting your hands dirty too soon. If you get worried and have second thoughts, tell me something in advance. No one will get mad at you."

Eric replied, "Thank you for your concern, but I will survive. I'm not surprised y'all have doubts about me. My weight is about one hundred and forty pounds and I never had a fight before. Tonight, the crew will see a different side of me."

Steven told him, "I hope it's the Hulk Hogan side of you. I'm worrying for nothing; if something goes wrong I will get involved. Look at the time; we should be heading towards the hide out, right now. I have to call the rest of the guys and let them know what's going on. Bring the "toys" with you and I'll see you there."

Eric walked to his bedroom closet and grabbed the garbage bag with the guns in it. Then he went into his mom's bedroom to look for the key, it went to her grey 2007 Toyota Land Cruiser. He found the key on top of her dresser. He got into the Jeep and headed to the hideout.

At 8:37, everybody was there. Steven told them, "It's about that time again. We have a change of plans. We are going to hit a corner store, but the first two robberies will consist of something different. We will randomly stick up people for their money. My only worry is a witness could see us. If a witness sees us, we have to take them out. Watching and waiting for someone to come by the ATM machine takes too long. I'm ready to get this thing started. We have everything set to go; Lewis brought the ski masks and Eric has the guns and our transportation."

Lewis rudely interrupted Steven. "I have a new idea; it will put us on the map. Every group has a name. The unknowns will not stay our identity anymore. For now on, we are The Teenage Mafia."

Willie asked, "Are we shooting up schools now? I'm not down for that shit."

Lewis stated to them, "We can't get paid by terrorizing a school. I wouldn't mind rubbing Principal Washington; he is "caked up"."

Steven was wondering why Lewis would do something like making a name when staying unknown was the best for everybody. Steven and Lewis had already talked about a name; both of them agreed the crew would not have a name. Steven became pissed off because Lewis didn't keep his word. Steven looked around the room and everybody had a smile on their faces. Lewis knew it would make Steven upset, but he did not give a damn.

James said, "It sounds like real gangsters with a little taste of swagger."

Johnny stated, "How did you come up with that name. I'll give it two thumbs up."

Eric wished he'd come up with the name. Willie said,

"The Teenage Mafia could easily become a movie's name; I'm down with it."

Lewis told them, "Everyone who wants to keep this name, raise your hands. If three of y'all want the name and three of us don't want it, we'll flip a coin. Put those hands up if you are down." Everyone raised their hands up and Steven kept his hands down. The crew had determined they would keep the name.

Steven told them, "I can't understand why y'all want a name. The cops are going to love it. If we stayed unknown, we could blend in with the rest of the crime. Everything is still good; I'm a team player. I want y'all to know we can't do this shit forever."

Lewis said, "Come on, Steven. You have said those words an thousand times. The pigs could know our group's name, but they still have to catch us in the act. I'm going to make sure they won't. I brought a pen and some paper; every place we hit, I will leave a message there. The news reporters would keep talking about us. Who are those guys? What is there next move going to be? The Teenage Mafia would become legends. The Trench Coat Mafia was a bunch of idiots. They were killing folks over some crazy shit. On the other hand, we are a special group. Working as a crew, we could have whatever our hearts desire. Money, hoes, and clothes are all a brother knows. Steven, would you continue to give us the plans for tonight?"

Steven told them, "Let's ride around until we see someone by themselves with nobody around. After we see someone alone, we'll attack them from behind. Shoot only if necessary, so don't get too trigger happy. Everyone should know who they are teaming up with; let's get the job done."

Once they went outside, they were looking for the car. Eric said, "I forgot that the car is parked around the corner. It wouldn't be smart if I parked right in the front of our hideout."

Steven joked with Eric, "You are very clever. If I had a sister, I would've hooked her up with you." The Toyota Land Cruiser had two front and three back seats. Behind the back seat was a large empty space. Steven wanted the ones who were teaming up to sit in the backseat; he was going to sit in the front passenger seat. If it was not your time to jump out, you would sit on the floor behind the backseat. Right now, Eric and Lewis were sitting side by side on the back seat. James and Johnny were sitting on the floor. As they continued to ride around, the sky was getting darker and the stars were coming out by the millions.

After about seventeen minutes into riding around, Willie spotted someone walking on the sidewalk with no one around. Steven told Eric and Lewis, "I don't have to tell y'all what to do." Both of them placed the ski masks over their head. Eric and Lewis slowly got out of the car. They started off walking fast and then they began to run. The guy on the sidewalk was a white male wearing a green t-shirt and blue pants. He was in his late thirties.

Eric was running faster than Lewis. Eric closed lined the guy from behind and the man fell down. He tried to get up but Lewis met him with some kicks to the stomach. The man fell back down. Lewis went into the guys pockets and took his wallet. Eric got on top of him and began throwing some punches, wildly. Lewis said to Eric, "Come on, man. I got the money. Let's go! Come on, man! Are you fucking theft? We need to get the fuck out of here!" Lewis's words went into one ear and came out of the other ear of Eric's. Finally, Lewis held Eric by his shirt and snatched him off the guy. Eric landed on the ground, on his back. The rest of the crew were watching and thinking, *What is going on out there?* Eric got up and stared at Lewis and then he ran back to the car. Lewis ran behind Eric.

Once Eric and Lewis were in the car, Willie drove away. Johnny asked, "What happened out there? Lewis, I couldn't tell who side you was on."

Lewis says angrily, "Eric lost his mind out there. I told him I found the money and he refuse to listen. Eric and I will never team up again."

Eric said, "I was trying to prove a point to y'all. Everybody saw that I'm not a soft person."

Lewis stated, "We'll you chosen the wrong time to prove yourself. This is not a game. We were supposed to take the cash as fast as possible and flee the scene. Eric, you better not pull a stunt like that again. The next time it happens, you will find yourself out of this crew." Lewis turned his head right and he saw an elderly lady. Then he placed the mask on again. It looked like she was heading to a corner store. She was walking very slowly and Lewis thought she would be an easy target. Lewis told them, "I'm getting ready to show y'all how it's done! Willie, stop this muthfuckin car." Willie didn't know what Lewis was getting ready to do, but he stopped driving. Lewis hopped out the jeep by himself. He slowly crept up behind the lady and pulled the .9mm handgun out of his pocket. When he approached her, Lewis pistol whipped the lady until she became unconscious. She had blood dripping from her head. Lewis took her blue purse and then he placed a letter in her mouth. The letter read: 'This is The Teenage Mafia; you are lucky we didn't leave our nuts in your mouth, Bitch!' Lewis stepped over the lady and ran back to the car. Lewis was feeling real good about himself.

Lewis started running his mouth, "Did y'all see that? It took me one minute to get the job done. Y'all need to sit back and take some mental notes. You have to become heartless with these muthafuckas." Lewis didn't care if she lived or died.

Steven felt sorry for her; he thought she could've been someone's grandmother. Steven told Lewis, "You have a head with no strews in it, man. The only thing you proven to me is how sick your mind can get."

Willie felt disgusted by Lewis actions and he let it be known. "How could you look at yourself in the mirror after that?"

James kept his mouth closed; he did not want to say what he felt. Johnny said what he had on his mind. "Lewis did what he was supposed to do. We are trying to get this cheese. He did not leave any bullet holes in her. She should've never come out this late walking, anyway. The lady is receiving social security money; she is not going to miss the bread we took."

Steven said, "We have to find another person to jack, no more elderly people. The middle aged and below, but no kids either, that is what we are looking for. Let's focus our attention on another hit."

Willie kept on driving them around. Johnny and James were sitting on the back seats while Eric and Lewis take the floor behind them. After eighteen minutes of riding around, they spotted another person. He was a black male in his late twenties. The man was wearing a pair of baggy black pants and a white t-shirt; his shirt was so long that it almost touched his knees. The man was walking on a sidewalk with a MP3 player plugged up to his ears. Willie drove behind him at a snail's pace and then he stopped. Johnny and James put on the ski masks. They hopped out the car and looked around; there was no one to witness the crime.

Johnny attacked the guy first. He punched him behind his head and the guy fell down and the MP3 player came out of his hand. The guy stood back up and Johnny delivered a powerful uppercut that took the man two feet off the ground and then he fell hard into a ditch. James jumped into the ditch and started stomping him.

Steven thought, *These guys haven't gone for the cash yet.* Steven gout out of the car and told them to stop. Johnny was kicking him from the right side and James was kicking him from the left side. It looked like they were playing soccer with a real person, instead of the ball. James and Johnny stopped once they heard Steven's command. Steven went into the ditch and checked the guy pockets for money. He found some cash and he told them, "I got the money." Then they went back into the car. The man was still lying in the ditch, feeling like a car hit him. Everything was going smooth for them. Steven said, "We are doing a great job out there, so let's keep it going. It's time for us to take on a bigger challenge. Robbing a store would put us on the right track to accomplish our goals. What store we are going to hit? Does any one of you have an idea?"

Willie answered, "I was waiting for you to pass the ball, Kobe. There is a 7/11 corner store near my home. Normally, two women work the night shift. I think they are racist. Every time I go in there, they watch and following me all around the store. The ladies are in the age range of 40 and 50 years old. The store has cameras inside. Some are at the front of the store, so shoot'em down if you can. Once you get close to the cash registers, the cameras should be in your face."

Steven told them, "The ski masks are going to protect our identities from the cameras. Shooting the cameras is a good idea. I want Lewis and Eric to go in with me. Y'all had a mis-understanding earlier, it's time to make thing right. I'm going in first with my gun already pulled out."

Eric said, "There are a few garbage bags under the driver seats." Eric gave Steven a .45 caliber semi-automatic handgun and he planned on keeping the other one for himself.

Willie drove them up the road from the 7\11, so the outside cameras would not see what car they were in. When Willie drove by the store, they didn't see any customers. Steven told them, "Lewis, I want you to watch the lady on the left and I will watch the one on the right. Eric, the only thing you have to do is empty both cash registers. Just like Lewis said, quickness is everything." They placed the ski masks over their heads and hopped out of the car. Steven, Lewis, and Eric ran into the store with their guns out. Steven yelled, "Hands up, so my eyes can see'em."

The lady on the left was white with blondish hair and the one on the right was also white with brunette colored hair. Both ladies wore khaki pants and navy colored polo shirts with their name tags on the right side. The woman on the right name was Mary and the woman on the left name was April. Both la-dies were terrified to have guns pointed in their faces. Mary screamed, "Please don't shoot us; we'll give you whatever you want." April broke out into tears and started crying.

Eric started empting the cash registers. Steven saw the cameras on both sides. He shot down the camera on his side and then he put the gun back in Mary's face. Lewis shot the camera on his side too. Eric was finished with one of the cash registers and then he started on another. April began shaking in fear. Steven said to both of them, "Turn around and face the wall."

April said, panicking, "Y'all don't have to kill us. You have taken all the money, already. Please. Please. Please don't hurt us. We have very young children at home."

Lewis yelled, "You two bitches are going deaf or something! My homeboy said turn y'all flat asses around! We are not playing at all!"

April thought once they turned around, they would kill them. Mary and April turned around to face the wall. Eric was finished with the cash register.

Steven told them, "Count to eighty and turn around." Then he waved with his right hand for Eric and Lewis to leave the store. Out of nowhere, Lewis went to the ladies and smacked both of them behind the head with the handle of the .9mm handgun. April was knocked out and Mary was holding her head on the floor. Lewis began checking their pockets while they are on the floor. He searched Mary's pockets first; he found $45. He searched April's pockets and he didn't find anything. Lewis told her, "You are broke with a job." Lewis pulled another letter out of his pocket and placed it in April's mouth and it read: 'I wish my dick was in your mouth instead of this letter. Criminally Yours, The Teenage Mafia.' Then Lewis shot up the store's phone. They left the store together. Once they got into the car, Willie drove away.

Chapter 8

They were going back to the hideout. Everybody other than Steven was happy about everything that was accomplished tonight. Steven was thinking about Lewis knocking out the old lady and what he did in the store. Steven believed Lewis was hard headed and out of control. He had planned on giving Lewis a piece of his mind, once they got to the hideout. Willie parked around the corner from the hideout. Lewis was proud of all the things he did tonight; he had never felt better. He was also trying to get in Steven's head. He still hated the fact that Steven called most of the shots.

They laid every item on the table that was stolen. There was a wallet, a purse, the garbage bag with the cash that was taken from the 7/11 store, and the money Lewis took from Mary on the table. Lewis was anticipating for Steven to speak with him. Lewis planned everything he was going to say in advance. Before they started counting the money, Steven told Lewis, "Tonight, you were acting foolish. Every time you left the car, something unplanned happen. It seems you did a lot of stuff to get under my skin and it worked. Why do you think we come up with plans? We have to stay organized as a crew."

Lewis said, "Why would I want to upset you? I did everything for this crew. There is a method to my madness. The old woman I jacked was at the wrong place, at the wrong time. It was just business. Damn, I didn't break those bitches' necks. The ladies at the store had it coming. After we would've left, they were going to call the cops. By striking them in the head with the gun, it gave us more time to get away. I even shot the phone up, so they couldn't call for help immediately. Must I explain more to you? Eric fucked up tonight and you are not mad at him. You are not an angel either, Steven. We pulled our guns out on them hoes at the store together. A matter of fact, we are all wilding out and I'm the lion."

Steven got in Lewis' face and hollered, "The lion is talking BS! You can fool them, but not me! Fuck that bullshit you are talking about. Eric was trying to prove something to us. He did it the wrong way, though. The show you put on tonight was in selfishness." Steven was ready to fight Lewis.

Willie stepped in between the two with both of his arms stretched out, trying to cool a heated situation, "Y'all are our leaders; it wouldn't make any sense to fight. If you cut the head off of a snake, the body would not have a chance. Lewis, some of the stuff you did tonight was off the wall, but you are far from being Michael Jackson. The old lady probably would've given you the purse, if you asked for it."

Johnny said, "Lewis's maneuvers weren't favorable, but smart. It's just business and y'all are taken it too personal. She is no kin to us. None of us even knew the lady. What's the big problem? Everything Lewis did we benefitted from it. Willie and Steven, y'all have to decide whether you want to become a thug or a teddy bear. A person can't be both of them."

Then Eric spoke, "I know I fucked up tonight. Johnny, you are right, but still we have to choose what's going too far. We want the almighty dollar and not to seriously hurt someone. The only time it would become right for us to seriously hurt someone, our lives have to be danger. I was whipping on a guy and knowing he was not going to get up no time soon; I over did it. My frustration was taken out on him."

James just stood there without saying what he felt. Steven said, "From now on, stop acting like an out of control psycho."

Lewis agreed, "Okay, man. If we didn't plan it ourselves, if our lives is not in danger, I won't get out of control. We put too much energy in arguing, so let's calculate this cash."

Eric said, "Now that's the best thing I heard all night." Lewis and Steven counted the money in front of the rest of them. The elderly lady had a picture ID, social security card, and three twenty dollar bills which made $60. The guy with the MP3 player had $203 in his wallet. Lewis took $45 from Mary at the 7/11 store. Eric took $1,688 out of the cash register at the 7/11 store. The total amount taken was almost $2,000. They split the money as equally as possible.

Lewis came up to Steven and wanted to shake his hand. Steven paused for about five seconds and shook Lewis' hand. Lewis apologized," I'm sorry for all the problems I caused tonight. It will never happen again; I promise."

Steven thought, *Is he serious or what?* He just accepted Lewis's apology to end the night on a good note. Steven told them, "Let us huddle up before we get out of here. We did well, but it could've been a lot better. More money would've made things better. We will "do it big" from now on. We will no longer jack people on the streets anymore. They are not guaranteed to have a lot of money. We will only rob stores and banks. Our pockets will bust open because it has too much money in it. Jacking people on the streets is alright, but people are not carrying a lot of dough on them. We have to jack fifty people to have a decent amount of money. Personally, if I hit one bank and get away, I'll be done with this shit. I would retire from being a thief. If you want to keep going, good luck to you. It will take a super master plan to hit a bank. If one of you have an idea about which bank to rob let me know."

Lewis stated, "The news will have a lot to talk about tomorrow. I can see it now; who is The Teenage Mafia? It's enough to last them a whole week. CBS and the local news channel should write us a check."

Even Steven had to laugh at that joke. Steven said, "We should visit different banks, just to look around them. Then we would talk about which one is the easiest target. Robbing a bank is the hardest thing we will ever do. I know I said that once before; I'm trying to express how difficult it is. Everyone has to stay on the same page with no mistakes. We had a busy night; it's time to go home for some R and R."

The time was almost midnight. Eric drove everybody home one by one. Everybody was tired from all the action.

Johnny came home to a crowded house. It was late and he was surprised to see everyone still up. Johnny's mom, dad, little sister, and two of his little cousins were watching TV inside the living room. The living room was large with three couches and a wooden four legged table. It also has family pictures hanging up on the walls. A picture of a black Jesus was on the walls above the 32 inch screen TV. His parents didn't care how long he stayed out because he never got into trouble before. Johnny lived in a one story brick house with three bedrooms. He was able to come and leave as he pleased.

Johnny went to his bedroom. He placed the money in a pocket, on a pair of pants. Then he folded the pants and placed it back into his dresser. Johnny was thinking about the night he had. He found his new lifestyle to be exhilarating. Johnny wanted the feeling of hitting a bank and getting away with it. He also remembered Steven telling him how difficult it will be. He wondered about his next move, after finishing school. Would he go to college? Or would he help Coach Thomas coach the football team? Or would Johnny continue to steal? Johnny took his shoes off and laid them down under the bed. He picked up the remote to find something to watch on TV. He stopped flipping the channels, once he saw that 'Sanford and Son' was on. He fell asleep watching the episode when Lamont was trying to move out.

When Willie arrived home, his mom and dad were asleep. His parents didn't care about how long he stayed out. Willie was the only child. His parents wanted to keep up with the Jones and that was the main reason why he never had much. Willie lived in a nice high class suburban neighborhood. Appearance was everything to his parents. Willie's parents made sure their house and cars looked great, so they could fit in with the neighborhood. Willie went upstairs to his bedroom. He had a wall covered with different UCLA posters. Willie had a king sized bed in his room. His bedspread had the NFL's logos all over it. He had a large dresser with a mirror on top. There was a 50'inch screen 3D TV in his room. Willie's bedroom was the same size of the average master bedroom. Willie was living like a king, but his parents had never given him over $80 before. Willie didn't like to bully other students, but he needed some cash in his pockets. He placed his cash in his Chuck Taylor Converse shoe box under his bed. Willie was so tired that he went to bed with all of his clothes on and fell asleep.

James was not supposed to stay out late. His mother was always gone at night for some reason. He could always tell whether she was at home or not. If her car wasn't there, she was gone. James lived in a condo and his mother owned the section they lived in. James went into his bedroom and it seemed like a hurricane with a category 5 came through there. James bed was not made up, he had dirty clothes on the floor, and his DVD collection was on the floor. He wanted to clean his bedroom, but he was just too tired. He took off everything other than his boxers and went to bed.

Lewis was kind of nervous. His parents had warned him about staying out late. It was sixteen minutes after midnight when he made it home. His steps were light walking up the stairs. He was hoping his parents would not hear him walking. He did not hear or see them and he wanted them to be sleeping. Once he stepped into his room, Lewis yawned and stretched his arms out. Lewis lay down in his bed on his stomach. He was feeling very comfortable. Lewis was getting ready to fall asleep and then something heavy got on his back. Sam had his knees down on Lewis's back. Jessica came into the room and pulled his pants and his boxers down. Sam tied Lewis's hands to the bed's rail. Lewis was struggling to stop Sam, but he was unsuccessful. Jessica watched the whole thing with popcorn in her left hand and a grape soda in her other hand. She was happy to see Lewis get what she thought he deserved. She took a seat on Lewis's chair to watch him in pain up close. Lewis yelled repeatedly, "Let me go! Let me go! Let me go!"

Lewis heard the sound of Sam unzipping his pants. Sam began to rape Lewis while talking trash, "I'll show you child molestation! Every time we get into a fight, you bring that old shit up. Damn Son, you have some good ass. Take it like a man you bitch. Don't get mad because you always had a little sugar in your tank."

Sam raped his son for eight minutes and then he squirted his semen on the back of Lewis's shirt. Sam started punching Lewis in his face until he passed out and then he untied the extension cord from around Lewis's hands. Jessica started feeling horny by watching her son get raped. She wondered did Sam have enough in the tank for her. She took Sam by his hands and led him to their room for sex. Tonight was the first time Sam had sexual intercourse with his son. When Lewis was just a little boy, Sam used to fondle with Lewis's penis. Sam put bruises on Lewis's face; he had one under his left eye and on the right side of his jaw. Lewis was just lying there without moving with his pants and boxers pulled down.

Eric stopped at a gas station before he went home. Normally sex would be on his mind, but all he could think about was going to sleep. He hid the money under his bed. He placed the garbage bag with the guns in the closet once again. Then he took a shower and half-way dried himself off; he still had bubbles on him. Eric was just too fatigued. He put his pajamas on and went to bed.

Lewis woke up in the morning feeling like he had a hangover. Lewis face was sore and some parts swollen. He used the upstairs bathroom to look in the mirror. He asked himself, "What in the hell happened to me?" Lewis started to notice a little pain around his anal area. All of sudden, Lewis' memory came back. He remembered his dad tying his hands up to the bed rails. He was begging his dad to stop, but he kept on going. Lewis whispered, "I was raped last night. That bastard has taken my manhood. Death is what I'm going to serve him. On my life, he will not get away with this shit. He went too far this time; I'm going to give him a first class ticket to hell. Only a sicko would get a hard on for their own son. Mom is going to die too, I saw her in my bedroom. I don't know what she did, though. I'm so mad right now; I need to cool myself down. I think some cocaine would put me in a better mood. I know this guy name Shannon Wilson. When he was in school he kept some drugs on him. We were tight back then. It's going to take the great sensation of cocaine to ease my pain. In the meantime, I will strategize on how to take them out of the game. I need a shower to get my dad's filthiness off of me." Lewis went ahead to take a shower.

James was asleep in his bedroom and his mother, Zenobia, walked in. Zenobia was a redbone who kept her hair micro braided. She was pretty in the face and thin in the waist. Her vitals were 33D-24-34. Zenobia's dress code was tight jeans, Nike snickers, and small tight shirts and she always kept her nails done. She was 35 years old and she was more of a friend to James than a mother. She saw that his room was a mess. She thought, *How did he get so sloppy?* Even though she didn't want to wake him up, Zenobia did it anyway. She yelled while shaking him, "Clean this bedroom, right now! I've seen pigs neater than you. Your daddy was a junky person too, for the small amount of time I knew him."

James spoke with dry slob on the side of his mouth. "You said something about my dad for the first time, ever. I've wanted to ask about him forever." Zenobia had opened up a can of worms. She was ashamed to tell him the truth. James began picking up all his things off the floor.

Zenobia told him, "Stop what you are doing for a minute." James took a seat on his bed. Then, she continued, "His name is Wilbert Bryant. We started talking like two months before I finished high school. He was 23 years old at that time. What made me fall for him; he was more mature than those guys in high school. We dated for five months. He was the first guy I fell in love with. You look just like him, James. It seemed like he said all the right things. Once I gave him some, he never called or spoke with me again. My heart was shattered like a mirror smashing against the concrete. I was pregnant and he was out of my life. He never knew about you because he didn't stick around."

James finally knew something about his dad. He had already assumed the worst because she had never spoke about him before. James gave his mother a hug. "Zenobia, everything is okay. I know it took a lot for you to tell me about what happen. I was expecting something bad. You shouldn't be a shame because things like this happen to good women all the time."

Zenobia became teary eyed because she thought her only son was growing up too fast. She wiped the tears from her eyes. James would like to meet his father, but his mom wouldn't know where he was. He would never wanted a relationship with his father because of the way he did his mother. She said to James, "Finish cleaning your room and I will make us some breakfast."

Eric was sleeping with his mouth open. He heard his phone ringing; he answered it while half asleep.

"Hello," said Rebecca. "I'm sorry for waking you up. It's all most noon and you are still in bed."

Eric replied, "Honey, I'm getting ready to get up."

Rebecca said, "You called me Honey and you never called me that before. How sweet of you, baby."

It finally hit Eric; he was not on the phone with Honey -- he was talking to Rebecca. Eric's eyes opened wide and he covered his mouth. He was hoping he hadn't told on himself. Rebecca asked, "Are you still there, Eric? Don't fall asleep on me."

Eric responded, "I'm not falling asleep. I was just wiping the crust out of my eyes. Last night my house was just like yours; it took me a long time to get this place cleaned. I should've had two or more people here to help me."

Rebecca wanted to find another way to get money from Eric, since she didn't want him to know she was still prostituting. Rebecca told him, "Soon you will see the surprise, I have for you. Do you remember my purple bra and panties?"

Eric replied, "Yes, I remember it like yesterday." His dick got hard when he imagined the way she looked in her bra and panties that night.

Rebecca told him, "I need a favor; my financial problem went from bad to worse. Every month it's becoming a challenge for me to pay my bills. Could you give me $250 to help me out with my bills?"

Two hundred and fifty dollars was a lot of money to Eric. He did not want to give that kind of money away. He thought, *She could be worth helping out. She needs to help me out with some ass*. Eric decided he would help her. "Okay, the money is yours. When are you coming over here to get it from me?"

Rebecca said, "Well, I was coming over there Monday.

Just give it to me on that day. Monday would also be a good day for us to have sex. It's been a while since I had some good loving."

Eric said, "You can compare my sex game to Michael Jackson on stage. I can perform great on any given day."

Rebecca started laughing and she was thinking, *He is acting like some kind of player. Eric can't fool me; he's still the sweet and soft nerd that I can get anything from him. At the same time, if I did settle down, he would be the one. With all the money I'm making, it's hard for me to quit. Every time I open my legs to a trick, it's seems like I'm hitting the lottery.* Rebecca was very smart. She was using her bangin' body with an angel face to her advantage. Eric had an IQ of a genius but he couldn't figure out what Rebecca was doing. Maybe she was the best at playing mind games. Rebecca told him, "I might call when you freshen up. You better rock my world, Eric."

Eric stated, "I'm going to rock it like someone is paying me. No one does it like me. I don't make love, I make magic."

Rebecca says, "We will both find out what you are made of. Holler at me later, boo." When was Eric going to realized that Rebecca saw him as another customer? Eric had to focus his attention on Honey. Honey had made plans to get with him tonight. He couldn't mess up and call Honey Rebecca's name. Eric hadn't chosen which one he liked the best, yet. He knew the only way to judge them was by spending time with both of them. Eric came up with an idea that he could use for Honey. He wanted to make things very romantic. He thought, *I need about five candles, a dozen roses, and one of those bottles of Bacardi Silver in the refrigerator.* He planned on spreading the roses all over the bed. Eric knew he could always go to Wal-Mart and purchased the dozen roses and the candles. Eric had a small blue radio in his bedroom with a CD player on it. He kept the radio on his dresser. Eric went through his large CD collection. He picked up two CDs, one was The Luther Vandross Essential album and the other one was the R. Kelly 12 play album. He was a big fan of R. Kelly, but Luther Vandross was the more romantic singer out of the two. He wanted to go with the Luther Vandross CD. If his mother asked him about the missing bottle of Bacardi Silver, Eric was going to tell her he dropped it and the bottle bust. Now he had everything planned; Eric had to go out and make things happen.

Lewis went down stairs after he took a shower. He saw that Jessica had made breakfast and left him something to eat; it was cold as usual. She made eggs, bacon, and toast. Lewis threw his plate along with his food into the trash. Lewis went back to his room and took some of his stolen money. He placed the cash into his pocket. He left home, on his way to Shannon Wilson's house. If Shannon couldn't give him what he wanted, he was going to stick up any drug dealer for some cocaine. His own father took his manhood and it was a hard pill for him to swallow. He knew it took 30 minutes on foot from his house to Shannon's house. He figured a long walk would give him even more time to think about his situation at home. Normally, when his parents made him mad at home, he would wish the worst on them. Killing them was a thought that came and left his mind. Over the years, Lewis had put up with a lot of BS. He was ready to explode on his parents like dynamite. The thoughts of him murdering his parents were not going anywhere, now.

Lewis had been over Shannon's house twice in the past, so he knew exactly where it was located. Lewis didn't know that Shannon was gang affiliated. They were cool at school, but they were not best friends. Once Shannon finished school, he and Lewis did not stay in touch with each other. Lewis would find out that Shannon was not the same person he was in school.

Redd was a crooked, shady, and non trustworthy kind of person. Making a deal with him was like making a deal with the devil. The knife would go through your back sooner or later. Lewis was almost at Shannon's home; he had to walk across the street. Shannon AKA Redd lived in a very large apartment complex. The name of the apartment was Blossoming Apartments. It took up a whole block. Shannon's mother used to stay there with him. She could no longer handle all the violence outside, different guys knocking on the door at all times of the night, drugs hidden all around her home, and her son gangbanging. Redd's mother was living in hell, so she moved as far away from Redd as she could. She raised Redd in the right direction and he chose the wrong direction. His environment molded him to live an uncivilized lifestyle. When Redd was younger, his mom would bring him to church every Sunday. She would make sure he studied his lesson for school, so he could pass. The older Redd became, the more he wanted to be a gangster.

Lewis walked up the stairs until he made it to the third floor. He took a left and walked pass three doors and the fourth one was Redd's apartment. Lewis was standing in the front of Redd's apartment and he saw the number 662. Lewis rung the door bell twice and he was hoping Shannon would be there; it would be a wasted trip if he was not there. He heard some footsteps coming to the door. Redd opened the door; he thought it was another crack head. Redd had a Glock .44 handgun in his left hand, behind his back. To Redd's surprise, it was Lewis at his door. Redd asked, "Man, what are you doing over here? Come on in, youngblood, and take a seat. So what brought you to these parts of the woods?"

Lewis answered, "I'm trying to get high like everybody else."

Redd said, "I have a few twenty sacks of weed with your name on them, homie."

Lewis told him, "Weed sounds good, but I want some cocaine. I'm trying to get high as I possibly can. Damn, you've changed since high school. Now you have more tattoos than Lil Wayne. What's up with all this red in your crib? You have a red couch, red cell phone on the living room table, red carpet on the floor, and a red bandanna hanging out of your back pocket."

Redd said, "First of all, let me pat you down for wires. You could be working for them "people"." Redd started patting him down for wires and he found Lewis's .9mm. He took the gun out of Lewis's front pocket. Redd told him, "This .9mm looks familiar, but I know you did not come here to kill me. A real ganster would've tried to shoot me while I was patting them down. I'm affiliated with the Piru Bloods; we are for real. I would not have it any other way." Redd placed the .9mm handgun back in Lewis's pocket and then he put his own gun back into his pocket.

Lewis said, "Shannon is a gangster. I always knew you had what it took to become one."

Redd stated, "My name is Redd; Shannon doesn't exist anymore. Look at me; this is who I am. Let me hook you up. Just give me $50 and I'll give you $60 worth of cocaine in your hands. Then I will give you a dime sack of weed for free. How did you know I was selling cocaine?"

Lewis replied," In school, you were selling a lot of weed and that was two years ago. I figured you would be selling other stuff too, by now. Apparently, your game has step up a lot. Give me $100 worth of cocaine and hook me up with $20 worth of weed for free."

Redd said, "So you want $100 worth of cocaine and a free $20 worth of weed. I got you covered."

Lewis told him, "$50 worth of coke wouldn't be enough for me. Thanks for being generous by accepting my deal." Lewis pulled out nearly $200 and counted $100 to give it to Redd. Lewis put the rest of the money back into his pocket.

Redd watched Lewis count and then place some more money back into his pocket. He thought, *Lewis could have some real money. His parents are rich. Lewis was known by some students has Richie Rich. Some kind of way, he's going to become a new customer of mine.* Redd kept his drugs and some of his cash in an iron safety box. The key to the safety box stayed in his pocket at all times. The safety box was under his bed. Redd went to his safety box to get $100 worth of cocaine and $20 worth of weed. After locking the box, he went back in the living room with Lewis. Then Redd and Lewis exchanged the money for the drugs. Redd said, "You must have walked a long way to get here. I am surprised that the sole hasn't come off from the bottom of your shoes. I did not see any car keys in your pocket. The average person from the rich people neighborhood would never come through here."

Lewis replied, "I have a heater for anybody trying to fuck with me. Why did you make fun of me walking over here? I have on a pair of Nikes and they could survive a two thousand miles walk."

Redd said, "You are still a cool dude. We can do some business together in the future. We could hang out like homies, just like old times."

Lewis told Redd, "Let's exchange numbers, man. Give me a call or I will give you a call to set something up." Lewis was glad to have someone to supply him with drugs. Redd was pleased to have another customer who could have plenty of money. After exchanging numbers, Lewis told Redd, "I'm ready to go back home; I'll get back in touch with you soon."

Redd asked, "Do you have a lighter?"

Lewis replied, "No, I don't have a lighter." Redd told him, "This lighter in my pocket is brand new." Redd took a green lighter out of his pocket.

Lewis said, "A green lighter, why isn't red?" Redd said,

"The store I went to didn't have any more red lighters. The guy who was working there tried to offer me a blue lighter; he made me want to smack his ass." Redd placed the lighter in Lewis's hand. Redd told him, "I almost forgot, here is two Black and Mild cigars. Take all the tobacco out of them and replace it with the weed. Tonight, you should get higher than a Georgia Pine Tree. Let me put on a t-shirt and give you a ride home."

Redd had a white shirt lying on his couch; he grabbed it and put the shirt on. Then he took the cell phone off the table and he placed it into his pocket. Lewis began following Redd to his car. Once Lewis saw Redd's car, he said, "Your ride is clean. An all black Chevy Impala, this must be a '64. Does this baby have hydraulics?"

Redd said with pride, "You know I won't have it any other way." Redd got into his car and opened the passenger door for Lewis. Once Lewis jumped in, Redd drove off. Redd had Dr. Dre's song name "Let Me Ride" playing in his CD player with the volume on low. Redd asked, "Do you live in the same big ass house? Your parents have a lot of bread. Someone like you was probably born with a silver spoon in your mouth. There is nothing wrong with your situation. It's a good thing to have all the aces in your hands, in the game of life."

Lewis acknowledged, "All my life, everyone at school thought I was the luckiest person in the world. If I was on the outside looking in, I would probably be thinking like everybody else too. Just remember, everything is not always what it seems. What looks like heaven can be hell."

Redd was not convinced that Lewis was having problems at home. "You know damn well, living large is the shit. After doing it big for so many years, you would commit suicide if you had to live like me. I'm selling drugs and doing a lot of crazy shit, trying to get on y'all level." After twelve minutes of cruising around, they finally arrived at Lewis's home. Lewis said, "I'll give you a holler, but feel free to call me as well." They gave each other some dap and then Lewis got out of the car. Lewis went inside his house. Sam was watching him through his bedroom window.

Sam was wondering, *Who is that guy driving an old school car? He might be bad news for my son. I bet he's a gangster or a street thug. Lewis has to stay away from guys like that.* Sam had a confused state of mind. He didn't know if he wanted to see Lewis rise or fall. Sam would get mad if Lewis would bring home Ds and Fs on his report card. At the same time, Sam would get happy to see a sign that his son would never become success. Sam couldn't make the decision to be a mentor or a menace.

Sam walked up to Jessica who was lying down in bed watching TV. Sam told her, "Our son hopped out of an old school car with some thug looking guy. I have never seen this guy before – he's bald headed with a lot of tattoos on his arms. He could've been a black guy. A lot of gangsters drive the old school cars like the one he has. Our law-abiding neighbors would've thought he was a thug too. Lewis should not get influenced by some tattoo-wearing gangster. If I see him again, I am going to send him a message to leave my son alone."

Jessica thought, *Sam is worst than Harvey Dent. One minute, he doesn't want Lewis in trouble. Then the next minute, he would love to see Lewis behind bars. Sam needed to make his mind up.* **She** said, "Lewis is going to be alright. We have raised him to know right from wrong; Lewis is not too bright at all, but at least he knows that much. Come and give me a kiss, Sam. Don't worry about our son; just give me your attention." Sam gave her a soft kiss on the lips. Sam was not going to let what he saw go away. Jessica was wishing Sam would leave Lewis alone.

James was at home watching the NFL. Three teams on his list were winning. His other two picks had not played. James was flipping from channel to channel keeping up with his picks. James thought about Alex. He disliked the guy, but he had to communicate with him in order to take more of his money. They played nine games of bowling yesterday. Even though James won seven out of nine games, he acted too cocky in front of Alex. James knew deep inside he was fortunate to get the best of Alex. Those games could've gone either way. James started thinking, *If Alex takes too long to call me, I will call him. I want every dime from Alex the Sore Loser and the rest of his friends. They used to be my friends; now the cash is my real buddy.* He reached down in his pocket and took out the money he won from Alex. Looking at the cash made him feel good about himself. He thought, *Maybe robbing and gambling is the blueprint to getting rich. I'm going to keep it up until I become filthy rich.* James knew he had a long way to go from becoming rich. James's mind was made up to make it a reality. At first gambling was for bragging rights. Just to say, 'Man, I took your money and I'm better than you'. It had become deeper than just bragging rights. James didn't want to see his friends with any money. James's obsession with money was altering him. His changes were not for the better.

Johnny arrived home from walking to the store. He heard his cell phone ringing and saw Willie's name and number. Johnny answered it, "What's up, Willie?"

Willie replied, "I have been thinking about last night. We really did make things happen. I finally got some change in my pockets and it feels great. This is my first time having a pocket full of cash. There's something else on my mind. I saw you on the bus talking to Coach Thomas. Players don't sit with the coaches. Tell me what y'all were talking about."

Johnny stated, "Coach Thomas was letting me know he

has my back. For the longest, I thought he was using me to win the state title and he did not give a damn about me. He said if I don't make it in college, he would give me a job as an assistant coach under him. He also said that lately I haven't been motivated about playing football. I plan on going all out for Coach Thomas on the football field, for now on. Coach Thomas deserves to hold the state championship trophy."

Willie said, "You sound very motivated. I guess Coach Thomas' words are a little better than mine. I'm glad you have seen the light. We have one more game left to play. It's our last game in high school. My prayers have been for both of us to play college football next year. If both of us don't make it, life will go on."

Johnny told Willie, "I am hoping for the best too. Making the fast money feels good. There is a small part of me that wants to keep robbing forever. My future is still pretty much undetermined. Helping Coach Thomas win the championship sounds good for now. In the back of my mind, I know the fast money will eventually lead to death or prison. What if we pull that bank robbery off? We would have enough money to leave the life of crime alone."

Willie told him, "Steven said we should visit a couple of banks and then we would pick the one that seems like the easiest target to rob. After we decided on which bank to hit, an excellent strategy must be made to dodge getting caught. If the police catch us, we will never see the light of day again. Can you imagine yourself as a felon in jail, who is getting old? The judge will show no mercy with all those assault and armed robberies charges. There's a chance we would have to use our firepower to get out the bank. Then we would face even more charges. I feel confident with Steven; we will not get caught doing a crime with him. I will quit after we hit this bank."

Johnny said, "Honestly, I don't know what I'm going to do after we hit a bank. Can you even imagine all the bread that would be in your pockets after every bank robbery? Working would never be an option. Money does make life a lot easier."

Willie told Johnny, "I was calling to see how you were doing. I'm going to call you later. Remember to keep your eyes on the prize."

Johnny responded, "My eyes will never leave the prize." They hung the phones up. Willie lay on his bed to watched TV. Johnny started eating the snacks that he had purchased from the corner store.

Eric was at home and it was getting closer and closer to the time his mother would go to work. He went to Wal-Mart about two hours earlier to buy a dozen roses and an eight pack of candles. Eric asked his mother for permission to use the Toyota Land Cruiser and she gave him permission. Molly cleaned and cooked before she went to work. Eric was excited because his mother was gone. He knew something special was getting ready to happen. Eric went upstairs to clean his room for the third time today. He sprayed the room with an air freshener. Eric was kind of shocked that his mother did not ask him about which store he was going to or what he was going to buy. Eric didn't ask for the car often. If she would've asked him those questions, he already had an answer waiting. Eric was going to tell her that he was going to buy some school supplies.

He opened the Luther Vandross Essential CD case and

placed the CD in his radio. Eric hit the play button on the radio and then he hit the repeat button. He turned the radio on a low volume. Eric was going to turn it up once Honey came inside of his bedroom. He took the dozen roses out of the bag. Eric sprinkled the rose petals all over the bed. Then he took the candles out of the bag. He took five candles out of the pack. He placed five of them around the room. A pack of matches from his dresser is use to light the candles. He didn't have a reason to use the matches other than the fourth of July. Eric had never been a smoker. Eric almost forgot he had a small amount of Sean John cologne left in the bottle; he sprayed some on himself, lightly. Eric realized he was missing one more thing. There was a case of Bacardi Silver in the refrigerator. Just like Nas needed one mic, Eric needed one bottle of Bacardi Silver. At the top of the refrigerator, there was an ice cube maker. He took his mother's salad bowl and placed a lot of ice in it. Then he placed one Bacardi Silver bottle in the ice. Eric carried the big bowl full of ice back to his room. Eric said to himself, *I need two glasses.* So he went back down stairs to get two champagne glasses out of the cabinet in the kitchen. Honey was the only thing missing from the puzzle.

An hour and a half later, Honey sent him a text message. The text message read: 'You better get ready for me, baby. I'm on my way over there to please you. Don't become shy.' Honey was playing a little game on him. She was not on her way to Eric's house. Honey had just hopped out of the shower. She knew the more he waited, the more anxious Eric would become. Honey figured the sex would be better that way.

Eric's anger was building up and he thought, *What is*

taking her so long to get here? Honey sent me a text message saying she's on her way. I hope all my work was not for nothing. Man, twenty five minutes has passed since she gave me a text message. It doesn't take a long time to drive from her house to my house. Eric called her on his cell phone and she did not answer. Then Eric heard the door bell ringing. Eric knew it was her at the door and he knew she played with his mind. Eric ran down stairs to open the door. When he opened it, Honey was standing outside of the front door with a huge smile on her face.

Honey said, "You probably thought I changed my mind. I would never do you like that, Eric." Eric was relieved to see Honey had made it to his house.

Eric told her, "Come on in, girl, and stop playing so much. Honey, I was worried about you. My bedroom is calling your name." As Honey walked up the stairs, Eric walked behind her, staring at her booty. Once she made it to his bedroom, Honey became amazed. She never had someone to do anything like this for her before. She had her hands covering her mouth while her eyes were wide open. Honey stood there like a statue. Eric was waiting for her to say something. Honey finally spoke, "This is the best thing someone has ever done for me. Eric, you have gone all out of your way for me." She turned around and gave him a hug. Then she asked, "What is the name of your good smelling cologne?"

Eric replied, "This is the best colongne P. Diddy has ever come out with. Sean Jean is the name of it." They looked into each other's eyes and started kissing. Then Eric said, "Wait a minute." He poured some of the cold Bacardi Silver in two champagne glasses.

Honey thought, *He went out and got some Bacardi Silver. I like drinking Alize'. It's the thought that counts anyway.* Honey had never tasted that kind of alcohol. Eric gave her a glass full of Bacardi Silver. Honey tried it and then she noticed how good it tasted. They kept on drinking until all of the alcohol was gone. Once again, they started French kissing. Honey took one step backwards and then she began taking her clothes off slowly. Honey wore a Rocawear outfit. Her shirt was red with a black Rocawear logo on the right side of the chest. It was one of those small and tight shirts that women wore to let their waist show. Honey's stomach was very firm. Honey's jeans were looking spectacular on her. The color of her jeans was dark blue with a black Rocawear logo on both of her back pockets. Honey was very horny; she wanted to have sex just as badly as Eric did. She took off her shirt, first. Her bra was designed with a strawberry print. Honey had to wiggle her hips to get out of those jeans. Her panties were also designed with a strawberry print. She took off her socks and her all white Nike Air Max shoes. Eric found her so attractive. He almost slobbered while he was watching her take off her clothes.

Honey asked him with her sexy and soft voice, "So what do you think about my body?"

Eric replied, "I have never seen a body as perfect as yours before in my life. Girl, you look fine, like a wide face Rolex, you just shines." Honey fell on Eric's bed backwards and opened her legs wide open. Eric told her, "Your perfume smells pretty good, baby."

Honey told him, "My perfume came from Victoria's Secret and I bought it for you. Enough of all this talking, I'm ready to fuck." Eric started taking his clothes off fast and then he turned up his radio. Luther Vandross's song name "Always and Forever" was playing. He got on top of Honey and pulled her bra down below her breast. Eric sucked her nipples over and over again. Then he pulled her panties down slow. Eric gave Honey oral sex while she was holding on tightly to the bed's rail with both hands. She was really enjoying Eric's tongue service. Honey had a sensational look on her face. This was Eric's first time giving oral sex. He was doing it like a professional. Honey told him," I have received enough tongue; give me some dick." Eric's dick was so hard; he could've smashed five bricks with it. Eric began kissing her on the neck and he was ready to swim in Honey's ocean. Honey said, "Hold up, Eric. Let me massage your dick." After three minutes of rubbing Eric's manhood, she put it inside of her. The way Eric was hitting it, you would think there was no tomorrow. Honey was so wet; you would believe someone poured a small bucket of water on Eric's bed. Their love making was very passionate; it could've sold a million copies on DVD and Blu-Ray.

Lewis locked his bedroom door because he didn't want any interruptions. Then he placed a white plate on his bed. He had a smoke detector above his bed. Lewis stood on top of his bed and took the smoke detector a loose, so he could smoke without the alarm coming on. He poured the $20 sack of weed on the plate. Lewis cut the cigar wrapper with his Boy Scout knife and then he emptied the tobacco out. Lewis replaced the tobacco with weed. He licked the cigar paper, so it could stick. Lewis took out the green lighter that Redd gave him and lit his blunt. Lewis went inside of his closet to smoke and he closed the closet door. He took his first hit and he started coughing. Then Lewis took another hit and he coughed once again. After the third hit, Lewis began smoking like he was doing it for years. He said to himself, "The Cali weed is the truth. Now I see why Snoop Dogg can't stop smoking." The weed made Lewis feel comfortable. Once he finished with his first blunt, he made another one to smoke. He smoked the other blunt in his closet too. He planned on using the cocaine for tomorrow night. After forty five minutes of getting high, Lewis became extremely hungry. Everybody would say he had the "munchies". He changed his shirt, so the weed scent wouldn't be so obvious. Lewis went into the kitchen. He took some bologna out of the refrigerator and made three sandwiches with cheese. Lewis brought the sandwiches and a grape soda back to his bedroom. Lewis's eyes were redder then a Chicago Bulls jersey. Lewis ate those sandwiches like he had not eaten in two days. Then he turned the smoke detector back on. Lewis lay down after he was done eating and went to sleep.

James was jumping up and down in his bedroom. All five of his teams won and made the point spread. It was the first time he had played with $50 and won. Frank called James's cell phone and James answered it joyfully, "I can't believe I won $600, after losing every Sunday last year! The point spread finally went my way!"

Frank said, "Congratulations, James, you are the only person who won this week. Don't spend it all in one spot. Save some of it for me, dude. You can come and pick up your money tomorrow. I don't have to say that twice."

James told him, "I'll scoop my money up tomorrow. My confidence level is high; I will play again next week. The money is coming home with me again. Thank you for helping me put my bid in. Without your help, it never would have been possible."

Frank said, "Your chances of winning two weeks in a row are kind of slim, but anything can happen. Our best gamblers wait a little while and then play again."

James responded, "I feel good about my chances to win every week. The odds of winning are against me; well, I'm going against the odds. I'm a true winner; losing is not in my vocabulary. Have some kind of faith in me; I can pull this thing off."

Frank knew if James continued to gamble he was going to lose, eventually. "Bring your picks to me before Sunday. Don't let this gambling thing control you, you should control it. I know rich guys who are now homeless because of their gambling habits," said Frank.

"I have it all under my control. Let me get back with you, so I can focus my attention on winning next week," James said. After their conversation, James was a little upset. *Frank is a hater. I finally won and he wants me to quit. Why he didn't say anything to me last year, when I was losing? That cotton picking bitch thinks he knows everything. Hell, I know a lot of shit too. I know these teams better than they know themselves. This is my money, not Frank's money.*

Frank had tried to help James but he took it the wrong way. Frank had been working at Touchdowns for 24 years. He had seen the best and the worst gamblers come and go. James's head was harder than a steel pipe. He could not see the major change in his attitude.

Chapter 9

The next day at school, Lewis wanted to speak with Eric. Eric was in line to eat breakfast. Lewis got into the line by hopping Eric. Lewis told Eric, "I don't hear from you until it is lights, cameras, and action."

Eric said, "Don't take it personal; it's hard to stay the number one student at this school. Books take up most of my time. Every since I gave you a "lighter" under the bleachers, you have never spoke with me alone again."

Lewis told Eric, "Expect a call from me tonight, if it is okay with you."

Eric was wishing Rebecca would give him a call tonight. He thought a short conversation with Lewis wouldn't hurt. Eric said, "It's okay for you to give me a call."

Lewis told him, "You and Steven have got kind of close. Everyone in our crew think y'all don't like the rest of us, sometimes it does seem that way. We all have to communicate with each other. Mr. Connection Man, will you please give someone other than Steven your attention." Lewis did not like the fact that Steven and Eric were cool with each other. Lewis knew Eric was the key to the operation. He wanted the key in his pocket, so he could be more in control of the crew.

Lewis and Eric received their breakfast and took a seat. Lewis said, "Make sure our lighters are not empty and they should be full tonight." Lewis never took one bite of his food.

He got up and threw his food in the garbage. Eric thought Lewis was acting very odd.

When the school's first break came, Steven and Eric were chatting about girls and the teachers they did not like. Then Eric remembered the talk he had with Lewis earlier. Eric told Steven, "I just remembered something; your boy Lewis was acting strange. He approached me talking about we are getting too close. He told me I should get closer to everybody in our crew. Lewis has never given a damn about hanging with me before. Then he tells me to make sure my lighters are full tonight. I guess he wants the guns to be fully loaded. We don't have anything planned for tonight. To me, Lewis sounds jealous of us."

Steven said, "He does have a point, though. But he's not sincere about the situation. You don't socialize with anybody other than me. At the same time, everybody is doing their own thing. Willie and Johnny are playing football. James was out there doing something by himself. Lewis was by himself too. Our relationship is deteriorating very fast. We don't kick it like that anymore. Lewis cannot be trusted right now. Who knows what he's going to do next? He could be jealous that we don't talk anymore; he needs to get his act together. Lewis is trying to kick up some dust. He is our crew's biggest headache. Lewis is becoming the David Ruffin of our crew." The school bell rang and they went their separate ways. Eric and Steven didn't have a clue about what Lewis had in store for them. Lewis was starting to not give a damn about anything.

Chapter 10

During the break, Lewis caught up with James. He told James, "It's my boy, the lone ranger. Out of everybody in this crew, your style shines the brightest. Every day I see you looking happy, but when it's time to get dirty, the vicious side of you shows up. People like Steven and Willie don't understand it. Your mind has to be like a switch; you have to know when to turn it off and on. Steven stupid ass thinks the switch can be turned off and on at the same time. We have to stop feeling sorry for strangers. Once we stop giving a fuck about these folks, money will come to us like it's falling from a tree."

James was down for anything that would increase his dollars. James didn't realize that Lewis had a hidden motive. James responded, "I have your back, Lewis. Anything you want to do, I will be down with it. As long as we are stacking that paper up high, we are good. If Steven thinks you are a psycho, wait until he gets a load of me."

Then Lewis said, "That's the kind of talk I want to here. Maybe, we should run this crew. Don't tell anyone about this conversation. Let our alliance stay a secret. I have to get in touch with Johnny; he might like the way we want to do things. If he doesn't like it, fuck him too. I have a master plan; it's better than anything Steven ever thought of. Tonight, I'm going to see how big their nuts are. Either we stand tall like killers or we are going to lie down like bitches. We must have a killer instinct to survive out here. Tonight, I cannot wait to see what these boys are made of. Be prepared for any time between 11pm and 12am. We better show some big nuts tonight."

James thought Lewis could help him quadruple his money. Lewis put in James's mind that Steven could slow them down because of his kindness. Steven was the person who made him a part of the crew but his greed was making him take Lewis's side. James said," My nuts are the size of bowling balls. We are going to stand tall, if I have something to do with it."

Lewis said, "It's not you that I'm worried about; it is Steven, Eric, and Willie whose hearts needs to turn blacker. If they leave me hanging, I'm going to leave them hanging, literally. I'll talk with you later on. I'm hungry as hell. Eric made me so mad today; I threw my breakfast in the trash."

Lewis knew Eric did not take the bait. Lewis thought it would have been hard to convince James to take his side, since Steven brought him into the clique. Lewis did not know anything about James personally. Steven and James were supposed to be cool with each other. It was very easy for Lewis to manipulate James. Lewis was hoping he could get Johnny on his side too.

Once school ended, Lewis was waiting on Johnny outside of the school's football stadium. He did not want to have a conversation with Willie because Steven and Willie agreed on everything. Lewis was getting impatient with standing outside looking for Johnny. *It has been 20 minutes since practice was supposed to be over with,* Lewis thought. Then he saw the water boy picking up paper. Lewis walked up to the waterboy and asked, "When is practice over it? I don't hear any noise coming out of there."

The water boy said, "We did not have practice today. Coach Thomas wanted the team to get well rested. The state championship is Thursday night; he wants them at their best."

Lewis replied, "I was waiting on someone who played on the team. Somebody should've told me there was not going to be a practice today. I guess it's time for me to go home." As Lewis walked away he said, "Damn!" He had waited on Johnny for nothing.

Later on that day, Eric was trying to set up another romantic occasion. He was eager to take Rebecca out to eat and then come back to his house and chill out. Eric didn't want to buy roses and candles this time. Eric started thinking, *Where's a good place to eat?* Applebee's was his favorite restaurant. He knew it would be hard to top the night he and Honey had together but he was going to try anyway. He washed the covers on his bed and now his covers smelled fresh. Eric still had a small amount of Sean John's cologne left in the bottle, he felt like things couldn't go wrong with it on. Eric thought, This is how Kobe Bryant feels when he goes for fifty points plus in back to back games. *It has been a long time since Rebecca and I had sex. Her name was Strawberry back then and I had to pay for sex. Ever since Rebecca told me that she was not going to charge me a fee for sex, we have not fooled around. If Rebecca doesn't give me some loving tonight, Honey will win this race. I will kick Rebecca's dishonest ass to the curve. It is time for me to give up on her. She must think I'm crazy. Those other trick daddies are having sex with her every day.*

It was 9:13pm and Rebecca did not call him. Eric gave her a call and she didn't answer her phone. Eric was so disappointed in Rebecca. He had no plans to talk to her again. Eric had his hopes up high and now he had fallen in heartbreak. He cared a lot about Rebecca and the time had come for him to let her go. The only good thing that came from her absence was that he got to hang on to his $250. Eric knew all of his attention had to be focused on Honey. While Eric was heated, Rebecca was having sex with a guy who was offering her $600 for an all-nighter. Rebecca considered herself a business woman. She was not worried about the way Eric would feel about her standing him up again. Rebecca thought her mouth piece was the best. Rebecca believed she could run game on Eric and he would talk to her again. She thought a good lie would make Eric cough up some cash. At first, she really was going over Eric's house. When she was driving over Eric's house, one of her new customers called her with a $600 opportunity. This guy was a true freak; he would do any nasty thing he was asked to do. Then Eric would not have a chance to see her tonight. While Eric was watching porn movies in his bedroom, Rebecca was having sex with her feet behind her head and she was screaming hysterically.

Lewis was in his bedroom with a plate again. He believed cocaine was heaven sent. Lewis had $100 worth of cocaine on his plate. He took his time to snort every bit of it with a rolled up five dollar bill. Lewis felt an incredible rush. Then he wondered, *I should buy $500 worth of cocaine the next time. Man, they need to legalize this dope. Cocaine is probably better than sex. James Brown never felt this good before. I need to call Mr. Connection and get the party started.*

When it is time to shoot, he better not freeze up on me. Lewis called Eric on his cell phone.

Eric was lying down in his bed falling asleep; his eyes are opening and closing. Eric's cell phone rang and it scared him. Eric said to himself, "I could've had a heart attack. Who is this calling me at 11:32pm? Lewis, what does he want? The psycho said he was going to call me." Eric answered his phone, "Lewis, what a surprise."

Lewis yelled, "Get those guns out and over load them with bullets! Hurry up because we don't have all night long. Don't ask me any questions, just do what I say." Eric did not say anything. Lewis continued to yell, "Are you deaf or there is too much wax in your ears? I said load the damn guns, right now! Call Steven punk ass and tell him to get ready. I want you to pick everybody up and take us to the hideout."

Eric said, "We did not plan anything." By the time Eric said 'We did', Lewis had hung the phone up in his face.

Eric called Steven's house and Steven answered the phone, "Man, what are you doing up this late? I'm on my way to bed. So what is going on?"

Eric responded, "It's your boy, Lewis, acting crazy. He gave me a phone call and he wanted me to load the guns up. Then he wants me to pick up everybody and take y'all to the hideout. Lewis is up to no good; I can feel it."

Steven told him, "Load the guns up because I'm curious about what he has on his mind. Let me call everybody."

Eric did not want to get out of bed. He had his mind set on going to sleep. Steven got off the phone with Eric, so he could call the rest of the crew. Eric loaded the guns with bullets. He took the key to the Toyota Land Crusier out of his mother's bedroom; it was on the dresser. Then he went outside and drove off to scoop up the crew.

Everybody was inside the jeep together. Steven was sitting in the front passenger's seat. Lewis and James were sitting behind Eric and Steven. Willie and Johnny were sitting behind Lewis and James on the floor. Eric parked around the corner from the hideout. Once they went into the large office, Steven told Lewis, "This better be good. I was at home relaxing and feeling comfortable."

Lewis said to Steven, "You are my best friend. Tonight, we will do it just for you. Your ideas are the main reason why we have been very successful. I have not forgotten what the pigs done to your father. It is payback time, Homie. We are going to send them a message and it will speak louder than words. We are going to light there station up; I'm not talking about Christmas lights, either."

Steven replied, "Since we are already here, there should be no bullets left in the chamber when we are done."

Lewis told Steven, "Those cops think they could screw someone's life up and no one would retaliate. Trust me my friends; they have the game twisted. I have a strategy that will be effective. There are many police stations. Most of the time, only the police officers who are stationed close to a minor incident will respond. When they get in their cars and leave, we are going to shoot their shit up. I know where a Family Dollars store is located near a police station. One of us will break the front glass of the store and it will cause a diversion. The store's alarm will signal the police officers to come. The pigs will think it is a burglary."

Steven was very impressed by Lewis's plan. James said,

"The plan is perfect, let's make it happen. Who will break the glass?"

Willie answered, "I will break the glass since I'm not really down for shooting up a police station. After I break the glass, where will I go?"

Lewis told Willie, "Just go anywhere, we are going to find you. Don't run for a long time because the pigs will come, full speed. The smartest thing is to run in the opposite direction of the police station. Make sure you know the name of the street, if you plan on hiding there. Hopefully, it won't take a long time to find you. Here's my .9mm handgun, use it to shatter the glass." Lewis handed his gun to Willie and Eric began taking the guns out of the bag.

Lewis and Steven had the Caliber .45 handguns. Johnny and James had the Caliber 380 handguns. All of them went back to the jeep.

Lewis told Willie, "I'm going to let you know when to pull the trigger." Willie got dropped off down the road from the Family Dollars store and the rest of them were on their way to the police station. Lewis said to Steven, "You are finally going to get some justice. We should've been did this mission. Look, there is the police station. I don't see any police outside. Are y'all ready for this?"

James said, "I don't have any doubt; I'm ready."

Steven replied, "Let the fireworks begin."

Lewis called Willie on his cell phone, "Willie, go ahead and handle your business." Willie ran towards the Family Dollars store and fired three bullets through the glass. The glass shattered in front of him and then he took off like the flash.

Three minutes later, two police officers came out of the station in a hurry. Once Lewis saw them running outside, he hopped out of the jeep, shooting at the police officers. One of the officers fell down with a gunshot wound to the chest. The other officer started shooting at them. Eric was ducking behind the wheel. Johnny stayed down low on the floor because he could not get out quick enough. Steven and James hopped out and started shooting back. The officer took a shot to the head and then he fell down to the ground. Lewis went against the plan again. The police officers were going to leave the station and drive to the Family Dollars store. Lewis was not supposed to stop them. Once the officers left, then they were going to shoot up the station.

All three of them jumped back into the jeep and Eric drove off. Johnny screamed, "Let's go and find Willie! No one is going home until we find him!"

Lewis called Willie on his cell phone, "Where are you, Willie?"

Willie replied, "I am inside of a trash can on Jackson Street."

Lewis told him, "I know you are stinky. Jackson Street is not far from Family Dollars. We are on our way to pick you up."

Steven had so much on his mind and he couldn't believe what had just happened. Lewis had created a shoot-out with the police. He took being a psycho to the next level.

Once they arrived on Jackson Street, they saw ten trash cans. All the trash cans may have to get checked to find him. Eric drove by the first one and Steven let the window down on the front passenger's side and said, "Come on, Willie." He did not get a response from Willie. Eric drove to the second trash can and the driver seat window was already down. Eric said, "Willie, can you hear me." Willie pushed the top off the trashcan and hopped out.

Willie opened the door and got into the jeep. While on their way to the hideout, Willie saw Steven with his head down and both hands on his forehead. Willie looked at Eric and he could've drowned in his own sweat. At that very moment, Willie had a feeling something went wrong. Steven could not wait to curse Lewis out for placing their lives in danger. Once they were in the large office room, Steven yelled at Lewis, "You are a son of a bitch! Your foolishness could've gotten us killed! I should kill your punk ass myself. All of that BS you are pulling needs to stop, now!"

Lewis said to Steven, "Don't try to play me like a chump. These guys will see you get knocked out unconscious. Now you better close your mouth before I close it to for you." Lewis got into Steven's face and now they were standing toe to toe. Both of them had anger written all over their faces. Steven shoved Lewis and then Lewis shoved them back. Steven punched Lewis in his mouth. Lewis tackled Steven hard to the floor. Everybody else broke up the fight and separated them.

Willie was baffled about why Steven and Lewis were fighting each other. He tried to talk some sense into both of them, "We are in this shit together. Fighting each other is a waste of time. Y'all need to swash this shit right now. So we can move on to bigger and better things."

Steven told Willie what happened, "Lewis tricked us about his plan. He opened fire on the police officers without giving them a chance to leave. He started shooting at them the moment they stepped out of the station. James and I didn't have any choice but to get out and defend ourselves, since they were shooting at us too."

Willie asked Lewis, "Is Steven telling the truth about everything?"

Lewis replied, "Yes, he's telling the truth. Tonight was a test for us; I needed to know what kind of heart we have. It was for a good cause. Steven's father's death is the reason I decided to get revenge that was so deadly. We severed them like a hamburger at Wendy's. Why do we carry guns for and we don't want to use them?"

Eric was extremely angry and he told Lewis, "Why did you put my mom's car in the way of flying bullets? Your jacked up plan placed our lives in danger and then it caught me off guard. I didn't have a gun to protect myself. I should take these glasses off and put my foot in your ass."

Lewis told Eric, "Nerd, come over here and kick it. I would beat your ass relentlessly."

Johnny kept his cool and said, "What Lewis did was not so terrible; he should've given us a heads up." Steven looked at Johnny like he spit on him. Steven walked towards Johnny and punched him in the face. Eric held Steven back while everybody else held Johnny back. Johnny tried to break free to get a piece of Steven.

Steven told them, "After we hit a bank, I'm out of this crew. Lewis is going to get someone killed. His crazy ass will not be the cause of my death."

James told Steven, "Please, stop acting like an angel. We were going to kill someone eventually. Don't try to run up on me and throw a haymaker. I have some fast hands and the odds of you winning a fight against me are very slim. Fuck shooting up a police station, I prefer an eye for an eye. They took your father, so we laid them to rest. Eric, you do not have to hold him back."

Steven told Eric, "I have heard enough of this shit, so take me home. I am hanging with these want to be gangsters. You all can follow Lewis around if you want to."

Eric said to them, "I had enough for one night too; it's time for me to take y'all home."

Everyone followed Eric back to the jeep. Eric checked his mother's vehicle for any damage and he didn't find anything. Everybody was quiet while Eric took them home. He dropped Lewis, James, and Johnny at home, first. He wanted to talk with Steven and Willie for a little while. "With all the fighting and arguing tonight, I am surprised, someone did not pull out a gun. Lewis has turned our crew upside down. We are the only ones with a leveled head. Even James acted idiotic tonight. He basically has taken Lewis's side. Lewis probably came to him like he did me."

Willie expressed his opinion, "Everything was going well until Lewis went wild. He will get somebody killed if he keeps it up. Lewis is a loose cannon; we don't know when he is going to let one go."

Steven replied, "I must admit, Lewis has gotten under my skin. My anger led me to hit Johnny and I wish he would accept my apology. I felt down to Lewis's level tonight."

Willie said, "I will speak to Johnny. It's going to become a challenge for him to let it go. Johnny is probably thinking about fighting you, right now. This crew is sinking like the Titanic. I am going to quit after we hit a bank too."

Eric said, "Some kind of way, we have to function as a team. How long can we get away with all this crime? I'm not trying to find out, either. The police officers are going to look hard for suspects. The Teenage Mafia could become the number one suspects. Lewis was leaving notes on our victims. A lot of smart criminals get caught by doing dumb ass shit like that. We have to be more careful. Alright Steven, here is your stop. Watch out man, Lewis could be waiting on you in your bedroom."

Steven responded, "If he's inside my bedroom, Lewis will leave through the window; his head will smash against the glass." Steven got out of the jeep and went inside the house. Eric took Willie home next. Eric checked his cell phone and it showed that Rebecca never called.

Chapter 11

The next morning, Johnny and Willie were sitting side by side in their first period class. Willie whispered, "I need to talk about what happened last night. Things did get out of hand. Steven told me that he is sorry for hitting you. He really wished it never happened. I told him I would talk to you about swashing the little beef between y'all."

Johnny whispered back, "I know Steven lost his mind when he put his hands on me. Everybody make mistakes and last night Steven made a large one. I won't hold a grudge against him. Attacking Steven is the last thing on my mind. It would be best if he would come to me and apologize himself."

Willie replied, "I'm going to let Steven know how you feel. He wants to speak with you, but he does not want to fight. Johnny, I know how hard it is for you to let Steven slide. Our program is already tumbling down. We don't need any more conflict. Lunch time is the best time for y'all to talk." Willie thought it was a little strange that Johnny would accept Steven's apology so fast.

When lunch time came, Willie was putting his books in his locker. Steven walked up behind Willie and asked him, "Did you get a chance to speak with Johnny about our situation? I hope he has cooled down, by now."

Willie said, "Yes, I did spoke with him. He is willing to accept your apology. He wants to speak you, personally. I set things up for you two to end the BS. You have to tell him what's on your mind. Look at him right there, hopping that little guy in the lunch line. I will stay right here to watch y'all talk." Then Willie pointed to Johnny. Steven got in front of Johnny in the lunch line. Steven told Johnny, "I'm sorry for what I did; it was uncalled for. Too bad that there isn't a way I can turn back time. We have to throw away what happened in the past, so we can go on with the future. We could go out and do something together." Johnny knew Steven was sincere with his regret. Johnny reached out to shake Steven's hand. Steven shook Johnny's hand and he thought everything was fine. Johnny pushed Steven and he slid six feet across the floor. Steven had a humiliated look on his face and he thought, **Damn, I might have to fight this big monster.** Steven was lying on the floor with both of his legs sticking up.

Willie was supposed to watch them talk. He was told by a teacher that Coach Thomas wanted to speak with him. Steven got up slowly and Johnny began walking towards him. All the students were excited to see a fight. One guy screamed out, "I have 20 bucks on Johnny!"

Johnny told Steven, "No one hits me and get away with it." Steven looked around for Willie and he was gone. Steven and Johnny put their guards up, ready to fight. Some students were surprised that Steven did not run. Johnny swung at Steven and he missed, but Steven connected with a straight right jab. Then Steven swiftly struck Johnny with a left jab. Johnny swung again and he missed. Steven hit Johnny with a combo; one right upper cut, a left and right jab. Johnny was dazed and he almost fell to the floor. Johnny realized Steven was too fast for him. All the students were stunned and it was like Mike Tyson and Buster Douglass all over again. Johnny came up close to Steven and gave him a bear hug. Then Johnny put his left foot behind Steven's feet and tripped him down. Johnny got on top of Steven and opened a can of whip ass. Johnny was punching like he was fighting for the UFC. Finally, Mr. Ross came out of his classroom to stop the fight. He pulled Johnny off of Steven. Steven had a black and swollen right eye and Johnny had blood leaking from his lips.

Mr. Ross told Johnny, "When will you learn that fighting is not the way to handle your problems. It seems like every time I look up, you are in another fight. Let's go to the Principal's office, mister." Steven got back up and Mr. Ross told him, "You have to come to the Principal's office too." Mr. Ross took both of them to speak with Principal Washington. The gossip went around the school that Steven was a better fighter than Johnny. Most of the students who saw the fight thought Steven won.

Mr. Ross went into the Principal's office and told Principal Washington, "These two students were fighting in cafeteria. Whatever punishment you decided to give them is okay with me." Mr. Ross walked away and closed the door behind him. Principal Washington was a 56 year old African American male. His head was bald and he wore eye glasses. Even in the summertime, he would come to work in a three piece suit. He had been working at Rosa Park high school for 25 years, as a teacher and as a Principal.

Principal Washington told them, "Y'all two knuckleheads still have not learned anything yet. Take a seat, guys. Both of you guys are seniors in high school. When you get in the real world and act unintelligent, you will go to jail. Seniors are supposed to set an example for the rest of the school. Earlier today, a few students came and told me Steven wanted to fight Johnny. I thought it was just a rumor."

Steven pleaded his case. "The fight was not planned by me. Johnny put his hands on me first and I was trying to defend myself."

Principal Washington said, "Everyone can't be telling a story on you. No one is going to hit you for no reason. You had to do something or say something to make Johnny snap on you. Johnny, I want you to stay out of trouble and find your classroom. Steven, you are suspended for two days. I'm going to write this up and place it in y'all student files."

Johnny got up and went to class like nothing ever happened. Principal Washington was on the phone calling Barbara, so she could come pick him up from school. After she spoke to Principal Washington, Barbara came to the school and picked Steven up.

On the way home, Barbara told Steven, "I can't believe you were in a fight. The most shocking part is you started the fight. Do not try to deny it because Principal Washington would not make up things. He has known Tim and me for a long time. Just because Tim is gone, you don't have to take it out on the world."

Steven kept quiet because Barbara's mind was already made up about what had happened. Principal Washington was not going to suspend Johnny because of the championship game this week. Any player who got suspended couldn't play that week. Principal Washington felt awful about the way he handled the situation. He already knew it was a 10 out of 10 chance that Johnny started the fight. He wanted the school's football team to win the championship so bad that he made up a lie to keep Johnny in class.

Willie overheard three guys talking about a fight, "That fight was the best one I ever saw. Someone was crazy enough to stand up for themselves against Johnny." "Steven reminded me of Floyd Mayweather with those fast hands. Steven almost knocked his head off. Johnny is not a machine after all. Anyone could probably beat Johnny ass with some quick hands" "I think Johnny got the best of Steven, even though he almost lost. Everyone will talk about this fight for a long time. When Johnny tripped him down, the fight was over with."

Willie thought, *I was supposed to watch them talk. Steven might think it was a set up because I left him. If I was Steven, I would think it was a set up. I'm happy to know Steven fought back. Steven showed Johnny he wasn't scared; it could be enough for Johnny to leave him alone. Johnny lied to me; he said he wasn't going to attack Steven. Johnny and I will have a real serious conversation. He has to stop bully other people; Steven has exposed his weakness.*

Rumors about the fight went around the school like a virus. Eric, James, and Lewis found out about it from different people. Eric wanted to get in touch with Steven to see how he was doing. James did not give a damn about them beating up on each other; as long as they were well enough to help him make some more money, he was okay. Lewis was surprised that Steven went toe to toe with the school's fighting champion. He thought Johnny should've dominated Steven.

When school got out, Willie talked to Johnny. "Why did you lie to me with a straight face? The only thing you accomplished was driving the dagger farther into the crew's heart. We can't trust each other and we are not getting along. Being a bully is becoming old. Many students saw what Steven did against you. Your invincibility is fading fast. The team saw me put you down in practice. If you keep on bulling people, it's a matter of time before you lose."

Johnny responded, "When someone put their hands on me, I have to handle my business. Steven came to me and he was apologetic. It did not matter to me. I wanted to fight him to get it off my chest. We have fought and my grudge against him is over with. I no longer have beef with him; you don't have to believe me. The crew is in turmoil and I wish I could take every punch back. Steven and I can bounce back from this to become cool again. He's not dead or paralyzed. Depending on who you speak with, some folks think he won the fight."

Willie and Johnny went ahead to practice. Willie still didn't know whether he should take Johnny's words serious. He figured time would tell everything. He had to speak with Steven to let him know why he was not there. Willie wanted to play the peace maker of the crew. He knew trust would build a good chemistry. Without chemistry, all of them could get placed behind bars. Willie didn't see a reason to speak with Lewis because he thought Lewis was too lost.

Lewis and James spoke with each other after school too. Lewis told James, "I heard the fight was good. Some people are saying Steven won the fight. Johnny must have been sick or something. Maybe his big ass did not eat. You know big people have to eat. Johnny should've crushed him like a bug."

James jokingly said, "Steven must have the eye of the

tiger. Johnny tried to kill him at the end of the battle. By the way, when is our next move?"

Lewis answered, "After we hit a bank, Steven will quit and we have to take over. With one less person, it would mean more green in our pockets. We don't need Steven at all." James told Lewis, "I hate to say this, but the boy is pretty smart. He has come up with some awesome ideas. Steven is good; we can be great. I'll catch up with you later."

Steven was at home thinking about the long day he **had**. *I actually had a fight with Johnny and lived to see another day. If Johnny wants a rematch, he will not get one. The next time, I will pick up something and lay his ass out. We have fought, so this shit should be over with. How did I get suspended for two days and Johnny was sent to class? Probably, one hundred students saw the whole thing. What if Willie played me like Jimmy Hendrix played the guitar? He disappeared when Johnny went nuts. Willie seems like an honest person. I'm sure he wants to tell me what happened to him. Hopefully, he has a good excuse.* Steven was at home watching TV in the living room with a towel full of ice on his right eye. The house phone began to ring. Eric's number was on the ID box. Steven answered the phone, "Do I have to be in critical condition for you to call? So what's good?"

Eric said, "You have to tell me what's good, Mr. Buster Douglass. You are lucky and unlucky. Everybody in our school knows about you. A lot of girls wouldn't mind hooking up with a gladiator. Don't be surprised when the students give you the superstar treatment. I told all the honeys you are my closest friend. Take advantage of your fifteen minutes of fame. Something like this only happens once in a lifetime."

Steven replied, "I don't think people will treat me any different. I really don't feel like the winner. I'm sitting at home with ice on my right eye and Johnny is at football practice. He is the winner in my opinion."

Eric said, "Everybody doesn't see it like that. Wait until you return to school, people who would normally not speak to you, will be talking to you. We could hang out on all the breaks together. Some people would think I'm a tough guy too."

Steven said, "It's fine with me. Don't get your hopes up too high about this. The fight wasn't the first or the last one they will ever see. Eric, no one could really think I won the fight. Mr. Ross was my guardian angel, flying down from heaven to save my life. When Johnny was abusing me, I saw more stars than an astronaut."

Eric told him, "Dude, you are funny. Let's get serious for a minute; I have two banks in mind. I'll check on them before they close today. We must know everything about the place before we hit it. Where are the cameras located? Are there any security guards? How many workers are there at all times? How close is it from the nearest police station? We must have knowledge on all these things."

Steven replied, "Go ahead and check on it".

Eric said, "I hope one of these banks have some flaws in security. Call me later, champ."

Willie called Steven ten minutes later. Steven told Willie, "I had a feeling you was going to contact me. Johnny went ballistic today. You said he was willing to talk things over. I told him how sorry I was about the incident at the hideout. Johnny shook my hand and then he pushed me to the floor."

Willie said, "I am sorry for what happen. Johnny told me a lie. He pretended like everything was alright; Johnny had a hidden agenda. He just wanted to fight you so bad. His pride wouldn't let go of the fact that you hit him and he did not get a chance to strike back. Fighting you is the only way he could get it off his chest. Coach Thomas sent a teacher to come and get me. He wanted to speak with me about a UCLA scout; who is interested in me. Coach Thomas told me I have a great chance to play football for them next year. It would be an opportunity of a lifetime. I have to keep up the good work. Maybe fifteen minutes later, I overheard three dudes talking about the fight. My bad, I should've been there to watch y'all talk. Johnny told me he is ready to make peace with you. He doesn't want a rematch or any other kind of altercation with you."

Steven asked, "Do you believe him this time? There won't be another fight with him. If he pulls that bullshit with me again, someone will get seriously hurt. It won't be me who get demolished."

Willie responded, "Don't worry about Johnny; he wants to keep this crew together. Another battle with you would break us farther apart. Everybody has to try keeping the crew together. I want to arrive on the UCLA campus in style, a tight car that the girls would love to look at and more money than any other student there. My parents do not give me anything. Who wants to arrive on a college campus being broke? In a little while, my name and being broke will not be in the same sentence."

Steven said, "I want you to go and check out a couple of banks. We need to make up a legit plan that is going to work. At the end of the day, it is still about the mighty dollar. Cash is the key to our hopes and dreams. Togetherness is going to help us become successful. Lewis thinks he could start some controversy any time he gets ready. I'm going to make sure our crew runs like a well oiled machine. With his stupid methods, our lives won't last too long. Lewis wants to make things work, even though its sounds weird. Lewis and I have to talk; it might not change anything. It could be effective enough to calm him down a little bit."

Willie said, "Calling Lewis is a waste of time. Your shot is better than mines to calm him down because you known him forever. I'll look for the next party to crash."

Once their conversation was over, Steven went to get some more ice for his right eye. He realized Lewis hadn't called him in a minute. They used to be close like brothers and now they were beefing like Snoop Dogg and Suge Knight. Steven had a lot of love for Lewis. He didn't want their relationship to end. Steven's mood was turning into depression over his fading friendship with Lewis. He started to reminisce on how good it was when Lewis and he were growing up as kids. At first it was playing at the playground and then it was chasing girls in middle school. Now they were bumping heads. Steven knew the only way to bring Lewis down to earth was to have a powerful and emotional conversation with him. Working things out with Lewis was the best solution for the crew. Steven gave Lewis a call on his cell phone.

Lewis was in his bed lying down when he heard a familiar ring tone coming from his phone. The ring tone was a 2pac song named "Never Had A Friend Like Me". Lewis knew Steven was calling him. Lewis wondered, **What does Steven** *want? He doesn't fuck with me anymore*. Even though Lewis was acting foolish towards Steven, he still loved him like a brother. Lewis answered his phone, "Hello."

Steven told him, "All of this crap between us has to end. You got to watch my back and I will return the favor. How did we go from brothers to enemies? There has to be a way for us to get alone better than what we are doing. I should've never put my hands on you, no matter how pissed off I was. We are a team with these other guys. Our group should strive to work as a unit, not two or three units. Can you imagine a car with the parts under the hood placed incorrectly? It's going to break down. If our crew don't do things right, we will break down. The car has smoke coming from under the hood right now. Do you want us to fall apart like a used Cadillac inside of the bank? Falling or balling, which one sounds more desirable to you?"

Steven had given Lewis an earful of things to put into consideration. Lewis opened up to Steven's worries. Everything Steven said made a lot of sense to Lewis. Lewis agreed, "Steven, you have never been this right before. It is possible for us to turn things around. I'm more than willing to get us back on the right track. We are the leaders of The Teenage Mafia. The body will only go where the heads leads it. Our communication skills must improve. I'm no longer going to be a problem. So let's make things happen. By the way, I walked inside of The Treasure Bank today and it looked so easy to pull off a robbery there. The bank has four workers with no security. I saw a few cameras there, but it doesn't matter. Everybody in the world would look alike with the ski masks on. The bankers are three women and one man; all of them could be middle aged. People like them wouldn't defend themselves against a bunch of wild animals with guns. Cooperation is their only option. The cash will be ours. This hit shouldn't take no more than six minutes, to complete."

Steven was pleased to see how good the conversation was going between Lewis and him. Steven thought, *Everything sounds good coming out of Lewis's mouth. At the same time, Lewis could be telling me what I want to hear. Could Lewis's mind change? I hope I really connected with him. There is no getting around Lewis; he has to straighten up his act*. Steven said, "I'm glad to hear you speak positive about everything. We can rebuild our friendship and make it stronger than ever. We will tell everybody about The Treasure Bank, so we could have a meeting about it, Thursday night. Everybody's input is very valuable. Someone could come up with a plan that is better than what we could come up with; it's possible. Everyone will say whatever they want. They are putting their lives in danger too."

Lewis told him, "Our strategy for The Treasure Bank will be better than the Phil Jackson's Triangle Offense. We are a six member crew, so six minds will work together. Everyone will know their roles and everything will happen in our favor. You can take that to the bank. I'll get back with you later; I'm tired. That favor I need is coming soon. Are you my brother?"

Steven responded, "I'm your brother forever." Their conversation was finished.

Lewis's mindset had changed. He wanted to be a team player now. At first he wanted to see Steven fall. Now, Lewis was saying that he was willing to make things work between the two. Lewis was confused about what his plans really were.

Part of him wanted to take over the crew once Steven left. Another part of him wanted to leave the life of crime alone. He would be happy if Steven let it go. Lewis thought, *Even though Steven comes up with most of the ideas. He doesn't have violence in him. Steven cares too much about other people and he's never going to become a ruthless criminal. You can't be like that and survive out here. Someone will kill him because he is too soft. As long as I'm with him, he's going home safe.*

Later on, Eric wanted Honey to come over his house. He gave her a call on his cell phone. Eric said, "Hey girl, what are you doing tonight?"

Honey replied, "I don't have any plans for tonight. If you want to hang out with me; it's cool."

Eric said, "This is a school night, but let's chill together, anyway. Let's go out on a date. We have to find a great restaurant. Then both of us could catch a movie. You and I are in a relationship now. We are going to get a chance to know each other better. The love making is incredible, but a strong relationship can't get built on it alone."

Honey told Eric, "I'm coming to get you. Every moment we spend together is a special one. I can't wait to see you. Ever since we started this relationship, I look at life differently. Life is not about hustling men out of their money. It's better to find someone who you care about and have a good life with them. I'll let you go, so I can get ready."

Eric was already dressed to impress. He had on a green Lacoste polo shirt with an oversized croc logo on the left chest area. He was also wearing a pair of brown khaki dress pants and a pair of wheat colored Timberland Euro Dub boots.

Honey took her time getting ready as usual. She went in her bathroom to take a shower. After the shower, she dried off with a big blue towel and wrapped it around her herself. She walked to her closet and chose to wear an Italian plum colored Rocawear Dark Romance Dress. She looked very intriguing in her beautiful dress. Honey placed a pair of Louis Vuitton high heels shoes on her feet and placed a Louis Vuitton purse over her shoulder. She put on her favorite pair of 24 karat gold loop earrings. She let her curly long blonde hair down. She sprayed on her Victoria Secret perfume. Honey looked in the mirror that was connected with her dresser. She instantly saw how magnificent she looked. She planned on showing Eric her classy side.

Chapter 12

Honey got into her light blue 2008 Chevy Malibu to drive to Eric's house. Once she arrived, butterflies were in her stomach. She said to herself, *I hope he like this outfit. If it doesn't make him love struck, nothing will.* She got out of her car and rang the door bell.

Eric was already in the living room waiting on her. He jumped up off the couch and opened the door. Eric saw her and said, "You must have left a modeling audition tonight." Eric gave her a hug and a French kiss.

Honey told him, "I am hungry; we need to eat first. What do you have in mind?"

Eric said with no doubt, "Applebee's." Then Honey drove them there. Honey loved going there to eat.

Eric ordered a bacon cheeseburger, French fries, and a Coke. Honey chose to eat a grilled steak, buttery mashed potatoes, salad, and a Diet Coke. They ate, laughed, and talked about their childhood. They stayed at Applebee's for an hour and forty minutes.

Eric and Honey went to the movies. They watched a scary movie titled "Bloody Murder," about a serial killer who terrorized the town. She held on to his arms tightly during the whole movie. Once the movie ended she insisted, "We are going to one of my favorite spots. Normally, I would go there to clear my mind. Trust me; it will put your mind at ease too."

She drove him to a boardwalk that was near an ocean

shore. The scene looked like it was cut out of a romantic novel. There were millions of stars shining bright. The wind was blowing cool air. You could see the moon's reflection on the ocean. They made-out while standing on the boardwalk. After being out there for two hours chatting, Honey and Eric were ready to leave.

She was driving back to his house to relax some more. Eric began thinking, *Our date is going well. Hopefully, it will get better. Even if we don't have sex tonight, our date would've still been a terrific one. Honey and I belong together.*

Honey was doing some thinking of her own. *He is the nicest guy I ever went out with. Those other guys were a bunch of assholes, who only wanted one thing. Eric is smart and sweet. He's the type of guy I can see myself spending the rest of my life with.*

They held hands while walking to Eric's front door. Once Eric and Honey entered into the house, they went upstairs to Eric's bedroom. Both of them were lying down in bed with Eric's left arm underneath her head. He told her, "Damn, I never thought it would feel this good to hold someone." Eric was using his right hand to run it through her hair backwards.

Honey became sleepy and then she closed her eyes. Eric was kind of tired too. He was fighting his sleep. Eric wanted the moment to last forever. The door bell rang and Eric was curious about who was at the door. He woke up Honey and said, "Someone rang the door bell and the time is 1:26am. I hope my mom isn't out there; she is going to be pissed off."

Honey told him, "Go and see who it is." She thought, *Eric's mother is outside. I did not want her to meet me like this. My car is parked in front of the house; I can't hide from her. She will know someone else is here, anyways.*

Eric went down stairs to see who was at the door. The door bell rang again. He opened the living room door and the person at the door was not his mom. It was someone he did not want to see. Rebecca was standing outside of the door.

For the first time, she came over his house without calling. Eric was speechless and he looked like he saw a ghost. Rebecca walked in without being invited. Eric finally had something to say, "Wait a minute, you stood me up and ignored my phone calls. I want you to leave my house and never come back. I told you that too much time apart was going to break us apart."

Rebecca had her story together. "Let me be honest with you. I am afraid of falling in love. My heart is always getting broken. My reason for showing up here is to apologize. It hurts me to know I hurt you. My car is in the shop getting fix. I came all the way over here to see you in a taxi. We can start over, boy." She almost had him fooled.

Eric said, "I want you to go, right now. Find someone else to use those excuses."

Rebecca didn't give up. "My heart is willing to give you a real chance. I have never cared about a guy more than I care about you, sweetheart." Then Rebecca gave him a tight hug. Honey came down stairs thinking that she was going to meet Eric's mother. She noticed a woman was hugging Eric but she did not look like his mom. Eric had a picture of his mother on the wall inside of his bedroom. Rebecca spotted Honey coming down the stairs and she asked, "Who is this girl coming down the stairs?"

Eric turned around and told Honey, "This is not what it seems like. I was just asking her to leave."

Rebecca became furious when she saw another woman at Eric's house. She yelled, "You are trying to ditch me for this bitch."

Honey responded, "Who are you calling a bitch? Bitch!"

Eric told them, "Y'all have to calm down. My neighbors are very nosey. My mom could find out I had y'all over here tonight."

Honey said, "Forget calming down because this bitch is over my man's house. Why is she over here at one something in the morning? She had her hands all over you. I did not see you putting up a fight, either." Rebecca knew that she and Eric were done with each other. She wanted to kick up some dust before leaving because she was jealous. Rebecca said, "You didn't know, Eric and I have been creeping around for a long time. Let me guess? He has been fucking you too. I bet you can't even spell class, bitch."

Honey had enough of Rebecca's disrespect, "Forget all this talking, I can show you better than I can tell you." Honey walked up close to Rebecca and took a .22 handgun out of her purse. She pointed the gun in Rebecca's face and screamed, "Call me a bitch again! I'll leave your brains on the floor!"

Eric saw things getting out of hand. He didn't know about the gun in Honey's purse. Eric had to stop Honey before something bad happened. Eric tried to talk some sense into Honey. "Please put the gun down. I want you and nobody else." Honey still had her finger on the trigger with the gun aimed at Rebecca. Honey asked Eric, "Have you fucked her before? Tell me the truth, now!"

Eric replied, "I haven't had sex with her since we decided to become a couple. Honey, can you put the gun down? We are going to have a lovely life together. Don't let her stop it by going to jail."

Rebecca was fearful about getting shot. She didn't want Honey to know how she really felt. Rebecca's mouth kept on running 100 miles per hour, "That little gun doesn't put any fear in my heart. Weak people who can't fight carry guns. Put it down and then we could "strap"."

Honey said to Rebecca, "Just take your ass back where you came from. I'm not going to jail over a piece of shit who can't dress. With that red skirt on, you should've stayed on the corner. Is it you or the dog shit under your shoes that stink?" Honey placed the gun back into her purse. Eric took a deep breath. He was relieved. Rebecca felt embarrassed because Honey won the war of words. Rebecca took out a .22 handgun from her red purse and then she aimed it at Honey. Instantly, Honey reached for the gun and she grasped it. Rebecca and Honey began wresting over the gun with both of their hands on it. Eric was watching them struggle over the gun. The gun went off and Eric ducked down to avoid catching a bullet.

The loud shot scared Rebecca and Honey, but Rebecca fell down with a fatal wound to the chest. Eric placed both hands on his head and said, "Shit!"

Honey stood over Rebecca and started to panic, saying, "O' my God, I killed her. We have to call the police. It is the right thing to do. I was struggling to take the gun from her in self defense. The police probably won't believe me. This is fucked up; I don't want to be in jail for life." Blood was coming out from under Rebecca.

Eric checked her for a pulse. He told Honey, "She is dead. I can't find a pulse and she's not breathing, either. Damn, what are we going to do? My mom will have a heart attack if she finds out what happens here. Shit! We have to think fast."

Honey asked, "What if we take the body and place it somewhere else?"

Eric replied, "Let's do it because I don't want to put our relationship in jeopardy. She came over here unexpected. Both of y'all have guns; times are changing."

Honey was crying and shaking. She said, "I can't help you move the body. Tonight turned out to be the wrong night to come over here. Everything was going good until she came over here and ruined our good time."

Eric told her, "Honey, get yourself together. Do you want a good life with me? Keeping the body hear would only effect our lives in a bad way. Her body is small enough to get placed in a garbage bag."

Honey continued to decline helping, "I'm not touching her at all. My love for you is deep, but touching her is too much for me. We should go ahead and call the police. There is a chance they could believe our story."

Eric said, "Fuck that; they may not take a word we say as the truth. Take a seat on this couch and I'll handle our problem." The blood increased on the floor. Eric knew he needed some help right away. He got on his cell phone and called the only person he thought would be trustworthy in a strange situation like this.

Steven was lying down in his bed, masturbating to a Janet Jackson poster. He heard the telephone ringing and he said, "It's bad enough I can't get no ass. Can I at least jack off? Who is calling here this late?" He walked into the living room to answer the phone. He looked at the ID box and then he said, "Eric, please don't let it be Lewis again. I am going to stay at home."

Steven answered the phone, "Eric, you have wakened me out of my sleep. It better be important."

Eric told Steven in a desperate manner, "It's an emergency. Something happened at my house tonight. Come over my house and help me out. I will get in big trouble if you don't come over."

Steven could hear the desperation in Eric's voice. Steven told him, "Tell me what's going on. From the way you sound something really bad must went down. Man, just spill the beans."

Eric spilled the beans and the corn. "Someone was killed at my house tonight. The story is very long and I will explain it to you, later. For right now, let me pick you up. Please say you'll help me out of this mess."

Steven thought, *He want me to help get rid of the body*. He said, "Come and pick me up; I'll help out."

Eric replied, "I'm on my way." Then they hung their phones up. Eric went to Honey and gave her a hug. He told her, "Everything will be alright. I'm fixing this problem. Just stay here, I'll be back."

Honey didn't want him to go. "You can't leave me here by myself."

Eric told her his plans, "One of my best friends will assist me in handling the situation. I got to pick him up. His name is Steven and I would place my life in his hands."

Honey accepted the fact he has to leave, "Go and get him. Would you please hurry back here? I'll be in your bedroom."

Eric kissed her on the lips and said, "Alright."

Honey thought, I hope Steven can be trusted. If he goes to the police, Eric and I are in big trouble.

Eric left the house as casually as he could. He did not want any neighbor to see him in a rush. He got into the jeep and drove away.

Steven took a peak in his mother's bedroom to see whether she was awake or asleep. Barbara was snoring; he knew she was sleeping. Then Steven stood by the window in the living rooming, looking through it and waiting on Eric. As soon as he seen Eric pulling up, he exited his home and got into the jeep with Eric. They were on their way back to Eric's house. While driving, Eric began telling Steven what had happened. "I've been paying prostitutes for sex. I was fucking a few of them at first and then two of them were making me fall in love. One of them kept it real and the other one had a lot of excuses. I was chilling in my bedroom with Honey; she is honest with me. The girl who told me many lies is Rebecca. Normally, she would call me first. For the first time, she came over without calling. I was trying to get Rebecca to leave, but she refused. Honey came down the stairs and saw her hugging me. They got into a battle of words. Honey takes a gun out of her purse and then she aimed it at Rebecca. I talked her into putting the gun away. Once she placed the gun back into her purse, Rebecca pulls her heat out of her purse. Both of them started to tussle over Rebecca's gun. Then Rebecca got hit one time in the chest and died. We have to get the blood off the floor and move the body to another location. There is a new pack of garbage bags in the kitchen. We are going to use how many as needed."

Steven asked him, "Honey is still at your place, right?"

Eric answered, "Yes, she is still there."

Eric and Steven arrived at their destination. Eric drove the jeep back into the garage. Steven was following Eric who was leading him to Rebecca's body. Once Steven saw the body, he stared at her face to see if she looked familiar. She did not look like someone he knew.

Eric said, "I'm going into the kitchen to get us a few bags."

Honey came into the living room teary eyed. She wanted to meet Steven and find out if he could be trusted. She saw Steven and thought, *He looks very handsome to me. These youngsters are looking better every day. I shouldn't think about one of his best friends like this. My friends always said, 'black men have big dicks'. I have to speak with him about this incident that happened here.* She told Steven," If anyone find out about this, my life is over. I will take all the blame. Thank you for coming over here to help us out."

Steven said, "Eric is my right hand man. He gave me a call and I'm here to lend a hand." Steven saw the .22 handgun on the floor. He asked Honey, "Is that the gun she brought over here?"

Honey told him, "Yeah." Eric came into the living room with four garbage bags. He put them together to make sure it was strong enough to hold the body.

Steven said to Eric, "We need to sit her up and place the bag over her head." Honey went into the kitchen because she didn't want to watch them take her away. Steven turned her around and pushed her head up until she got into the sitting position. Eric placed the garbage bags over her head and down to her waist. Steven laid her back down on the floor. Eric pulled her legs into the bag and tided the bag into a knot. Then he picked up Rebecca's gun and placed it in his pocket.

Eric asked Steven, "Do you think we should get the blood off the floor with a mop?"

Steven stated, "We can use the mop with bleach and whatever y'all been mopping the floors with. Just know the mop has to go soon; before someone thinks it looks kind of reddish. It's dark outside, so maybe no one saw her coming over here."

Eric added, "Another good thing is she didn't drive her car over here. The only bad thing is a taxi driver brought her over here. Well, they pick up many people every day. They won't remember everybody who rides with them. Look at the time; its 4:39 in the morning. Time is rolling. My mom will make it home at about 7:20. I'll get the mop and the rest of the cleaning material."

Eric went to get a mop, a bucket, some water, a jug of bleach, and the Lysol. Steven cleaned all the blood off the floor. Eric told Steven, "I know a place where we can dump the body. Let's get her into the jeep." Steven and Eric dragged the garbage bag with Rebecca's body into the garage. Eric opened the back door on the jeep. Eric and Steven picked up the bag together and placed it on the floor at the back of the jeep. Eric got into the driver seat and Steven got into the front passenger seat.

Eric got back on the road to get rid of the body. Steven thought, *The dumping spot better be a good one. I'm pretty sure he knows that already. I have my hands on more dirt than a worm. I don't even live a normal life anymore.* They arrived at the same boardwalk that Honey had taken him to earlier. Eric told Steven, "We are going to toss the body into the water." They got out and placed the bag on the boardwalk and then pushed it into the ocean. Eric threw her .22 handgun in the ocean too.

Steven saw dried blood on his hands and arms. He told Eric, "Now I look like the killer. It seems like I'm living out a movie. My life is going downhill. A few months ago, I was a normal teen. All of us are a menace to society." Eric and Steven entered the jeep and headed to Eric's house. Steven kept on talking, "What if we took the legal way to getting money. Our lives wouldn't be upside down. We are on the road to hell. I wish my mom already had a nice house with a dependable car."

Eric said, "I thought we should've done things the legal way too. We are in too deep to turn around and do things the right way. Everybody is so motivated to getting this dirty money. Maybe, the good Lord will forgive us for our sins. At least you and I have a conscience. Lewis loves all the drama coming his way. He must be thrilled about robbing innocent people"

Eric placed the jeep back into the garage. He and Steven entered the house and went to Eric's bedroom. Honey was sitting on the bed, trying to calm down. Eric said to her, "We have taken care of the problem. You are going to be shaken up for a while; that's normal under these circumstances."

She stood up and gave Eric a hug while staring at Steven. Steven was checking out all the pictures on the wall. Honey told Eric, "Our future will be bright. Tonight has to get left in the past. The past is just a memory. It's our big secret and no one has to know, but us. A matter of fact, we have to pretend like this incident never happen."

Eric smiled and he figured she would be alright. He said to both of them, "The school bells will be ringing soon. What happened here is beyond complicated. Complicated is an understatement. Honey, would you take Steven home for me because I'm very fatigued? He will give you the directions."

Honey said, "Giving him a ride home would not be a problem. Come on, Steven, let's go."

Eric took a quick shower and went to bed.

While Honey was taking Steven home, she wanted to talk with him. "I have never seen you before. It is a good thing Eric has a friend like you. I wish I had someone like you. I mean, a friend like you. The average person would've never done what you did tonight."

Steven told her, "I'm not the average person. Eric is such a great friend; I had to help him out. Eric has found himself a fine girl and I'm still solo. One day it's going to happen for me."

Honey said, "It could happen sooner than you think. Let's exchange phone numbers, so we can keep in touch."

Honey and Steven were outside Steven's house. She wanted to take Steven to bed and rock his world. She gave Steven a hug and told him, "Thanks for being there for us. I will be forever grateful to you. If you ever need anything, I will be there for you. No matter what it is, I will give it to you. If you want me to come in, I will."

Steven did not have a clue that she wanted to get with him. Steven said to her, "I'm okay. Sleeping is the only thing on my mind, at this moment. Let's go ahead and exchange phone numbers. We could be good friends too like Eric and I."

Honey was disappointed that Steven did not invite her

in. Steven told her, "Bye." Then he went into his house. Steven thought as he entered his house, *It's all good, as long as the incident stays a secret. What a fuckin' night. Just when I thought I couldn't sink any lower, something like this happens. My father would roll over in his grave if he knew what I was doing.*

Chapter 13

In the morning, Lewis and James caught up with each other before school started. Lewis explained, "There's a slight change in our plan. We will wait until Steven leaves the crew, first. When we hit the bank, he's going to disappear like a crack head mother's TV. All of the beefing can cause us not to function as one. I really wanted to finish driving them crazy, but it could hurt our chances to succeed. Whatever plan we come up with, I'm going to stick by it. We are real thugs and most of our crew members are sweet hearts. Steven's absence will silence the peace talk. For example, we shouldn't try to kill nobody. Fuck all that half stepping shit. If you are going to be a G, be a "G". The Teenage Mafia will have a take no prisoners' attitude. To be feared is greater than to be loved. People would know we are not playing games with them and they would take us very seriously. Our victims will hand over whatever we want to stay alive."

Later on that day, the word got out about The Teenage Mafia. All the teachers and students were whispering about them. Everybody was wondering if the criminals could be going to school here. At 12:00pm, the local news broadcast made people aware of The Teenage Mafia. They talked about a crime wave of several robberies and a possible deadly attack on two police officers. The news reporter spoke about letters that were found on some victims.

The entire buzz was like music to Lewis's ears. One guy

told Lewis during the lunch break, "We don't have anything to worry about because no one here has those kinds of balls." Lewis replied with a small smirk, "I wouldn't put anything pass these students at this school. The police have to stop them before more damage is done. Who would go around hurting innocent people?"

Eric wouldn't admit it, but all the talk about them made him feel cool and tough. Eric had always wanted to feel that way. He felt kind of eager to keep the people talking. Willie and Johnny spread rumors about The Teenage Mafia to fit in with everybody else. Johnny had in mind that his crew was becoming the modern day outlaws. Willie did not like the drama their actions cost, but he liked the attention. James didn't care about whether people talked about The Teenage Mafia or not. He wanted the money and he didn't care about the fame. His goal of being rich was his main focus in life.

Steven hadn't heard anything because he was at home sleeping; he had a very long night. After he woke up, Steven checked the ID box on the phone and he had nine missed calls. He said to himself, "That broke my old record of six missed calls. I'll watch a little TV; there is nothing else to do." As soon as he turned on the TV, he saw a Latino detective with a black three piece suit, a black pair of casual shoes, a white long sleeve button up shirt and a red tie. He was on stage behind a podium with other police officers, talking during a conference.

Detective Lopez was speaking, "My name is Hugo Lopez and I'm a detective. I chose to handle this case. I personally want to bring these bad guys down. There is a new gang on the rise in our community. We already had our hands full with the Bloods and the Crip gangs. The Teenage Mafia must be brought to justice. With the youth depending on crimes to be their oasis, the future is looking shaky. These thugs knocked out an elderly lady and took her purse. Someone should've taught them job seeking skills. They may have or had nothing to do with the murder of two of our beloved police officers. At this time, there is no evidence that links them to the crime. The Teenage Mafia is definitely our prime suspects. We know for a fact, two ladies working at a store were rob and assaulted with guns by them. These monsters could be prepared to keep hurting innocent people. We must stop this newly formed gang before they grow by adding more members. If you decide to go anywhere at night, especially walking, please be careful. Times have changed people; walking late at night is becoming dangerous. The Teenage Mafia is wearing white ski masks and they are armed and dangerous. If anyone seen or know anything, contact your local police department. I would like to thank you all for listening to this urgent message."

Steven was impressed by Detective Lopez because he displayed so much charisma. He demonstrated the true meaning of being highly intelligent. Steven knew Detective Lopez would become a thorn in his side. It will get harder since the law enforcement knew about them. At first, they were a secret. Then Lewis wrote those letters and placed them on some of their victims. Making those letters was an unwise move. Steven felt like setting up another meeting. He wanted to tell Lewis to stop writing the letters, so the police wouldn't know who did the crime.

Once school ended, Steven gave Eric a phone call. Eric said, "Man, I called you twice. We made the headlines on the news today. I bet we are going to make the front page of the newspaper too."

Steven told Eric, "You sound kind of happy. The news will increase our chances of getting caught. I know it feels good to get the media attention. A thug's lifestyle is very attractive. Put on your thinking cap; staying unknown would've been the best thing for us. The pigs will come after us with everything they have. Lewis's poetry is their first evidence against us. We have to be slicker than grease and quicker than lighting."

Eric said, "Why didn't I think about it the way you did? We need to hurry up and rob a bank, so we could let it go. If we keep on going, something bad is certain to happen. Our families will attend our funeral services if we keep it up."

Steven responded, "Now you see the bigger picture. Would everybody be able to see it too? I want to call a meeting soon to let everybody know what is on my mind. I wonder what the crew would be like without me. Lewis would try to call all the shots. He would be too confused to make the right decision. Everybody needs to quit after we rob The Treasure Bank. Lewis told me the bank is an easy target. I'm ready to come up with my final plan. A Detective name Hugo Lopez was on TV saying he will bring us to justice. He seems like a very smart man and he's not some old guy who is just reading from a card behind the podium. Detective Lopez is creating a clever plot to bring us down. I will get in touch with Willie and Lewis. James hasn't spoken with me in a minute, so I will call him too."

Eric said, "Thank you for helping me out last night. You really are a good friend. I'll call you back later."

Steven said, "Bye."

Steven called James's cell phone and said, "Are we strangers? I'm just messing with you. We might have a meeting Thursday to go over the details for the next mission. Lewis has already found us a bank to hit. We are going to collect more cheese than any other mission, we ever been on."

James told him, "I don't have a problem with robbing any bank. Making money is so important to me. We are going to strike, so fast that they won't know what hit them. Fuck the police. The boys in blue can't stop us. They would be too busy eating donuts and drinking coffee. When the pigs make it to the scene, The Teenage Mafia will have already escaped with the green."

Steven told him, "Yep, our plan is to get away with the green. I will quit once we hit this bank. It is good to leave on a high note. Thanks for being a part of this crew. Don't forget I picked you to join our clique. How long will you be a part of this?"

James answered, "Becoming rich is my goal. I have no set time to quit, but I want a few million before retiring. When everything is said and done, my great-great grand kids will be taken care of for life."

Steven told him, "I'm not trying to sound weak or scared, but sometimes you have to look at history. There have been criminals smoother than us. The ones who did not know when to quit eventually got caught, most of the times. If anything happens to you or Eric, I will blame myself. It was me who brought y'all into this bullshit."

James stated, "We have this thing "down packed" (under control). Nothing is going to happen to us. History doesn't mean anything to me. Those other guys are not The Teenage

Mafia. We are a clever unit. When we put our heads together, the impossible becomes possible."

Steven realized James was going to stay a criminal for a long time. He had a feeling that something devastating would happen to James because he didn't know how to quit. Steven's attempt to bring James down to earth did not work. Steven said, "Don't forget we might have a meeting Thursday. Holler at me, whenever." James knew Steven was telling him the truth, but he was willing to risk everything against all odds.

Steven tried to give Lewis a call, but he was already on his cell phone talking to Redd. Lewis wanted some more drugs from him. "I don't have any more coke or weed. When can you hook me up with some more? It's time for a refill, Doc."

Redd said, "Boy, you are not playing. I have an unlimited amount of both. The only question is how much do you want."

Lewis answered, "Give me $200 worth of cocaine and throw in $40 worth of weed."

Redd responded, "I will hook it up. Whenever you do something, go all the way with it." Redd believed Lewis could become one of his high paying fiends. Redd thought if he could get close to Lewis, he could take every dollar he had.

Lewis said, "Well, the transportation is in your hands. Flint Stoning or should I say walking to your crib takes too long."

He told Lewis, "It's okay to get high on weed. There's another kind of drug that will get you even higher. The "rocks" are the next level. I might give you a little sample with the pipe for free. Smoking rocks is better than doing any other drugs. I promise it will be too good to go a day or two without it."

Lewis replied, "On TV, that crack does more harm than anything else. Crack heads are considered as people who are throwing their health and life away."

Redd responded, "Those people are actors pretending; it's their job. What a person does in their free time is nobody else's business. Make up your mind; these rocks are going faster than turkeys in November."

Lewis agreed, "I guess it won't hurt to try crack. Give me my sample with the rest of my order."

Redd said, "It will be worth your time. I'm on my way to scoop you up." Lewis went outside to wait on Redd with his cash already in his pockets.

Sam was watching Lewis through his bedroom window. Sam thought, *Lewis is waiting on someone because he's looking both ways. Why he's not in his bedroom studying or doing homework. The teaching at these schools has changed. When I was in school, my teacher gave me homework every day. There's that tattoo wearing thug, again. Lewis must be mess up in the head. Out of all the decent people in L.A., he prefers hanging out with him. This is the last straw; Lewis will have to speak with me. Jessica and I have given him a comfortable life. Why would he take that route? Steven was coming around every weekend. He probably ran him off to hang out with the thugs.*

Redd decided to hit a few corners before taking him to his apartment. Redd said to Lewis, "Man, I like your style. The real, recognize the real. We are connecting well because of that. Let's hang out next weekend. I know a girl Tammy. Damn, the bitch is fine. Her ass is bigger than J. Lo's. She is having a house party; dime pieces from all over L.A. will show up. I will try my best to fuck all of them. My D.I.C.K. will be inside of somebody's daughter."

Lewis burst out laughing. "Boy, you are retarded. I want to put them under the bed covers too. I have never been to a house party before. It better be a "tight" party. There is an outfit in my closet; I have to find it. The shirt is an all red Jordan Still Jammin' Tee with a red pair of Jordan jogging pants. My pair of Air Jordan shoes is so sick. They are the Flight 45 Edition; the color of my shoes is red and white."

Then Redd told him, "We will look like a team. Any kind of red clothes is the style. Once people see you with me, automatically you're considered a gangster. No one will get out of line with you, hopefully. I'm going to be affiliated with the Piru Bloods for life. It's blood in, blood out."

Lewis and Redd arrived at the Blossom Apartment Complex. They walked to Redd's apartment. Lewis took a seat on the couch and Redd went to get the drugs out of his bedroom. He unlocked the box with his key and grabbed ten sacks of crack; each one was worth $20. Then he grabbed two sacks of weed; each one is worth $20. He also grabbed two dime sacks of rocks which were worth $10 a piece. Now he was looking all over for the crack pipe, from the closet to the dressers. Redd finally found it in his bottom dresser. Lewis had $240 in his hands waiting on Redd to exchange with him. Once he came back into the living room, Lewis exchanged with him. Lewis told him, "You are holding more drugs than the pharmacy."

Redd told Lewis, "I'm a dope dealer, so it's what I do. The bills will not pay for themselves and some food must go down my throat. I handle my business like a real professional."

Lewis said, "I can see that. Wow, this is enough drugs to last a few weeks. We could get high right now. Let's open both sacks of weed."

Redd took out a pack of Black and Mild cigars. He was getting ready to make a blunt. Lewis was watching him closely. Redd poured the tobacco out of the cigar into a small trash can. Then he replaced it with the Chronic. Redd licked the wrapper until it wouldn't unroll. He took out a lighter and lit the blunt. Since Lewis had already paid, Redd wouldn't mind smoking. He would never get high on his own supply. Now that he was finish making the blunt, he said, "Have you ever played 'Puff-Puff-Pass'? Why are you looking at me like I'm speaking Chinese? We are going to take turns passing the weed back and forward. Everybody around here smokes the green, damn near. I smell it every day." Both of them took turns, puffing and passing the Chronic. The apartment was filled with smoke.

The smoke detector was never on at Redd's home. Lewis was coughing and Redd was laughing at him. Lewis said, "This shit is the bomb, blood."

Redd told him, "I know why Dr. Dre made two albums called The Chronic. The weed is so good; it make me wonder why I sold it to you in the first place. I feel high enough to touch the sky." Lewis was just as high as Redd. He was talking very slow and calm, "We could go to the party and have a threesome with ten girls. One girl would suck my dick, another one would lick my nuts, and two of them would lick my nipples." Redd started laughing and then he said, "I have a thing for Chinese women. Most of them look very good; I would sale my soul for five of those bitches. Open your legs baby and show me the sushi. If I owned a van or something large to drive, all of those women from the China restaurant would come home with me. They will "run a train" on me. Pass the blunt, stop trying to hog it."

Once they were finished with the first blunt, Redd made another one. Lewis told him, "California should become the weed state. The best green is grown around here. I feel like I'm floating in the air. The weed scent is all over my clothes. If my parents smell this shit on me, my dad and I might break the house down. My dad will never get the best of me again. Fuck my mom and my gay ass daddy."

Redd told him, "That sticky is making you say anything. My mother loved me and I can't deny it. She moved out of here because of me. I was so careless when I first started slanging drugs. All the violence outside played a role in her leaving too. I miss all the home cooked meals. Most of my food gets put in the microwave. She begged me to stop slanging drugs, but this is what I was born to do. Getting a 9 to 5 job has never crossed my mind before."

After they were finished smoking, Lewis was ready to go home. Lewis said, "I'm so high; my buzz will last three days. The munchies have creeped up on me. Take me home, so I can eat."

He told Lewis, "Okay, but the weed will become off limits for a while. I'm fucking with you. Give me a call, when you want to get high again. My phone lines are always open, 24/7." Both of them went to the car and Redd took Lewis home.

Lewis went inside his house and went straight to the refrigerator. He made three ham and cheese sandwiches and a cup of grape soda. As soon as he turned around, Sam was standing behind him. Sam questioned him, "Who is that guy that you've been hanging with? Did you remember anything we taught you? I can see through him like a glass. He is a thug who could cause some trouble. You smell funny, Lewis." Sam walked closer to Lewis and started sniffing him. Sam recognized the smell of weed and looked at Lewis's red eyes. Then Sam said to Lewis, "It is bad enough your brain cells barely work; now you are becoming a dope head. This thug is also a drug dealer. Where does he stay, so I can curse his ass out?" Sam upset Lewis by trying to get into his business.

Lewis told his father, "Leave me the fuck alone. Before you judge me, look in the mirror. First, I was molested as a kid and then raped a week or two ago by you. The father of the year award won't touch your hands. I should've called the cops. Keep your muthafuckin' mouth closed and let me handle my business, bitch." Lewis walked away from Sam and went to his room. Sam's feelings were hurt. He screamed, "As long as you are staying under my roof, the rules will be obeyed. I will not allow a dope smoker to live here. Make the right decision for a change."

Sam went to his bedroom and told Jessica while she was getting ready for bed, "Our son came home smelling like weed. His new friend has introduced him to drugs. Lewis is easily influenced. He did not get that trait from my side of the family. There is no way in hell I will let him do drugs and continue to live here. Something has to be done about this. I need to strangle him. We have to take back control of the house. Lewis thinks he could do whatever he wants." Jessica was lying down in the bed, trying to get some sleep.

She said, "He is a young man and mistakes will happen. You were seventeen and eighteen years old before. Let him run free for a while. His new friend will get him into big trouble. The only people he could call is us and we are going to let him burn. Jail is his next destination. If he wants to become a jackass, don't stand in his way. He will learn the hard way because of his hard head. Why are you so stressed out, babe?"

Sam started to cool down, "He will need us to help him. I'm not pulling any strings to bail him out of jail. Some people have to learn the hard way. It is a matter of time before he hangs himself."

Johnny and Willie were speaking to each other on their cell phones. Johnny said, "I can't believe high school football is coming to an end. Just yesterday, I was a freshmen starving for a starting position on the team. Every year we were in the playoffs losing. Every year we were getting farther and farther in the playoff. Now our team has finally cracked the can open."

Willie replied, "Our high school days will become great memories. You were always the best player on defense. No matter how hard I played, the newspapers would only show your face and your accomplishments. I had to wonder when the journalist would show me a little love. After each game, my dad talked about you a lot, Johnny this and Johnny that. He had no doubt that you were going to college and then the NFL. Do you know how bad I wanted him to brag about me?"

Johnny didn't have a clue; his uncle had such high expectations of him. Johnny said, "A lot of people are looking for me to do great things. They believe in me more than I believe in myself. All the newspapers made my head big by showing my great stats and giving my face more than enough exposure. My ego got out of hand. I treated my teammates like they were beneath me."

Willie told him, "I would've become overconfident too. Both of us put in a lot of time and effort to get where we are now. Thursday night will be remembered forever. Coach Thomas has always been there for us. The man is like a second father to us. He helped us elevate our game on the field."

Johnny responded, "When we win the championship, I'm going to make sure both of us are in the newspapers. If Coach Thomas knew we were behind The Teenage Mafia, he would be hurt and disappointed."

Willie said, "My parents are so "tight" with the bread. If they weren't so cheap, I would have never been a part of the crew. All of their money goes on material things. During Christmas time, they want the most expensive decorations to out shine the neighbors. What about having more food in the refrigerator than the neighbors?"

Johnny told Willie, "Our refrigerator stays full. We can't open it without food hitting the floor. I don't want to sound like I'm bragging. Our house can't touch y'all house, though. I must admit, the crew will never be the same without Steven and you. Eric might quit too, after the bank robbery. It will take more than three of us to get the job done. Lewis would bring in new members. I would have a serious problem with it. It was hard for us to trust anybody in the beginning. We will continue this conversation later. My mom cooked pork chops, sweet potatoes, biscuits, and macaroni. My bad, I will never mention any statement about food again."

Willie told him, "It's cool. I'll speak with you later." Willie dialed Steven's number and he answered by saying, "What's up, Willie." Willie responded, "Everything is going good, but how is your eye?"

Steven replied, "I can see out of it, so everything is alright."

Willie told him, "I looked at a few banks and all of them has top of line security. I'm talking about armed security personnel and surveillance cameras."

Steven told him, "Lewis has found us a bank to hit. The Treasure Bank seems like an easy target. They have four workers, three women and one man. All of them could be in their middle ages. I was going to call you first, but you beat me to the punch. The meeting is Thursday night." Willie said, "Damn, the championship game is Thursday night. Johnny and I can't miss it. Just have the meeting without us." Steven said, "I can respect your wishes. The state championship game is Thursday night; it slipped my mind. Y'all better win. The meeting would become the first one without you and Johnny. Eric, James, Lewis and I will come up with a plan for Friday after noon, hopefully. We need some more ammunition for the guns. Every since our shoot out with the cops, we have been short of bullets. Maybe Eric can get us some more. I hate to ask him for anything under short notice."

Willie asked, "How does Eric get his hands on so many weapons? He is just a nerd. Can you picture Screech with an AK-47? We don't know anything about his connections, it is a mystery."

Steven replied, "I made him a part of the crew because he was always telling me about his connections, over the years. Our guns have to be fully loaded before we put one foot inside of the bank. We would "spray" the bank down if necessary.

A shoot out could go down and we must get prepared to open fire. Those bankers shouldn't put up a fight. Our crew has to stay flawless, leaving no evidence behind."

Willie asked Steven, "Have you heard anything from James? That dude doesn't socialize with none of us until it's time to get some money. In my opinion, he is still a stranger. How much do we really know about this guy?"

Steven answered, "James and I have been cool with each other for years. I don't know him personally. He is always talking about money. Greed can make a person lose his mind. Look at us for an example; we were regular teenagers. Now we are the scum of the earth. Lewis was right; there is not a good criminal. Robin Hood is still a fairy tale. Being hungry for currency is making us go wild. We are a bunch of animals and the city of L.A. is our jungle. My mom always said that money is the root of all evil. I never understood it until now. If someone gets caught will they snitch? The cops would offer a great deal to bring the rest of us down. Who's bold enough to take the charge like Ray Allen? Someone could "sing" to the police like he's on MTV's Making The Band."

Willie sad, "I hope no one gets caught and rat us out. If someone gets arrested, it is a good chance they will spill the beans. Our story can only end real good or tremendously bad. What make things even more complicated, even if we quit, someone could still get caught and give up information about us. The smartest thing for everyone is to stop after we rob the bank. We both know it won't happen. Our lives could be in their hands for a minute."

Steven said, "I thought everything was planned to perfection. Snitching is a topic and we will speak about it in the next meeting. It could ruffle a few feathers, but it has to get addressed." Steven couldn't wait until he got back to living a normal life. He knew now that he didn't have the answers to everything. Steven was going to anticipate everything working out for him.

Once Steven came back to school, he felt like a superstar. Many students were asking him about the fight. He realized Eric was right. The battle had given him popularity. Steven had some of the finest girls in school wanting to speak with him.

Eric was looking for Steven during lunch time. He found Steven putting his books in his locker. Eric said, "I told you so. Everyone is talking about you coming back to school today."

Steven said, "The fight made me famous. A lot of people were asking me questions. What was going through my mind during the fight? Why did I fight back? Did I take boxing classes before? Who is going to the prom with me? It's funny to me because I see those same people Monday thru Friday and they were never interested in me before."

Eric said to Steven, "I'm your closest friend. Let's go into the cafeteria, so people could see us together. It would make me look cool."

Steven agreed to do it, "Come on, we can share the spotlight." The cafeteria was serving pizza, corn, and mixed fruit. Steven told Eric, "They are having my favorite lunch. It feels good to come back to school. That's something I thought would never come out of my mouth. Too bad, the royal treatment won't last forever. At least everyone knows my name. It's like I'm a movie star, Will Smith and Brad Pitt rolled up in one."

Steven and Eric made it to the front of the lunch line and received their plates. They sat down beside each other. Eric asked Steven in a low tone, "Have that incident crossed your mind? I think about it every day and night. My girl is handling the situation better than me."

Steven responded, "What we did was fucked up, but it was for a good purpose. I would help again to save your life. Look at what I talked you into doing for me. We are even. Damn, my pizza is cold. The cafeteria workers must have been cooked this food. Do they even know who I am? My food should be hot every day. I'm Steven Ward, bitch."

Eric said playfully, "My food is cold too. Do they have any clue about who I am? I'm Steven Ward's right hand man, bitch. You got to fight every week to get the respect of the cafeteria's workers. If you need a manger, I'm here for you. The folks around here would call you Ali."

Steven told him, "If you were helping, both of my eyes would be swollen. I would walk around the school with a cane like a blind person. I will fight like Holly, not Ali. The state championship game is Thursday and our friends can't make it. We will have the meeting without them. Friday morning, we will let them know what's up. That way, they won't be lost about everything. Have you heard from Lewis or James?"

Eric answered, "No, I have not heard from them. Those guys are weird. James doesn't holler at nobody; he stays to himself. Lewis should be alright when he stops pissing people off. The last time he talked to me, he was trying to start some shit."

After finishing their food, Eric and Steven left the cafeteria. They went into the gym to hang out before their first period class. Both of them were sitting on the bleachers far from everyone else. Steve said, "Me and Willie had a long talk. Someone could snitch if they get caught by the cops. I plan on quitting and someone could still tell on me for a lighter sentence. I'm going to talk about dropping dimes in our meeting. We will also come up with the best strategy for the bank robbery."

Eric said, "A lot of my cash will go on helping my girl out. She won't have to worry about anything. I'm going to find me a little job, so it would seems like I worked for everything. The economy is jacked up, so it might not be possible. Lewis can do whatever he wants because the world knows his parents has money."

Steven told him, "My living conditions are not too good. With my cash, my mom and I are going to stay high off life. Right now, the homeless people would not change places with me. My reason for coming up with good ideas is that I'm so motivated to help my mom." Eric told Steven, "It never occurred to me that we had a real reason to rob people. I thought everybody was just full of greed. Look at me; I'm trying to get rid of my nerdy image. At home, my mom spoils me. She gives me everything she thought I wanted. We are living very comfortable in our suburban neighborhood. There goes the bell ringing. The sound makes me want to "call Earl"."

Steven told him, "If you run across Lewis and James, tell them the meeting is at 8:00 tonight and on Friday after noon, we will stick the bank up. Please get some more bullets; we are almost out."

James was at home in the bed, pretending to be sick to avoid school. He was on his cell phone talking to Frank. James asked him, "Do you want me to go over my teams again? I want to make sure my bets are placed right. On Saturday, you'll get my $50."

Frank said, "Someone belongs in school. An education is very important these days. Many African Americans from the past had to fight for us to get that chance. You won't believe how many black people was beat down and killed for our rights. I know someone has talked to you about our history. The police officers used dogs, blackjacks, and water hoses on black people who were fighting for their freedom."

James told him, "Get over it. The year is 2011, not 1934. I get enough history lessons at school. Don't take it the wrong way, but I don't want to hear it from you. This conversation was supposed to be about me trying to win Sunday, not how the white men treated those weak black people."

Frank shook his head because James did not understand the past. Frank was a part of the struggle for freedom. He still had scars on his right arm from where the police officers made a German Shepherd attack him.

James kept running his mouth, "How could they let the white man kick their ass like that. Someone should've taught them how to stick and move. If it was me, I would've punished them."

Finally, Frank had enough of James's stupidity. Frank was extremely angry, but he kept his cool. Frank said, "I have your teams written down. Business is picking up fast, so get back with me later." Then they hung their phones up.

Frank thought, *James doesn't have a clue about black history, but he could tell you everything about the rapper 50 Cent. If James was living back in the days, he wouldn't* think, so foolishly. *He better straighten himself up, before he throws away his life. When will the young black male learn to do the right thing?*

James thought, *Man, Frank is tripping hard. He is always trying to preach. He needs to become a pastor for a church. The white man has never harmed me. They are the ones who received a beat down not me. I should not care or think about the past. This is the present and I'm trying to get mines in full.*

Chapter 14

Willie and Johnny were on a charter bus instead of the school bus they normally traveled on. The team was "crunk" saying, "We can't be stopped! We can't be stopped!" Johnny was yelling along with the rest of the team. Coach Thomas noticed Johnny's attitude had changed for the better. His little talk with him worked out for the better. Willie and Johnny were sitting side by side at the back of the charter bus. Principal Washington let them leave early, so they could get a good warm up before the game. Coach Thomas was very proud of his team. Win or lose, he would walk away from the game with his head up. The team wanted the state championship just as much as he did. Coach Thomas felt confident about his team's chances of winning tonight.

After school, Lewis gave James a call on his cell phone while he was walking home from school. Lewis said to him, "Eric sent me a text message saying we are having a meeting at 8:00 tonight and the bank robbery will go down Friday after noon. Willie and Johnny won't be there because of the big game to tonight. The Treasure Bank robbery is my idea. I bet some elementary kids could stick the place up. A couple middle age people work there with no security."

James said, "I like the way you talk. We are always on the same page. After we hit The Treasure Bank, our crew should stick up another one. Our "dough" will rise like it's in the oven. Steven will regret leaving the crew. Why would he quit when everything is going so well? We make this shit look easy. He thinks the longer we keep robbing people, our chances of getting caught is greater. Fuck that, the Teenage Mafia is the smartest muthafuckin' criminals of all times. We'll drain every bank dry if we have too. A person like me would break in someone grandmother's house and rob her old ass for every valuable thing she own. As you can see, I don't give a fuck anymore. Being relentless is my new way of life."

Lewis stated, "Everybody in our crew should think like you, but some people wants to wear the halo on the top of the horns. Steven thinks he can do both. He's my brother and I love him. God bless his heart."

James began snickering and then he said, "Steven is as soft as a pillow. You are right, everyone can't be a thug. I wonder who is the gayest, Steven or Elton John."

Lewis told him jokingly, "Leave my brother alone; he's not around to defend himself. Be ready for tonight. Feel free to put your two cents in. Everyone can say what they think needs to be done, so don't bite your tongue. I'll see you tonight."

Eric was at home, wondering how he was going to get some ammunition for the guns. He didn't want to call Redd for help, but it was his only option. While walking around his bedroom, he said to himself, "Redd is the last person I want to speak with. If I don't come through for the crew, nothing can get accomplished." He was staring at his cell phone. Eric knew for a fact that Redd would get suspicious. He would ask him about what happened to those other bullets. Then he thought about asking Honey to bring him some bullets because she owned a .22 handgun. Honey was also 24 years old which made her old enough to purchase the item. He had narrowed his choices down to Redd and Honey. Who would he call? Eric had decided to contact Honey instead of his gang related cousin. He dialed her phone number.

She answered, "Baby, what's up."

Eric replied, "I need a favor from you. Would you bring me some bullets? It doesn't matter where you get them from. My mom has a few guns and she doesn't have too many bullets. Everybody is carrying some heat; I want to feel well protected too."

Honey said, "I'll do it for you. After that shit went down in your house, I might want some more protection. When do you want me to get it for you?"

Eric responded, "Today, I would like to have them as soon as possible. I'm going to meet you around the corner because my mom is at home. I will use my own money for the ammunition."

Honey thought, *Something is wrong with this picture. Maybe, someone is after him*. She asked, "Are you paranoid?"

Eric said, "No. Have you ever heard of the old saying; it's better to be caught with it than without it?"

Honey told him, "I'm already driving around, so give me about eleven minutes to pick you up."

Willie and James were on the football field jumping up and down, after their team won the state championship. It was the school's first title in twenty six years. One player poured an orange cooler full of red Gatorade with ice on top of Coach Thomas. Coach Thomas had both of his hands up in victory. Then he started hugging all his assistant coaches and players. Willie and Johnny stood still for the journalist's picture camera. She wanted a picture of them holding the trophy.

Then Willie kissed it and raised it in the air. He passed the championship prize to another teammate. Everybody on the team had a chance to hold the trophy. The prestigious trophy was the color of gold with the top portion the shape of California. The base portion of the trophy was black with the name of the title in gold, District #4 5A State Championship. The score was 16-10; it was a great defensive game. Johnny stopped the other team's Running Back on the goal line with the time running out. The next day, Willie and Johnny would make the front page of the newspaper.

While Johnny and Willie were on the football field, the rest of the posse was at the hideout. They were in the building's main office as usual. Steven told them, "I wish Johnny was here, so we could end the beef. I'll get a chance to talk to him one day. Let's get to business. Everybody knows tomorrow is my last day being a part of the crew. I'm trying to move on with my life. Even though I come up with some good schemes, this shit is not for me. If y'all get caught, don't give the "5-0" (police) any information about me."

James became offended by Steven's statements. He thought Steven was trying to call him a rat. James said to Steven, "Hold up, man. No one will go against the G code by snitching on you. I would rather be killed before I let the police capture me. There are no bitches in this group, I hope. We are supposed to trust each other. Remember? Talking like that is a slap in the face to all of us. We have done a lot of dirt together. I thought we had a brotherhood."

Steven explained himself, "All I'm saying is if the cops place someone behind bars, don't use my name for a lesser sentence. In other words, keep my name out of your mouth.

Frank Lucas was a kingpin and he ratted on everybody. Telling on someone is a dirty thing to do. History shows some dudes mouth run like hot water. Don't take it personal; I'm just saying what's on my mind. Talking hard doesn't mean anything to me. I wish everybody the best of luck."

Lewis told Steven, "I understand where you are coming from. We still have to trust each other. It's too late to think like that. Our lives are in each other hands. Now let's move on with the program and The Treasure Bank is the topic." Everybody was brainstorming to come up with a plan.

James said, "We should go in and shoot everybody. Then we would take the money and run; I'm kidding."

Eric told them, "My mind is blank and no idea has come to me yet. I hope no one sees us because we never done "dirt" in the day time. The last thing I want is a high speed chase with the law in my mom's car." Eric wasn't the only person who didn't have a clue about what to do. James and Lewis were thinking hard and couldn't squeeze out an idea.

Steven said, "Basically, We can use the same formula in the bank that we used on the corner store. Robbing any place during the day time is a major problem. Leaving the scene without anyone seeing us is the hardest part. Sticking the place up is easy. We have to go in with our guns out to get their immediate attention. Watch their hands to make sure they don't hit an emergency button. We would run away if that happens. In this case, using force is very acceptable, slapping, choking, stumping, and punching. It would make them give up the cash quicker than yelling. We have to get in and out as quick as possible. The jeep has to get parked around the corner because every bank has cameras outside. As we walk to the bank, look around for cars driving by and people on foot. If we don't see any one, put the masks on and run into the bank. I'm ready to pull one of Lewis's numbers, let's break'em off something proper like after the money is ours. It would take a while before they call the cops. We can use the head start. If there is traffic outside, we will wait a minute. A minute is all the time I'm willing to wait. I'm counting on no one to be outside; when we leave from there. Eric, remember to take the license plate off the jeep; someone could try to take a good look at it. I chose to rob the bank, tomorrow afternoon; we are getting out of school early, so the students can travel for the game. What do y'all think about everything I said?"

James agreed convincingly, "It sounds good to me. You are pretty good at being the general. Finally, Steven has given us the authorization to kick someone ass."

Eric said, "Steven should write a book on how to become an excellent criminal. You were probably trained by Rick Ross, the real Rick Ross."

Lewis told everybody, "Hell is freezing right now; we are all on the same page. Steven has seen the light. The Teenage Mafia is ready to handle business. With the dough we are going to make, we will be straight for a long time. Fuck Detective Lopez; that Latino can barely speak English. If he gets into my way, my .9mm would barbeque his ass. Fuck the rest of the police officers too. The boys in blue will turn into the "boys in red", if they get in our way."

The meeting was over and they felt confident about their chances of getting the job done. Everybody walked home because Eric's mother was off work. She didn't trust him driving on the road at night.

Once Steven arrived home, he thought Barbara would be sleeping, but she was sitting on one of the living room couches watching TV. Barbara told him as he walked through the front door, "You are hanging out late on a school night. Well, you're getting older. Just yesterday, I remember taking you to school for the first time. There is something I must tell you. The LAPD has awarded us with $40,000. They felt sorry about what happened to Tim. The good news doesn't stop there. We will receive Tim's pension from Motel 6."

Steven was so happy that he wanted to jump for joy around the house. Steven gave her a tight hug. She told him, "God doesn't let his people down. Everything will be alright. We can move to a better house and I can get a better car. We are going to move on up like the Jeffersons. One day, we will look at different houses. I always wanted you to have the better things in life. The feeling was terrible, to see other parents give their children the better things in life and I could not do the same thing for you. Tomorrow, tell me some things you want. I'm heading to bed."

Steven had not seen Barbara this happy since before Tim's death. He thought about telling the crew he wanted out but he knew he could not let the crew down. Everybody was depending on him. He was the one who came up with most of the plans. Steven began thinking, *Why is all of this good luck is starting to happen? I was putting my life on the line for nothing; money was already coming my way. Damn, there is no way I could've known.*

Eric and Honey were on the phone talking to each other. Eric told her, "I miss you. It has only been a few hours, but it feels like days. Our next night together will be a perfect one without the interruptions. You mean everything to me."

Honey responded, "You mean everything to me too. Next weekend is a great time for us to chill with each other. What happened on that messed up day will stay on our minds forever. I tried to forget about what went down in your living room. It's impossible to forget something like that. You would need a bad case of amnesia. We still have to live our lives like nothing happen. Life can get complicated sometimes. Crazy things happen all the time. Your friend, Steven helped us out a lot. I have faith that he will not go to the police. Steven is now a good friend of mine too. Maybe, you can invite him over my house for dinner. It is the least we could do for a guy who saved my life."

Eric replied, "Steven proved himself as a true comrade. No one else would have helped out. I'm tired of you talking about Steven. What about us getting together this weekend? We are going to have a wonderful time. I expect us to have some more incredible sex. I'm at my happiest when we are spending quality time together. In a little while, I will be able to give you anything your heart desires."

Honey thought, *How will he be able to give me anything? Maybe those bullets I purchased for him will get used. I doubt it; he's not a killer.* Honey said, "My legs will always open for you. You'll rock my world like an earthquake. I have to use the bathroom. I can't hold it anymore."

Eric told her, "Alright, I'll call you tomorrow." Eric got off the phone with Honey and he just remembered, *My mom will be at home tomorrow afternoon. If she don't loan me the jeep, our plan is ruined. I don't have any choice, but to ask for it. She doesn't want* me behind the wheel too much. I'm going to ask her for permission as nicely as I can.

The next day, Lewis was pumping himself up by playing The Notorious B.I.G.'s song name "Somebody Gotta Die". Lewis figured after today his life would change for the better. He would not have to depend on Sam and Jessica. With the amount of bread he was expecting, Lewis could become the man he always wanted to be; a made-man. Instead of going into the kitchen for a plate, he kept one under his bed. Lewis took the plate from under the bed and placed it on the bed. He went into his dresser and took two $20 sacks of coke out. He was wishing the coke would pump him up even more. After he rolled up a one dollar bill, he inhaled every last drop of the cocaine. He became higher enough to touch the clouds. It pumped him up like he wanted. **He thought, Man, this coke is amazing. I heard sex is the best feeling in the world. Cocaine will challenge that theory. When Lewis finished the** drugs, he went to school.

During the lunch break at school, Steven and Eric went into the restroom together. Steven wanted to use Eric's cell phone to speak with Willie. Willie said to Steven, "I'm still in bed. Last night, we won the state championship. We stopped at Pizza Hut to celebrate the win. The excitement lasted the whole night. Holding the trophy in the air was one of the best feelings I ever had. It took four years to play at the championship game."

Steven said, "Congratulations, you deserve it. On another subject, we decided to go into the bank and kick some ass. We need more time to get away. Driving fast would bring more attention on us. We have to drive cautiously. The jeep will be parked around the corner, but not too far away. So the cameras wouldn't show what kind of vehicle we came in. Bring your A game. The first thing to watch inside the bank is the hands of the workers. We don't want them to hit an emergency button. We would have to run away if that happens. Someone could walk into the bank while we are sticking the place up. If they walk in, they can't leave out. Everything is going to work out fine. I am going to make sure of it. We have too much life to live. You are going to the NFL and I am going to be at home with my wife, watching my boy make tackles. At around 12:50pm, our crew will get this paper. Just follow my lead; five of us are going in and five of us are leaving out. Now, you better believe it."

Willie said, "Let me get up and get this room clean. We'll hook up in a few minutes."

James was sitting down in the living room watching the movie name "Higher Learning." He began thinking, *Steven is harder than what I expected. I was flabbergasted when he gave us the green light to break our foot off in their asses. It shocked Lewis because I seen the look on his face too. When it came down to making important decision; I was lost. Eric and Lewis did not have anything to say. Steven knew exactly how to handle the situation. Lewis and I have the heart and not the brain for this job. What are we going to do when Steven leaves the crew? Perhaps I could find a new hustle to get paid. Alex hasn't called me in a minute. When Alex was beaten me in every game, I had to cut my phone off because he was calling me too much. None of my old gambling buddies are contacting me. They are upset with me because I was taking all their cash. Fuck them. I'm not calling them anymore. Their money is childlike and my money is full grown. Those punks are not on my level. Today, I will give Frank my money to place a bet. Hopefully, he won't try to teach me about history. My million dollar dreams will come true. What I'm doing right now are just baby steps to reaching my goals.*

Once school got out at 12:00pm, Eric was under some pressure. He was nervous about asking his mother for the jeep. He knew there was a chance she could say no. Molly was watching The Bold and The Beautiful on TV in the living room. Eric peeked in the living room to see what kind of mood she was in. Eric saw her and he couldn't tell what kind of mood she was in. Eric took a deep breath and found the guts to ask his mom for the jeep. He approached her and said, "Did you lose some weight? Your hair looks nice."

Molly saw through Eric and she knew he wanted something. She asked him, "How much money you want? Do you want the jeep? It has to be something."

Eric realized his mother knew what he was doing. Eric told her, "You are one smart cookie. I didn't want any money, but can I use the jeep, please."

Molly thought about it for a moment and then she said, "You can drive it. Be careful, you are still a rookie driver. I don't completely trust your driving skills. Keep your seat belt on at all times. Don't try to show off in front of some girls."

Eric told her, "You are the only girl I care about."

She replied, "Son, save that lie for someone else. I have seen you looking at those honeys up and down with your tongue hanging out of your mouth."

Eric asked his mom, "Where did you learn how to speak hip?"

Molly laughed and told him, "You'll be surprised if you knew."

Eric took the key off of her dresser and now he had to bring the jeep back in one piece. When Eric went into the garage, he used a screwdriver to take the license plate off.

Eric had picked up everyone. Steven was in the front passenger seat, Willie and Johnny were sitting on the back seat, and Lewis and James were loading up the guns while sitting on the floor behind the back seat. Steven said, "When I say kick their ass, go ahead and demolish them. We are going to get our money, first. We are not playing any games; it's time to collect."

Eric said worriedly, "Whatever y'all do, help me bring my mom's car back without a scratch. She will kill me if something happen to the jeep."

Steven asked James and Lewis, "Are y'all finish loading up the guns?"

James answered, "We are almost finished with them. If things get out of hand, we'll light the bank up like it's the fourth of July." All of them were feeling a little apprehensive.

Lewis said to them, "We're finished loading the guns. I bought some gloves for everybody; one size fits all." Lewis and James started passing out the guns, the white ski masks, and the black cotton made gloves.

Steven asked, "Is every one ready?" The rest of the crew said, "Yes." Steven said, "Drive us to The Treasure Bank. Eric, you will stay inside the car. Your mom's car is in your hands. No one can protect it, the way you would. When you see us coming back, go ahead and crank the jeep up, so we can get the fuck out of here."

They arrived around the corner from the bank at 1:30pm. Everybody had a ski mask and a gun in their pockets other than Eric because he was staying in the car. Steven told them, "Let's go! Let's go!" They hopped out of the jeep. While walking to the bank, they looked around to make sure the coast was clear. Steven told them, "Put the masks on and let's go in." The crew ran into the bank with their guns out. A 36-year-old African-American male security guard who had started working the previous day was caught off guard. He was in very good shape, 185 pounds of muscles. They thought the bank didn't have any security. He raised his hands up.

Steven did not let the guard being there take him out of his game. Steven told the bankers, "Y'all are not special, get your hands up too. Any wrong move, you will meet your maker."

Lewis pulled three black garbage bags from his pocket and handed Steven one of them and then he yelled, "Y'all better fill these bags up." Lewis put his .9mm against one of the lady bankers head. She was giving him the money out of the register as fast as she could. Lewis told her, "Take me to the vault."

The lady replied, "Don't hurt me. Take all the money you can. Come on, follow me to the vault." She took him to the vault. It took her eight seconds to put in the code to unlock the vault. Once the steel door opened, Lewis saw the cash stacked from the floor to half way up the wall on one side and there were a lot of steel boxes with keys holes, looking similar to the ones at a post office on the other side. Inside of the vault was entirely made of steel. The money was put together in 6 feet blocks. He knew there wasn't any way he could get every dollar and check every box.

Lewis told the woman, "Help me fill these bags up and don't try anything crazy. You better not slow down." Then she started helping him get the money. No matter how fast she was going, Lewis kept on rushing her, "Faster! Faster!" They filled the bags up with money. Then Lewis began to walk back to the front with her.

The security guard was staring at Johnny and he didn't even notice. He saw that Johnny had made a mistake. Johnny was holding the bag with money inside. He was paying too much attention to the bankers behind the counter. A Caliber 380 handgun was in Johnny's right front pocket. At this point, all four cash registers had been emptied. Now they were waiting for Lewis to come back. The security guard wanted to sneak his gun out so he could use it. In a split second, the guard went for his Caliber 357 Revolver and Johnny saw him. Johnny and the guard started to wrestle over the gun. Willie came to Johnny's rescue and commenced to striking the guard as hard as he could. The gun fell to the floor and then he turned around to give Willie a powerful uppercut to the jaw. Willie retaliated with an uppercut of his own. Willie and Johnny double teamed the guard. He was swinging wild and connecting some punches on both Willie and Johnny. James and Steven were tempted to help out, but they had to watch the other three bankers to keep them from hitting a possible emergency button and running away. Lewis hit the guard behind the head with his .9mm handgun and he fell to the floor. Willie, Johnny, and James stumped him every time he tried to get back up. Finally, the tough guard gives up and stays down. One of the ladies started praying. Lewis showed Steven the two bags full of money. Steven said, "Kick their asses."

Lewis walked up to the praying woman and said, "We are going to see if God will stop me from fucking you up." Lewis grabbed her head and banged it against the cash register repeatedly. Then he slanged her to the floor. Everybody other than Steven began a violent assault on the people who worked there, pistol whipping, punching, and stumping.

Steven thought, *They have received enough punishment. It's time to roll.* He screamed, "Let's get the fuck out of here. Everybody, it's time to go." Steven looked out the glass door and no one was out there. All of them ran out the bank and jumped back into the jeep. Then Eric drove off. Once they were in the jeep, the masks came off.

Six minutes later, they heard the police sirens, but they were gone far away already. The crew was very delighted to get away. Steven and the crew were satisfied with the results from the bank robbery. Only one thing in Steven's mind bothered him, he could still see the thrashing his boys put on the bank workers. He felt remorse.

Johnny asked, "When will we cut this pie? We can't go to the hideout during the daytime. Someone can easily spot us going in."

Eric told them, "We can keep the money in the back of the jeep, on the floor. My mom never drives it. We have to hurry up and get this vehicle off the road. The cash is safe back there until we meet tonight."

James liked the idea of getting the jeep off the road but he had a little problem with letting Eric hold all the money. James asked Eric, "Can we trust you with all this bread? Some crumbs could be taken out and no one would ever know."

Eric replied, "I would never do y'all guys like that.

Everyone has to put some faith in me. Bring a bag or two with you at hideout tonight." Eric dropped them off at their houses, but Willie was taken to Johnny's house.

When Eric arrived home, he wanted to look normal. Molly heard him driving into the garage. She wondered, *What took him so long to come home? Where are his bags of junk food from the store? He doesn't have anything in his hands; I find that to be strange*. Molly had smelled a woman's perfume on her couch before. She was waiting on him to tell her about his new friend. She wanted to see how long Eric was going to keep her a secret. Eric went to his room, happier than a kid in a candy store. He had brought his mom's car back in one piece and he would have more money than he ever had in his life. Eric took paying Honey's bills, taking her shopping and taking her on a vacation into consideration.

James felt like he had more juice than O' Dog and Bishop put together. His ego had out grown him. He believed nothing or no one could stop him. He still didn't fully trust Eric with the money. He decided to give Lewis a call to chat with him. Lewis was feeling as cocky as James. Lewis answered his cell phone excitedly, "These muthafuckas can't stop us. If we want something, we'll just take it. We are sitting on a lot of money. That bank held so much money inside. Once she opened the vault, I saw my new lavish lifestyle flash before my eyes. Having money, "sporting" (wearing) new clothes, and having fine hoes are becoming a reality. It's on and poppin' forever."

James said, "You are damn right. We have one major problem; Eric has all the money in his hands. I find it hard to believe that Eric will do the right thing. He could keep the money and say fuck us. Do you really believe Eric will do the right thing? If the nerd double crosses me, he won't live to talk about it."

Lewis told James, "I don't think he would do something that foolish. Let me say it better, I know he won't do something that foolish. The money isn't going anywhere in his hands. I couldn't bring that money home. My parents are some nosy bastards. Steven and you didn't know if y'all moms were at home. We do not have to wait, too long. Tonight is not two days away. Some of us are kind of soft, but I trust everybody in our crew. If I didn't trust everyone, Eric would've not taken the money home with him. You need to worry about other stuff; how is your slice of the pie going to get spent?"

James told him, "Some kind of way my money will multiply. My dough will produce even more dough. My hopes and dreams are very huge. You can say I'm obsessed with getting money. I do not have a set time to get out of the game. Being filthy rich is my true purpose in life. I'll see you at the hideout tonight."

Lewis replied, "Don't worry about nothing. All the cash will be there tonight."

Willie and Johnny were still on cloud nine from winning the championship last night. They had to talk about the two major events that happened. Willie was in Johnny's bedroom watching TV. Johnny came back into his bedroom with two 20 oz Sprites and two big bags of Doritos. Willie got his soda and chips from Johnny. He started the conversation by saying, "These two days have been amazing. Last night we won the District #4 5A Championship and that's big enough by itself.

It took four years for us to get there. In four years, do you know how many regular season and playoff games we have played? Think about all the practices in that time span. It's impossible to remember all of them. We put a lot of blood, sweat, and tears into playing football."

Johnny showed him the newspaper he received from his father. The front page has Willie and Johnny holding the championship trophy in their hands. The title of the page was the word "CHAMPIONS" in all big and bold letters. Johnny told him, "I told you we were going to share a spot on the newspaper. We are probably the best thing that happen to this school in twenty something years. I wish we were juniors, so we could come back next year and defend the title. The team should be just fine next year. I expect them to go all the way. They have learned enough from us to make it happen. Today, a different kind of luck happened. We successfully rob a bank. We can go to college with money and without worrying about any financial problems. I will hold on to my money until I find something good to invest it in. We need to find a bag to put our money in. Did you know the school is throwing us a parade? I do not know the date of the parade."

Molly was getting ready for work. She was doing her last minute cleaning as usual. Molly's conscience was telling her to check the jeep. She told Eric, "Take care of the house while I'm gone." Molly opened the door to the garage and walked through it. Eric was walking to the garage; he wanted to tell his mother he loved her and bye. Eric opened the garage door and saw his mother opening the jeep's driver door. Eric thought, *Damn! She is getting ready to drive the jeep. This is hard to believe; normally, she wouldn't touch the jeep.*

The guys are going to kill me. She'll find the cash. Mom will ask where the money came from. Molly jumped inside the jeep and cranked it up. The palms of Eric hands were sweating; he was scared and nervous. Molly checked the gas hand, the mileage, and she turned around to look at the back seat. She figured he went joy riding because she couldn't pick up a perfume scent. Molly got out of the jeep and hopped into her car. When she drove off, Eric's heart stopped beating fast and it was a sign of relief. He said to himself, *She almost found it.*

Later on, the crew met up at the hideout. Eric started the meeting off by pouring the money out on the table. A red money band made of paper was wrapped around the dollars. Lewis said, "It is time to start counting. That bank has so much money; the cash we took is maybe 13% of it. I took whatever I could with two garage bags. The guard who was there took me by surprise. We showed him a thing or two." Eric took out two calculators, and he and Steven began the counting process. After two hours of counting, they came up with a total of $701,125. Everybody grabbed over one hundred grand. Steven told them, "It's time for me to leave the crew. We had our fun. The Teenage Mafia took this city by storm. No one saw us coming. I would like to thank y'all for being down with me. Especially Eric and James, y'all guys could've turned me down. You could have said 'no'. Instead, y'all joined the crew and put in some work. We could not have done this shit without them. Our lives were on the line every time we done something. We argued and fought, but what family doesn't. A hundred grand a piece should be enough for us to move on. Dirty money can always turn into clean money. I want everybody to quit; the decision is not mines. Do y'all remember when Michael Jordan hit the game winning basket on the Utah Jazz? He retired after the shot. I want all of us to finish on top." Steven started showing all of them some love by shaking their hands and wishing them the best of luck.

Before Steven could make it to Lewis and shake his hand, he stopped Steven by saying, "Hold up. There is one more obstacle in your way. Then after that, you would officially be out of The Teenage Mafia. This time we won't hit a store or a bank. I promise you and everybody else three hundred grand a piece. Does the deal sound sweet to y'all?"

James said with poise, without even knowing what the deal was, "You can count me for $300,000. I would put on some armor and slay a fire breathing dragon for that amount."

Lewis told Steven, "This is the big favor I been talking about."

Steven agreed, "Okay Lewis, you can count me in too. Alright, there are no second and third big favors. Just like Mike said, 'this is it'. I can't wait to return to my normal life and live by the rules of the law."

Lewis stated, "Once I formulate a great strategy for the mission, I will let y'all know. Even though, I can't speak on it right now. The mission will have more of an effect on Steven than the rest of you." The money had been separated in individual bags. Steven had his money in a green and black duffle bag and the rest of them had garbage bags.

Eric said, "I'm taking everybody home. It's not smart to walk around with this kind of money. I almost forgot, congratulations to Willie and Johnny for winning the state championship. You two are the truth." Johnny said, "Can't nobody get on the football field and dominate like us. Only Steve Young and Jerry Rice made a better duo than us." Everybody laughed because they found what Johnny said to be funny. Then Willie added, "And you know this, mannn!"

Lewis was enjoying the moment and a thought crossed his mind, *If we get away with this, I will be rich. I wouldn't have a reason to keep terrorizing people. We are robbing these people to live large. Once my mission is completed, I would have more paper than a paper mill. On the other hand, Steven is the only one of us who has the smarts to stay a criminal. There is no way we could do this without him. James wants to keep The Teenage Mafia going for as long as possible. He would get pissed off if I quitted on him. I must agree with Steven; leaving this shit alone is the smartest and safest thing to do.*

Steven said, "I'm going home to think about my money. Before we get out of here, don't go on a shopping spree. The police will look for someone who got rich, all of sudden. It won't be smart to buy a car until you get a job. Do not spend too much cash at one time. Do not buy the mall out like you are a rapper signed to Cash Money Records. Trust me; the battle is not over yet. It will be tempting to buy a car and expensive clothes. Keep your heads in the ball game. Invest the dough into your future."

Willie said, "My bread is going to help me out in college. You could call it an investment. I hope everybody caught Steven's words, 'everybody should quit'. If you have $50,000, pretend like you have $50. Everything we done should be kept in the dark. Remember, with stolen money comes responsibility."

James hated when someone tried to tell him what to do or how he could do it. His mother was the only person he felt comfortable with telling him what to do. James said, "I will try my best to do the right thing. Why would we steal this money and can't buy anything? Our hard work would be for nothing and it wouldn't make any sense."

Steven said to James, "I never said we shouldn't buy anything, but not to purchase enough to bring too much attention on yourself."

James thought, *No one will tell me how I should spend my bread. These dudes must don't know who I am.*

Lewis told them, "Last but not least, don't forget less than three weeks from now I will make you all $300,000 richer. Does anybody here have something important to say?" No one did. Then Lewis said, "I'm ready to go home and spend some quality time with my money. Eric, can you please get us out of here?" Eric took everybody home in the jeep.

Chapter 15

In the morning, Willie placed his money on the bed, the money from The Treasure Bank. He knew the amount, but he wanted to count it anyway. All of a sudden, Willie heard a knock on his door. Willie's mother said, "I know you are awake because I heard your footsteps. Hurry up and open this door. I don't have all morning long." He got a little nervous and quickly placed the money under his bed.

He told Susan, "Give me a minute and I'll be out." After Willie finished placing the money under his bed, he opened the door for his mom.

Susan told him, "Willie, we are so proud of you. Son, you have turned out to be everything your dad and I hoped for. Ricky, step in here for a moment."

Ricky was Willie's father and he came into the room with an envelope in his right hand. Ricky said, "I wanted to be the first person to congratulate you on your scholarship to UCLA."

The school was offering him a football scholarship with books, dorm fees, and other expenses paid for. Willie's dream had finally come true. Willie screamed, "UCLA! UCLA! Let me read that." After reading the letter Willie told them, "Hard work does pays off. UCLA, here I come."

Ricky told Willie, "I saw Johnny and you on the front page of the newspaper. I know I haven't cheered you on like a real father. Susan and I are very proud of your accomplishments.

Keep up the good work. Don't feel any pressure because we just want you to try your best."

Ricky gave his son a hug and then Susan joined them with a big hug of her own. For Susan, the thought of her son leaving was both bitter and sweet. Her only child was heading to college. Susan's tears began to drop slowly from her eyes. She knew it would never be the same again. Ricky saw Susan getting emotional and he said to her, "Don't worry about nothing; he will still be in the same city as us. Some children have to move far away from home. Willie is going to visit us whenever he can."

Willie told his mom, "Of course, I will come home every chance I get."

Ricky said to his son, "Over the years, we have been short-changing you. There is a reason why we did that to you. We knew one day you were going to college and you would need our help even more. Son, take a deep breath." Ricky reached into his right pocket and pulled out a key. Willie just stared at the key. Ricky gave Willie even more good news, "This key is to your new grey 2010 Nissan Altima." Ricky went into his right pocket again. He pulled out a debit Master Card. Then he said, "The card is holding $15,000. It should last a long time if you spend it wisely."

Willie was so shocked; he couldn't believe what was happening as he stood there speechless. Finally, Willie asked his dad, "Do I really have a car? Stop playing with me, Dad. Are you sure I have a car?"

Ricky put a huge smile on his face. Then he told Willie, "Yes, Son, there is a new car outside that belongs to you."

Willie yelled, "Outside! Where is the car located outside?"

Susan answered, "Oh it's located in front of the house."

Willie ran down stairs and went out of the front door. He stood beside the car and kissed the hood. Willie started jumping around with excitement like the night his team won the state championship.

Barbara and Steven were sitting down in the living room, discussing their plans. Steven said, "I have not thought about college. Moving out of this house and you driving an upgraded car has been the only things on my mind. I am ashamed to get dropped off at school in that 79' Caprice. It made me feel good about walking to school."

Barbara was attached to her car. Just because the car was old, had paint coming off, it still belonged to her. The car had sentimental value to Barbara. She did not like the fact that Steven was talking trash about her car. Barbara told him, "Alright Son, your message is clear. When your father bought the car, he paid for a paint job on it too. The car looked clean as you and the rest of the kids would say. I will get another one, but I won't get rid of my 79' Caprice. Today, we could look for another house and a car. I have to see what is in my price range."

Steven told her, "Let's look around our neighborhood first for a house. This neighborhood is very peaceful, plus I love being around here. It's best to look for a house that you could rent to own. That way, you wouldn't pay rent all your life. Apartments are cool, but you wouldn't want to stay that close to other people. You can't rent to own an apartment."

Barbara said, "I'll know the right house when I see it."

Steven figured Barbara would choose another old school car. He asked her, "What kind of car would you search for?"

Barbara responded, "Nothing too fancy, a Honda or a Mazda." Steven was thinking about a Lexus or a BMW. He said, "There is nothing wrong with those cars, you just named. I thought you could've raised the bar just a little bit. Here's your chance to finally ride in style for a change. You have one life to live and it's time to act like it. The majority of your life, you were struggling to pay bills and providing food. Come on, Mom. Out with the old and in with the new. We shouldn't spend like there is no tomorrow, but we need a serious upgrade."

Barbara said, "Hard times have overwhelmed us through the years. Tim and I always had to take the cheap route with everything. We couldn't really afford to have a child. When it was just him and I, we were still struggling. Even though the doctors told me I couldn't give birth, I still wanted a child. At first, Tim did not want a child. He knew financially things would get worst and things did get worst. Before we adopted, Tim and I would argue almost every night about it. I was in high spirits when Tim agreed with me and brought you home. Once Tim wrapped his arms around you, for some reason, he did not remember that adoption was a bad idea. Instantly, he felt like a father. He loved you, so much that sometimes he didn't want to share you with me. He would jokingly say, 'hey, it's a father and son thing'. Sadly, Tim isn't coming back. I'm getting up in age, Son. Steven, you will have to carry the family's legacy. For now, let's get out of here to begin our search." Barbara and Steven left their home with the thought of upgrading in mind.

James was sitting on a black leather couch in his bedroom, writing down a list of everything he wanted. He had different kinds of cars, clothes, and jewelry. He had made up his mind to buy two necklaces with the matching gold and silver Jesus Piece medallion, a gold Rolex watch with diamonds around the face, Coogi clothing, and a Dodge Magnum or a Dodge Avenger. Guns were added to his list, so if the Police tried to stop his shine, he would make their life expire. James felt like a baller and he wanted to look like it. He refused to let Willie and Steven dictate how he would spend and handle his money.

James's mother, Zenobia, came into his room and said, "You are doing homework; I can't believe it."

James told her, "I can't believe it, either. Don't underestimate me. I can fool you and make the honor roll every six weeks. I'm very sharp when I pay attention in class. Being in a classroom is boring to me. Sitting down in a desk, listening to a teacher for an hour makes me sleepy. After about twenty five minutes, I'll just lay my head down."

Zenobia told him, "School is the key to a bright future. Selling drugs can make you successful. Big time drug dealers can make lots of money. It is a very risky thing, getting involved with drugs. If you are interested in the dope dealing business, I know someone who could hook you up. He could keep you safe from getting killed or going to jail. Your Uncle Larry is a kingpin on the streets. No one could flip those "quarters" like him. I'm not talking about twenty-five cents."

James looked at his mother and asked, "Are you okay? I never heard this side of you before. Your name should get changed to Miss Thug life. This is a bigger surprise than Hulk Hogan joining the NWO."

She stated, "You have to be clever; anybody can't succeed

in selling drugs. As long as you are not a bomb on the streets, I'll be proud of you. Respect the game and the game will respect you."

James asked, "Where have you been hiding the real you. Now you call yourself "spitting game" to me. I knew we always had more of a friendship than a mother and son relationship. Can't too many thugs say their mom is harder them."

James's mom went ahead and broke a secret to him, "I have something to tell you."

James said, "I'm all ears, Zenobia."

She continued to talk, "All of this time you have been thinking my child support money and welfare was our only source of income. That's not the truth; my brother Larry and I have been slanging dope together. He is full time and I do it when I feel like it. Look at this condo and our neighborhood; our legal income says we should live in the projects. We are not supposed to be living in a middle class or a high class neighborhood."

James replied, "Wow! Montel Williams would love to have us on his show. You kept more secrets than an undercover brother. It's about time for Uncle Larry and you to pass down the family's business to me."

His mother acknowledged, "Drug dealing is not a game at all; it can get dangerous. If something happens to you, I would never forgive myself. James, you are all I have other than my Brother Larry. Your school has been sending me letters. All the letters say that you skip classes and don't show up to school some days. Graduation couldn't be in your plans. Doctors distribute drugs, but the Police want to fuck with other people, who are trying to do the same to make a living.

We sell the same shit that Dr. Richard prescribes at his office. Some job applications will tell you to write down any medicine that been in your system lately. So when your urine comes out dirty, they would know what it is. The white man feels like if his hands are not in the cookie jar, your hands shouldn't be there either. Putting you in the game would've been my last option. I would rather see you in college, James. You don't go to classes and your jump shot isn't wicked. No one will hire your black ass without a high school diploma. I will be your mom and boss. You could help me knockout some of these bills around here. The dope game is shady, but if you can't trust your mother, you can you trust. I'm reliable and dependable. When the dollars start pouring in your hands, don't forget who took care of you for all these years. I sent your bad ass to school with the best name brand clothes money could buy. Sean John, Rocawear, and Nike got rich off of me alone."

James loved his mother and he would do anything for her. Dope dealing was another way he could become rich. James said to her, "We have a deal, boss. When do I start work?"

She responded, "I must teach you some things first. Your uncle and I have to discuss the situation. He should be giving me a package soon. I'm going to put you under my wings, so you would learn from one of the best hustlers that ever put on a pair of Jimmy Choo shoes." Then she walked out of his bedroom. James truly believed he was on the road to riches. He thought robbing banks, gambling, and now getting ready to become a drug dealer was going to make him a millionaire. James saw himself as a money machine that couldn't produce counterfeit dollar bills. He could feel his luck getting better every day. James already knew a little about selling dope. He knew he could use his own money to make it multiply over and over.

Eric was watching a flick called "Suck Me". He was starting to feel a way that he hadn't felt in a little while. He thought about all the money he had in his possession. Eric realized he could have sex with how many dime pieces or prostitutes he wanted. He was deeply in love with Honey, but more women were starting to sound better than just one. Eric knew he could live out his fantasies as many times as he wanted. His fantasy was to have sex with four or more women at the same time. He never had that kind of money before, so he always settled for one woman. Watching his flicks was inspiring him to trick again. Eric's sex addiction was creeping up on him again. Eric said to himself, "If I bring some bitches over here, Honey will never know about it. With the hoes I would bring in, I could make my own porno flicks and my life would be the shit. The name of my movie would be 'Eric in Pussyland'. It would include me and three or four women. Damn, that is a genius idea. The only thing I don't have is a camera to record. Wal-Mart and Best Buy would have plenty of cameras. I will hide one of them somewhere in this bedroom, so they won't see it. Fuck it; I have one life to live and I'm really too young to settle down. I'm going to live this one muthafucka to the fullest." Eric pulled out his black note book from inside of his shoe box, which was kept under his bed. He had twenty-nine numbers for prostitutes in the notebook. Eric had made some promises to Honey, but his sex drive had taken over him.

Barbara drove Steven around for thirty four minutes before she stopped at a house that looked like it was made for them. The house was light green with a black roof. The house was made of boards on the outside. It also has a front and back porch with concrete steps connected. The front porch was smaller and the back porch. Barbara thought the house was just right, not big and not too small. The ditches were located in front of the house and on the left side of the house. The yard around the house was full of green grass. A red and white sales sign was in the front yard and it read: 'for sale or rent to own'. The sign also said the house had three bedrooms. Two little trees were in the front yard and three huge trees were in the back yard. The trees were so small in the front lawn that you could grab some of the limbs.

Steven said, "Look at all that shade, it would be good to have it during the summer."

Barbara and Steven got out of the car to get a better look at the house. Barbara said, "I can't wait to see the inside of this house. The house was made for us, Son. We can't let the opportunity pass us by." Barbara took out a pen and a little piece of paper to write down the address and the contact number.

Steven told her, "Now this is an upgrade, Mom. We should've been staying at a house like this. Three bedrooms are more than enough room for us. I hate to down talk our house, but it has too many major problems. Our house is too small and rain always comes through the ceiling in rainy weather. We deserve to live in this nice house. It's our dream house. When we get home, you have to call the landlord's number immediately. On another day, we could continue with the car search. The house that stands before us is our first priority. It's not in our community like we hoped for. I have walked through this neighborhood numerous times and never saw anything abnormal. It shouldn't be a problem for us to get used to living around here."

Both of them jumped back into the car and Barbara drove them home. Once Barbara made it home, she called the contact number. The landlord wanted to set up an appointment with her the next day. Barbara agreed to meet him at the house she wanted. After the conversation with the landlord, she was more than happy to tell Steven the house was indeed obtainable. Barbara told Steven, "The house will cost $40,000 and I agreed to rent to own. We will get our first look inside the house tomorrow."

Steven asked, "Why can't good news come every day of our lives? Sometimes it seems like the rich people have all the luck. Poor people like us always get the short end of the stick. Why God didn't make everybody rich? People would not have to steal or be homeless if they were rich."

Barbara told him, "You have made a good point, but God is good and he does everything for a good reason. His intentions are always wonderful, Son. Only in heaven, we will find out why catastrophic things happen to innocent people, I think."

Lewis was trying to think of a master plan because he wanted some more green in his hands. He was lying in bed. Killing Sam and Jessica was a hard task for him. Lewis thought about pulling the trigger on Sam and Jessica. He decided he wouldn't be able to aim the heater at them. He would let someone in the crew take them out. Lewis began to think, *How can I get away with murdering my parents? They have done more harm towards me than good. My mom took a back seat while my dad done everything, but kill* me. Once they are out of my way, it will be smooth sailing. As the only child, their cash will be my cash. For all the pain and suffering they put me through, I deserve every dime those muthafuckas own. The $300,000 a piece that I'm giving the crew will be nothing compared to the millions of dollars going into my pockets. I'm getting ready to become a millionaire and my future is looking lovely. My age is eighteen; I have many years ahead of me. I would never have to work. Every day, the video game controller will be in my hands. All my clothes would be name brand and custom made. Parties would be at my crib on the weekends. All the bad bitches are invited. There's a chance I could start my own business. As long as the Police don't make me a suspect, everything will be great. Sorry James, but robbing is a thing of the past. Steven and I would exit out the crew at the same time. James and whoever wants to keep this shit going will have my blessing. I put in James's mind that I would be doing dirt for a while. Fuck being a part of this crew; people change their minds every day. If I am rich already, there isn't a reason for me to keep on stealing. Living in another house is my plan. Living at my parent's house would keep the old and bad memories alive. I don't have school today, so I should get high. The crack along with the pipe is in my dresser. Redd said it would get me higher than I have ever been before. Crack has always been some powerful shit. Weed and "powder" is my thing; I will never use rocks. People who smoke rocks lose their mind. They would invest everything just to get high off it. Crack would take a fine dime piece woman and make her look like the lady at the beginning

of Tales from the Crypt. My homeboy was courteous by try-
ing to help me out, but my lips will never touch a pipe.
My parents taught me how to drive and helped me get
a driver license. They should have bought me a car. Any
nice looking car would have been good enough for me. My
walking days are coming to an end; it's just a matter of
time. I want both of my parents to die execution style. My
dad has molested me, rape me, beat me, and treated me
like a dog. Sam and Jessica needs to die. I will take the
law in my own hands. Our whole community thinks we
are living this fantasy life style. I would rather live an
average lifestyle than to live here with these assholes. I'm
going to have an optimistic mind set while watching their
demise.

Later on that night, James realized he didn't give Frank
$50 for his bet. James became mad at Frank because he didn't
call to remind him. He thought Frank was jealous over his last
win. James called Frank and told him that he was on his way.
James took out two twenty dollar bills and one ten dollar bill
out of his dresser. The time was 9:58pm and the sports bar
didn't close until 11:00. James left his house to meet up with
Frank. Frank was already outside waiting on him. James gave
Frank the money without speaking to him and walked away.
Frank wanted to call James back and return the cash to him,
but he did not.

Chapter 16

In the morning, Willie took his new Nissan for a cruise. He was "bumping" Jay-Z's "Dead Presidents II" song. Willie felt like a new man. He couldn't think of a time where he had been more fortunate than now. He was on top of the world. Willie added the $15,000 to the $100,000 plus that he already had. Willie thought about Steven and went to his house. He wanted to show him the car. He arrived at Steven's house and rung the door bell.

Steven answered the door by asking, "Who is it?"

Willie replied with enthusiasm, "Open the door, man. This is your boy, Willie."

Steven opened the door and Willie told him, "Come outside! I have something to show you." Steven came outside and saw the car and he knew it belonged to Willie by the joyful look on his face.

Steven gave Willie his opinion. "Damn! That car is tighter than Kanye West's jeans. It looks like the one I seen on the Nissan commercial. Boy, you have come up. Did you pay for this car?"

Willie replied, "No. Let me tell you what happen. I'm going to make a long story short. My mom and dad came in my bedroom with the scholarship letter I have been waiting on. Then they surprised me with $15,000 and this car. All this time, I thought they were being cheap for nothing. Secretly, my parents were saving some money up for me. My scholarship will cover my books and dorm fees."

Steven was unsure about telling anybody about the money he and Barbara would receive and already received. He went ahead and told Willie about his luck. "My luck these days has changed for the better. The police department gave me and my mom some money; they did scare my dad into a heart attack. The hotel he worked for will give us his retirement money. We should be moving into our new house soon. My mom is also looking for another car. Why are all these good things happening to me now? If this happened a few months ago, I never would've done any crime. I can't change the past, but it's the future I have to worry about now. It seems like the rain was full of pain and it has stopped; now the sun is shining bright with better days. I guest every dog has its day. With all this good news, you, I, and Johnny need to go out and celebrate. Yes, I said Johnny because he and I didn't get a chance to squash the little beef we had. It would give us a chance to talk about everything. We have plenty of money to blow, as long as it's not on jewelry or any other thing that would portray us as ballers. Your car made you look like one, but your mom and dad bought it for you and that is a legit excuse."

Willie asked Steven, "Do you want to go over Johnny's house and holler at him? We don't have anything else to do."

Steven replied, "Let's get out of here. I'll tell my mom I am leaving, first."

After Steven spoke with Barbara, Steven got into the car with Willie and they left. Willie drove directly to Johnny's house. Johnny was already outside sitting on the steps. Johnny saw a gray Nissan car parked in front of his home. He thought it looked smooth. Steven hopped out first and Willie hopped out next.

Johnny got up off the steps and walked over to the car. He told Willie and Steven, "Y'all are jacking cars now."

Willie said, "We are not stealing cars. My parents gave me this car because they are proud of me. You can call it a going to college gift."

Johnny did not believe his parent would buy him a car, "Your parents would not give you $50 and then unexpectedly, they gave you a new car. A Nissan is one of the top brand cars. Willie, I'm a lot smarter than what you think. I think you took some of that bank money and made things happen."

Willie said to Johnny, "I know you are far from being dumb. You know my house number. Call it and speak with one or both of my parents. They would tell you the truth. My mom is so religious; she would make The Pope look like a thief. I'm already tired of talking to you about this car. What are you doing outside?"

Johnny responded, "I'm catching some fresh air. My mind is on everything from school to myself in ten more years."

Steven approached Johnny and said, "I apologize for everything that happened between us. We can put the past behind us and continue as good friends. I have been thinking about speaking to you face to face. We are supposed to be each other's crutches, so no one would ever fall. Even if we don't get dirty anymore, The Teenage Mafia is forever."

Johnny was calm and he didn't want to hold on to a grudge against Steven. Johnny explained to Steven, "We are good, homeboy. There are no hard feelings here. My family taught me that if anybody put their hands on you, make sure you hit them back. It was more of a pride kind of thing. When you "stole" on me, I thought wow, Steven really hit me. Once we fought, my beef with you was over with." Johnny put his right hand in the shaking position and then Steven shook his hand. Steven was glad that he and Johnny talked things over.

Willie humorously told them, "I'm glad to see black people in harmony these days. Now Johnny, the last time you said it was over, Steven went home with a black eye. Are you one hundred percent sure this time. If you darken his other eye, he won't be able to see shit. He would come back to school with a Seeing-Eye-Dog, leading him in the right direction."

They all had to laugh at that joke. Then Willie said to Johnny, "The reason we are here is to pick you up and find a restaurant to celebrate all the good things that's been happening lately, our one hundred grand plus and the state championship victory. I know we already did something for winning. We're not finish with celebrating yet. I'll eat pretty much anything, so where y'all would like to eat?"

Johnny stated, "We could hit Chili's up."

Steven agreed, "Everybody likes that place. It sounds good to me. Willie, get us out of here, so we can eat." All three of them entered the car and Willie was behind the wheel.

Once they arrived there, Willie, Steven, and Johnny ordered the same thing -- cheeseburgers with French fries and Cokes. The crew ate and joked around the whole time they were at the table. Johnny said, "Willie did not like you because all the decision came out of your mouth. He thought you saw us as dumb jocks."

Steven replied, "I did not know that. To tell you two the truth, I was against bringing y'all into the crew." Willie chuckled hard and he choked on his soda. Then Steven continued to speak, "Y'all had a bad reputation at school. Johnny was knocking guys out in the cafeteria and then he would start back eating like nothing never happen. Johnny is the 80's version of Mike Tyson. People were shock to see me fight back. If I go down, I would rather go down swinging. Willie is known as the nice bully. As long as you gave him what he wanted, everything would be okay."

Willie added, "Johnny and I had a hard time trusting and believing anybody other than each other. Everything we done as a crew worked out for the better."

Johnny said, "Let's get back to the fight. Steven's hands are so fast that I thought three men were hitting me. Steven showed me that I'm not invincible. I thought the fight would be another first round knockout. I almost got knockout in the first round. My bulling days are over with. What if a guy comes along and he's faster and stronger than Steven?"

Steven said, "Damn, I hate to cut you off, but this cheese-burger is off the chain. Chili's is my new dining spot. I have to ask y'all a question. Does one of you have any idea about what Lewis has on his mind? For $300,000 a piece, it is something major. He says it doesn't have anything to do with robbing banks. If Lewis's plan gives us that kind of money, he's a smarter criminal genius than me. $300,000 a piece, that's almost a $1,000,000. It is more money than we took from the bank."

Willie answered, "I'm just as lost as you are. Lewis and I don't call each other. I only hear from him when we all meet up. Steven, you supposed to know him better than anybody else."

Johnny told them, "It's hard to believe Lewis could offer us close to $1,000,000. He has never told me anything about his plan. Knowing Lewis, things can get very interesting. Expect the unexpected, guys. Lewis is always confused about what he wants to do. You never know which Lewis will show up."

Steven told them, "Lewis has been telling me for months that he will need a big favor. I should have made him tell me what the secret is in the beginning. We all have to wait on him to say something. Lewis and I basically grew up together. He would normally tell me what's on his mind and not keep things a secret."

Willie said, "I'll pay for everybody's food." Willie waved at the waitress to stop her and then he told her that they were ready to pay. He gave her a hundred dollar bill and she went to get his change. After Willie received his change, he took Steven and Johnny home.

Lewis was at Redd's house, going over the plans for Tammy's party. Redd was over-confident about the party, "Man, it is going down. Tammy told me she is inviting all her best looking friends. They are just looking for a good time. Do you know what I mean?"

Lewis answered, "A good time means dancing and drinking."

Redd told, "You don't really know what this party means for the both of us. We are going to dance and get our drink on. We are getting laid at this party. I'm going to bring twenty- five rubbers with me. How many girls have you fucked before?"

Lewis had a puzzled look on his face because he was thinking too hard to come up with a lie. Redd asked Lewis, "Are you a virgin? Wow, a real virgin. I thought y'all no longer exist."

Lewis put on a cocky front, "Many girls have "got down" with me before because I'm a pimp by blood, not by rela- tion. Y'all chase'em and I be replace'em. I keep them at The Heartbreak Hotel." Lewis was a little too late.

Redd had already figured him out. "Now that is a good line; it's a Notorious B.I.G. rhyme. You never had a piece of ass before in your life. Well, your luck will change this Saturday night."

Lewis admitted it, "I am a virgin, but not by choice. A few times, I have gotten close to getting some. I kept on saying the wrong things and the panties kept on coming up. My game is very weak. Can you teach me what to say?"

Redd explained to Lewis, "Sometimes less is more. A woman knows she is going to fuck you the moment she sees your face. If it's going down, don't say shit. Just let the fuck- ing begin."

Lewis asked, "How would I know if she wants to do something?"

Redd answered, "A woman would show a man no inter- est if she doesn't want sex with him. The bitches who want to speak with you, would smile at you or give you a constant stare. Sometimes they are bold enough to holler at you first. If that happens, she is yours for the taken."

Lewis wondered, *How does he know so much at such a young age?* Then he said, "You are not that much older than me. Where did you learn all that game from? I don't think Playstation have more game than you. Your brain should've been in my head. They would call me Kobe because I would score too much."

Redd reassured him about the party. "Don't try too hard

at the party to score. You don't want to look too desperate. Those hoes are trying to get laid just like you. I know Tammy personally, man. We were fuck partners. She is one of the best women I ever had in my bedroom. She would do any freaky thing I ask her to do. She would ride me and then let me hit from the back. Her blowjob is mind blowing. Tammy would let me nut in her mouth."

Lewis was getting horny listening to him. He cut him off, "That is enough and I get the picture. I bet you are rubbing it in on purpose."

Redd with a small smirk on his face replied, "Maybe a little bit. Your time to shine is coming very soon. I won't rest Saturday night until I know you had some ass; that's my word. I'm not going to tell anybody you are a virgin. The secret is safe with me. Don't forget to wear the red outfit you told me about. We are going to be like Tango and Cash in that mutha-fucka. Those hoes won't know what hit them. Let me warn you again; it's very dangerous to kick it with me. A punk ass Crip could try to send me to Thugs Mansion. I carry a few heaters everywhere I go. Are you still willing to hang out with me?"

Lewis said, "I'm still down for Saturday night. I carry a heater everywhere I go too. If one or both of our lives are in danger, I'm going to blast with no hesitation."

Redd told him, "Shit can break out at any minute. It is good to know we have each other backs. When the drama goes down, don't freeze up on me. Anybody can't be a gang-ster. Have you ever heard of the old saying for the gangsters?"

Lewis said, "No, I have not heard of it before."

Redd responded, "It is said that if you live by the gun, you will die by the gun. I already know how my life will end. A lot of Crips hate me and they would love to pop three in my back. What kind of gun do you own other than that .9mm handgun? Carrying a vicious heat is important in these streets."

Lewis said, "My nine is not the best gun out there, but it will get any hater off me. It follows me everywhere I go, just like my shadow. If a clown wants to get cold, my gun will heat his ass up."

Redd asked Lewis, "Do you need a refill on anything? What about the crack I gave you?"

Lewis would not say he didn't use the crack. He stated, "The crack was good and it put me on a higher level of being high. But the weed and cocaine is the only way I want to roll. It doesn't feel right to put a crack pipe to my lips. Give me $200 worth of cocaine and $60 worth of weed."

Redd was a little upset because he wanted to get Lewis hooked on crack. He thought, *At least he is still buying my products. My crack should have been enough to turn him into a real fiend. My ecstasy pills could do the trick.* Redd went into his safety box which was still kept under his bed. He grabbed the items Lewis requested. Every sack was a twenty dollar sack. Redd went back into the living room and exchanged the drugs for the cash. He asked Lewis, "Have you ever heard of X pills before?"

Lewis answered, "I have heard of X pills before and I have never tried it. Cocaine and the green is my thing right now. I might try one at another time." Redd wanted him to try some.

He decided to convince Lewis that the X pills were cool. He told Lewis, "Dog, you have to try this shit. It's more of a party kind of drug. A lot of people take them in clubs or any fun event where alcohol is being served. X pills can make you a Fucking Machine. The bitches would scream for more. Have you ever drunk Crown Royal with Coke, gin with orange juice, or vodka with Red Bull?"

Lewis answered, "I have never tried any of those drinks. My dad keeps beer in the refrigerator and sometimes I would steal a beer from him."

Redd said to Lewis, "Now we are getting somewhere. I keep a case of those bottles of Old English 40 oz. As long as you could drink some kind of alcohol with the pills, you would feel amazing. Taking X pills with the alcohol will place you in the zone. The zone is a great mood that would give you confidence. You will be high and feeling like your swagger is better than everybody else. The ladies love a man with some swagger. The truth is that confidence and swagger is the same thing." Redd knew a good lie was damn near ninety percent the truth. Since Lewis was young and inexperienced, he fell for the game Redd ran on him.

Lewis was wondering about the X pills. *Since Tammy's party is coming up soon, I need some swagger to help me score while I'm there. This zone you are talking about better work or I will leave the party still a virgin. Do you have any more pills? I could use a few before the party Saturday night.*

Redd could've been a salesman because of the way he advertised his products. He tells Lewis, "I don't have any at this moment, but some will be in my hands before Saturday. I'm expecting a package soon."

Lewis asked, "Do you get high on your own supply?"

Redd replied, "Sometimes I would think about it. Getting

high on my own supply would be unintelligent. Some people have the game twisted. I would lose money doing my on drugs. My money is too important to waste by not using my head. Bitches have to be fucked and bills must be paid. The only problem I have is selling drugs out of my home. Shouldn't any dope dealer sale from their home. Finding a corner to post up on was my first option. These dudes out here are tripping. They are going to want a certain percentage to use their corner. If their offer is decline, they will send some young gladiators to come after you. Two things would happen if they catch you slipping, a beat down and you would get rob or they'll kill you and rob you. That's why I slang at home most of the times, to keep the haters out of my business. They would have to kill me before I hand over anything."

Barbara and Steven went to meet the landlord about the house. Barbara and the landlord negotiated for fifty minutes while looking around the house. Finally, Barbara agreed to a payment plan that would last 48 months. She could move in as soon as possible. The landlord told her he would let his people help with moving their stuff. He knew Barbara did not have a truck to move her own things with. Barbara accepted his offer to help. Barbara and Steven took almost half of the day to move. She was directing traffic, telling them where to place all their things. Steven was helping the four guys the landlord sent to help them. Barbara called all the utility people to get her electricity, water, gas, and cable on.

Eric felt his phone vibrating. He looked at it and saw Honey's phone number. He answered the phone, "What's up, girl?"

Honey said, "I was just thinking about you and felt the

urge to hear your voice. I can't wait to the weekend to see your face. We have to choose between Friday and Saturday. Fireworks will spark up no matter which day we pick. Thoughts of you have been running through my mind. This must be what love feels like. I want Steven to come over with you one day. We have to finish showing him our gratitude. He is such a great guy. I wish we could do something for him."

Eric said, "We don't have to do anything special for him. Friends do each other favors all the time. I do not want to sound jealous, but focus more on me and not Steven. Every time I think of you, the night under the stars comes to mind. When school gets out for the summer, we should take a trip somewhere. The places I thought of were Las Vegas, Miami, Seattle, and the Big Apple, New York City."

Honey would love to visit those places and she let it be known, "It was always a dream of mines to visit New York City and Miami. Don't "gas me up" if you are not planning. In other words, don't get my hopes up high and let me down."

Eric stated, "I'm serious as three heart attacks on top of a stroke. We can go where your heart desire."

Honey said, "I wish we could hop on a plane right now. Believe it or not, I never went outside of LA. Most guys won't think outside the box like you. I know you really care about me. Eric, my heart can't take anymore betrayal and abuse. If you are looking for a fling or a good time, please let me know. It's very understandable; a lot of guys don't want to get in a committed relationship. Here is your chance to let me know; I would have no hard feelings. At least you could be a man about."

Eric was confused about whether he should have sex with

some of the finest prostitutes or not. He didn't want Honey getting in his way of fulfilling his fantasies. At the same time, he loved Honey with all of his heart. He couldn't tell Honey how he really felt because she would leave him. Eric said to Honey, "I will be a man about our situation. It's impossible for me to picture my life without you. We need each other. If I'm not the man of your dreams, mold me to be him. Honey, you know I'm a sensitive dude. My heart can be broken just like yours. You are taking a chance on me, just like I'm taking a chance on you. Any trip we take in the air will be a first class trip. You are going to love shopping while on vacation. It might sound like I'm running game, but everything I said is for real."

Honey believed every word that came out of Eric's mouth. She did not want Eric to know she had a crush on Steven. She would like a chance to see what he was like in bed. It was something about Steven she found irresistible. She wanted Steven to become boyfriend number two behind Eric's back. Honey told him, "Only time will prove the real from the fake, the platinum from the bronze. The fake people can only pretend to be real for so long. After a while, he or she will say fuck this shit and go back to being their true selves. History has proven it time after time. Even if you are telling me lies, what's done in the dark will come to light. You'll get the benefit of the doubt. Keep on loving me and our future will be great together. My hair is a mess, so you know what I must do. Boy, your voice is always good to hear. I love you and take it easy."

Eric responded, "Okay. I love you too." Then they hung their phones up.

Eric began to feel guilty because Honey had high expectations of him and he was leaning towards cheating on her. Eric knew if he cheated, he wouldn't be different from the other guys she been with in the past. Honey would be destroyed if she found out he fooled around with all those women. Eric was one hundred percent sure about making his sexual fantasy come true. He didn't have any more second and third thoughts about what he was going to do. Eric just wanted to freak them other girls and keep Honey by his side. Eric had sex with over twenty prostitutes before and he was still thirsty for more. The only questions on his mind were which prostitutes he wanted and when would it happen.

James chose five teams for the second week. Four of his teams had already won and made the point spread. The last game he had to watch his team blowing out the other team by twenty four points. James was going nuts in his bedroom and he was yelling, "No one can pick these teams like me! For the second straight week I'm picking winners! Frank is really going to feel like a jackass. The only thing he is going to tell me is stop while I'm ahead. Why not keep winning when you are hot?" Then finally he lowered his tone, "I know Peyton Manning better than his coaches. That boy is a fool with a football. He should have five Super Bowl rings by now."

His mother came to his bedroom, wondering why he was making so much noise. She asked, "Boy, have you lost your mind? Why are you hollering like someone is torturing you back here?" She glanced at the TV and saw that he was watching a football game. Zenobia said, "You are going crazy over a regular season game. Normally, folks would act like that over a playoff game or a super bowl game." You don't even have a dollar on the game and yelling loud. Just keep the racket down a little, Son."

Zenobia didn't have a clue about James's gambling habits. James had never told her about all the cash he lost over the years. A lot of Christmas and birthday money went down the drain. His mother gave him too much freedom at an early age. James had grown up before his time. James was only seventeen years old. He had already skipped school many times, lost his virginity, smoked weed, and committed armed robbery. James was far from the average teenager. Pretty soon, he would add selling drugs to his resume.

James's last team won the game and then he left home to get his money from Frank. The amount was $600.

Later on, Redd dropped Lewis off at home. Both of them were high after smoking $40 worth of Lewis's weed. Lewis used his key to get inside the house and then he went into the kitchen looking for something to eat. He had the munchies again. Lewis opened the refrigerator looking for some bologna. There wasn't any bologna in the refrigerator. Lewis said with frustration, "Fuck! We are out of bologna. My mom probably ate it all. That bitch eats up everything around here." As Lewis kept looking for food, he discovered some salami meat. He hated salami. Tonight, Lewis didn't have any other choice, but to settle with what he could find. Lewis took four slices of light bread out of the light bread bag that was on the table. Then he placed some mayonnaise on his bread and added some cheese with his sandwiches. He placed two sandwiches in the microwave to heat them. Lewis took the two sandwiches and a can of orange soda to his bedroom.

Sam watched him the whole time he was in the kitchen.

He even smelled the weed scent from Lewis. He noticed Lewis was walking like he was intoxicated. Sam was steamed at Lewis. He came home high and he was eating up all the sandwich meat. Sam wanted to put a lock on the refrigerator to keep Lewis out, but first he wanted to tell Lewis what was on his mind. Sam walked up the stairs and went into Lewis's bedroom. Sam opened the door and stared at him. Lewis looked at his dad and then he turned away from him.

Sam was disgusted with the fact that his son was high, "Lewis, why are you turning into a junky? Your mother and I taught you right from wrong. Why pretend like we taught you nothing at all. We should take our last name back and replace it with Slow. We are humiliated and uncomfortable with the reality of you being our son. Instead of hitting the books harder, you have chosen to hit the weed harder. I might be dead and gone, but the lifestyle you are living will lead to self destruction."

Lewis cursed his father out, "Can you get the fuck out of my room? Find another child to rape. My ass is still sore from the last time. Go talk to someone who will listen to you. Sam, there is no respect here for you. Muthafucka are you deaf? Go park your car in front of an elementary school. I'm sure some little boy is going to like it, you faggot."

Sam was hurt by his son's remarks and he wanted to kill him with his bare hands. He began to retaliate with some words of his own, "The next time I fuck you, I am going to nut in your mouth, faggot. Then I would make you swallow it." Sam walked out of Lewis's bedroom feeling like he got the best of him with harsh words.

Lewis thought he had to get rid of his father before his

father got rid of him. *Sam is trying to irritate me, so I could fight him. Every since I slammed him the last time, he has been dying for a rematch. I was in my bedroom chilling and then he comes in here messing with me. In due time, Sam will get what is coming to him. His punk ass belongs to me. Just because I am his son, Sam doesn't have the right to harass me when he feels like it. With those losers out of my way, life will be much sweeter. Sam wants a piece of me, so I'll give it to him.* Lewis went ahead and ate his food.

Sam and Jessica were lying down in their bed under the covers. They started to hear knocking on the door. They wondered why Lewis was knocking on the door. Then the knocks became louder and harder. Jessica said to her husband, "I'll get up and see what he want."

Sam already knew he had made Lewis mad by coming into his bedroom messing with him. As soon as Jessica opened the door, Lewis came in and bumped her out of his way. Lewis screamed at Sam, "Talk that shit now! Don't look stupid; you should have never come in my room fucking with me. You are going to make me place my foot in your ass."

Jessica tried to calm Lewis down by getting in front of him. She told him, "Go back to your room. I'm certain you misunderstood what he said. Please go back to your bedroom, right now!"

Sam began to get out of the bed and he was thinking, *I was waiting on the day when he would cross my path again. I'm going to beat him like I would a full grown man. He could barely walk to his room and he wants to rumble with me.* Sam told Jessica, "Move out of the way and let me handle this problem."

Jessica was thinking, ***All hell is getting ready to break loose. Lewis is extremely infuriated and Sam is not thrilled either.*** She moved out of the way, so she wouldn't get hurt. Sam walked to Lewis and now they were face to face.

Sam threatened him, "If you don't calm down, I will put you down. Your mother and I are letting your ass get away with murder. So close that smart mouth and go back to your room. Stop knocking on our door like you are crazy. You've been warned so good bye."

Lewis wanted to show Sam he was not scared of him. He pretended to walk away from his father. Then he turned back around quickly and punched Sam in the mouth. The unexpected blow dropped Sam to his knees and then he got right back up. He grabbed Lewis and they started to wrestle. Sam began connecting some punches behind Lewis's head. Lewis rammed Sam into a big mirror on the wall. The mirror shattered to the floor. Sam grabbed Lewis by his shirt and slanged him to the floor. Lewis got back up and Sam slanged him to the floor again by his shirt. Lewis got up half way and gave Sam a good shot between his legs. While Sam was holding his nuts, Lewis gave him an uppercut to the jaw. Sam fell on his back and Lewis got on top of him. Lewis was going for the knockout; he was serving Sam with some solid left and right blows. Sam had his guards up, but Lewis was still connecting. Sam got lucky and landed a powerful straight jag while lying on his back. Lewis fell down backwards; the jab left him in a daze. Sam got up off the floor and placed both of his hands around Lewis's neck to help him off the floor. Lewis had both of his hands on Sam's left arm. Sam pulled his right hand back as far as he could. Then he delivered a Lennox Lewis like punch to the jaw of Lewis and knocked him out on the floor. The battle between father and son was over.

Sam had gotten the best of Lewis. Jessica was looking at the positive side of the fight. If Sam lost, he was going to take his frustration out on her. She would rather for Lewis to get hurt than herself. Sam dragged Lewis by his feet until he was out of their room. He left him on the floor, outside of their bedroom. Sam was breathing hard while he locked the door. Then he climbed back into bed with Jessica.

Lewis awakened after being knocked out for seven minutes. He gradually got up on his feet. The whole fight played in his mind as he went back to his bedroom. Lewis said to himself, "He won that round. I thought I had him beat. The next time, it won't be a fight, only bullets traveling through his body. I must admit, Sam was stronger than I expected. Jessica stood there and watched the fight as usual. She is probably happy I lost, so Sam wouldn't knock her ass out. Just like an inmate on death row, her days are numbered too. Sam won this fight because I was still high. Under normal circumstances, Sam knew he would lose a fight against me. He knew I was high and he took advantage of me. Sam has gotten what he wanted. My stupid ass fell right into his hands. There will be school tomorrow; I hope I'm not too fucked up." He went into the bathroom to use a mirror; he did not see any new bruises, but his jaw was sore. Lewis took a shower and went to bed. He went to sleep with payback on his mind.

Chapter 17

The next day at school, Steven and Lewis were eating breakfast together. Steven said to him, "It's been a long time since we chilled in the cafeteria together. What's wrong, man? Normally, you would be talking up a storm. You are quiet like a black person who accidently walked into a KKK rally."

Lewis wanted to talk with Steven about what happened last night. His pride was hurt after being knocked out cold by Sam. Lewis told Steven, "There is nothing wrong with me. I'm trying to enjoy these waffles, eggs, and bacon. A lot of my thoughts were on perfecting my plan. You all probably done a lot of guessing and I bet none of y'all came close to what I have in store. Y'all are going to stay wondering how to break the code. Do you remember when I said less than three weeks?"

Steven answered, "Yes, I remember when you said that."

Lewis told him, "A sudden change in my plan has come up. So make it about two weeks. In two weeks, instead of making it rain, we can make it flood. Make sure everybody knows about the changes. It is getting ready to go down. So don't change your mind about helping once I tell you what it is. We are going to live lavishly for the rest of our lives."

Steven said, "Damn, I forgot to tell you something." Then the bell rang for their first period class. "I will talk to you later about my situation because it is a long story."

Lewis replied, "Get with me during lunchtime or after

school." They did not get a chance to meet while school was still going on.

Eric and Johnny did get a chance to meet up during lunchtime. They were in the gym hanging out by the bleachers. Johnny was always in the mood for joking around. He could easily become a comedian. Johnny playfully said, "A telescope would cost a lot of money. With your glasses, I could save a thousand bucks. I will put those bad boys on and see every galaxy out there. Your glasses could help me see the future."

Eric stated, "I don't know how to roast. Your momma is so fat she has to take showers inside a car pool. She is so ugly that guys wouldn't date her if you paid them like a NBA superstar. Don't get me started, fool."

Eric caught Johnny off guard. He did not think Eric could come back with some lines of his own. He told Eric, "My street credit would be gone if folks found out I was kicking it with you. You would make Prince look like John Cena. Now it's time for me to put you in your place. You have been beating your meat for so long that your right hand is still trembling."

Eric had to bow down after that one, "Where did you get those jokes from? Those jokes can't be your punch lines."

Johnny said, "They are mine. Sometimes I would sit around the house thinking of new ones. On a serious note, I would rather make good grades by myself than telling good jokes. How do you make the honor roll over and over? I don't know shit in class."

Eric explained, "Well, everybody is different. I catch on to things in school very fast. After the teachers shown me a few examples, I am ready to ace the test. Some people take longer to learn. For me, math is the most challenging thing in school."

Johnny stated, "Everything seems difficult in class. All the testes become too complicated for me to pass without help."

Eric thought about tutoring Johnny with his schoolwork. He saw it as a real challenge. Getting good grades in school was too easy for him. He believed teaching Johnny and helping him make good grades would be more impressive than making a 4.0. Eric realized that Johnny was discouraged and he needed some confidence. He said to Johnny, "You are looking at the smartest tutor at our school. If anybody can teach you, it's me."

Johnny responded, "I would really look like I don't have any knowledge. All of the slow students have tutors and the last thing I want is to look slow."

Eric said to him, "You are wrong about that. If you refuse my offer, then you would look slow. No one has to know anything. Let me secretly teach you a few things. I could make you an average student or better. On the weekends, in the mourning time, we can hook up."

Johnny felt desperate to get better with his school lessons. He told Eric, "We have a deal, homie. Keep everything on the D L. My street credit is on the line. We need to start on Saturday; I'll come over to your "crib"."

Lewis and Steven got a chance to talk after school. Steven had to tell him about the good things that happened to Barbara and him. Lewis was going to find out about his improved living conditions anyway. Steven said, "You won't believe how my luck has changed for the better. My mom will receive dad's retirement money. The police department has given us a nice piece of change. The police officers must have felt sorry for the pain they cost. My mom and I have moved to a better house. The house isn't spectacular, but it is good enough for us."

Lewis felt suspicious about all the money Steven said they were receiving. He thought the bank money played a big role in getting another house. Lewis let his suspicions be known. "Come on, man. Do you expect me to believe that shit? Out of the blue, y'all move into another house. How could you say one thing and do another? No one in our crew will believe your story."

Steven thought, *I just know he is not trying to talk about somebody. He is the king of being confused.* Steven said, "Have you learned anything over the years about me? I will not lie about serious matters. My mom would not tell you a tale, either. She loves you, like you are another member of her family. Wait until you hear about Willie's story and then you really would get into a doubting mood. I'm going to let him tell his own story."

Lewis told him, "My time to shine is coming too, watch and see. It's time for me to dip into a little of my money. My parents are rich, so the Police wouldn't expect me to be a part of a robbery spree. I need a car because I'm tired of walking. My parents would never buy me a car to drive. I could use some new clothes too because I have to stay "fly". My wardrobe is the very best of Jordan and Sean John. You have to step your clothing game up. The gear you are wearing has expired a long time ago. Barbara needs to take your ass to the mall, ASAP. What are you doing later?"

Steven answered, "Ms. Obey gave me some homework. I

have to complete three pages. I thought seniors wouldn't get a lot of work when school is getting ready to be out. You have to check out the new house. It is definitely an upgrade from our old house."

Lewis said to Steven, "Maybe, I'll show up at your crib tomorrow. You haven't come over to my house in a minute. Every since we started running the streets, things has changed. The only thing that will never change is us being brothers. Are you still my brother?"

Steven responded, "I'm your brother forever".

Then both of them walked home. Steven didn't know how bad things really were at Lewis's home. Lewis had kept his biggest secret from Steven for years. Lewis finally came up with a solution to his problems at home -- a plan to murder his parents while he was in his third period classroom. He decided to stage a burglary-homicide at his home. Lewis did not want to become a suspect. He figured if the front door became broke and valuable items were missing, his chances of getting away with the crime would be greater. Someone in his crew could rough him up to look like he was assaulted. Lewis was going to make sure the police thought he was the victim. Since Lewis had been staying with his parents for all these years, he knew them very well. He knew their normal time for going to bed was 8:50. Lewis would be in his bedroom while the crew would be on their way. Lewis had multiple keys to the house; he could give them one ahead of time. He would come downstairs to meet up with them and then he would cause some type of diversion to make his parents open their bedroom door. Once their bedroom door was open, they would slaughter Jessica and Sam. His parents always slept with the door locked; it could become a major problem for him. Lewis had to figure out how he would lure one of them to open their bedroom door. Lewis knew he needed a little more planning to make it really look like a buglary-homicide. He needed a story to tell the police since he was going to be there during the murder. They were going to interview him to get some information hoping it could help solve the case. Whatever story Lewis chose to use, he had to stick with it. He was told that a lie changes and the truth stays the same. Lewis realized with all that money he could buy anything he wanted or thought he wanted. Lewis would buy another house and he would no longer live where he took so much abuse, mentally and physically.

A part of him wanted to show Steven that he was a real criminal genius too. Lewis had something else in his favor; everyone believed their family was living in harmony like the family on "The Cosby Show". It would be difficult for the neighbors and the police to see him as a suspect. Steven was the only one who knew his family's dysfunctional ways. He would have two weeks to get the mission ready.

Steven thought as he walked into his yard, *Why would his plan be harder on me than the rest of them? It must be something personal. I probably won't like it, but I have to keep my word.* He entered the house and went room to room looking for Barbara. He noticed she was not at home. Steven wondered where she could be. Then he heard a car horn blowing outside. It sounded like the horn was blowing in front of their house. Steven went out the front door to see who it was. Barbara was outside, behind the wheel of a black four door 2008 Chevy Cobalt with a sunroof. It looked brand new with only 39,899 miles on it. The car had black leather seats. The Chevy Cobalt was not the best car in the world but it was fifty times better than driving her '79 Chevy Caprice. Steven had a big smile on his face. He was happy to see his mom in another car. Steven walked up closer to Barbara, so he could speak to her, "Where did you get this great looking car? This car was made just for you. My mom has good taste after all."

She answered, "I purchased this car from a car dealership name "Cars for you". This baby can save me a lot of money on gas. I'm going to let you drive it sometimes. Everyone needs to know how to drive and have a driver license."

Steven always wanted a driver license. His mom's old car wasn't eligible to take the driving license test in. This was the chance he needed to start back studying the driver license handbook, so he could past the written and the signs part of the test. Steven knew he could drive well, so passing the actual driving test would not be a problem. He told her, "I have to get a driver license handbook from the DMV. Most people say they cost two or three dollars. The book is not big at all. In my free time, I would learn everything there is to know."

Barbara got out of the car and dropped a bombshell question on Steven, "Why haven't you brought a nice young lady home? I'm getting up in age and I have zero grand kids. At least you can give me a little hope for the future. Steven, have you looked in the mirror lately. You are a very bright and handsome young man. Girls should throw themselves at you."

After both of them walked into their house Steven responded, "For years, I thought my clothes were the reason girls don't speak to me. Now that I think about it, my clothes were okay and they just were not name brand. Why I don't have a girlfriend is a mystery. Even guys who are not attractive are holding hands with their girlfriends at school. When I get some "fresh gear", it will increase my chances to meet that special someone. My whole style needs a makeover."

Barbara told him, "Things have changed a lot since I was a teenager. Name brand clothes are only a portion of it. Your conversation must consist of superb communication skills to find an intelligent and respectful lady. Another thing, I'm going to buy you some cologne. Women love men who smell good. Your teeth are white like a dentist goes to work on them every week; that's a plus. I don't know how you keep your teeth so white."

Steven was glad someone had noticed. He proudly told her how he kept his teeth white, "At home, after each meal, I use Scope, floss, and then I brush my teeth."

Barbara said to Steven, "No son of mine is going to stay girlfriend-less. We could go shopping at the mall. The mall has all the latest fashions that attract younger and older people. This weekend coming up, you'll get an upgraded on your clothes. Don't pick any pants that would sag on you; it would look tacky. I might be old, but I'm still a fashion genius. Back in the days, most of the girl at my school wanted to dress like me. The boys used to say I was pleasant to eyes. Being classy was and still is my style. The younger generation of men wants chicken heads with big booties. Very few guys are looking for classy women who you could take home to your mother."

Steven thought, *Barbara is too old-fashioned to know what is tight these days. Back in her days was a long time ago. On the bright side, she is a female; mom could give me some pointers. I have been trying to figure girls out since becoming a teenager. I still don't have a clue. Once I change my style to a better one, it's going to be on.*

Barbara said, "I know you think my ways are too old-fashioned. Many things have changed since I was the hottest girl out there. It doesn't change the fact that I'm a fashion expert. With my help, you could easily become one of the smoothest guys at school. Most girls want mature guys, so dress like you is going to college not high school."

Steven was taking in everything that Barbara was telling him. Hopefully with her coaching him, he could find someone to take out on a date. Steven was not worried about the dough because he had enough to take her anywhere. He was overexcited to choose the name brand clothes he had been thirsting for.

Barbara began to tell him things she thought he didn't know. "Did you know most girls favorite color is light blue? Wearing all black would make you look even cooler."

Steven stated, "Wow! You have been keeping all this knowledge from me. How could you do me like this, Mom? I'm your only son."

Barbara giggled and said to him, "Son, you never asked me anything. Just like most young people, you think all the answers are floating in your head. Over the years, I watched you go to school without ironing your clothes, wearing dirty shoes, and not studying. If you would have put more effort in studying, I would be talking to an honor roll student right now. In the past, girls did not like the nerdy type. These days, girls like smart guys. Steven, find a girlfriend; I'm getting older not younger. Remember everything I told you and things will happen the way you want them to. Don't bring home any chicken heads; they think their big booties can take them to the top. They don't believe in using their brains, only sex to get what they want out of life. Most of them are gold diggers who are looking for their next spot to dig. Be sure to look for a wholesome young lady because they will stick by your side. In the long run, she would handle your business if you are not able." Both of them took a seat on the living room love couch.

Steven was hungry for more knowledge. "What would a classy girl talk about?"

Barbara replied, "That's an easy question. A girl with class would talk about positive things. Her mind would be on her future. She would prefer going out to the movies and having dinner, not going to the clubs. You won't meet too many single good women inside of a club. Most decent women have a strong relationship with their mother. Another good sign is a woman who goes to church almost every Sunday. Be a strong, respectful, and truthful man. There are so many men treating women like property. Don't be one of those fools. Women are getting beat, lied to, and cheated on every day. You could become the man that all women dream about. Honest, lovable, and romantic are some traits that real females are looking for. Finding a good man is like searching for a needle in a haystack. I'm sure a lovely girl has been watching you at school. Son, you are not showing enough for them to step up to the plate. Most of the time, men speak to women first."

Steven told her, "My heart starts racing when I get close to speaking with a girl. They say a close mouth won't get fed.

That statement is very true. Mom, talking to you has given me confidents. I feel like I can get with Tyra Banks."

Barbara responded, "Don't be too confident; it could back fire on you. Never pretend like you are more than your-self. Act like Steven and everything will be fine."

Chapter 18

Friday came again. James took his time and picked some more teams he thought could win. For the third week in a row, James was ready to gamble again. He was convinced he could not lose. But this time around, he would bet differently. James had an idea to bet on the same five teams, three times. He would win $1,800 if things went in his favor. James already had over $100,000. He did not have to gamble on games any more but his greed refused to let him stop. All he could think about was more money. For an example, $10,000 sounds good, but $18,000 sounds better. He wouldn't be satisfied until he reached his goals. James did not want to quit while he was ahead. He had enough money to start a legit business and make his money work for him. It never crossed his mind about what he was going to do once a million plus dollars was in his hands. How would he stay a millionaire? James was so cocky and young, he thought he could get away with anything. James also thought he could out smart any police officer. Being rich was the only outcome he could think of. Those robberies placed so much cash into his pockets; James's ego had skyrocketed. His gambling habits were turning major.

He tore one sheet of paper to make three pieces, then left his home to speak with Frank again. While walking, he gave Frank a call to let him know he was on his way. James was bragging on the cell phone, "Your boy is going for a three peat, similar to Scottie Pippen in '93. No one could pick the right teams, the way I can."

Frank gave James his props, "You are getting good at this. The record is five weeks in a row and it has been standing for ten years. Believe it or not, very few people could say they won three weeks in a row."

James overconfidently said, "Getting good is an understatement. I'm already great, so get it right. I'm on my way down there with the winning teams list. They might ban me from playing because I'm winning too much. It is a good thing you are placing my bets; they would not give me anything if the owner knew my age. Come outside and holler at me."

Frank came outside to meet James. After James showed Frank his list, he told him, "These teams will dominate this week. If you want to win, put some bread on them too. At this point in my gambling career, it's impossible for me to lose."

Frank detected something different in the way James placed his bets. He told James, "I have worked here for over twenty years. No one has ever chosen the same five teams, three times. Most of the time, they would change two or three teams to have a greater chance to win."

James said, "Well, I'm different from everybody else. The record is five weeks, so six weeks and above is what I am aiming for. My mouth has been running, so much that giving you the cash did not cross my mind." James reached into his pocket and gave Frank $150. It was the most money he had ever betted on football. James said, "I know you must get back to work. I'm not going to hold you up any longer. Thanks for helping me out with everything. Without your help, my age would've destroyed my chances of gambling at Touchdown.

Here is a $100 tip to show my appreciation." James reached back into his pockets to give Frank a $100.

Frank became happy and thought, *Now that is how you are supposed to appreciate someone for helping out.*

James jokingly stated, "Frank, are you crazy? There is no way, I would give you $100 tip or any other amount; please don't take it personal. Don't look so bitter; I was only fucking with you. Tips come your way every day. Go ahead and place my bets. You will see me when it's time to collect." James walked off, heading back home.

Frank wanted to call him a son of a bitch. Frank did some thinking. *Every time I place a bet for him, my job is on the line. He really isn't thankful that I'm helping him. Whether James wins or loses, he can't fuck with me anymore. That bastard will have to find him another sucker.*

Chapter 19

The next day was Saturday and their school was having a parade. It was very sunny, but the wind was blowing. The parade was a celebration for the school's football team. They have won the District #4 5A State Championship. The parade was large, with a little over 12,000 people there, holding blue and gray balloons. Blue and gray were the school's colors. Five news reporters were there to get the story. Cheerleaders, the boy's scouts, the girl's scouts, the pep squad, the school's marching band, the basketball team, the baseball team, police officers, and firemen were a part of the parade. The police officers were walking and driving in front, behind, and on both sides of the spectacle. About 97% of the student body showed up, including the teachers. The festivities stopped at a large white courthouse's front lawn. Mayor Rudy Henderson and Principal Washington were already on stage waiting on them. The football team with all their coaches joined them on stage. The Mayor and the Principal gave speeches. Then Coach Thomas and his players received the key to the city from the Mayor. The bronze key was 37 inches long and 6 inches wide with a red ribbon wrapped around it. Coach Thomas gave an inspirational speech. He thanked the entire team for playing for him. He wanted the senior players to go on to bigger and better things. At the end of the program, Coach Thomas raised the key to the city high and Johnny raised the state championship trophy high. The journalists took many pictures of the event.

A tear fell from Willie's right eye because he knew his high school football career was over. Willie looked around at all his coaches and teammates and thought, *Man, this could be the last time that all of us will be together. It was a great ride from start to finish. Coach Thomas said it is time for the seniors to go on to bigger and better things. Even thirty years down the line, this school and its football program will have a place in my heart.*

Eric followed the parade on feet, from the school to the courthouse. He left once the program ended. Then he used his cell phone to call Honey. She answered her cell phone by saying, "Where are you, Eric? I hear many people in the back ground."

Eric responded, "I'm at my school's parade. The football team won the championship, so it's for them. To tell you the truth, I did not think, so many folks cared about football. The crowd is very large. The entire school is here, possibly. My school's marching band put on a great show. They played some old and new songs. The football team was treated like the modern day Beatles. Smiles were on a lot of faces. Today almost felt like a holiday. It did take our school over twenty years to win another championship. If they were winning the title every year, it would not be so much excitement. Most of the players are seniors. That means, back to the drawing board for next year. It might take another twenty plus years to win the championship. We need to hook up tonight. What you think about that?"

Honey replied, "I do not see a problem with it. Tonight is a good time for you to finally come to my crib. Forget going out because we could just chill at my place. I'll make the popcorn and rent some movies from the Video Express."

Eric told her, "Please buy some soda pops if you don't already have some at home. We have to wet our throats after eating popcorn. I can't wait to see your bedroom. You could be a neat freak. I was looking forward to going out tonight, but we can do that another time. Do you want me to drive over there or will you pick me up from my house?"

Honey said, "I'll come over there to get you. We'll have a good time at my home."

Eric asked, "What kind of movies you are going to snatch. I trust your taste; the movies will be straight."

She answered, "There is one scary movie and one romantic comedy movie I have in mind. Hopefully, you have not seen them before because I haven't. Baby, I'll see you later. I have to clean my place up and get those movies. Don't worry about the soda pops, it's some here already." After they both said bye and I love you, it was the end of their conversation, for right now.

Barbara and Steven were also at the parade before they decided to give The South Coast Palace mall a visit. Steven liked almost everything he saw. He was like a kid in a candy store. At the Vibe store, Steven grabbed every pair of Nikes he saw trying to get a better look at them. Barbara thought it would be a challenge for Steven to find exactly what he wanted. Steven was not use to going into the mall with the mindset of getting any clothes he wanted.

Barbara decided to help him out the best she could by using her judgment. She told him, "Look for clothes that mature and older guys would wear. It is going to give you a sophisticated appearance. Leave the long t-shirts and sagging pants on the rack." As they kept walking, Barbara spotted a store named

"Gentlemen's". Barbara said, "With a name like that, it got to have casual clothes in there. Let's see what they have in their store." Steven and Barbara went inside of the Gentlemen's store. They saw different color dress pants, Lacoste clothes, Timberland boots, Lugz boots, Stacy Adams three-piece suits and casual shoes, Northface shirts, Coogi clothes, Sean John clothes, and Eastland clothes.

Steven picked up a pair of brown colored Eastland boots and then he said, "These babies are coming home with me. That light blue Lacoste long sleeve shirt is a keeper too. Those light brown dress pants is a great match to go with it."

Barbara told him, "Now find one more casual outfit, Son." After searching the Gentlemen's store for seventeen more minutes, Steven's choice were a gray Sean John polo shirt with the grey Sean John jeans to match. Barbara spent a total of $303.84 at the Gentlemen's store. Barbara and Steven went to the Footlocker store. He wanted to get the rest of his clothes from there. He did not waste any time looking for some tennis shoes. He picked up the new Air Jordan shoes and said, "Where have you been all my life?" The shoes were mostly white with red and black. Then he told Barbara, "I need a black and a red Jordan shirt and then I would be straight." Steve found the two shirts he wanted quickly. The two Jordan shirts and the Air Jordan shoes cost $204.29.

Barbara purchased all of it. She had one more thing on her mind. "We cannot leave the mall without some type of cologne. It's hard to believe you had forgotten about it."

Steven said, "My mind was on getting the best looking clothes. I must have become over excited because some of my hopes and dreams are coming true. Macy's are known to have cologne and perfume. A lot of students say they get their fragrance from there. I saw a large Macy's sign when we first came in. We could go to the front of the mall to check it out." Steven and Barbara headed to the front of the mall. Just like Steven said, they ran directly into Macy's in the front of the mall. It would have been impossible to miss. The Macy's sign was in large red letters. Steven said to Barbara, "This is our last stop." They saw that the fragrances were setup in the front of the store.

An African American woman asked, "May I help you?"

Barbara answered, "Yes, we can definitely use your help. My son is looking for cologne with a scent that is not too loud. His cologne must have a light and fresh smell."

The lady responded, "I know just what he is looking for. A matter of fact, it just arrived yesterday. He could be the first person to buy Giorgio Armani's new cologne name "Acqua Di Gio' from here. I think it's Russian. Smell this sample and tell me whether you like it or not." Barbara and Steven sniffed the little sample paper. Both of them had something positive to say about the fragrance.

Barbara stated, "It could be the best cologne I ever smelled."

Then Steven told them, "The popular guys normally have a smell that is similar to this cologne."

The lady told Steven, "Trust me; smelling like this will get you a lot of girl's attention. Women love guys who smell very good. With a little of this on, you will be at the top of your game."

Barbara said, "He will take it and thanks for your help." Barbara paid $57.05 for a 1.7 FL oz bottle of Giorgio Armani's cologne. She spent a total of $566.18 at the mall.

Barbara said, "My legs are getting sore. I'm ready to get out of here."

Steven was ready to leave the mall too. They walked out the mall together. Both of them got into the car and headed back home with Barbara behind the wheel. While going home, Steven began to feel guilty because his mom did not buy herself anything. Her mind was on Steven the entire time at the mall. Steven asked Barbara, "Why didn't you buy yourself anything? We used up all our time on me."

Barbara responded, "I brought joy to my son. There is not a better feeling than that. I'm an old fashion woman. My clothes at home are good enough for me. If I had a million dollars, my mentality would not change. Never let money or anything else change you. Rich people have problems just like poor people. In other words, make the money and don't let the money make you. There have been rich people who killed themselves. Money does solve some problems. It solved my transportation problems, look at my Chevy Cobalt. It will get me anywhere I want to go. The old Caprice classic of mines has been breaking down for years. I hope your new clothes help you stand out at school. You are my only focus since Tim's death. In a little while, real decision will face you. Steven, you are becoming a man. I can't tell you what to do forever. Take the knowledge and wisdom that your father and I installed in you. Always make positive choices and live a righteous life. Be better than Tim and I put together. Think about going to college for a higher education or find a trade at a technical college and then before you know it; success will knock at your door. Don't put too much pressure on yourself because anything beats selling drugs and robbing people. In the future, you look back at the past and say I made it. The hard work has paid off."

Barbara and Steven arrived home. Steven asked, "What do you mean about not being here forever? You scared me talking like that. I hope it was not some kind of hidden message. Don't tell me you are feeling sick. I know you are getting older."

Barbara responded, "You took it the wrong way. Soon, you will become a fully-grown man. Life is going to get real serious. I can't always be responsible for your actions. It is all about growing up and learning how to stand on your own two feet."

Steven showed signs of relief. "Why didn't you explain it like that the first time. Losing another close relative would be too much to take."

Barbara told him, "I'm not going anywhere, Son. Someone has to be here to decorate your wedding. The name Barbara is also French for babysitter."

Steven stated, "It will be a long time before I have kids. I was just a kid myself not too long ago. Just hold on Mom, one day it will become a reality."

Both of them went into the kitchen and Barbara was ready to cook dinner. Barbara told him while getting the spaghetti with meatballs, sweet potatoes, and pork chops ready, "The money we received from the police department was a gift from God. We have to spend every dollar of it wisely. Thank God we can finally live comfortably. I will not waste our money on unnecessary things." Steven knew that Barbara had given him enough knowledge in one week to last a lifetime.

Lewis was inside of his bedroom playing a game on the

PlayStation 3. He had a visitor at the front door. Sam yelled, "Lewis, someone is at the front door waiting to speak with you!"

Lewis wondered, *Who could it be? Redd did not call, so I know it's not him. My dad would've been upset if he showed up to this house. I'm tripping; Steven comes over here out of the blue, every now and then*. Lewis put the game on pause to see who wanted him. He went downstairs to the front door. He opened the door and to his surprise, Willie was waiting on him. Lewis said, "I can't believe you even remember where I stayed. Your new car is off the chain. Whose change really paid for this car? Steven said you had some unbelievable luck. So go ahead and explain everything to me."

Willie explained to Lewis, "My mom and dad saved up some money for me. For years, I thought they were just being cheap with me. They were cheap for a good reason. The reason is parked on the roadside of your house. I am still shocked that I have a car."

Lewis told him, "You and your parents could be living well off that bank money. Even if you did spend some of that dough, it is your money and no one could tell you how to use it." Lewis and Willie were standing on the steps until Lewis wanted to get a better look at the car. Lewis was impressed by the 2010 Nissan.

Willie said to him, "Every time I look at this car, it feels like I'm dreaming. If I am dreaming, I hope to God I don't wake up. My parents pulled a rabbit out of the hat."

Lewis began to think, *My parents couldn't get me a car. I guess they thought I was not special enough for them.*

Willie never had anything and all of a sudden his parents buy him a smooth car. My parents are some sorry mutherfuckas. They could have bought me two cars and would not miss the money. My time to cruise is coming. Lewis said to Willie, "Congratulations, someone like you deserve something good to happen to them."

Willie thought, *Lewis lives in a big ass house. His house is probably the coldest one on the block. His parents' cash would make my parents' cash look like chump change. Why doesn't he have a car? All the other students with rich parents are driving their own car. Something is fishy about this situation. His parents can't care too much about him, if they are letting him walk to school and back home every day. Maybe I should ask him when his ride is coming.* Willie said, "Why your parents are keeping you careless? Everybody knows they have more money than Uncle Scrooge. Then you are walking to school. That's fuck up, man. I remember one day, on the way to school, my mom and I saw you walking in the drizzling rain. We wanted to give you a ride, but you were already about fifteen yards away from the school."

Lewis did not want Willie knowing his personal business at home. He responded, "My parents are on a paper chase. Nothing is getting in their way of making money. They are not going to be late for work by bringing me to school. Dad promised me a car and he has not gotten it yet. Yes, we leave in a big house. There are a couple of luxury cars outside of our house. No one could see the hard work and dedication they live by. A lot of work is used to keep this kind of lifestyle up. Some nights, my father comes home late from work. I know my role and I play it well. As long as I keep taking summer vacations, eating lobsters and shrimps, getting all the latest video games I would not mind walking to school. The relationship I have with my parents is almost perfect. We are such a happy family and I would not trade them for nothing in this world."

Willie believed every word Lewis said. He said, "My home is a happy one too. The only problem I had with them is not having much over the years. I guess it workout better for me that way. My ride is fresher than "Johnson & Johnson". Just last week, I was wondering why my parents kept my pockets in the great depression. In the blink of an eye, they made me happier than I have ever been. It used to hurt me to see other people my age having money and driving by me as I'm walking. Your dad needs to hurry up and give you one of his cars or buy you one."

Lewis stated, "Having my on wheels would be great. I try not to think about my dad's promise too much. The longer I ponder about it, the longer it seems like I'm waiting. One day when I am not thinking about it, bam, there it is parked outside of the house. Have you been cruising around today?"

Willie answered, "The road and my car are becoming best friends, but I just left my house. Earlier today, we had a parade and it was fun to be a part of it. Watching all my teammates celebrate for the last time was an exciting and sad moment for me. After four years of losing in the playoffs, we finally brought home the title. One of my dreams came true. The average person doesn't know how much hard work goes into a championship. The next step for me is to dominate on a college level. It's more difficult than a high school football level because guys are much bigger, stronger, and faster."

Lewis told him, "Football is your life. Hard work would make you bigger, stronger, and faster too. Look at all the football experience you have under your belt. There is not a level of football you could not master."

Willie placed the back of his right hand on Lewis's forehead and asked, "Are you feeling well today? I don't think I ever heard words of wisdom coming from you. Let me write this down. Have you ever seen 'Entourage' on HBO? A bunch of young guys with a lot of money and they are always partying with models, actress, and videos vixen. Everybody remembers Nelly's 'Tip Drip' video on BET's Uncut. We could live that kind of life, surrounded by the most beautiful women in the world."

Lewis said, "A man would have to be gay to forget that video. The best part of it is when Nelly swiped a credit card down a woman's ass. What are you doing for the rest of the day?"

Willie replied, "Johnny wanted me to holler at him today. His house is my next stop when I leave here. Get with me if you feel like getting out of the house later on."

Lewis told him, "Alright now, when you see my number on your phone, answer it." Then Willie left Lewis's house on the way to Johnny's house.

Eric was in the shower preparing for tonight. He had a lot of sexual positions he wanted to perform on Honey. He could see himself banging her from the back over and over again. After the doggy style position, he wanted to try the sixty-nine and the froggy-style positions. Those were his favorite ones to watch on the flicks. Eric was so ready that he had pre-nutted on himself. He kept on thinking about a foursome;

the thought would not go away. *A few times would not hurt. Honey won't know a thing if I play my cards right. With many women, the different fucking styles would be endless. Hell, I can create new ways to fuck.* Eric got out of the shower and dried off with a navy blue towel. Then Eric put on the clothes he had already ironed. A dark blue pair of Levi's jeans and a royal colored Duke shirt with the Duke's symbol and a Nikes symbol in the middle of the shirt, in the front. Eric's shoes were a pair of all white Nike Air Max. He wanted to change his style up a little bit. He normally wore casual clothes. His mother had been gone for an hour already.

Honey rented two motion pictures, a romantic comedy titled 'The Heartbreak Kid' and a horror movie titled 'Halloween'. She already had the soda pop and the popcorn at home. The popcorn needed to get popped in the microwave. Honey was wearing a pure white Adidas trefoil mid Tee with a light blue pair of Apple bottoms jeans. Her shoes were a pair of all white Adidas original hood mid with the Adidas symbol being the color of metallic silver on both sides of the shoes.

While driving, she picked up her cell phone and dialed Eric's number, "Eric, are you ready to come over my house? I don't want to wait any longer."

Eric responded, "I'm ready to be in the presence of your prettiness. Do you have the movies, the sodas, and the popcorn ready?"

Honey said, "Of course, but the popcorn needs to be popped. Give me about twelve minutes to make it there."

Eric said, "Okay, but don't keep me waiting forever." They got off the phone with each other.

She arrived at his place in ten minutes. Eric walked out

of his house and jumped into the car with her. She drove with her left hand and held his left hand with her right hand. After thirteen minutes of driving, they were at her apartment complex. The apartment complex was not large at all. It consisted of twenty-five apartments with no upstairs. It was made with light and dark brown bricks, mixed together. Eric and Honey got out of the car. Eric was holding a little plastic bag with the movies in it. Eric saw the inside of her place for the first time and then he said, "I knew it. You are a neat freak or it's clean because I'm over here."

Honey told him, "I am a neat freak, so take your shoes off. My carpet has to stay white, Eric." She took her shoes off and he did the same. Both of them were standing up in the living room. She told Eric, "Do you know how to work a Blu-Ray Disc Player? My things don't need get be broken."

Eric replied, "There is nothing I don't know how to work. You should know firsthand that I can work things really well. The people at school call me a nerd and there is a good reason behind that. My nickname should have been Mr. Technology. You are looking at an advance student."

Honey said, "Alright Mr. Technology, put in one of those movies, while I get the popcorn and soda pops ready." Eric placed 'The Heartbreak Kid' movie inside the Blu-Ray Disc Player. He took a moment to look around the living room. All three of her couches were black. A see-through glass table was in the middle of her living room. She had many pictures of herself on the walls and on top of the table. A gold and brown ceiling fan was hanging up above the table. She had a Sanyo 32 inch screen TV in there too. Her living room walls were black. Eric realized Honey treasured all her things because everything looked brand new. He thought the living room's black and white decor looked nice.

Honey came back into the living room with a large red plastic bowl full of hot and buttery popcorn. She told him, "Hold this bowl and don't drop any popcorn on the floor." Honey went back in the kitchen to grab two large red cups filled with ice and strawberry soda. They took a seat on the three seated couch. The single seat couch was on the right side of them and the Love Seat was to their left side. They laughed at The Heartbreak Kid movie. The film was very hilarious to both of them. Honey was happy she chose that movie. Once the movie went off, Eric put in Halloween, the modern version. Michael Myers scared the hell out of both of them. When Eric and Honey started watching the movies, they were sitting side by side. During the second movie, Honey laid on top of him with her head on his chest. They kept jumping during the entire film. Eric and Honey went from laughing to being scared to walk into the kitchen. They joked around saying, "Michael Myers is in there."

Now that the movies were watched, the popcorn was eaten, and the sodas were drunk, Eric was ready to get it on. He asked her, "How does your bedroom look?"

Honey knew he gave her a hint that he was ready for sex. She said, "There is one way to find out how it looks. Let's go in there, Eric." Eric was more than just ready to find out.

Honey took him by the hand and walked him into the bedroom. The bedroom was the color of the living room. The carpet and the walls were black. The dressers and the top cover on her bed were white. She had a 16-inch TV on top of her dresser. Eric told her, "You must love the colors black and white. Personally, I think it looks cool. Maybe you can decorate my room."

Eric went ahead and climbed in her bed and then Honey climbed in the bed after him. They begin kissing passionately. Eric's dick became harder than a steel pipe. He helped Honey take her shirt off. She reached both of her hands to her back and unhooked her bra. Eric was happy she took it off herself; he normally struggled with taking them off. Eric started squeezing and sucking her beautiful breast. Honey had her left arm behind his head while he was pleasing her. He was sucking her breast like it was his true purpose in life. Eric took a Trojan condom out of his pants pocket. He pulled down his pants and boxers to his knees. Honey took off her clothes as fast as she could. Honey took the condom and placed it on his dick with her mouth. While Honey was down there, she gave him a blowjob. Eric's toes began to curl as he grasped her hair tightly. After nine minutes of getting his dick sucked, he told her, "I'm ready to fuck now." Eric lied on top of her and grabbed his dick; he was getting ready to make an impact. Honey knew what she was going to say will bring Eric's excitement down. She had to deliver some bad news.

Honey yelled, "Hold up! We can't do this right now because I'm on my period. Sorry, but it slipped out of my mind. We won't be fucking tonight. I came on my period early this morning. I wanted to make love as bad as you did."

Eric thought, *You have to be fucking kidding. How could you forget some shit like that? I should call those hoes numbers in my little black note book. She has pumped me up for nothing. This is some bullshit.* Eric cared too much about Honey to tell her how he really felt. He acted cool about it, "Baby, everything will be fine. We are going to have a million other chances. I still had fun tonight, Honey. Seriously, I enjoyed myself and you did too."

Honey stated, "That's why I love you so much. Any other guy would have flipped out by now. Damn, I'm happy you are different from the rest. Some guys would make up an excuse to leave after receiving news like that. Eric, you are a special guy." She placed her arms around Eric and gave him a hug. She did not know Eric was ready to go home. He was very disappointed in the way the night was going to end. Honey got up and put all her clothes back on. She recognized the dissatisfaction in his face. Eric pulled his boxers and pants back up while he was still lying down in bed. While she had Steven in mind, she said, "Wait a minute, let me finish sucking your dick." She took a small green towel out of her dresser. Then she took the condom off of Eric's dick. She said, "You better not cum in my mouth. Tell me when you are ready to explode." She grabbed his dick and gave him some more head while fantasizing he was Steven. She sucked his dick like it would save her life.

Eric thought the blowjob felt five times better without the condom. His mood changed from disappointment to 'Damn, this is the shit!' Eric's eyes rolled behind his head in ecstasy. After fifteen minutes of Honey giving him The "BJ" special, Eric screamed, "I can feel it coming, baby! I'm cumming! I'm cumming!" She placed the towel around his dick and then jerked it up and down until he exploded. Eric was shaking similar to getting electrocuted. Honey definitely gave him a rush he would never forget; his mind was blown away. Eric had a huge smile on his face. Eric told her, "When you get off your period, I will return the favor. Girl, I didn't know you could do it like that."

Honey said, "I'm delighted to see you enjoyed yourself, Steven, I mean Eric." Eric did not think long about her calling him Steven. He thought it was just a simple mistake. Eric took the towel off of his dick and told her, "I believe this towel belongs to you." Honey took the towel and placed it in a small white dirty clothes basket that she kept in her room. Eric began to deliberate, *Tonight turned into a sweet dream instead of a nightmare. I'm addicted to sex, so I had to get some kind of loving. Maybe Honey could give me some head whenever I'm horny and she's on her period.* Eric's lust was outweighing his love. He was starting to see her as a sex object and not the person he fell in love with. With every day that went by, Honey wanted Steven more and more. They were planning to betray each other. After another hour and a half of cuddling in bed, she took him home at 2:09am.

Chapter 20

The next day was Saturday and it meant party time for Lewis and Redd. Lewis was lying down in bed going over everything Redd told him. He basically gave Lewis a manual in words of how to act at Tammy's party and get women. He promised Lewis he would score tonight. Lewis was hoping Redd could get him some ass or he could use the game Redd taught him and get some without his help. Lewis thought he had to get some at the party and anything other than scoring was a massive let down. Lewis knew he couldn't blow an opportunity like this. He went into a deeper thought. *There will be plenty of girls at the party. So what can I say to make the panties drop to the floor? Most of the girls who are going to the party will use alcohol and drugs, so they won't be in their right state of mind. Redd said the women are coming over there just to strew. Everything is in my favor to get laid. As long as my game is tight, I will get down in dirty. If I say the right things, it's going down. It would take a complete idiot to fuck this up. My mind is always on drugs and sex; I really have not given any thought to how dangerous hanging with Redd can get. I carry a .9mm everywhere and if drama comes my way, I will handle my business. When a hater step up to me, he'll get the same thing I gave those police officers. At first it was just drugs and now it alcohol and sex too.* Lewis began to snicker. DELETED *My dad was right about Redd, he is a bad influence on me. Fuck it; I'm my own man. A real man has to live and die with the decision he makes. If Redd brings some X pills, it would be a big plus. He has not call and said anything yet, but he would probably have some pills tonight. We are going to get some alcohol before we hit the party. Redd and I will get in the zone; we'll stay both high and confident at the party. The life I'm living is unique. Growing up, I never saw myself as a thug or a gangster. The truth about me, I have never been rich. I'm a poor kid with rich parents.*

Redd was preparing for the party too. He was trying to figure out which guns were going with him. Redd placed most of his guns on the kitchen table and loaded them. He normally carried his .22 handgun inside of his socks next to his ankle, when he was in the clubs. His AK-47 always went in the trunk of the car. The package he was waiting on came earlier today. The items inside the package were X pills, crack, and weed. After scaling the drugs, he bagged it up. Redd would make sure everything was calculated right to know the amount he would make. He planned on making a killing at the party. Redd did some thinking of his own. *Lewis is becoming a man tonight. The first piece of ass is always unforgettable. He is the student and I am the teacher; Lewis could take over the world with my knowledge. Sometimes, students get big headed and challenge the teachers. I hope his head don't swell up too much. After having sex for the first time, it's a life changing experience. Lewis will never be the same again, after tonight. His chest will stay poked out and he would have more swagger than he ever had. Enough about Lewis, I have to focus on myself.*

What will I wear to the party? It is time for me to bring out my all red Boston Red Sox Manny jersey with the all red Boston Red Sox cap. Manny doesn't play for them anymore, but the jersey is still bad. Lewis is not the only one with a pair of Air Jordan shoes. A pair of black and red Air Jordan XVI will be on my feet. My kicks will out shine anybody else's. I was told to bring some cash everywhere I go, even if I don't plan on spending. I'll bring about $2,000 in hundreds to Tammy's house. It isn't much, but it's something. What kind of pants will I wear tonight? Oh, that an easy question for me to answer. I have an all black pair of Red Monkey jeans. The Red Monkey jeans are my most expensive jeans. I wrote the book on being so fresh and so clean. Hell, I'm not only a client, I'm the player president. We are going to act like Dr. Dre and Snoop Dogg at this party. Or should I say, Dr. Dre and Eminem. Fuck it, Dr. Dre and anybody. I'm Dr. Dre and no matter who I work with, I'm going to make good things happen. Lewis has a lot of guts; it's a great thing to have. My strategy for my ex girlfriend's party is simple. I want to dance with some hoes, make some money, and put a few bitches to bed. Once my ex sees me with my fly gear on, she would want me back again. After we hook up, her friends will receive some of this thug loving too. What kind of alcohol will Lewis and I sip on? Lewis probably can't drink hard liquor. Ciroc Vodka and Red Bull is a match made in heaven. I'll fix it up, so he won't call Earl. Back to my fire power, my Caliber 380 and my .22 Revolver handgun are coming into the party with me. The AK-47 is going in the trunk as usually. Hopefully, a lot of pill poppers show *up tonight. I have to get paid. Another drug dealer could show up and he could hurt my sales a little. Lewis might get approached by him with a better deal. He seems like a man with some loyalty. I have confidence that he won't fuck with any other dealer other than me."*

Johnny went over Eric's house to study. Eric was taking his time, slowly showing Johnny different ways to break down his math examples while sitting down at the kitchen table. Eric said, "Math is the hardest thing students have to learn. In the classroom, teachers teach at their own paste. Everyone will not learn like that. Every individual learn at their own paste, some fast and some slow. Just because I learn faster than you, it would not mean shit because we both know the same thing. In a boxing match, a fast fighter could hit the slower fighter two hundred times. The slower fighter can connect eighty punches and knockout the faster fighter. The race is not always won by the swift. You should always keep that in mind. Take your time and learn; this is not a race."

Johnny listened to every word coming out of Eric's mouth. Johnny was motivated for the first time in years. He thought, *Eric is right; if I stop rushing and take my time, maybe there is a chance for me to learn. The teachers are not teaching at my paste; they are moving too quick. I will work my way up to being the student I used to be, before I became lazy. Willie did not make things better for me by doing my homework and studying for the both of us.* For three and a half hours, Eric continued to give Johnny examples on getting the correct answers.

After going over so many problems, they became tired and watched 'Welcome Home Roscoe Jenkins' on TV. Eric had gained a lot of Johnny's trust and respect. It was hard for Johnny to trust anybody. Johnny told Eric, "Y'all are living well here. Everything is so clean; the floor and the table have a shine to it."

Eric replied, "My mom and I are a team. I mess up everything and she comes behind me to clean up."

Johnny responded, "That is not a team. She is doing all the work. We need to watch 'The Revenge of the Nerds'; I'll cheer for the jocks and you would cheer for the nerds."

Eric said, "I see what you are trying to do; a joke fest won't start today. I learned my lesson from our last battle. My punch lines are good and yours are better. One day, things will change. Until then, just cancel me out from roasting against you. Don't let me find out your jokes are not original; all the battles you won will have an asterisk beside it. Then Johnny Moffett will be known as the biggest cheater of all time. You would pass the New England Patriots and Mark McGuire for the top cheating spot. On a more serious note, what are your plans after high school?"

Johnny didn't want to hear that question. School was getting closer and closer to being out, so he would be hearing it more and more. Johnny told him, "If someone gave me a dollar for every time I heard that question, I would become a millionaire. The answer you're looking for doesn't exist. The time to make a decision is coming soon. My parents are on my case daily about my next move. College is the best choice. Why go to college and you don't know shit. Failing in college is a bigger let down. Sometimes I think robbing and stealing could be the best thing for me. We all heard that a thug lifestyle will lead to a sad ending. What if I could beat the odds?"

Eric did not like how Johnny was talking. He replied, "Johnny, you need to pump your brakes. Don't be foolish. Why continue to roll the dice with your life? Having money coming in stacks is tempting. I had thoughts of doing this shit forever. My common sense kicked in; it's just too risky."

Johnny said, "I've been holding a three weeks secret from my family. On a Saturday, the mailman brought a letter from USC. They want me to play ball for them."

Eric's eyebrows rose. He said, "USC! It's a no brainer, take the opportunity. They are one of the top colleges in the country. Even the celebrities come to their games, Diddy, Snoop, and Paris Hilton. I'm going to get you college ready even if it kills me. The NFL recruits many players from their school every year."

Johnny's learning abilities made some progress. His confident blossomed like a flower in the spring time. In one day, Eric had done more for Johnny's self-esteem than Willie in three years.

Zenobia and James were going over their partnership. Zenobia said to him, "The eagle has landed and I have a location for you to post up at. Larry and I discussed everything to get you started on the right track. The dope is bagged up and ready to go. Don't steal any money from your uncle and me. Seeing all that money could make you want to take a few stacks. We know the exact amount of "dough" you are supposed to bring back."

James wanted to prove he was trustworthy. He told her, "I have never stolen from you in my life. Although, I had many chances to steal. You should not worry about a thing. I will have the game down packed. The streets are mines for the taken."

His mother told him, "You are mighty cocky for a person who never been involved in the street life. This world is totally different than what you are custom to. Its okay to act like a tough guy, but don't overdo it. Act weak and the haters will eat you alive." She pulled out a Glock .40 handgun and stated, "I promise, this heat will get the haters to wave the white flag. It would swat them away like flies. If something happens and you have to pull it out, go ahead and put them to sleep. They could be carrying heat too. Never give a crack head or anybody else some credit. Most of these folks have a hard time paying their debt. Do not give up anything until you get the money first. It is the only way to conduct business. Someone might try to snatch your dope and if that happens, the money will come out of your pockets. Here's a mask to protect your identity."

James said, "You are trying to turn me into the Joker with this clown masks. The movie was cool, but the mask is ridiculous." The mask had a white face, red lip with a big evil smile, and the hair colors were green and black. The mask had five small holes in it, two where your eyes could see through, one in the middle of the big smile, and two more in the nose part. The mask was made to cover a person's entire face and head.

Zenobia responded, "It's kind of unorthodox, but take it and go to work. Here is the duffle bag with the products already inside. Tonight will be your first time on the job. Let me teach you how things will be operated." The black duffle bag was made of leather. She took out a sack of weed and two sacks of crack. Then she explained, "Every sack is worth twenty dollars other than the weed. The smaller sacks of weed are dime-sacks which are worth ten dollars. Five of the other bags are worth $100. Do you understand how we want this business handled?" James replied, "Yes, I remember everything you said and showed me." Zenobia said to him, "I had to show you how it's done. People take drug money very seriously, including your uncle. Both of us don't want to hear any excuses. Call me when you get finished. I'm going to drive you to the location."

Zenobia's car was a black Chrysler PT Dream Cruiser. Zenobia and James entered the car with her behind the wheel. She drove him to a small abandoned house. The house was used for drug dealing and prostitution. She told him on the way there, "Use the back window because it won't alloy people who are passing through to see what you are doing. All the fiends know to meet you back there." She gave him a key that could open the front and back door. It was turning night when she dropped him off. James went behind the house and used the key to enter. Once he walked in, he looked around the house to get familiar with everything. He found a chair and brought it to the back window. Now he had to wait on customers.

Redd and Lewis were on their way to a 7/11 store. Redd said to him, "I have the best X pills in my pocket. How many pills you want? My pills would normally cost $15 a piece. I'll give you the homeboy discount and make it $10 a piece."

Lewis responded, "Give me fifteen of those pills." They made the exchange, $150 for fifteen X pills. Redd went inside the store and purchased .5 of Ciroc Vodka, a six pack of Red Bull, a bag of ice and some red plastic party cups. He got back into his car and told Lewis, "Let's find a park, so we can get wasted." Redd drove off with the Peace Park in mind. Lewis gave Redd three X pills, so he could get in the zone too. He knew Redd would never use his own dope. Redd surprised him when he pulled out $40 worth of weed, so they could smoke. He mixed the Ciroc Vodka with the Red Bull inside of two cups filled with ice. He took the weed and made four blunts. They swallowed three X pills a piece and then the drinking and smoking started. They smoked up all the weed and drank most of the alcohol. Both of them were intoxicated and they felt good. Redd said, "Now it's time to party, dog."

James had customers coming back to back. James was shocked that he did not think selling drugs would be so easy. Even more stunning, one of his former teachers was a crack head. Mr. Smith was always telling him right from wrong in middle school. Mr. Smith was a great role model and all the students looked up to him. He used to be James's favorite teacher. Selling crack to Mr. Smith bothered him a little, but it was a part of the job. He thought, *If I refused to serve him, he would find someone else who will. It is just a matter of time before someone else I know comes up to me for some drugs. I guess no one is perfect after all.*

James made $250 in an hour and forty-five minutes. In his first night, James was already thinking about going into business for himself. He knew all the money he made working for his mother would get split unevenly three ways with him taking the short end of the stick. For right now, he was going to take this opportunity to learn everything about the dope game. James wanted to find another spot in the same area and charge the customers a cheaper price.

Redd and Lewis were walking on Tammy's yard and they were headed towards the front door. The closer they got to the house, the better they could hear the music. There were twelve people on the front lawn drinking beer. Redd knocked on the front door and he did not get an answer. He told Lewis, "Fuck it; let's go in." Redd opened the door and they heard 50 Cent's "In Da Club" song. A disco ball was hanging from the center of the ceiling. Most of the cheerleaders from Lewis's school were there. All the girls at the party were wearing a t-shirt with their panties on. The guys were wearing a t-shirt with their boxers on. The party took place in the living room and the dining room. The living room and the dining room did not have a door or a wall separating the two. Lewis and Redd were the only people there fully clothed. They stood side by side, watching all the fat asses shaking. Tammy spotted Redd and she began to walk over to speak with him. Redd told Lewis in his hear, "The girl with the purple shirt on is Tammy; she is heading our way." Her measurements were 36D-25-40. Tammy gave Redd a hug and a kiss on the face. Redd said in Lewis's ear, "I'm going to kick it with her for a minute. Enjoy yourself, man. Get behind one of these bad bitches and dance. One of them might want to fuck. Don't forget what I told you."

As soon as Redd left, a girl came up to Lewis for a dance and she grinded her booty on him. He placed his hands on her waist and his dick became hard while dancing behind her. The girl he was dancing with was a sexy blonde, but she could not stop him from thinking about how fine Tammy looked. She was a black girl with an enormous booty, huge breasts, and natural long curly hair. Tammy looked like Deelishis from the Flavor of Love Show. Tammy took Redd into the kitchen, so she could hear him better. He said to Tammy, "I have not received a call from you in minute. Me and my homie could be looking crazy out there. We are the only people with our clothes on. You could have given me a heads up."

Tammy replied, "I'm sorry about that. At least you are standing out in this crowd. It is how I found you, so quickly. Boy, I told you about wearing all red too much because it could get you "knocked off". It does look very good on you, though."

He responded, "Trust me; I'm waiting on someone to get out of line with me. My guns will be raid to these cock roaches. They will get exterminated fucking with me. What about you and me tonight? Are we going to fuck or not?"

Lewis had taken over the party. Once he stopped dancing, another girl came along and took him by the hand. Tammy handpicked DJ Roy Lee to DJ for her party. His music kept the party "crunk". Tammy used blue light bulbs for the party; she thought it would look more exciting. There were people dancing on the stairs and on top of the speakers. Tammy's home was a two-story house. Her mother and father were gone to New York City on vacation.

Tammy acted hard-to-get, but she wanted to screw just as bad as Redd did. She said to him, "We have not kicked it in almost two months. Out of the blue, you are here to fuck me. Your eyes are so red. You have been getting high and you are probably drunk too." She walked up close to him and stated, "That smells like the best weed California has to offer. I can get high just by standing next to you. I'm not some hoe you could fuck when you get horny. You know I am tired of having a sex partner; why can't you step your game up. Living like a gangster has your life messed up."

DJ Roy Lee played an R. Kelly song named "Feeling on Your Booty". Lewis was slow dancing with both hands full of ass. The women were coming to him because he looked very thuggish, attractive, and he walked with swagger. He did not look like the average white boy. The alcohol and drugs made him feel relaxed. He was sweating like he was running a marathon. Lewis was having so much fun that he forgot his number one goal to get laid. Redd was using his mouthpiece on Tammy, "You should be used to getting dick down by me. I know you are getting bored dealing with them. I know you miss my thug loving. Dr. Love prescribed this medicine for you to take. Let me lick that pussy until my tongue fall off. I'll have you speaking in French and you have not even taken the class."

Tammy was getting wet from listening to him talk dirty. She finally stopped playing hard-to-get, "Let me freshened up and then we could get freaky."

Redd said, "I need a big favor from you. My homeboy Lewis is still a virgin. The boy needs some ass bad. Talk to one of your friends and make sure she shows him a real good time."

Honey's eyes became big and she replied repeatedly, "He is a virgin. He is a virgin."

Redd acknowledged, "Yes. He has not had sex before. I know you though they did not exist. I've given him my word he would score tonight. He could be out there scared and too nervous to approach a female. Can you hook him up with some ass? He is a white boy; they are known to commit sui-cide if things do not go their way."

Honey agreed, "Boy, you are crazy. I will give him the

finest girls this party has to offer. He is getting ready to have a night that's impossible to forget. Now that is a promise from me to you. Tell your friend to walk up the stairs and turn left. Go to the last door; it will be across the hall from the bathroom. Wait about thirty minutes and then tell him someone is waiting for him in there." They separated, so she could take a quick shower.

A few people approached Redd for some weed and X pills, since he looked like a drug dealer to them. He started selling sacks of weed and X pills; the X pills were sold for $15 a piece and the weed was sold for $20 a sack. Redd and Lewis were dancing with some girls side by side. He looked at Lewis and he knew he was in the zone. Redd thought, *The whole time I've been gone, Lewis was having the time of his life. Damn, I trained him well. In twenty minutes, he will really have some fun. Both of us will knock some boots.*

Once the buzz spreaded around about Redd having drugs, about 80 percent of the party wanted something from him. His pockets became full of money in twenty minutes. He needed to get some more drugs; he had some more dope in his car. When Master P's "Freak Hoes" song went off, Lewis and the girl he was dancing with stopped. Redd came to him before another girl could grab his hand. He told Lewis in his ear, "There is a fine bitch waiting to fuck you upstairs. Listen to me closely. Once you make it upstairs, turn left. Go to the last door; it's across the hall from the bathroom. Handle your business. If you smash it good enough she would want to fuck again. Before you know it, you'll be given her booty calls in the middle of the night." Then Redd gave him three Lifestyle condoms. Redd went to his car while Lewis headed up stairs.

Thanks to Redd's X pills, the party became even wilder. Some girls were standing on the wall with their mouth wide open while the guys were shooting X pills in their mouths from five feet away. Girls started making out with other girls. Guys were trying to stick their dicks inside of the girls while dancing with them. Lewis had to squeeze between the people dancing on the stairs. He made it to the top of the stairs and went left. He could see the last room; it was across the hall from the bathroom. The bathroom door was open with the lights on. There were two bedrooms before the last one across the hall from the bathroom. His heartbeat began to pick up speed. As he walked down the hall by the first bedroom door, he heard a woman screaming, "Fuck me harder, baby! Make it hurt! Don't stop, keep it going faster!" He could also hear the bed squeaking. Then he continued to walk down the hall. As Lewis passed by the second door, he heard a guy yelling, "Ride this dick, bitch! Keep on riding this dick until you run out of breath!" The lady was screaming like someone was stabbing her with a butcher's knife.

Lewis was standing in front of the door that he was supposed to go in. He took a deep breath and opened the door. Then he walked into the room. The light was very dim, but he could see her sitting on the foot of the bed. He strained his eyes trying to see who she was, but he still was not able to see her. She said, "Come on over here, Sweety. I promise I won't bite, only if you want me to." Lewis lay next to a girl in bed; he didn't even know who she was. While he was lying on his back, she hopped on top of him. She said to him in a sexy voice, "Feel on my body." Lewis took both of his hands and squeezed her tender breast. Her breasts were so big; both of his hands could not cover one of them. He placed his hands on her waist and then he felt her flat stomach. The woman was wearing a bra and a pair of panties. He grabbed her ass tightly and he noticed out of all the asses he touched tonight, her ass was the fattest and the softest. Even her long curly hair smelled good. She said, "I know my body feels soft. Sometimes I can't keep my hands off myself. My body is the bomb."

Lewis said, "Girl, even though I can't see your face, I can tell you are a dime piece. Baby, you have it going on." They started making out and she placed her hand on his chest. His heart was beating faster than Sugar Ray Leonard on a punching bag. She could tell he was not use to being in a situation like this.

The woman wondered, *So he is a real virgin. I wanted to make sure he's a virgin before I have sex with him. He doesn't know how to kiss, but I can teach him. Making passionate love to a virgin is a fantasy of mine. He will be burning my phone up after tonight.* She stated, "One of my favorite positions is the doggy style. Can you fuck me like that? Get behind my ass and pull my panties down." She didn't have to tell him twice; he went straight to work. Lewis got up and pulled her panties down. Then he pulled his pants and boxers down. Lewis struggled to put the condom on. She wanted to laugh at him and she thought, *He does not know how to use a rubber. I'm really going to have fun with this kid. Since he is a virgin, I'm sure he doesn't have a STD.*

She told him, "Put the rubber down and go in me raw. It feels better that anyway."

Lewis threw the condom down on the floor. The woman

was already wet, so he went in with no problems. Lewis was giving it to her as hard as he could. He thought, *This feeling is incredible. Her pussy is better than any drug I ever took.*

She told him, "Wait a minute, let me turn around." The woman finished taking her panties off and turned around. She said, "Come on, I'm ready." Lewis climbed on top of her and she wrapped her legs around him. He went to work on her again. She had her eyes closed while moaning with enjoyment. She got on top of him and placed both of his hands on her ass. She tried to bang every inch of it inside of her. Lewis could no longer hold back from cumming. He said to her, "I'm getting ready to cumm; let me pull out. I held it back for as long as I could."

She told him, "Don't pull out and keep on going. I'm on birth control, so you won't have to worry. I want you to fill my pussy up with nut." Lewis came inside of her and it gave him an ultimate rush of a lifetime. She said, "Lewis, you are so wonderful in bed."

Lewis asked her, "How you know my name? Do I know who you are?"

She told him, "Turn on the lights if you want to see who I am. The switch is on the right side of the door."

Lewis got up and turned on the light. He was surprised to see the mystery woman's face. It was Tammy. He placed his right hand over his mouth and said, "Damn! I just had sex with someone who's too fine."

Tammy climbed out of bed with just her bra on. She walked up to him and said, "There's plenty more where that came from. You were pretty good for a white boy. The person who said white men have small dicks lied. I think you are cute, so this is not our last time meeting. Redd told me your name and I remembered how you looked when he was talking to you. Y'all came to my party being the only people fully dressed. Give me your phone number."

Lewis was still stunned. He forgot his phone number. Lewis told Tammy, "Give me a minute to remember my phone number. I have never seen a woman who looks better than you. Girl, you are all I need to get by. I'm more than willing to hook up with you again. What about Redd?"

She answered, "Redd should be dead soon. He knows the "crabs" on the eastside want him to rest in peace. They are going to keep coming after him until he is six feet deep. A target will be on your head and chest next, if you continue to hang out with him. Redd is cool, but I can't deal with all the crazy shit he does. He has to watch his back everywhere he goes; that's not a life worth living. Lewis, you could be what I'm looking for. Most women like older guys; I have a thing for younger guys."

After Lewis gave her his number, he said, "I will become whatever you want me to be and more." They started back hugging and kissing again.

Chapter 21

Redd was dancing with a girl and he was wondering, *Where did Tammy go? She was supposed to take a shower and come back to me. It has been a little over an hour since we talked. I think the bitch stood me up. I'm going to see what this black pretty young thing with her ass on me wants to do.*

He told the girl, "Come outside, so we could talk." Her height was 6'1 and she had the complexion of Rihanna. Her measurements are 32D-23-33. She had a body like a model. She was not thick, but sexy and slim. Her hair style was a small Afro. Both of them went outside together. Redd said to her, "I know you came to the party for the same reason as me, to have a good time. We can take our good time to a higher level in the back seat of my car. Tell me your name, boo."

She told him, "My name is Shemeka. You are mighty bold to ask a girl for sex that you don't know. You are right; I am here to have fun. My man is at home giving Kevin Durant all of his attention. He picked watching basketball over going out with his fiancé. What is your name?"

He answered, "My name is Redd." Then she said, "Well Redd, don't tell anybody we fucked. My fiancé and I are getting married next week. He is a very good and honest man. There are not too many guys like him around. Do you have a rubber?"

Redd replied, "I have a few of them. My car is parked

close to the corner." They walked to his car. Shemeka said, "Your car is cool and it looks like a gangster ride." She hopped in the back seat while he let the convertible roof down. Then Redd took a seat on the back seat. Shemeka took off her tight white t-shirt and her black silk panties. She lay down on her back and then Redd put on the condom. He got on top of her with the thought of beating the pussy unconscious. They began having sex with each other. He was drilling it better than a construction worker.

Redd's luck had changed for the better. Shemeka came to the party just to have sex. As long as there were no strings attached, she was ready to spread her legs as far as she could get them. Tammy was the only girl Redd had strong feelings for. In reality, he loved her ever since they were together in high school. Tammy used to be in love with him too and now she saw him as a sex partner. Redd just wanted to fuck all the rest of the girls with no emotional connection. He was more than willing to have sex with no strings attached.

Redd had made over $800 at the party. Everything other than not hooking up with Tammy went his way at the party, he made some money, danced with a lot of ladies, and he had sex.

Lewis also had a fantastic time. He danced with more girls than any other guy at the party. Having sex with Tammy was like winning the lottery for him. Tammy took a shower and then she put on a red t-shirt and a different pair of panties. Lewis and Tammy went back down stairs together. While Lewis and Tammy were dancing together, Redd was still showing Shemeka a good time in the back seat of his car.

James had made $1,060 and his duffle bag was still kind of full. He became tired, so he called his mother. She answered her phone by saying, "I thought you were going to spend a night down there."

James responded, "My first night on the job was good. I am ready to go home. My eyes are dropping lower and lower."

Zenobia told him, "I'll pick you up. Did you make a least $1000, we were hoping so? Today is the 15th; a lot people cashed their checks."

James said, "I made a little over $1000 because people were coming all night long. Don't worry, the mask stayed on like it's a part of my skin. Let me stop lying; it came off when I was not doing business."

His mother wanted him to stay out there until the fiends stopped passing through. Since it was his first night, she decided not to be hard on him, yet. She told James, "I am proud of you, Son. Keep up the hard work if you want to be successful in this line of work. I am on my way, so sit tight." Zenobia jumped in her car to get James.

Redd and Shemeka came back in the party together. He saw Lewis dancing behind Tammy and he did not think anything was suspicious. DJ Roy Lee playfully said on a microphone behind the turntable, "I would like to thank everybody for coming out tonight. Tammy, keep on having these amazing parties. I love you, girl! Now where is my check? I have not received a dime since I been here. Now you know this bullshit is against the minimum wage law." Then DJ Roy Lee began to laugh, he received $400 a week ago. Then everybody in the party started laughing. People began walking out of the house.

Redd told Tammy, "You have done a disappearing act."

She responded, "My mom called and she would not stop talking. She was telling me about the great time they are having in New York City. We will get another chance to have some fun." She gave Redd a hug and when he turned his back, she gave Lewis a tight hug and a kiss on the lips.

Redd turned back towards Tammy and he said, "Have your cell phone close by tomorrow. I am going to give you a call around 10:00am. Tonight, something kind of special was supposed to happen between us. You know I'm your first and last true love. It's impossible to get me out of your system. Let's bounce, Lewis; Tammy, I'll deal with your sexy ass later."

Lewis said to Tammy, "Your party was off the chain. It was nice to meet you. Take it easy."

Tammy told both of them, "Y'all need to make it home safe. There are a lot of drunk drivers out there. Most of them left my house a few minutes ago."

Redd and Lewis headed back to the car. Lewis started bragging before they could get half way off the road that Tammy lived on. "Tonight might be the greatest night ever. Every girl at the party wanted to dance with me. The X pills with the Ciroc Vodka and Red Bull mixed are a damn good combination."

Redd said, "Mr. Luck, I know you danced a hole in the floor. What I don't know is what happened in that bedroom. Did you use your anaconda? How was your first piece of ass?"

Lewis was not going to tell him about the spectacular sex he had with Tammy. Lewis wanted to tell him something and leave Tammy's name out. Lewis answered, "Hell yea, it went down. She was so fine; she'll give Megan Fox a run for her money. Baby girl wanted me to smash it from the back. Being the man that I am, her wishes were my command. After that, she lied down and let me beat it out the frame from the front.

Having sex was ten times better than I expected. She climbed on top me; I all most nutted right way. I thought she was a jockey the way she rode my dick. What about your night?"

Redd said arrogantly, "Do you even have to ask? I am the one who trained you. All the bitches at the party wanted me. I could've fucked any girl there. Thanks to my drugs, there is over $800 in my pockets. When you went up the stairs, I went to my car for some more drugs. The chicken head who gave me some action is bad. Her name is Shemeka and she's getting married next week. We could have made a baby in my back seat. She became so wet; I thought I had to crack these doors and let it pour out. Look at the time, your parents is going to disfigure you."

Lewis stated, "I'm a grown ass man and they better not fuck with me. The night has been perfect and it will stay that way."

Redd said to Lewis, "My tank is on E -- help me find a gas station. We just passed one five minutes ago. If gas prices get any higher, I'm going to Wal-Mart to buy a bike."

Lewis was getting very tired; Tammy took most of his energy from him. The time was 3:03am and Lewis was getting even more exhausted as time passes. Lewis said, "I'm extremely tired. My soft bed seems like the best place to be. Please hurry and find some gas."

Redd spotted A Texaco with six gas pumps outside. He told Lewis, "I have to go inside the store because I don't have a card." Redd drove to the Texaco for gas. He paid for $30 worth of gas inside the store and then he went back outside to use a pump. While pumping the gas, Tammy crossed his mind. He really was looking forward to fooling around with her at the party. He figured there would be another chance to bend her over. A dark blue 81'Cadillac Deville with four doors drove by them slowly. Then a hand reached out of the front passenger window, holding a Glock .44 and making the bullets fly. Redd dropped the gas pump and ran to the front of the car. Then he ducked down.

Lewis got scared when he heard the shots. He pulled out his .9mm handgun. Most of the back window of the car was already shattered, leaving glass on the back seat, trunk, and on the ground. Two armed guys hopped out of the '81 Cadillac Deville back seats and started to walk towards Redd's car. Lewis turned around and started blazing his .9mm handgun through the back glass; what was left of it. The two men ran back into the Cadillac and the car drove off fast. Redd was a gangster and he did not fire one shot at his enemies. He stayed hidden by ducking down on his knees like a coward. Lewis got a good look at the car as it drove off. Then he asked himself, **Where is Redd? I hope he did not get hit.** Lewis got out of the car to search for him. He did not have to search too long at all. Lewis saw Redd hiding in front of the car, shaking while ducking down. Lewis thought, **This fool is not a gangsta, he's a "wangsta". He has two guns on him and one in the trunk; I believe he did not shoot one muthafuckin time. He is too scary to gang bang. Tammy is correct; he will be dead soon. He will not get me caught up in the mix. If I keep hanging with him, those Crips will eventually use their toasters to heat me up. Then my face will be on Steven's t-shirt.** He said to Redd, "They are gone. Let's get the fuck out of here."

Redd got up breathing hard, sweating, and his heart was

pounding as he entered the car. The workers at Texaco called the police while Redd and Lewis were leaving.

Redd placed his right hand on his chest and said, "Those sons of bitches tried to smoke me. The Eastside Crips finally caught me slipping. I tried to shoot back, but it seems like every time I looked up a bullet was flying over my head. They shot out all the windows on my ride. We need to retaliate on those crabs because this bullshit means war."

There was no way Lewis was going to help him fight against any gang. He knew Redd was not going to fight back because he saw him in action, first hand. He found out how risky chilling with Redd could be. Redd showed him he was completely spineless. Lewis pondered, *Steven and the rest of my crew are not real gangsters, but if their lives are in jeopardy, they would open fire on anybody. Redd needs to turn in his Bloods membership card. It must have taken only good health to become a Blood. The only thing that's keeping him alive is his mother's prayers. I want to tell his sorry ass, hell no, fight your on battles. There are no plans of revenge going on in my mind.* Lewis said to him, "I'm not a member of the Bloods. There are many of them and one me. Living in fear is not for me."

Redd became a little upset about Lewis not wanting to get involved, "Man, you are a little shook up, that's all. We did not get hit by any shots. Look at my windows, it will cost over a "G" to get them replaced. Fuck! Those Crips were aiming at your head too. In my world, payback is called an eye for an eye. They lit my car up, so we should do a drive by on their "cribs". I seen that dark blue Cadillac Deville; it belongs to a guy name C-Loc. I'm one hundred percent sure it was him and his boys. Some fools just can't get over the past. About five months ago, I done a stick up on him and took his dope. Something told me to kill his ass when I had a chance."

Lewis stated, "Five months ago is not the past. C-Loc should be steamed; he was robbed for his dope. They spit a few bullets my way. Give me a chance to think about whether I want to retaliate or not." Lewis told Redd a lie, so he would stop talking about it for right now. He would never jump in a war between the Bloods and Crips. It would definitely be foolish because Lewis had enough money coming his way to be rich. After one night with Tammy, he would rather pick up a rose than a gun. Plus, Tammy would stop fooling with him if she knew he was gang affiliated.

When Lewis entered his home, he did not hear anything, which was a good sign. Lewis was also looking around everywhere because he knew Sam could have another trick up his sleeve. Lewis walked up to his bedroom and went to bed. Lewis thought, *I will never forget this night, for as long as live. In one night, I transformed from a man to a legend. Redd has to fight his on war and I will try to stay my distance from him. Tammy and I will get a lot closer. When my eyes first caught a glimpse of her beauty, I knew she was the one for me. Redd is stupid for choosing gang banging over her. Redd will turn green if he finds out that Tammy and I are getting it on.*

In the morning around 10:00, Redd gave Tammy a call on his cell phone. Her phone rang until the answering machine came on. Redd said to himself, "She ignored my phone call. What is wrong with that bitch? When I met her at the party, everything was cool. She even agreed to drop those panties for me. When we separated, something must have happened. I do not believe she stayed on the phone with her mother for that long. Tammy doesn't miss my calls when I tell her the time to expect it. I will get to the bottom of this shit. She could have fucked another man at the party. Maybe I am jumping into a conclusion too soon. Tammy might have a legit reason for not answering my call. I'll try to contact her in two more hours. A mechanic has to fix my car because I can't drive it around with all the windows shot out."

Tammy did not answer her phone because she was already on the phone talking to Lewis. Lewis gave her a call the minute his eyes opened. "Those Crips came out of nowhere and attack us. I was changing the radio station in Redd's car and he was pumping gas. Their guns sounded like the ones Rambo be shooting. The bullets shattered his windows and caught both of us off guard. There was something else that pissed me off, Redd had two guns on him and he did not do shit. While I fired back at them, Redd hid in front of the car, ducking down. I had to shoot through the back window. We would have been dead if I did not carry any heat. When they noticed another person was shooing at them, they disappeared."

Tammy said, "It is a good thing that you didn't get hurt or killed. Hanging with that clown is suicidal. You have to lose all contact with him, to stay alive. There is a weak spot I have in my heart for him because we known each other for a long time. He will notice that both of us stopped talking to him. If Redd gets smart enough to put two and two together, he will come after you. Scary people are indeed the most dangerous people. You are a nice guy and I would not want you to get hurt. My ex will try to make sure I don't start a relationship with you or anybody else. Walking away from me would not be such a bad idea. He is going to have a serious problem with us going together. You would be dating me at your own risk."

Lewis responded, "I am not scared of Redd. He taught me a lot things and I do respect him. If he tries to hurt me, I will defend myself the best way I know can. Redd carries a gun around and so do I. We can battle with the guns or man to man; it's whatever he wants to do. He knows I'm not a push over. A real man would move on if a woman doesn't want him anymore. Hopefully, he's an authentic dude. Enough of talking about him, it is all about us. When your parents coming back home?"

Tammy answered, "They have another five days on vacation. Let me guess; you want to come back over here. As long as they are gone, you are more than welcome to come over here. We can have a good time chatting over a nice dinner."

Tammy had changed the way Lewis thought. Her effect on him was very positive. He wanted to put the thug life behind him and live an honest life style. Just the sound of Tammy's voice placed a smile on his face. He truly believed that Tammy was the finest-looking girl in the world. He told her, "There is one stipulation before I come over; you must cook all the food."

Tammy said, "Of course you can depend on me to prepare a meal. Only a professional cook is supposed to stand over a stove. The first time I saw your face, I hoped we could get a chance to talk. Instead, something better happened between us last night. My friends would be shocked if they found out, me and a white boy hook up. My girlfriends are into thugs and rough necks, but I'm more opened minded about different men. The color of a person skin doesn't mean anything to me. As long as he could treat me like a lady, we won't have any problems. Can you treat me like a queen and always show me some respect? If you can, my heart will belong to you."

Lewis told her with poise, "I would run through fire for your love. There is not a mountain I won't climb to grab your heart. Do you have a car? My ride is coming soon."

Tammy replied, "You noticed how big my house is; the real question should have been what kind of car I have. I have a blue Lexus. It's my second car, Lewis. My first car was a Pontiac and it was traded in for my Lexus. Give me the directions to your house. I'll pick you up when it's time." Lewis gave her the directions, so they could meet up later on.

Redd called Tammy again, but she did not answer her phone. Lewis sent Eric, James, Willie, and Johnny a text message and it read: 'We have a meeting tomorrow night. I will announce my plans for the next mission. Let's get this money.' He would have sent Steven a text message, but Steven didn't have a cell phone.

Eric called Steven and gave him the message. Steven was glad to know that the big favor Lewis had been talking about was soon to be revealed. He was tired of guessing what was on Lewis's mind. Steven had a feeling it was going to be shocking. Steven took his brand new clothes out of the bags and laid them on the bed. He tried the outfits on to see how they would look on him while staring at himself in his bedroom's mirror, on the wall. He was very pleased with the choices they made. He started to think about how God had been so good to him. He and Barbara moved to a bigger and better house. He finally got his hands on some name brand clothes.

Steven had his mind set to never be poor again. He had a feeling that all those crimes would come back to haunt him and he was worried about it. Steven was starting to wonder often, could God forgive him for his sins?

James was at home watching the NFL games and for the third week in a row his teams did what he wanted them to do. James was dancing and jumping around in his bedroom. He was also hollering, "Wooo! Wooo!"

Zenobia could hear him in the living room. She said to herself, "He must be watching the NFL games again. It seems like his team is always winning. He did a great job selling dope for his uncle and me. Hopefully, James can stay focus and every dream he has will get achieved. I counted the money and saw the amount of drugs he had left, everything is the correct. He did not take anything from us. Now he has proven himself to be trustworthy. Trusting someone is hard to do these days, when it comes down to money."

Once James claimed down, he wondered about different ways to become his own man. His mother and uncle only gave him $260 out of $1060. He felt like they pimped him. James's greed blinded him from seeing a lot of the money coming back to him. Zenobia would pay bills and buy food for the both of them. James didn't invest any money on the drugs he sold and he expected them to break bread with him evenly. After one night of a little success, he wanted to operate a better business than his uncle and mother. He wanted his mother to work for him. James pondered, *I have to get deep into the streets to find some else with a mass amount of drugs. Uncle Larry is not the only person who can pull some strings around here. My shit will be better* *and cheaper than Uncle Larry. I can be a kingpin, if I put my mind to do it. I'm seventeen years old with over a $100,000 in my hands. My uncle could dislike my move, but he can't knock the hustle. Lewis had a lot of time to think about the crew's next move. He will come up with something that's going to work. Soon, I will have $300,000 on top of what I already have. My uncle could teach me how to weigh, bag, and cook dope. Once he teaches me, I will immediately stop fucking with him. Anybody who's on top, had to double cross a few people. It's time to call Frank about my money. With my winnings, I have to go shopping.* He grabbed his cell phone out of his pocket and called Frank.

Frank was too busy to answer his phone. James decided to visit the Touchdown bar. He wanted to speak with Frank. As he became very close to the bar, he called Frank on his cell phone again. Frank answered his cell phone, "Hello."

James replied, "Come outside, I'm already out here."

Frank said, "Give me five minutes to come outside."

Once Frank came outside, he had some bad news to give James, "Sorry, you did not win this week. The point spread went up on the Colts and the Titans game before it began. I should have called you and said something."

James didn't believe Frank was telling him the truth. "Stop joking around and give me my money. My cash and I are a duo like Kobe and Gasol. I know you are tired of me winning, but that is what a winner does."

Frank explained again, "The point spread changed before the game. At first the Colts had to win by two points and then it changed to three points. I can't give a person who lost some money. You were mighty close, but only one game stopped you from collecting your money."

James saw the expression on Frank's face and knew he was serious. James lost his cool. "Y'all are some cheating sons of bitches. You and this bar can kiss my ass. These stupid bitches knew I could not lose. Frank, your old ass probably told them to change the point spread to keep me from winning. Jealousy is written all over your face."

Frank responded, "Look at all the things I have done for you and this is how you repay me. Goodbye and don't call me again. Don't come up here to bother me again." Frank turned around, getting ready to walk back into the bar.

James grabbed his arm and said, "Do not walk away from me because we are not finish talking."

Frank turned around and told him, "Are you retarded? We are done! Let me get back to work!"

James agreed, "Alright, we are done." James let his arm go and pretended to walk away. Then he turned back around swiftly and sucker-punched Frank. He hit Frank with a "One Hitter Quitter" in the face. While Frank was laid out counting sheep, James jetted away.

Meanwhile at Tammy's place, Tammy and Lewis were eating dinner together. After one night of sexing Tammy, Lewis was ready to give her the world and more. He really didn't know Tammy, so tonight he wanted to get that chance. They were sitting down at the kitchen table, eating and talking. The kitchen was huge; everything in the kitchen was large from the refrigerator to the stove. The wooden kitchen table was ten feet long with ten wooden chairs under it. A wooden cabinet was over the white sink with the clear faucet and knob. There was also a black and blue colored marble floor in the kitchen.

Tammy and Lewis were sitting across from each other at the middle of the table. Tammy fried shrimps and French fries for them to eat. Lewis told her, "Tell me something about you."

Tammy responded, "I'm twenty-two years old. My favorite color is purple. As you know, I'm into younger guys. My dream is to become a lawyer because women who work a profession like that are considered smart and strong. Shrimps with French fries are my favorite dinner. So it is your turn to tell me something about you."

Lewis replied, "I am eighteen years old and my goal is to become some type of business man. I would love to own a business that belongs to me. Even though this word can kill the mood, red has always been my favorite color. My choices for food are pizza, hamburgers, pasta, and I have love for shrimps too. Most of the time, I'm confuse about things. For example, which directions I want to take with my life. The next question is for you. Why did you have sex with me on the first night?"

Tammy answered, "In the back of my mind, I knew that question had to come up. I'm far from being a hoe. You and Redd are the only guys I had sex with. He told me that you were a virgin. It is hard to find a guy with less or no sex experience. Every guy wants to be a player these days. The average good looking guy probably had sex with over thirty women. To train a virgin how to make love was always a desire of mine. I saw you; a virgin who looked good which made you hard to resist. The temptation made me give it up; meeting another young virgin might never happen. I have a question for you; did you come to my party just to screw?"

Lewis answered, "Do you want the truth? You can't handle the truth! I'm just playing with you. Redd promised me it would happen at your party. He said my virginity was going to be kept a secret. Redd leaked my business for a good reason and it worked out for me. One day, I will be able to give you the world. I will take you shopping and get your nails done, including your toes. We could find the best spa. And last, but not least, give you my heart."

After they ate dinner, she gave him a tour around the house while holding his hand. Then she took him back home.

Chapter 22

The next night, The Teenage Mafia went to their hideout and Lewis was ready to lay down his master plan. Lewis started the meeting by saying, "It feels like a long time has passed since we met up like this. All six members of The Teenage Mafia are here. Our journey had some ups and downs, but we pulled through it all. What I'm about to say is going to be very sickening. All of us will have a part in murdering my parents."

Steven was in disbelief. "The big favor is to kill Sam and Jessica. Man, you can't be serious about that. Parents are supposed to get on your nerves. The money sounds good, but your parents living sounds better. Your parents treated me well, all these years. Maybe you need some more time to think."

James did not give a damn and he showed it. "Maybe Steven should shut the fuck up. I don't mean to be rude, but Lewis is his own man. He doesn't need anybody to help him make decisions."

Steven wanted to bust James in the mouth, but he kept his cool. He told James, "I know nothing can get between you and your money, but this situation is very different."

Johnny said to them, "We have already killed two policemen, knocked out an old lady, and robbed many people. All of us are on the road to hell; we might as well go in style. Lewis has a good reason for coming up with this idea. Lewis, tell us why you want them to be gone."

Everybody other than James was waiting on a real excuse to kill Lewis's parents. Lewis knew they would want to know the reason behind this mission. He was not going to tell them about him getting child molested and raped a few weeks ago. Lewis was willing to tell them about the abuse he suffered growing up. "My dad has been putting his hands on me for years. He would come home drunk and give my mom and me a hard time. My mom was happy to see us fight because he was not beating her head in. She hit me in the head with a vase when I tried to stop him from fighting her. For years, she watched him abuse me mentally and physically, without helping me by calling the police or trying to stop it herself. My dad and I had a fight recently; it was a great battle. I thought I had that bastard beat, but he got the best of me. When you fuck over a person for a long time, eventually they will get a chance to fuck over you. Especially, if that person has never cost them any harm; the revenge is even worst. My life has been a living hell and I can no longer deal with it. Willie, I lied to you. The reason my hands are not behind the wheel is that my parents don't give a fuck about me. Why am I walking to school with four cars parked outside? Steven only knew about the verbal abuse and the non-support I endured over the years. Basically, they are rich and I am poor. It never crossed your minds that Lewis is rich, but why is he committing armed robberies."

Willie said, "Come on, Lewis. Everything can get worked out. Have you ever thought about getting you and your parents some kind of counseling? Think about the future; this is something you will regret forever. Do you think getting back at them like this is a little extreme?" No one could have guessed that he wanted them to kill his parents.

Johnny stated, "Lewis has been through a lot of shit. The way his parents done him, they don't deserve to live. Real parents would never neglect their child."

James said, "It is Lewis's parents and if he wants them to disappear, we have to ride for him. Some of y'all are taking this shit too personal; it is strictly business. I look at it like another day at the office. Let's go ahead and waste them. They are not real parents, anyway."

Lewis told them, "I heard enough of everybody's opinions. We have to vote on this shit. If a tie happens, a coin has to be flipped. Everybody who thinks my parents should die, raise your hand up."

Lewis, James, and Johnny put their hands up. Steven and Willie kept their hands down. Eric was the last vote they were waiting on. Eric's right hand was going half way up and down. Then he said, "Fuck it." He raised his right hand all the way up. Eric told Lewis, "You can count me in. They will feel the wrath of The Teenage Mafia. That punk ass dad of yours will never put his hands on you again. Your mom will wish she had put up some kind of effort to stop him."

Lewis said to them, "Four to two, we are going to kill them. Everyone come in closer, so you could understand me better. I have a few house keys and Steven will get one of them. I will cut the alarm off before y'all even get there. My parents gave me the code when they wanted me to turn it on and off. Most of the times, my parent goes to bed early. Before y'all come over my house, the ringer on y'all cell phones should be off or left in the car. Before turning the ringer off, wait for a call from me. I will let someone know when to come over my house. We have to make it look like a burglary-homicide. My parents sleep with the door locked. I am going to make one of them open the door. Then all of you will run in there and kick their asses. My dad has a gun in there somewhere. The best thing that could happen is for him to open the door. We could hurry up and get him out of the way. You all will do the dirty work while I watch. The reason is that no evidence can get on my clothes or skin. Someone will give them one shot to the head, apiece. I would not waste too many bullets on these pieces of trash. Someone will have to rough me up too. I want to look like I was attacked. The police have to see no evidence that could lead them back to me. The only thing that could fuck my plan up is if they never open the door. If we break the door down, it will give Sam enough time to get his gun. Trust me; we do not want his hands on a heater. I have been haunting with him before; he is very accurate when shooting at his targets. Sam is good enough to be a sniper. Any money or other valuable things that you find in their room, it's yours. Since I am the only child, I will own everything they have and that is how I plan on paying you all $300,000 apiece."

Steven began thinking about all the good times he shared with Sam and Jessica. They had shared plenty of laughter together over the years. Now Lewis wanted them taken out of the game. Steven had a lot of love for Sam and Jessica. He started to believe he wouldn't be able to help them murder Sam and Jessica. Lewis said it would be harder on him than everybody else.

Steven said to Lewis, "It is never too late to change your mind. We have all had some bad times at home. You are almost out of school, so moving out would be a better idea. I have been around you long enough to know there is a smart brain inside that head of yours. We have made enough money to start a business together. Success would be the best and the sweetest revenge in this case. It would crush them to know you are doing great things without them."

Lewis thought, *Steven is making a lot of sense. My parents saw me as a dummy and an embarrassment to our family. Those jackasses failed to realize that not everyone will make the honor roll in school. I have given school my best shot and they never motivated me to do better. My parents have done too much damage to me. Murdering them has been on mind for a long time. Even though Steven is right, my parents must die.* Lewis told Steven, "Thanks for your concern, but I will not change my mind. Does anyone have any questions? Friday night will be the last chapter in their book. Around 10:30, they should be sleep. Fuck my parents; think about $300,000 and what you could do with it. This meeting is officially over with."

James was very angry because he thought Steven was going to change Lewis's mind. Lewis and Steven didn't need the money if they put their cash together and started a business, James knew it. He did not want to miss out on three hundred grand. Being around Steven was starting to irritate him because he was always talking positive. James thought Steven should become a kindergarten teacher.

Eric took Lewis and James home while Steven and Johnny were in the car with Willie. Willie said to Steven, "Lewis has gone too far this time. Killing his parents is the most insane mission we ever faced. There is something else Lewis is not telling us. He is living in hell, but I don't think it's bad enough to kill them. Why not move out? He has more than enough money to live on his own. My opinion, Lewis is hiding an even darker secret. What that secret is? We may never know. He will not tell us because it could be too embarrassing. I have a lot of secrets that I'm taking to the grave with me."

Steven replied, "Willie, you are right. Lewis is hiding something else from us. There is a darker side to his story. He probably told us half of it. It could have been a million different things that could have happened at his home. Whatever happened there had to be very serious. Sam and Jessica hid their problems at home well. You would think they have a perfect relationship."

Johnny finally spoke, "Y'all are wasting time trying to play Sherlock Holmes. No one will figure this shit out. There are so many things could happen behind closed doors. Only Lewis and his parents know what is going on behind closed doors at their home. After Friday, Lewis will be the only person who knows what happened there."

Steven added, "Lewis and I are like brothers. I always thought he would never keep a serious secret from me. Even as kids, we would talk about everything. He knows me better than anybody and I know him better than anybody. One day, he will tell me the rest of the story. Whether its tomorrow or a couple years from now, he is going to spill the beans."

The next day after school, Redd gave Lewis a call while he was walking home. Lewis wondered if he should answer or not. He decided to answer the call.

"What's up?" Redd said, "Every since you got some pussy, your head gotten bigger. I'm just fucking with you, man. When will we get high again? There's plenty of that green sticky icky icky over here. The cocaine and X pills are calling your name. I can come over there to pick you up. My windows were replaced with new ones. They even cleaned the inside of my car, so when you take a seat, it want cut your ass."

Lewis told him, "That's sounds good, but I'm tired right now. We can get together later on. I'll holler at you around 7:30pm. Then we can get fucked up."

Redd said, "Alright, that time is okay with me." They got off the phone with each other. Lewis said to himself, "Why he had to call me? I don't want anything to do with anymore. It would be smart to stop hanging with him at a slow pace. Hopefully, he won't have any hard feelings towards me. Tammy won't like the fact that I have to kick it with him a few more times." Actually, Lewis was not tired. Once he made it home, he played NBA Live 2010 on his PlayStation 3 in his bedroom.

Eric was sitting in the living room watching TV. He was trying to find something good to watch. Eric stopped flipping the TV because he wanted to look at the news. Jessie Ross, a news reporter said, "Just in, there was a body of a white female found in a black garbage bag. She was fatally shot in the chest. The police department said the shot could have come from a .22 handgun. After being murdered, she was thrown off shore. The young lady looked like she is in her early twenties. The body has not been identified yet. If anybody knows anything, contact your local police department." Eric was frightened because he started to believe the police would soon find out what really happened. Eric thought Rebecca's body would never be found. He put the accident behind him.

CSI Miami was one of Eric's favorite shows but it raised his belief that the murder could be traced back to him. Eric began to panic while he walked all around the house. Eric said to himself, "Damn! I am going to serve a life sentence behind bars. The pigs will snoop around here, asking my mom and me some questions. Rebecca should have never come over here without calling me. Damn, I have to call Honey and Steven to let them know what I heard on the news. I am going to call Steven first." He grabbed his cell phone out of his pocket and called Steven.

Steven answered the house phone, "Hello."

Eric told Steven nervously, "I was watching the news and they said the body has been found. We could be in some serious shit, man. I'm too young to spend the rest of my life in prison. Look at how skinny I am; someone could easily make me their bitch. You know I could not survive in jail."

Steven could hear the panic in Eric's voice and he wanted to calm him down. He thought Eric sounded like he was the one who pulled the trigger. Steven was a little shaken up by the news too, but he kept his composure. Steven calmly said, "Look at the bright side, I'm pretty sure the people who known her knew she was a prostitute. People come up missing all the time; anybody could have done it. A fine girl like that probably had a million clients. As long as a witness doesn't come out and say something, everything will be okay. Cool down, man, you are not going to jail and neither is Honey and I. Speaking of Honey, have you told her anything yet?"

Eric replied, "No, I have not said anything about it to her. I was going to tell her next, right after we get off the phone. She's always talking about you and how your help save the day. Maybe you should give her a call."

Steven stated, "I might give her a call to see how she is

doing. But for right now, telling Honey what you seen on the news would be a bad idea. She might not be truly over what happen to Rebecca. If you tell Honey, it would make her worry even more. There is no reason for anyone to panic right now."

Eric said, "Steven, you are unbelievably smart. Sometimes it seems like you are the guy with all the answers. Just like me when it comes down to a test in school. It is a good thing I spoke to you first instead of Honey. Honey and I would have been two terrified and worried people."

Later on, Lewis went to Redd's home and bought more dope. Lewis was snorting cocaine and smoking weed while he was there. Redd helped Lewis smoke up his weed as usual. Redd told Lewis, "Every since the party, Tammy has not said a word to me. She has been ignoring all my calls and text messages. What is wrong with her? I thought about coming over her house unexpectedly last night. She makes me want to stalk her ass."

Lewis said, "I thought you were a player. Why are you stressing over her like that? Why would she be pissed off at you for? Just think about it hard and it would pop up in your mind."

Redd responded, "Shemeka could have told her something. I should rough up that chicken head feathers. Shemeka is a private person; she would never put her business in the streets. She loves her fiancé too much to put their relationship at risk. Then their wedding day is next week." As Redd continued to get high off the chronic, he began to relive the night at the party, in his mind and he started with talking to Tammy in the kitchen. *The conversation was going good between us. I asked her to hook Lewis up with one of her friends. She agreed to get him laid. Then she gave me the directions to give him. The directions were to go all the way up the stairs. Then turn left and go to the last door across the hall from the bathroom. Whose bedroom is across the hall from the bathroom? It is Tammy's bedroom! We always fucked in her bedroom and her friends were never allowed to get busy in there. The guests always used the two guest rooms, garage, and the bathroom. Lewis went up stairs and fucked my bitch in her bedroom.*

Redd stood up and yelled, "At the party, you fucked my girl! You are a no good, back stabbing son of a bitch. Muthafucka, I was going to find out, once all the pieces of the puzzle were put together. Both of y'all need to be slapped by me."

Lewis was already standing up and he said, "She is just one girl. What happened to all that boss player talk? It won't be hard for you to find another girl. You talked about Tammy like she is just another girl on your list. We should not be beefing over her."

Redd pulled out a .45 handgun from his pocket and aimed it at Lewis. Then Lewis pulled out a .9mm handgun and aimed at Redd. Redd screamed, "I should shoot your monkey looking ass! Everything you know, I taught it to you. Without me, your virgin days would have lasted ten more years, cracker. All you will ever be is a piece of white trash."

Lewis was not going to keep quiet while Redd talked trash, "Look coward, when those real gangsters came after you, I swear you disappeared like a magician. There was a gun in your pocket and another one in your sock. Why didn't you bust back at them? I grabbed my heater and made it blast. Your worthless life was saved by me."

Redd said, "Get the fuck out my crib and walk your Fred Flintstone ass home. Watch your back because I will be coming for you."

Lewis told him, "Watch my back, fuck that sneaking shit. Let's go at it with the guns right now. Tammy gave me some pussy and it was delicious. Do something about it, bitch! Do something about it."

Redd just kept his gun aimed at Lewis. He did not want to have a shoot out or a fight with his hands. Lewis walked out backwards with his gun still pointed at Redd. As Lewis walked down the stairs, he could not believe Redd figured out everything so quickly. Lewis knew a beef with Redd could cost him his life. Redd's plan would be to catch him slipping. He had to call Tammy to let her know what happened.

She answered his phone call, "Hey baby."

He said to her, "We have a major problem on our hands. Redd figured out everything."

Tammy asked, "How did he find out?"

Lewis told her, "I don't know how he found out. We had words and now, he is coming after me. That clown pulled a gun out on me and then I returned the favor. His eyes turned dark red and if my gun wasn't on me, he would have killed me. Everything went down in his living room. I told Redd he should move on and it went in one ear and out the other. This situation can only end in blood. Either, he is going to smoke me or I'm going to smoke him. He's deeply in love with you."

Tammy responded, "The way that shit went down, he must be dangerously in love with me. Redd needs to wake up and realize that it's more women on this earth than me. I'm sure somebody wants to be in a relationship with a gangster. Redd and I need to have a serious talk. He will have to leave us alone. We haven't been together for that long and shit is getting out of hand. I am kind of worried about your safety."

"You don't have to worry about my safety. Defending myself has never been a problem for me. Let's hope Redd will just move on. If he doesn't leave us alone, something bad will happen to him, not me. This is a promise from me to you; everything is going to be okay. Redd doesn't put any fear in my heart," Lewis said. "Are you walking?"

Tammy said. "I can hear the cars passing by."

"Yes, I am out here walking," Lewis responded.

"Tell me your location, so I can give you a ride. Redd's house is a long way from your home,"Tammy said.

"I'm near the 99 cent store on Wilson Street and it's not far from where Redd lives at. A matter of fact, it is around the corner from Redd's home. You must really care about me to hop out of your bed to pick me up at night."

"I'm not lying down; actually, I'm watching my favorite T.V show. Stay put, Lewis; give me a few minutes to get there,"Tammy told him.

Tammy got in her Lexus to pick him up. Once Lewis jumped into the car with her, he gave her a soft kiss on the lips. Tammy noticed the strange smell on his clothes. "What is that strange smell on your clothes? You and Redd have been smoking weed together. Smoking it every day is a problem," Tammy stated. Tammy drove Lewis home because he had school tomorrow.

Redd was sitting down on the couch heartbroken. He

was only trying to help Lewis out and it backfired on him. All he could think about was Lewis betraying him. He thought they were developing a true friendship. He was on the couch crying a river. Redd was in disbelief because Tammy dropped her panties faster than you could blink. Maybe he gave Lewis too much game. Redd began to think about the night he took Tammy to the prom, the two Christmases they celebrated together and the day that they lost their virginity together. Redd said to himself, "My bitch can't leave me for a cracker. She doesn't know he is a junky. Tammy has to come back where she belongs. No one could love her more than me. There is no way in hell I would give her up. Fuck it; if she doesn't want to be with me, she won't be with anybody else. Tammy is my property and Lewis won't take it from me. Lewis better have eyes behind his head. He will die for betraying me. One day. Just one day, he will slip and I will be there to blow his brains out. Tammy is confused right now; she'll see the light and come back to me. If she doesn't see the light, her brains will be blown away too. Just the thought of her with another man is making me very furious. Lewis and Tammy might turn me into the next O.J. Simpson."

Chapter 23

The next day, Redd gave Tammy a call. Tammy was not in the mood to speak with him but she saw it as a chance to tell Redd to move on. "Look Redd, we had some good times together. You can be a sweet guy when you want to be. Some other girl would love your company. Why are you taking things so hard? Our relationship has been over for months. I'm sure you have been sleeping with other women."

Since Redd finally had her on the phone, he planned to make the best out of this opportunity, "Tammy, I know you still have feelings for me. Lewis could never love you better than I can. He is still a high school student. Lewis would not know what real love is. He is just trying to have a little fun with you and then throw you away like yesterday's newspaper. How could you leave me for a junky; an X pill popping, weed smoking, cocaine snorting junky? Soon, he will keep a pipe in his mouth like Popeye the Sailor Man."

Tammy said in denial, "Lewis would never take those drugs. Many people don't consider weed a drug; it is grown naturally. He has a bright future ahead of him. Stop trying to brainwash me with lies -- they are not going to work."

Redd told her, "You have only known this guy for a couple of days and talking like y'all are in love. Our history together has to mean something. Do you remember the time we lost our virginities together? Wow, it seems like that day was seven years ago. We were so scared of getting caught by your parents. What about the heart shaped diamond ring; I gave it to you last Christmas and you have been wearing it every day since?"

Tammy was starting to feel those old feelings coming back. Then she thought about his gangster life style and it shot those feelings right back down. Tammy replied, "Before we broke up, I gave you a choice. The option was between me and the streets. Your ass chose to stay a drug dealer; you kept on hanging with the Bloods. You chose to fuck multiple women behind my back. It is time for me to give another guy a chance. Your chances of getting back with me went up in smoke a long time ago. I don't mean to be cruel, but I would never go out with you again. Please leave me and Lewis alone. Love me enough to let go."

Redd knew Tammy's mind was made up. There was nothing he could say or do to bring her back to him. He hated the fact that she didn't want him anymore. Redd could not stop selling drugs because it paid all his bills. He could not picture himself working a 9 to 5 job. The dope game had him sitting on some real cheese. He told her, "Good luck, he better treat you right. Bye." After the conversation, Redd wanted to throw his cell phone down and break it. His feelings for her were still strong. She placed him in a situation to make a decision. He had to kill either him or her and maybe, both of them.

Tammy thought Redd was over her and he was willing to move on. She only added more fuel to his fire by not taking him back. Redd felt like things had to go his way or no way at all.

Friday finally came and Lewis had been waiting for this

day for a long time. Lewis was walking to school thinking about catching up with Steven; he wanted to go over the plans again. He wanted to make sure the plan went perfectly. Lewis couldn't wait to count his riches once the deed was done. During the lunch break, Lewis caught up with Steven. He spotted Steven using the water fountain. Lewis crept up behind him and said, "Damn man, save some H20 for the rest of us." Then he looked left and right to make sure no one was around. Lewis gave Steven one of the extra keys to his house. He said to Steven, "Do you remember everything we went over? We have to treat this mission like a regular night for us, trying to get paid. The car has to be parked around the corner and you have to do everything on my command. I know you still want me to change my mind, but that will not happen. The same money my parents refused to help me out with will be mines. Fuck my parents; everybody thinks their good role models, but they are far from it. They may have won the battle, but the war belongs to me. They will regret mistreating me."

Steven said, "I think your problems at home can be worked out; unless, there is something you're hiding. Deep down in their hearts, Sam and Jessica love you. Once they are gone, they will never come back. It will be something you have to deal with forever. The pain of losing one parent is terrible."

Lewis told him, "Stop feeding me bullshit. Tim and Barbara love you and they gave you whatever their income could afford. If Tim and Barbara had the same kind of cash my parent got, you would have been spoiled. Yes, my parents liked you a lot. It could have all been an act. Sam and Jessica always acted well mannered around other people. I guess it was to hide their true selves. Stop trying to convince me not to murder them. Don't turn soft on me now because we have business that needs to be taken care of. When your dad died, it was me who helped you get revenge on the pigs. Even though, you did not like the way I had done it. Steven, it's your time to ride for me. This is your last time breaking the law with our crew. With $300,000, you would go out on top of your game. If your mind changes about helping me, our friendship is over. Real brothers have each other backs, no matter what."

Steven said, "I have not changed my mind about helping you. There's just other ways to handle this situation. I'm your brother until the casket drops and there is nothing changing that. A person who doesn't give a fuck would have quickly taken the money. I am making sure it is what you want to do. There aren't any magic tricks to turn back the hands of the time."

Lewis stated, "At least we are on the same page this time. Are you my brother?"

Steven replied, "I'm your brother forever. I know you very well. There is something you are leaving out of the story, Brother." Steven walked away from Lewis.

Lewis thought, *He's one smart boy. Steven knows there is something else. It is hard to tell someone a man molested and raped you, if you're a guy yourself. A secret like this is very embarrassing. It makes me feel like my manhood was taken from me. People would think I'm some kind of faggot. I never had a problem with gay people, but it's not my style. My skeletons will stay in the closet for right now.*

Later on, The Teenage Mafia got ready to make things

happen. Lewis was at home in his bedroom; he was trying to give Sam and Jessica enough time to fall asleep. The time was 10:32pm. Lewis walked down the stairs, through the living room, through the kitchen, and finally, he was standing at his parent's bedroom door. He placed his left ear on the door and he heard both of them snoring. He walked back into the living room and called Eric on his cell phone. Eric answered his cell phone, "Are you ready for us?"

Lewis responded, "Go ahead and pick up everybody. Remember to treat this like any other night we are out handling our business. Bring the white ski masks and the white t-shirts. Get pumped up because we are at it again."

Eric told him, "We should be there in about twenty minutes."

Lewis wondered, *Eric has been down from the start. When Steven brought him to our group, I thought he was going to be a scary nerd. He probably has bigger nuts than the rest of us. Never judge a book by its cover.*

Eric took the license plate off the jeep. Then he called everyone and picked them up. He drove around the corner from Lewis's house. Lewis started having second thoughts about murdering his parents. Steven's words were echoing in the back of his mind, *There is a better way to handle the situation. Success would be the best revenge. Losing one parent feels terrible.*

Lewis called Eric's cell phone about their location, "Where are y'all? It's show time and y'all should be looking at the back of my house. Don't walk around the corner because we have too many nosy neighbors. Climb the gate and walk through our back yard; it will decrease the chances of anyone seeing what you all are doing. Come on, I'll meet you guys in my living room."

Eric got off the phone with Lewis and said to the rest of them, "Lewis is ready for us to enter his home. I will be the lookout man and the getaway driver."

Lewis was fixing his room up like he had been asleep. Steven, Willie, Johnny, and James placed the ski masks over their heads and put the guns in their pockets. They hopped out the jeep and climbed over the 6'4 iron made gate. The crew walked fast through the grassy back yard to the front yard. Lewis had turned the alarm off earlier. Steven used the key Lewis gave him at school to get in. Once the crew walked into the living room, Lewis came down the stairs to meet them. Lewis whispered, "Follow me." They followed him making the least noise as possible. All of them were standing outside of Lewis parent's bedroom. Lewis said in a low tone, "As soon as one of them opens this door, show no mercy." Lewis knocked on the door three times but he did not get a response. Then he knocked four times on the door, even harder.

Sam yelled, "Why are you knocking on this door, so fucking hard?" Sam got out of the bed to see what Lewis wanted. Sam turned on his bedroom light. Lewis heard him unlocking the door. When Sam opened the door, Johnny hit him so hard in the mouth that saliva flew out and he fell to the floor. Jessica heard the sound of Sam hitting the floor. Then she saw some people wearing white ski masks and white t-shirts standing over Sam. Jessica started to scream, "Don't hurt us! We have plenty of money! Stop! Stop!" James walked to Jessica and dragged her out of the bed. Her head and back smacked the floor. James wanted her to stop screaming and he got on top of her. He used both of his hands, punching her senseless. Blood started coming from her nose and mouth. Sam got up trying to fight back, but he was no match for Steven, Willie, and Johnny. They punched and kicked him until he stopped getting up. He just lay on the floor with both hands covering his head. Jessica was knocked out. Both Jessica and Sam were wearing light blue pajamas.

Lewis watched the entire beat down in the doorway because he did not want any evidence getting on him. Lewis ordered the crew to kill them, "It is time to finish the job; give them one to the "dome"." James took a .45 handgun out of his pocket and stood over Sam. He shot Sam directly in the middle of his forehead. Then Lewis told Steven, "Steven, it's your turn. Don't think, just shoot." Lewis gave Steven his .9mm handgun.

Jessica had regained consciousness. Steven stood over her while she begged and pleaded for her life, "Don't kill me. I didn't do anything to you. Take whatever you want." The palms of Steven's hands began to sweat. The gun looked like it was vibrating in Steven's right hand. Steven said in his mind, "Lord, will you forgive me?" He shot her in the left side of the head. Lewis ordered them to go in their dressers and throw their clothes around the bedroom. He wanted them to keep any cash or valuable items they could get their hands on. Lewis wanted them to go all out to stage a burglary-homicide. The crew went through all ten dressers. James found a pearl necklace and two diamond rings. Willie found a Rolex watch with diamonds going around the face. Johnny grabbed a small treasure box full of gold earrings and a woman's gold bracelet and $260. Steven did not take anything; he helped with throwing the clothes around the room.

After seven minutes of stealing, Lewis told them, "Someone has to open a can of whip ass on me. I want to be seen as a victim who escaped. On the count of four, somebody get it done. I'll say when to stop." Steven, Willie, Johnny, and James were looking at each other, wondering who will attack him. Lewis began to count slowly, "One-two-three-four." James went wild on Lewis; he was punching so hard that Lewis almost got knockout. Lewis's face had a couple of bruises. Lewis told James, "Stop and rip my shirt!" James ripped Lewis's shirt like Hulk Hogan. Lewis was in pain, but it did not stop him from giving the next command, "Get out of here, so I can call the police. Steven, shoot the door knob from the outside." The crew ran back to the living room and went out the door. Steven stopped outside of the door and shot the door knob twice with the .9mm. Then they dashed through the back yard and climbed over the gate. They jumped in the jeep and Eric drove off.

For the first time, a witness heard the shots and saw them climbed the gate. He also saw them entering a jeep to get away. Lewis waited five minutes before calling 911. He wanted to give them a little more time to get away. The lady operator said, "This is 911, how may we help you."

Lewis pretended like he is out of breath and said, "Help me! Someone please help me! My mom and dad could be dead."

The operator told him, "Can you clam down and give us your address?"

Lewis told her, "Please come now. Those guys could still be here. My address is 1183 Rose Garden Street."

Another operator called the police while Lewis stayed on

the phone with the lady operator. She said, "Can you tell me what is going on at your home?"

Lewis replied, "Are the police on their way here? Some masked people were fighting my parents and me. They fought my parents in their bedroom; they also had guns. I was attacked outside of my parents' bedroom. I escaped and ran back to my room."

Lewis heard the police sirens outside. Five police cars surrounded the house. The door was already wide open and most of the officers went into the house with their guns out. Within a few minutes, they discovered the bodies. Detective Lopez knocked on Lewis's bedroom door four times and said, "This is the police; is anybody in there?"

Lewis screamed, "I'm in here!" Then he unlocked the door and started crying. Once Lewis saw Detective Lopez, he gave him a hug. Lewis played his role well without any rehearsal. He should have received three Oscars for his performance. Lewis was breathing hard like he was in the fight of his life. Detective Lopez thought he was calming him down. Finally, Lewis became relaxed and he was ready to talk. Detective Lopez spoke with Lewis before taking him to his parents' room.

Steven and the crew were still on the road. James was exhausted for real. He beat up on Jessica and Lewis. James used up a lot of his energy going through those dressers and running from the scene of the crime too. He told Eric, "Please stop at a store, so I can get something to drink. I never been this dehydrated before in my life."

Eric was on a mission to get everybody home quickly. He told James, "Hold on, you are going home first. We should not be making any stops other than y'all homes. There are many stores that have cameras in them, so it won't be wise. Some dude saw us tonight, leaving from Lewis's crib. He was standing near the road, behind us. It was a good thing the license plate wasn't on this jeep. There are a million of these jeeps in L.A."

Steven hated the fact someone saw them, "Fuck! There should have been no witnesses. Whoever the person was could be following us right now. For the first time someone seen us."

Eric told them, "Before anyone asks me, it was too dark for me to get a good look at the person."

James had the seat behind Eric and he had the look of a person who boxed for 20 rounds. Willie was also pissed off, "This is my last time jeopardizing my life. I quit. You all can have this shit. We could have caught the witness and murdered him or her. That person was lucky most of us did not see'em. I would have ordered Eric to chase'em down."

Johnny started thinking, *The person who seen us can't identify anybody. We all wore masks and it's impossible for him to indentify us. It's still not good when someone sees you leaving the scene, though.*

Steven stated, "Tonight should be the last time we get our hands dirty. Even Lewis will throw in the towel after this, watch and see. He's on his way to being rich. Lewis won't have a reason to continue a life of crime."

James didn't believe Steven. "Lewis is one of the realest guys I know. The man loves money as much as I do. He and I are guaranteed to keep the cash flowing with or without most of you. Steven, you get scared when every mission is completed. Even if there were not any witnesses, the words 'I quiet' would have still come from your mouth."

Steven responded, "Tonight, I murdered someone who cared about me. I'm not in the mood, so leave me the fuck alone. Everybody knows you want to be Mr. Bad Ass."

Eric pulled up to James's condo home. James wanted to curse Steven out, but he hopped out of the jeep and went inside of his home instead. Steven said, "I'm glad we were at his house; he was begging me to kick his ass."

Eric told them, "I have proved my toughness. No one here can say that Eric is a soft nerd. I will join Steven and Willie; my days of committing crimes are over with."

Back at the scene of the crime, Detective Lopez with the rest of the law enforcement was taking pictures of the bodies. Both of them were laid out with a bullet to the head and blood was on the floor. Clothes were scattered all over the room. Some dressers were still opened with clothes hanging out of them. They saw an empty jewelry box on the floor. Officer Butler, a 37-year-old Caucasian man who worked side by side with Detective Lopez, was tracing around the bodies with some chalk. Detective Lopez noticed multiple shoe prints made of dirt from the living room to Sam and Jessica's bedroom, the bruises on both of the victims face, the gunshots to the front door's knob from the outside and what seemed like a heartbroken Lewis.

All the neighbors came outside to see what was going on. Before their eyes, they saw two body bags carried out the house and Lewis's painful look. It had finally sunk-in to the neighbors that Sam and Jessica were dead. From looking at all the evidence, Detective Lopez was almost convinced that what happened here was a burglary-homicide. He wanted to bring Lewis to the police station for more questioning.

Detective Lopez and Lewis were getting ready to drive off, but they got stopped by Officer Butler. "Hold up, we have a witness. Tell Detective Lopez what you heard and saw." The witness was a 32-year-old Caucasian male named Robert Marco. His hair was reddish and there were freckles all over the guy's face. He wore eye glasses, a red t-shirt, a dark blue pair of pants, and an all black pair of Reebok Classic tennis shoes. Robert was more than willing to tell what he saw. "I saw at least six people wearing white ski masks and white t-shirts. I heard gunshots first, but at that time I was unsure about it. We live in a very peaceful neighborhood. The only reason I was outside is to catch some fresh air. As soon as I stepped in my front lawn, I saw them climbing over the gate. Then I walked to the roadside and they jumped into a jeep with no license plate and drove off. It was too dark to see the color of the jeep. There could have been someone all ready in the driver seat waiting on them. Because of their ski masks, I was not able to see who they were."

Lewis heard everything the witness was saying. It angered him, but he did not let it show. Lewis wanted to wrap some duct tape on his mouth and kick him in the nuts. Detective Lopez wanted to take Lewis and Robert to the Police Station to see if their description of the killers and their stories matched.

About twenty-two minutes later, they were at the police station with the recorder out. Detective Lopez really wanted to hear what Lewis had to say because he could have some important information to catch whoever done the crime. Lewis was sitting on a wooden four- legged chair in front of a small wooden four-legged table. The recorder was turned on and placed in front of him. Detective Lopez was sitting on another chair across from Lewis. Detective Lopez told him, "Please relax, I know this situation is very upsetting. Remember whatever you can about the events that happened tonight."

Lewis said, "I was in my bed sleeping. The yelling and screaming woke me up. Then I went down stairs to see what's going on. The screaming became louder as I got closer to my parent's bedroom. I went down stairs with the mind set of breaking my parents up from fighting. Four or five people were in my parents' room with white ski masks on. Their t-shirts were white too. They started fighting me, once I put one foot into the room. I tried to defend myself, but there were too many of them. My dad came out of nowhere and slangs them off of me. Before getting away to call for help, I saw my mother on the floor motionless. You are looking at a true coward. What kind of person would let that happen to his parents?"

Detective Lopez asked, "Did you call 911 as soon as you escaped from them?"

Lewis answered, "Yes. My cell phone was in my bedroom. It took me about three minutes to find it. Usually, my phone would be on the charger beside my lamp. While searching for my phone, I heard some gun shots. When I found my cell phone, I called 911. My parents' deaths are my fault. I should have stayed there and helped my father fight them. I went to my room, too chicken to come out. Then I heard the police sirens coming from outside. I heard your voice telling me you are a police officer and I opened my bedroom door."

Detective Lopez asked, "Did you hear the killer's voices? Did you see anybody's face?"

Lewis said something that would sound believable to a cop. "All of them sounded like young black men. Their masks never came off when I saw them. Everything happened so fast. I need more time to concentrate better. If something comes back to me, you will be the first person I call."

Detective Lopez said, "Your home will belong to us for a little while. Some officers and I will go back there to find more evidence. Once we are finish with the house, we'll get in touch with you. Leave us a contact number we can call. Do you have another place to stay in the meantime?"

Lewis searched his mental index and said, "My friends, Steven and his mother would let me stay there for a while. All of my things are at my house."

Detective Lopez told him, "The only way we could let you back into the crime scene, an officer will have to accompany you."

Lewis said, "It's okay with me."

Detective Lopez hit the stop button on the recorder. He took Lewis home to get his personal things. Lewis cried while getting his things together. Detective Lopez felt sorry for him. He thought Lewis was too young to lose both of his parents. Detective Lopez had seen this happen a lot, especially with all the gang violence in L.A. He solved many cases and some were still unsolved. Detective Lopez had a strong feeling that it was the work of The Teenage Mafia. The white ski masks and t-shirts were a possible sign of their involvement. This could be one of his toughest cases because there were millions of teens in their city. Detective Lopez knew he was dealing with some smart little bastards. Attacking mostly at night, taking the license plate off the car, and keeping the masks on were some very clever moves. He pondered, *I have to catch them in the act. They are going to slip and when they do, their asses belong to me. The Teenage Mafia is collecting a lot of money. Those little street thugs will not know when to quit. I will not let them out smart a well trained detective as myself. These punks have robbed a store, robbed a bank and now, pulling off a Burglary-Homicide. Even at a young age, criminals are getting much smarter. The Teenage Mafia is different from the Bloods and the Crips gangs. If a member of the Bloods gets killed, normally the rival gang committed the murder. The Teenage Mafia is going after money. They should be sitting on between $600,000 and $800,000.*

Once Lewis had gathered his things, he was taken to Steven's house. Lewis rang Steven's door bell at 1:59am. Steven had just taken a shower and went to bed because he was tired. When Steven heard the door bell, he thought it was the police. Steven was very timid about answering the door. He got out of the bed with his gray shorts on and placed a pair of black house shoes on his feet. Steven went to answer the front door, "Who is it?"

Lewis replied, "It's me, Lewis."

After Steven realized Lewis was at the door; he opened it. Lewis walked in with two large blue duffle bags filled with his things. Steven was curious. "What are you doing over here?"

Lewis responded, "Well, Detective Lopez told me I can't go home until they finish looking for evidence in there. We are going to be seeing a lot of each other. I have some bad and some good news. The bad news is a witness saw y'all leave my crib. The good news is he doesn't have a clue about who y'all were. The police only know about the white ski masks, the white t-shirts, and that y'all left in a jeep. They don't know the color of it. The pigs can only wait for us to make a mistake. We are too smart to make mistakes. I'm joining the retirement club for criminals. Your boy is getting ready to collect some real cake. My girlfriend and I are waiting to live in luxury."

Steven said, "You have a girlfriend. Man, you've been living a double life. Your relationship was kept in the closet."

Lewis stated, "Things change and sometimes people get older. Her name is Tammy and she's the bomb with a capital B. Baby girl is a ten."

Steven told him, "James said that you two were still chasing paper. He became mad at me when I told him you were not taking part in criminal activities. He almost made me put my foot in his ass tonight."

Lewis replied, "It is my fault because I led him into thinking like that. He has over $100,000, some jewelry, and plus another $300,000 coming his way. James has to chill out because Detective Lopez is on our asses. As far as I'm concerned, The Teenage Mafia doesn't exist anymore. We are the head of this operation and without the head the body can't continue. Everybody can say they left the crew with plenty of cash. We have reached our goals. Would it be okay to leave my bags in your room?"

Steven said, "Of course it would be alright to leave them there. This city never saw us coming. The only thing left for us to do is enjoy life. I need a girlfriend. Does Tammy have any friends, sisters, or cousins?"

Lewis was unsure about that question, so he told him, "I'll find out something, dog."

Steven asked, "Where is all your money? They could find it at your house."

Lewis told him, "You are underestimating me. My bread has been right under y'all noses for a few days. I placed it under this house. One day, last week, I followed you home from school. It's called thinking ahead of time. Do you really think I would leave my money there with all those pigs snooping around? I'm tired; give me a cover, so I could fall asleep on the couch."

Steven gave him a blanket, and both of them went to sleep.

Chapter 24

In the morning, Eric gave Honey a call, "Hey baby, what are you doing?"

Honey responded, "I just hopped out of the shower. Are we going to hang out tonight? Every moment spent with you is special."

Eric told her, "We can hang out together. Have you ever thought about meeting my mom? It would be a big step for us."

Cindy called Eric on her cell phone while he was talking to Honey. She used to be one of the prostitutes he was fooling around with. Eric saw her number showing up on his phone. In a split second, Eric told Honey he would call her later because his mom wanted him to do something for her. Then he clicked over to speak with Cindy, "What's up, girl? It has been a while since I saw you last. Why did you decide to call me now?"

Cindy answered, "I was just thinking about you; we did have a lot of fun. Our fun should have never ended, boo. Our nights alone were legendary."

Eric said the first thing he thought of, "You are calling to get some more of this, I bet. There is no need to be greedy; I have enough to feed the needy."

Cindy giggled and said, "Your confident level is higher than what it used to be. They must teach swagger at your school." Eric thought about his fantasy of getting down with a few girls at the same time.

He told her, "We have a swagger class at our school and I'm the teacher. With you, it has always been business before pleasure. What if I paid you to have sex with me and some more girls?"

Cindy was caught off guard with that question. She thought, *I'm a business lady. Eric probably can't afford to have me sexing him and other girls at the same time. If the price is right, I can make it happen.* Cindy said to Eric, "I never had sex with a girl before. It will cost more than a regular session. My price is $2,000." She thought he would not be able to come up with that amount of money.

Eric said, "The money is yours. Make my fantasy come true. Bring about three fine ass women with you. Can you handle it for me?"

Cindy stated, "I want my money up front and the women I'm going to bring will want their money up front too." Cindy was so fine that she could easily make the front cover of the Ebony magazine. Her measurements were 34C-25-39 with the height of 5'7. Cindy's booty was big enough to be in the next T.I. video. Her skin complexion was caramel brown with long straight black hair. She was mixed with black and Dominican.

Eric told her, "We are going to make things happen at my house. The girls you bring better look sexy. I am paying y'all a lot of bread."

Cindy said, "It's easy to find some beautiful girls to join us. Most women in my line of work are motivated by money. We'll be worth the money, I promise."

Eric said, "Give me a call, when you get all three of the girls together. Hopefully, it can go down as soon as possible."

For Eric, the urge was not going anywhere. When he saw Cindy's number, he saw an opportunity of a lifetime. Cindy was going to find three of her freakiest friends.

Lewis called Tammy, sounding sad. "Hey, how are you doing?"

Tammy could hear the depression in Lewis's voice. She replied, "I feel good, but you don't sound okay."

Lewis told her, "Something terrible happened at my house last night. My parents and I were attacked by some guys wearing white ski masks."

Tammy said, "O' my God, did someone get hurt?"

Lewis acted emotional. "They are gone. My mom and dad were killed. I don't know what to do. My dad saved my life. It was just too many of them. At first, I was asleep and then the noise awakens me. I went to my parent's room, to see what the commotion is about. Those guys started attacking me. Then my dad came to my rescue. He could have run away, but he chose to save my life instead. He took those dudes off of me. I went up stairs to call 911on my cell phone. Then I heard some shots; my parents were hit in the head. Leaving my parents behind is something I will regret forever. Blood was all over their bedroom floor. The murderers took cash and some valuable items. Out of all the houses in our neighborhood, why would they stop at my home? My life will never be the same."

Tammy felt the need to console him. "I need to stand by your side, right now. We need each other, more than ever. Let me try to brighten up your day. Where are you, Lewis?"

Lewis responded, "I'm over my best friend's house; his name is Steven. We are close like brothers. I have to freshen up now and you will get a call from me later on. You are right; we need each other more than ever."

Tammy told him, "What happened to you was very tragic. No one should lose their parents like that. I hope the police catch whoever took their lives. Even if the police don't catch them, they can't hide from God." After they hung their phones up; the words "they can't hide from God" were still in his mind.

Barbara came to Lewis and gave him a hug. Then she said, "Everything is going to be okay, if you keep your faith in God. He will make a way for you to get through any obstacle. You can stay here as long as you want. We have plenty."

Lewis had tears falling down his face. He could feel Barbara's love. It was the feeling he always wanted. His parents never showed him any kind of affection. All he ever wanted was for them to show him some real love. Lewis became emotional for real, this time. He wiped his tears away, but the more he wiped the more they fell.

Steven walked into the living room and saw what looked like a mother and son moment. He asked himself, *I wonder if those tears are real. Mom and I have already talked about what happened to Lewis's parents. She is cool about letting him stay a while. He is not a stranger; she has known him for most of his life. Mom is crazy about him. Lewis always wanted parents like my mom and dad.*

Redd became a stalker. He wanted to know Tammy's every move. Later on that night, Tammy went to pick up Lewis from Steven's house. Redd bought another car, so he wouldn't be noticed. The car was a candy apple red '89 Lincoln Continental. The seats were red and it was made of leather.

The rest of the interior was white. Everything under the hood was brand new and the car had some brand new spinning rims on 22's. Redd knew about the murders of Lewis's parents. He was disappointed because Lewis didn't get eliminated.

Tammy and Lewis went to grab a bite at the Extravagance Dinning restaurant. It was one of L.A.'s most elegant dining places. Redd said to himself, *This is some bullshit; Tammy wanted KFC when she was with me. Tammy must have lost her damn mind, treating him better than me. Well, she did mention going to better places to eat and my mind was on going to the cheaper restaurants. But still, she shouldn't have done it big without me, though. They just don't know; I could walk in there and start "dumping". Too many witnesses are a bad thing to have. It's fucked up; I have to stay in a car while they are having a good time.*

After an hour and a half, Tammy and Lewis left Extravagance Dinning. Redd followed them to the Galaxy Cinema; they wanted to watch a movie name "Love Sucks". Love Sucks was a romantic comedy film about a desperate young man; who's searching for love in all the wrong places. Redd thought, *She didn't feel like going to the movies with me. Well, she used to beg me to watch a movie at the cinema with her. I like to stay at home and catch a bootleg movie on my DVD player. Tammy should have waited on me to take her here.* After one hour and fifty five minutes, Tammy and Lewis left the Galaxy Cinema. Tammy drove to Steven's house and dropped him off. Redd was happy she took him there, instead of her home. *Lewis isn't getting any ass tonight. She brought him there because she still has feelings for me. Maybe, I should give her a call or give Lewis a warning.* Redd sent Lewis a text message and it read: 'I'm happy your parents were murdered. If you keep hanging with my bitch, you will be next. Fuck you, cracker.'

Lewis read the message and began to think, *Redd will be a thorn in my side. I might have to deal with him before he deals with me. Tammy thought he was going to leave us alone. Tammy said she spoke with him and he agreed to let her move on. I realize the beef between me and Redd is still cooking.* Lewis started wondering about death and how anybody could be touched. Lewis loved Tammy, but he did not want to die for their relationship.

Steven walked in the living room to speak with Lewis. "You hid your girl from me again. I want to meet the fine girl who has you sprung. What's wrong? Either you seen a ghost or she broke your heart already."

There was a worried look on Lewis's face. He told Steven, "I'm okay. I have a lot on my mind, that's all. When Tammy comes back over here to pick me up, she'll get the chance to meet you and Barbara."

Steven said, "Alright, she better look damn good. I'll catch you in the morning."

Chapter 25

A week had passed and James was becoming anxious about getting his $300,000 from Lewis. James was inside his bedroom, counting some of his money and he was wondering, *What is taking Lewis so long to pay me? He hasn't called me yet. Lewis could keep all the money for himself. He already knows that I'm the last person to play with about their money. Lewis and I were supposed to take over the crew. He has not said anything about that either. I will visit him and talk about our future plans.*

James's mother let him use her PT Cruiser. He drove to Steven's house. James rang the door bell and Steven let him in.

Steven said, "Hell will freeze over twice. You actually came over my house. What's up, man?"

James asked, "Where is Lewis? I have to speak with me."

Steven went into his bedroom and told Lewis, "James is standing in the living room and he wants to holler at you. Let me take over the game controller while y'all talk. You already know I'm the best at NBA Live."

Lewis said, "Yeah right." He walked away from Steven to speak with James. James and Lewis greeted by shaking hands.

James didn't waste any time, "Where is my money? Why is it taken so long?"

Lewis told him, "You are going to get your money. A lot of business has to be handled first. My parent's insurance company and the people that handle their money at the bank have to get back with me. There's a bunch of paper work I have to sign once they get back with me. The money will come soon."

James stated, "Soon isn't good enough for me. Right now sounds much better. Why haven't you spoken to me about our plans for this crew? What spot will we hit next? Hitting another bank is the best move we could make."

Lewis responded, "I'm sorry. This is my fault; I led you to think we should keep robbing. We all should chill out and enjoy our money forever. I'm going to stop living a life of crime. We accomplished everything in that line of work already. Everybody has made a lot of money and that was our goal."

James was heated; every word that came out of Lewis's mouth was an insult to him. James told him, "Don't become a lying muthafucka. Don't turn into a pussy on me. Since you are waiting to be rich, help me become rich too. It's time for you to return the favor, since I helped you. I found another bank we should rob."

Lewis said to him, "You didn't hear anything I just said. I won't steal anymore. It is over for me, James. Be your own man; nothing is stopping you from doing it yourself. We had a good run. Now is a good time to quit."

James responded, "You haven't heard what I said. You are going to help me. Step up and be a man of your words. I was down with every idea you came up with and this is how you repay me. My boy has turned into a fucking coward."

Lewis said, "You have made a lot of money. Steven was right about finishing on top. When I get my new crib, you are more than welcome to come over."

James pulled out a Glock .40 and aimed it at Lewis. James told Lewis, "Have you ever wondered what God looks like? If you fuck me out of my money, you will find out."

Lewis didn't have his gun on him; it was left in one of his duffle bags. Lewis yelled, "Put the gun down, so we could talk! Without me, you would have never made $100,000. Steven and I took you in and we all were successful. If you use that gun, you better kill me."

Steven dropped the controller and went to see what was going on between Lewis and James. Steven saw James with his gun pointed at Lewis. He told James, "Put the gun a way, we are supposed to be better than that."

James said to Lewis, "If you don't have my money by next week, your ass is mines. Lewis, I thought you were real. I guess my judgment isn't too good. Both of y'all can kiss my ass. Y'all are not the only people who could have pulled that shit off. I don't need you two!" James placed the gun back into his pocket and left Steven's house.

Lewis thought, **Damn. James is the second person who pulled out a gun on me. Maybe, my life is coming to an end. It seems like everybody wants to kill me.**

Steven said, "Are you okay? I heard some yelling and I came right away. James is spiraling out of control. It was a mistake to recruit him. It's a good thing that my mom went to the store. She would have been so upset. James is a bitch for bringing that drama over my house. He sounds for real about taken you out of the game. Do you believe he will try to kill you, if he doesn't get his money next week?"

Lewis answered, "I don't know, Steven. Fuck him; he will get his cash the same day I get mines."

Eric and Cindy had finally got things together. Cindy's choices were three of the best prostitutes she had as friends. Their names were Ice Cream, Cupcake, and Passion. Eric was already thinking about positions he could use dealing with four girls. He bought a handheld camera from Best Buy. He would record the whole thing, so he could watch it over and over. Eric and Cindy planned to get it on tonight. Eric had to come up with a lie because he didn't want Honey to come over his house. Cindy was starting to like the idea of freaking with some ladies. She thought of it as exploring her sexuality.

Eric picked up his cell phone to give Honey the bad news. "Honey, I'm not feeling too well. I have been throwing up all day. It could be something I ate. My mom thinks it was food poisoning. We can chill once I'm feeling better."

Honey didn't know Eric was telling her a lie, "Now is the perfect time for me to cater to you. I'll bring you water, food, and whatever you want."

Eric stated, "My mom said it could be contagious. My heart won't allow me to put you at risk. I'm lucky to have a girl who's willing to help out. Give me a few days to get better. Sweat has been dripping down my face all day long."

Honey said, "Alright, get your rest and call me, so I won't be worried. Don't be surprised if I blow your phone up with calls."

Chapter 26

THE GRAND FINALE

The time was 7:45pm and Eric was getting his camera ready. The camera was hidden in the closet on top of five shoe boxes. Eric placed some clothes on top of the camera, but he kept its lens out. He was already on hard thinking about what was going to happen. He sent Cindy a text message: 'Come over here, girl. Don't forget your three friends. Tell them that my rocket is ready for takeoff.'

Cindy responded with a text message of her own: 'We are on the road right now. Your house is the next stop. Keep your rocket on the ground, for now. It has a long journey ahead.'

Cindy and her crew arrived at Eric's house. They hopped out of Cindy's 2005 sky-blue Infinite and entered the house. Ice Cream, Cupcake, and Passion followed Cindy to Eric's bedroom. Eric said, "Wow, three dime pieces are in my room. Introduce me to your friends, Cindy."

Cindy replied, "Okay, Ice Cream is the blonde. She loves sucking dick and I bet she could make your toes curl. If giving head could sell records, her mouth could easy go triple platinum. Don't be fooled by looking at her baby face; the girl is a freak. Cupcake is the dazzling brunette. The guys nicknamed her Cupcake because they say her cumm has a sweet taste. She can also ride a dick faster than the speed of light. Cupcake has the desirable coke bottle shape like me. She is one of the finest bitches on the street. Please don't fall in love with her because that pussy is very good. She even stole some of my clients with it. Many people say Cupcake favors Jessica Simpson. The last girl name is Passion. This black chick has an ass that is bigger and softer than mines. Look at those big lips; can you imagine what she can do with them. Passion used to be a stripper until she found out there is more money in selling pussy. She loves when a guy hammers their dick in her ass. Passion would swallow your nut for a good amount of cash. All of us have beautiful breasts, no stretch marks, and some great pussy. Give us the money, so this thing can go down. We all want $2,000 apiece; will that be a problem for you?"

Eric did not answer her question; he broke bread like a true trick daddy. He gave all of them $2,000 a piece. All three of the women started taking their clothes off. Eric started having second thoughts. *Honey is at home and she thinks I'm sick. I'm becoming a dog like those other guys she dated. Why did I place myself in this situation?*

Cupcake walked up to Eric and whispered, "Take them clothes off because I came over here to fuck." Eric stood there with a confused look on his face. Cupcake got on her knees and unzipped his pants. Then she started sucking his dick like a lollipop. Cindy, Passion, and Ice Cream climbed into the bed to make out. Cupcake bended over and Eric went inside of her with no protection. He watched Cindy give oral sex to Passion while hitting Cupcake from the back. Cupcake had cum dripping down her legs. Ice Cream started licking Cindy's ass and pussy from behind while Cindy was still giving Passion some tongue action between her legs. Ice Cream got out of the bed and went to Eric and Cupcake. Ice Cream took

Eric's dick out of Cupcake's pussy and placed it in her mouth. Then she sucked it two times better than Cupcake. Eric used all of his strength to lift up Ice Cream. Her legs were wrapped around his waist while he carried her to his bed. He was on top of her, nailing the pussy. Cindy and Passion were lying on the right side of them, but they had switched places. Passion was giving Cindy oral sex and fingering her too. Cupcake was watching the action and wondering, "How can I get back into the action? Coming over here to watch wasn't my goal." Cupcake went to Eric and pulled his head up. Then she turned around and placed her pussy in Ice Cream's mouth. It looked like she was sitting on her face. After a few minutes, Cupcake's cum began to run down Ice Cream's chin. Cindy said, "It's my time to get some dick." Eric and Cindy started fucking and she was on top of him. You could hear her ass slapping against his upper legs, over and over again. Passion and Cupcake were sucking and licking Ice Cream's breasts while Ice Cream fingered herself.

Eric got out of the bed and said, "Let's play a game. It is called 'Who Can Suck My Dick The best'. Y'all have seven minutes to do your thing." One at a time, they sucked his dick like it was the only one that existed. It was no surprise that Ice Cream won because it was her specialty. Eric told them, "I'm tired. Which one of y'all is going to make my volcano erupt?" Passion grabbed his dick and placed it in her mouth. Passion sucked it until his volcano erupted in her mouth, then she swallowed his lava.

Everybody started putting their clothes on. Cindy had such a great time; she was thinking about going both ways permanently. All the ladies other than Cindy gave Eric their phone numbers. Cindy had it already. Eric said to them, "Thanks for coming to my place tonight. Y'all have made my fantasy come true. We all had a spectacular time." All the ladies gave him a hug before leaving his home. He stared at Passion's ass until she walked out of the house.

Eric was the happiest guy on earth and he said to himself, "I will make a sequel to 'Eric in Pussyland'. Those ladies made me forget about Honey. I was supposed to give her a call."

Eric went into the closet and picked up the camera. Then he pressed the stop button. Eric called Honey, "Hey baby, how are you doing?"

"I should be asking you the same question. Look at the time, it's 11:12pm. I was kind of worried. A little voice in my head was telling me to come down there. Are you doing alright now?" Honey said.

"Maybe, the rest was the best thing for me. I'm no longer sweating and my energy is almost back to normal. Drinking plenty of orange juice probably helped me out a lot. Tomorrow night, we can reschedule our appointment. I'm still a little tired, though," Eric replied.

"Go ahead and get your rest, so you could be 100% tomorrow. Hurry up and get well because I miss you. Don't die on me, so stay away from the white light; I'm just kidding. I'll holler at you later," Honey said.

Eric and Honey got off the phone with each other. Eric thought, *I'm glad she did not come over here. The first thing she would have seen is Cupcake big breast. She would have walked in on a freak show. I had the time of my life. Tonight, I went from a nerd to the pimp of the decade. Can't too many dudes say they had sex with* four women at the same time. I guess it was a five-some. Eric pressed play on the camera, so he could watch 'Eric in Pussyland'. Eric did not fall asleep. He watched his personal flick all night while jerking off.

On Tuesday morning, James stayed at home while the rest of the clique went to school. He was bagging up weed and cocaine on the kitchen table. His mother Zenobia trained him how to do it. James had a lot on his mind. *Steven and Lewis think they could pull the plug on the whole operation. I am my own man. Lewis really believes that without him I would be broke. That want to be black fool has the game twisted. He just doesn't know how bad I wanted to put him away with my Glock .40. If Lewis fucks me out of my dough, his life will come to a halt. Steven can run his punk ass up to me too. They always make caskets for sensitive muthafucka too. What if Johnny and I are on the same page? We would be a dynamite duo. Eric is always down for putting in some work. Eric and Steven seem to agree with each other a lot. Willie is acting like a hoe. I can't be like Michael Jordan in the 80's, a one man show. It would be nice not to slice the pie six different ways. If I did all those robberies myself, my pockets would have been fatter. Lewis fucked everybody; he is giving us $300,000 apiece while his gay ass could possibly collect a few million. Why couldn't we break bread equally? Nobody said anything to him about cheating us, out of the cash. I need to hol-ler at Eric and Johnny to see what's shaking. They could see things my way. Breaking down this powder and weed takes time; Zenobia left me a pound of each. She probably wanted me to do it because I have so much time on my* *hands, since I dropped out of school. Zenobia should've left me a helper. I've give Eric and Johnny a call after school. The Teenage Mafia could be done.*

The time was 4:22pm and James knew they should have made it home by now. He gave Eric a call first. "Eric, it feels like we have not spoken to each other in months. Do you want to stay on the paper chase? There is much more money to collect. Think about sharing the dough, two or three ways, not six ways. We know the pigs can't fuck with us. Are you in or are you out, man?" James asked. James had given Eric an ear full.

"We can't keep rolling the dice with our lives forever. Something bad will happen sooner or later. Normally, I would accept a great offer. It's too risky; people know about The Teenage mafia now. Take your bread and run with it. Have you ever thought about running a legit business? A lot of successful people started off drug dealing. Once they made a certain amount of money, they wiped the dirt off the money and made it clean. Put your money into something positive, so the boys in blue won't try to bother you," Eric responded.

James realized that Eric will not jump on his band wagon. "Eric, you used to have some heart. Steven has brainwashed you too. Y'all have turned soft on me. We were like the new N.W.A. (Niggaz with Attitudes) at first, but now we are the Backstreet Boys. You can save that positive talk for the little kids. This crew is finish. We had a great thing going. It takes stupid muthafuckas to fuck it up." Then James hung the phone up on Eric. James had one more call to make. If Johnny refused to join him, James would have to carry the load by himself.

He had faith that Johnny would accept his offer. James dialed Johnny's number on his cell phone.

Johnny answered, "James, are you feeling well? You must have called my number by mistake."

James replied, "It's not a mistake at all. I wanted to speak with you about a chance of a lifetime, so listen carefully. What if we did not have to share the money with a lot people? With two people, we would be rich in no time. We can bomb rush small banks. Both of us can go inside of the bank and handle our business. We are professional bank robbers with a lot of heart. Come on, man. The pigs can't stop real G's."

Johnny responded, "Are you crazy? It will take more than you and me to get the job done. Getting more money always sounds good."

James kept trying to convince him. "This could be our big opportunity. Think about it harder; this is about us living large. We made some money, but we can do much better. Don't quit early like everybody else. Look how those guys are "stunting" on the rap videos. They're always flashing money and surrounded by beautiful women. Their jewelry is platinum watches, necklaces, and bracelets. Did you see Baby the Birdman's earrings? They are the same size of a golf ball."

Johnny began imagining himself inside of a club surrounded by ladies and he was making it rain by throwing money up. Then he saw himself walking out of a mansion and getting into a black Rolls Royce. He had diamond earrings in both ears. Gucci shades were covering his eyes. His watch, ring, necklace, and bracelet were made of platinum with diamonds, with the glow that never stopped. He was wearing a Coogi authentic track jacket that was designed with green and blue patterns. Johnny thought he could capture The Notorious B.I.G.'s swagger. Johnny told James, "We have a deal. Two people can put this thing together. Every dime would get split two ways. Once I'm sitting on some millions, I'll stop."

James was thrilled to know Johnny would have his back. "That is what I'm talking about, someone who is willing to keep it real! We have to discuss what our plan is going to be. It will be easy because we are criminals by nature. Steven and the rest of them will wish they stayed thugging a little while longer. A few hundred G's won't last too long. We must strike while the iron is hot. Our crew has been on top of the game, lately."

Johnny added, "Next Wednesday, our school will get out early for its last teachers and parents meeting. After 1:00pm, we will hit a bank. We will dress like we normally do. You have to find us a vehicle to use. The Teenage Mafia formula will always work. James, we better know what we are doing."

Lewis decided to get a car because the police wouldn't get suspicious about a rich kid driving a new car. Lewis and Tammy visited a car lot named Car Fever. The car lot had Chevy and Toyota cars. Lewis did not want a Suburban or a jeep; he wanted something smaller. He was smart enough not to get a very expensive car or any other car that would cause too much attention. He saw an all red 2010 Chevy Camaro Coupe and it was love at first sight. There were seven all red Camaros parked in a straight line. The car dealer told them it would cost $25,000. Lewis took his book bag off of his back that was holding $60,000. After counting $25,000, he gave it to the dealer. Then the dealer gave him two keys to his new car. Tammy was impressed when she saw him go into a book bag full of money. Lewis, Tammy, and the Car Dealer went into the car dealership building. Lewis was ready to sign all the paperwork.

Redd was hating on him from a distant. He was still stalking Lewis and Tammy, following them like a shadow. *Lewis is wild for that shit. The cracker wants to be like me so bad. He wants my girl and he wants to "sport" my favorite color, red. If I would have known he had that kind of money, I would have killed him and took everything he had. Lewis is not a blood or affiliated with them. He does not have the rights to even pretend like he is a gangster. I'm a real gangster because I earned my stripes. I have been in street wars against the Crips and Lewis would never be able to duplicate me. That white boy will get his issue, soon.*

Tammy followed behind Lewis in his new Camaro and they were heading back to Steven's house. Once again, Redd was trailing them in his '89 Lincoln Continental without being notice. When they arrived at Steven's house, Tammy and Lewis were holding hands while Lewis rang the door bell. He wanted to introduce Steven and Barbara to his new girlfriend. Steven got up off the couch and opened the door. He saw Lewis holding hands with what could be the finest girl in the world. After looking at Tammy, the only thing he could say in his mind, *Damn! She looks good.*

Barbara went in the living room to see who was at the door. She told Lewis, "Come on in and introduce us to your company." Then Tammy and Lewis walked into the living room. Tammy had butterflies in her stomach. She acted as if

Barbara was his real mother. Lewis said, "Barbara and Steven, meet the love of my life and her name is Tammy."

Barbara told her, "Tammy, you are a beautiful girl."

Tammy was wearing a grey colored Rocawear 'History in the Making' t-shirt. The shirt also had light and dark golden colored rhinestones on the front. Her black jeans were also made by Rocawear. She was not wearing any socks with her Chanel high heels. Tammy replied, "Thank you; I am always trying my best, to look my best."

Barbara told them, "Steven has to step his game up now. Then he could find a fine young lady to bring home, too."

Lewis and Tammy started laughing, but not at Steven. They were not expecting an older white lady to know any kind of slang. Steven felt ashamed because he thought they giggled at him. Steven felt jealous too because he did not have a girlfriend. He wondered, *Tammy looks too good for Lewis. He must be paying her to be with him.*

Barbara told all of them, "Let's sit down and talk." Lewis knew the question would come up; where did they meet? Tammy and Lewis agreed to say they met at a 7/11 store, while talking on the way there. Steven kept his silence while Tammy, Lewis, and Barbara laughed and talked on the three seated couch. Their conversation lasted fifty-four minutes.

Lewis said, "I almost forgot, my new car is outside." All of them including Steven went outside to check it out.

Steven looked at the car and thought, *How much luck can one person have? Lewis must have God on speed dial.*

Barbara liked the car. "They need to put you in the next 'Transformer' movie. The Camaro is very stylish. My son will have a car with style next. Tim always wanted a Camaro. It's a good thing someone he loves is living out one of his dreams." Barbara gave Tammy and Lewis a hug.

Steven was envying over it in his mind. *She doesn't even show me that much love. Maybe Mom wishes Lewis was her real son. I can't wait to bring a classy girl home, so she could be proud of me.*

Barbara said to Steven, "Let's go back in the house; so we can give them a little time alone." Tammy and Lewis stood outside hugging and kissing until she became ready to go home. When Tammy left, Lewis started walking back towards the house. Redd drove behind him and kept on going. He decided to follow Tammy around some more. Lewis came into the house with a huge smile on his face.

Steven and Lewis were sitting side by side on the couch, watching the MTV Top Twenty Videos. Steven could hear a change in **Lewis.** "Everybody who is doing wrong needs to change their lives. Doing the right things is my new way of life because I no longer want to break the law. Tammy has been so nice to me. She could bring out the best in anyone. She could be the one I been waiting on forever. Tammy is a combination of being smart, sexy, and caring. We could get married and have children one day. Tammy is my main focus right now. I'm going to get a big house, so we could live in it together. I always wanted two or three kids. Who knows, I could join a church one day."

Steven had a puzzled look on his face. He had never heard Lewis speak like that before. Lewis turned a whole 360. He was not the same person anymore. Steven pondered, *Lewis has aged ten years overnight or Tammy has the magic potion between her legs.* Steven said, "It's a good thing that your life is turning around for the better. We are going back to living a normal life. I hope God forgives us for all the dirt we have done. I hope the man upstairs grant us our wish. We and the rest of the clique have sinned, so much that it feels like we were working for the devil."

Lewis added, "I wish we had gotten this money another way. It's too late; the damage has already been done. Being involved in criminal activities, made me lose my mind. It turned me into a monster. I thought becoming ruthless was the key to being a successful criminal. A person can do anything if they don't care. I will take the blame for poisoning James's mind. That fool pulled a gun out on me; now you know he lost his mind."

Steven said, "The name James is starting to get me upset; I would rather talk about Tammy. She seems like a wonderful person. Just make sure she's the right person before you get your hopes up too high. How long have y'all been talking?"

Lewis responded, "Tammy is a wonderful person. We have been talking for a few weeks, but it feels like I've known her forever. It is something about her that makes me want to be a lover and not a fighter. Tammy and I have done a lot of talking about you; which one of her friends we are going to hook you up with? We started with eight and now we are down to three. I'm going to make the choice for you. I know the type of girl you like. Growing up, we talked about different girls all the time. Barbara made Tammy and I laugh, tonight. It was funny when she said 'Steven has to step his game up'. We are going to be double dating soon."

Steven replied, "You better have great taste in women. Tammy could have been just luck. Don't fix me up with a chicken head. Your judgment might be alright. Hurry, I'm dying from being womanless."

Lewis laughed and stated, "Bro, you sound desperate. I need to find a crack head to please you. Your itch has to be scratched. Those crack heads will do anything for a special low price. The head is $10 and the cat is $5."

Steven said, "You have to stop talking that nasty shit because it's making me feel sick. Getting some head sounds like a good idea." Both of them began to chuckle. Steven told Lewis, "I'm tired and I have school in the morning." Steven got up off the couch and went to bed.

Lewis checked his cell phone for any missed calls. Instead of finding missed calls, there were three text messages. He did not hear his phone because it was on off-ring. The first message was from Tammy: 'I love you, baby. Barbara and Steven are cool people. They will get a chance to know me better. Don't try to become a player because you are driving a new Camaro. Bye.' He checked the second message and it was from James: 'What part of the words 'next week' that you don't understand. My patience is wearing thin. You are going to find yourself in a casket. Why are you fucking with the wrong man's money? This will be the last warning.' Lewis checked the last message and it was from Redd: 'Leave my girl alone. Tammy is my property and not yours. I could have killed your dumb ass. Keep playing with fire; it's a matter of time before the flames burn you. When I attack, you will die a slow and painful death. Step out of my way or feel the wrath of a real muthafucking G.' Lewis didn't get scared at all. He was not afraid of Redd and James. He thought James tried to scare him into giving up the money because if he killed him, he wouldn't get paid. He truly believed

Redd would kill him because of his obsession with Tammy. Lewis knew Redd would do anything to get her back into his arms. Lewis felt that he would be ready when Redd grew some nuts and came after him.

The next day at 4:30 pm, Lewis received a call from Detective Lopez on Steven's house phone, "Hey Lewis, we are finish with the autopsy on both of your parents. We're done with the investigation at the crime scene. You can come back to the house when you're ready. My team and I have done a thorough search in the house. We discovered some important evidence. We are on the right track to find out who committed these murders."

Lewis asked, "When can I have a funeral for my parents? It's time for me to get some closure. I'm going to let God deal with whoever murdered them. Mom and Dad will live in my heart forever. I'm not going to live in that house anymore."

Detective Lopez said, "You are in control of the funeral arrangements. Since the autopsy has been done, we are turning them over to you. Their will read that if anything happened to them, everything will go to you. They must really love you. My parents died and they did not leave me anything. Lewis, your parents have giving you a great head start in life; please use it wisely. I hope I can bring you some justice by taking the killers to jail. Be careful, those thugs are still out there. It's possible they can come after you; the only witness to see them close up."

Lewis replied, "I'll be real careful. Those bastards don't want to see me right now. My parent's funeral will take place the day after tomorrow. I have to get in touch with my family and neighbors."

Detective Lopez told him, "Keep your head up. Better days are on the way. If you remember anything new or you just need someone to talk with, give me a call. Have a nice day. Bye."

Two days later, Sam and Jessica's funeral was held at the Mount Zion Baptist church. They were members of that church. Lewis was the only family member there. All the neighbors were there too. Sam and Jessica did not keep in touch with their families. Their families did not like them because they changed over the years. They stopped answering their calls. Sam and Jessica felt like they should only chat with folks with the same amount of money as them or more. Barbara, Tammy, Lewis, and Steven were sitting on the front row seat.

The following week, on a Wednesday, school ended at 12:00pm for the last teachers and parents meeting. The meeting was about graduation and summer school. Around 1:35pm, James was driving his mother's PT Cruiser with her permission. Johnny was with him on the passenger side. Both of them were wearing white t-shirts and Johnny was holding both white ski masks. They were headed to Capital One Bank on Robert Street. James had a Glock .40 handgun and Johnny had a Caliber 380 Semi Automatic handgun. They had two black garbage bags on the back seat.

When James and Johnny arrived outside of the bank, they placed their ski masks on. They ran into the bank together with their guns out. James yelled, "Y'all know the mutha-fuckin routine! Put those hands up in the air and wave'em around like you don't care!" The bank's manager, Ms. Afeni, left her office to see how things were going in the front. She saw the bank getting robbed and then she headed back to her office quickly to call the police. Detective Lopez answered the phone. He was eating some glazed donuts and drinking a cappuccino while sitting down in his office. He said, "This is the police department; how can I help you?"

Ms Afeni replied, "I'm the manager of the Capital One Bank on Robert Street. We are getting robbed, right now. I have seen two guys with white ski masks sticking the place up."

Detective Lopez stood up and asked, "Where are you located inside the bank?"

She responded, "I'm in my office." Then he said to her, "Lock your door, we are coming to help."

Detective Lopez hurried and told every officer there about the bank robbery. Detective Lopez and the rest of his men left the station fast. He knew The Teenage Mafia was at it again. A young Caucasian guy was behind the counter. He was giving up the cash swiftly, putting it into James's garbage bag. An older Caucasian guy in his 60's was placing the money in Johnny's bag slowly behind another counter. Johnny was getting pissed off because he was not moving quick enough, "Hurry the fuck up, old man! I don't have all day!" Then the guy started trembling and Johnny knocked him out with a straight jab. Johnny started taking the cash himself from the cash register. There were four bank customers lying down on the floor. All of them were forced to keep their hands behind their heads, one man and three women. Once they took all the money from the four cash registers, they got ready to leave. Johnny said, "Let's go." Both of them began to flee from the bank.

The PT Cruiser was parked in the front of the bank with the license plate taken off. Johnny got into the PT Cruiser and cranked it up. James's greed kicked in at the last minute and he decided to go into a customer's pocket while she was on the floor. Johnny could hear the police sirens getting louder. He said, "Shit, James has to hurry up!" Johnny saw the police and he took off like a bat out of hell. Detective Lopez and three other officers stopped at the bank while Officer Butler followed the fast moving PT Cruiser. Detective Lopez yelled at James, "Put the gun down!" James was shocked to see four police officers standing in front of him. They caught him trying to take the bank customers' money out of their pockets. James stared at the police officers and his heart was beating fast. James knew he was going to prison for a long time. In a split second, James decided he would rather go out in a blaze. James busted one shot and he missed, then Detective Lopez and the rest of the officers gunned him down. He took six shots; the bullets hit him in the stomach and the chest. Detective Lopez checked his neck for a pulse but he did not feel anything. James was dead.

During the high speed chase, Johnny threw the ski mask out the window. Officer Butler was on his trail, but Johnny had a good head start. Finally, Johnny hopped out of the car and placed the white t-shirt in the trashcan. He had on a blue shirt that was under the white one. Johnny walked slowly with hopes of throwing the Police off track. Officer Butler saw the PT Cruiser parked near an alley. He took his .44 handgun out and went by the car. He wanted to see if the driver was still in there. Officer Butler did not see the driver, but he knew the person was somewhere close by. Johnny was in his neighborhood and he wanted to make it home before the Police caught up with him. Johnny could see his house 20 feet away from him and then Officer Butler drove up behind him and yelled, "Freeze! Put your hands up and don't move!" Then he said on his walkie-talkie, "This is Officer Butler. I'm on Woodson Street. I stopped a possible suspect from the bank robbery." He told Johnny his rights and placed the hand cuffs on his wrist from behind him. Then three other officers came to him for back up.

Johnny said to the police, "Y'all racist pigs grabbed the wrong man! I guess it's because I'm black!" Officer Butler put Johnny in the back seat of his police car and took him to the station for questioning.

Rumors about James's death and Johnny's arrest were passed on like a disease. Everybody was saying that they were a part of The Teenage Mafia.

Eric told Steven what happened to James and Johnny. Steven received the news while he was in the Camaro with Lewis on the passenger side. They just came back from the store and parked in front of Steven's house. Steven felt so bad, but he had to tell Lewis what had happened. "Eric told me that James was killed trying to stick up Capital One Bank. Johnny was arrested and he is a suspect. The news said the robbers were wearing white ski masks and t-shirts. James probably convinced him to participate in the robbery."

Lewis said, "That's fucked up. I hope Johnny can be strong and don't snitch on us to the "5-0". If he does, we are screwed. Steven, I have been keeping a secret from you, for a long time. The real reason I wanted my parents dead, my dad was molesting me as a kid. Then the faggot raped me, a few months ago and my mom watched the whole thing. She didn't do a damn thing to help me. My life has been one huge rollercoaster ride. My dad and I had many fights and some were very physical. Sometimes I would not show up to school because of it."

Steven was heartbroken to hear what Sam did to Lewis. He never would have guessed that Sam was a rapist and a child molester. Steven was in so much pain mentally. He knew James was dead and Johnny was at the Police Station. Now Lewis wanted to come out with his big secret. Steven and Lewis didn't know what to do. They were looking depressed. Out of nowhere, six thunderous sounds came. The sound came from the .22 handgun of the shooter. Lewis's face and t-shirt were covered with blood. Steven saw a red colored old school car getting away. All the bullets went through the driver side of the car. The shots scared Steven and he ducked down to avoid getting hit. Steven asked Lewis, "Man, are you okay?"

Lewis was gasping for air, "I can't. I can't breathe." Then Lewis blacked out. Steven got out and pulled Lewis to the back seat. Steven turned on the emergency lights and drove Lewis to the hospital.

Once he arrived outside of the hospital, he ran inside to get help. With blood on his shirt, he screamed at the nurses, "I need your help! My friend is outside in a car; he has been shot a few times! He could bleed to death if y'all don't act quickly!"

The nurses went to get three doctors to help out. They followed Steven back to the car. They carefully placed Lewis on the stretcher and then he was taken inside the hospital to be work on. Once he was placed in the emergency room on a respirator, the doctors were working on him non-stop. Steven used Lewis's cell phone to call Tammy to he let her know what happened to Lewis. She arrived at the hospital at eight minutes. Lewis's heart rate began to drop. The doctor used the defibrillator on Lewis's chest and his heart rate dropped lower. Steven and Tammy were sitting down in the waiting room talking. Steven and Tammy became quiet once they saw the doctor heading their way with a face full of sweat. The 65-year-old Caucasian male had on a pair of glasses and a white, long, and cotton made jacket. The jacket had two large pockets on both side of the bottom. The doctor had a picture ID on his right chest. The doctor said, "He's in critical condition....

Acknowledgements

First of all, I would like to thank God for giving me the gift of story writing. He gave my mind more ideas every time it went blank. God kept me writing even when I did not feel like it. The Teenage Mafia story took me a year to create. This book is only the beginning for me. I want to become a legendary Author and The Teenage Mafia story is my first step. Katrina Tyler would hurt me if I did not mention her name. She told me what a good book is supposed to have in it. Her knowledge about books led me into writing some amazing scenes. To my nieces and nephews, Waymon, Desiree, Malik, Maresha, and E'Zaven, don't let anyone shoot your hopes and dreams down. Remember this; people are always going to say what you can't do. To my brothers and sisters, Sherry, Hulk, Dee Dee, Nobi, Jetta, and Da'Shinta, now you all can say that my brother is an Author. I would like to give a special thanks to Nakita Nixon. She gave me a lot of confidents and Nakita was the first person who told me I could write my own book. I would like to thank my mother Linda Johnson, my step father Michael Johnson and my father Henry Tyler Jr. for taking me seriously when I told them I was writing a book. I almost forgot my cousin Jermaine; he always believed I could do anything in life that I wanted to do, even when we were little kids. ONE LOVE to my friends: Wu, DJ Roy Lee, Boom, Greg, David & Cynthia Turner, Mack, Datravis, Lt. Skinner, & Rudy. ONE LOVE to Reuben McCall High School-Class of 2003. My email address is htyler3@att.net